Like Dandelion Dust
This Side *of* Heaven

KAREN KINGSBURY

Like Dandelion Dust
This Side *of* Heaven

CENTER STREET

New York Boston Nashville

Scriptures are taken from the HOLY BIBLE: NEW INTERNATIONAL VERSION ®. Copyright © 1973, 1978, 1984 by International Bible Society. Used by permission of Zondervan Publishing House. All rights reserved.

Karen Kingsbury is represented by the literary agency of Alive Communications. 7680 Goddard Street, Suite 200
Colorado Springs, CO 80920
www.alivecom.com

Center Street
Hachette Book Group
237 Park Avenue
New York, NY 10017
www.centerstreet.com

Printed in the United States of America

Like Dandelion Dust and *This Side of Heaven* originally published in paperback by Center Street.

First Compilation Edition: April 2012

10 9 8 7 6 5 4 3 2 1

Center Street is a division of Hachette Book Group, Inc.
The Center Street name and logo are trademarks of Hachette Book Group, Inc.

The Hachette Speakers Bureau provides a wide range of authors for speaking events. To find out more, go to www.hachettespeakersbureau.com or call (866) 376-6591.

Library of Congress Control Number: 2011940635

ISBN 978-1-59995-403-5

Like Dandelion Dust

Josh, my tender tough guy. This is the year you'll enter high school, and I know you'll make a huge impact on every sports field you play on. But more than that, I look forward to the impact you'll make in the lives of your peers. Keep standing firm for what's right, Josh. God has bigger platforms ahead with every turn.

EJ, my chosen one. This year you have become the one most likely to encourage a family day for the eight of us. I love that you have the most fun when we're all together, no matter what the activity. God is drawing you out of that shy place where you once lived. The young man you are becoming is a delight to all of us!

Austin, my miracle child. You are growing up so quickly. It's hard to believe you're starting middle school. But what's been most fun for me as your mom is watching you exhibit such leadership among your peers. At the last baseball tournament, they created an award on the spot just for you. They said anyone with that sort of character needed an award whether your team won or not. Keep being a leader for Jesus, Aus.

And to God Almighty, the author of life, who has—for now—blessed me with these.

ACKNOWLEDGMENTS

This book couldn't have come together without the help of many people. First, a special thanks to my friends at FaithWords who have worked diligently with the producers of the movie *Like Dandelion Dust* to make sure this version of the book came out in a timely fashion, and with the right cover art.

Also a big thank you to my agent, Rick Christian, president of Alive Communications. I am amazed more as every day passes at your great integrity, your talent, and your commitment to getting my Life-Changing Fiction™ out to all the world. You are a strong man of God, Rick. You care for my career as if you were personally responsible for the souls God touches through these books. Thank you for looking out for my personal time—the hours I have with my husband and kids most of all. I couldn't do this without you.

As always, this book wouldn't be possible without the help of my husband and kids, who are so good about eating tuna sandwiches and quesadillas, and bringing me plates of baked chicken and vegetables when I need the brain power to write past midnight. Thanks for understanding the sometimes crazy life I lead, and for always being my greatest support.

Also, thanks to my mother and assistant, Anne Kingsbury, and to my sister Susan Kane, for having a great sensitivity and love for my readers. And to my sister, Tricia Kingsbury, who runs a large part of my business life. The personal touch you both bring to my ministry is precious to me...thank you with all my heart.

Also thanks to my marketing assistant Olga Kalachik, and to my daughter, Kelsey, who helps with so much of the publicity and mailings that go out as part of our many donation programs.

And thanks to my friends and family who continue to surround me with love and prayers and support. Of course, the greatest thanks goes to God Almighty, the most wonderful author of all—the Author of Life. The gift is Yours. I pray I might have the incredible opportunity and responsibility to use it for You all the days of my life.

FOREVER IN FICTION™

A special thanks to my **Forever in Fiction™** winners whose character names appear in this book. I created **Forever in Fiction™** as a live-auction item for charities. Every penny of the winning bid for **Forever in Fiction™** goes to the charity that holds the auction. So far, more than $100,000 has been raised for charities across the country from people winning **Forever in Fiction™** If you or your group is interested in the donation of a **Forever in Fiction™** package, visit my Web site at www.Karen-Kingsbury.com. I donate approximately six of these packages per year.

As much as possible, I try to give my characters identifying features that correlate with the person for whom that character is named. Still, the **Forever in Fiction™** characters in this novel are entirely fictional.

And so thanks go to the two **Forever in Fiction™** winners whose names appear in *Like Dandelion Dust*. The first package was won by a group of friends at the Summit View Church auction. Anne Fraser, Jaymi Sutton, Vicky Dillon, Joan Smith, Barbara Seifert, and Michael Petty combined for the winning bid and presented **Forever in Fiction™** to Beth Petty for her fortieth birthday. Beth is a wonderful wife, mother, and friend. She and her husband, Michael, have four children: Cammie, 14; Blain, 10; Braden, 7; and Jonah, 5. They have a female golden retriever named George Brett and a life that is full of love, laughter, and devotion to the Lord. Beth, your friends and family love you very much. They pray that this gift will remain as living proof of their feelings for you.

Also thanks to Kym Merrill, who won **Forever in Fiction**™ at the Discovery Church Women's Christmas Brunch auction. Kym chose to honor her sister, Allyson Page Bower, by having a character named after her. Allyson, 45, is mother to Tavia, 21; Travis, 15; and Taylor, 7. She is also grandmother to Harley, 4. A hard worker whose sole focus is caring for and loving her children, Allyson loves digging in the garden and sitting on the beach, and is known for baking the best banana pudding in the state. Allyson, your sister loves you very much. She prays that you will catch a glimpse of that love in the honor of finding your name **Forever in Fiction**™.

ONE

Once in a while Molly Campbell wondered if other people saw it. When strangers passed by her and Jack and little Joey, maybe they could actually see a golden hue, pixie dust on the tops of their heads or a light emanating from the air around them, telling all the world what the three of them inherently knew.

That life couldn't possibly be more perfect.

Sometimes when Molly walked through the Palm Beach Mall, hand-in-hand with four-year-old Joey, her purse holding a couple hundred dollars cash, two debit cards and a Visa with five figures open to buy, she'd see a tired-looking, disheveled man or an aging woman with worn-out shoes—hollow-eyed and slack-jawed—and she'd wonder what had happened. How had life placed these people in their separate worlds, and how had she and Jack and Joey found their way to the right side?

The good side.

Molly felt that way now, sitting at the Cricket Preschool parents' conference, listening to Joey's teacher rave about his progress in math and spelling. She held the hand of her quick-witted, rugged husband and smiled at Joey. "That's what we like to hear, buddy."

"Thanks." Joey grinned. His first loose tooth—the one in the middle, upper left—hung at a crazy angle. He swung his feet beneath the table as his eyes wandered around the room to the dinosaur poster and the T. rex. Joey loved the T. rex.

The teacher continued, "Your son is charming, a delight to everyone." Mrs. Erickson was in her sixties, silver-haired with a gentle hand, a teacher who preferred to use colored marbles or M&Ms rather than a stern voice and repetition to teach the alphabet. "He's reading at a first-grade level, and he won't be five until fall. Amazing." She raised her brow. "He's computing beyond his years, as well. And he's extremely social."

Then the teacher shared an anecdote.

One day the week before, Joey came to class a few minutes early, and there sat Mark Allen, a child with learning disabilities. Mark Allen was staring at his empty lunch box, tears streaming down his face. Somehow his mother had sent him to school without any food for snack time.

"I was in the supply closet," the teacher explained. "I didn't see what was happening until I returned."

By then, Joey had taken the seat next to Mark Allen, pulled his Batman lunchbox from his backpack and spread the contents out on the desk. As the teacher walked in, Joey was handing the boy his peanut butter crackers and banana, saying, "Don't cry. You can have my snack."

"I can only tell you," the teacher concluded, her eyes shining at the memory, "Joey is the kindest, most well-adjusted four-year-old I've taught in a long time."

Molly basked in the glow of the teacher's praise. She let the story play over in her mind, and when the conference was over and they left the classroom, she grinned at her husband. "He gets it from me, you know." She lifted her chin, all silliness and mock pride. "Sharing his snack with that little boy."

"Right." Jack's eyes danced. "And the social part." He gave her a look. "He gets that from you, no doubt."

"Definitely."

"But the smarts"—he tapped his temple, his voice full of laughter—"that's my doing."

"Wait a minute..." She gave him a shove, even if she couldn't keep the smile from her face. "I'm definitely the brains in this—"

"Let's go, sport!" Jack took hold of Joey's hand and the two of them skipped ahead as they reached the parking lot. It was a beautiful South Florida May afternoon, cooler than usual, all sunshine and endless blue skies and swaying palm trees. The kind of day that made a person forget the humidity and unbearable temperatures just a few weeks away. Molly could hear Jack and Joey giggling about recess and playground rules and tetherball. As they reached their blue Acura SUV, Jack gave Joey a few light pokes in his ribs. "So, sport...got a girlfriend?"

"No way." Joey shook his head. "Us boys have a club. The Boys Are Best Club." He put his hands on his waist. "No yucky girls."

"Oh...good. Boys Are Best." Jack gave a few thoughtful nods. He opened the driver's door as he pulled Joey close and gently rubbed his knuckles against Joey's pale blond hair. "You boys are right." He winked at Molly. "Girls are yucky."

Joey looked at her and his expression softened. " 'Cept for Mommy."

"Really?" They climbed into the car. From the driver's seat, Jack looped his arm around Molly's shoulders and kissed her cheek. "Well..." He grinned at her. "I guess Mommy's not so bad. As long as she stays out of the kitchen."

"Hey!" Molly laughed. "It's been a month since I burned anything."

Jack raised his eyebrow at Joey. "Today made up for it. Flaming cinnamon rolls—that'll go down in the family record book."

"They shouldn't put 'broil' and 'bake' so close together on the dial."

Jack chuckled. "We shouldn't put you in the kitchen. Period."

"You might be right." Molly didn't mind her reputation for foul-ups at mealtime. Cooking bored her. As long as they ate healthy food, she had no interest in creating elaborate recipes. Simple meals worked just fine.

When they were buckled in, Joey bounced a few times on the seat. "Can we get pizza, huh? Please?"

"Great idea. That'll keep Mom out of the kitchen. Besides"—Jack gave a pronounced tap on the steering wheel—"anyone who gets a perfect report in preschool should be allowed pizza."

"Pineapple pizza?"

"Definitely pineapple pizza."

As they drove to Nemo's Deli a few blocks east of the school, a comfortable silence settled over the car. In the back seat, Joey found his library book, a pictorial on the Great White Shark. He hummed *Here We Go 'Round the Mulberry Bush* as he turned the pages. Molly reached over and wove her fingers between Jack's. "So...isn't it amazing?" She kept her voice low, the conversation meant for just the two of them.

Jack grinned, keeping his eyes on the road. "Our little genius, you mean?"

"Not that." Sunshine streamed through the windshield, sending warmth and well-being throughout her body. She smiled. "The kindness part. I mean..." There was laughter in her voice. "I know he's a prodigy in the classroom and a natural on the playground. But how great that the teacher would call him 'kind.' "

"The kindest boy she's seen in a long time."

"And well-adjusted." Molly sat a little straighter.

"Very well-adjusted."

They were half-teasing, bragging about Joey the way they could do only when no one else was around. Then the smile faded from Jack's face. "Didn't you think it'd be harder than this?"

"Harder?" Molly angled herself so she could see him better. "Preschool?"

"No." Jack gripped the steering wheel with his left hand, more pensive than he'd been all afternoon. He glanced at the rear-view mirror and the fine lines at the corners of his eyes deepened. "Adopting. Didn't you think it'd be harder? School trouble or social trouble? Something?"

Molly stared out the window. They were passing Fuller Park on their right, a place they'd taken Joey since he came into their lives. Home was only a block away. She squinted against the sunlight. "Maybe. It seems like a lifetime ago."

"When we brought him home?" Jack kept his eyes on the road.

"No." She drew a slow breath through her nose. "When we first talked about adoption, I guess." She shot a quick look at Joey in the backseat, his blond hair and blue eyes, the intent way he sat there looking at shark pictures and humming. She met Jack's gaze again. "As soon as they put him in my arms, every fear I ever had dissolved." A smile started in her heart. "I knew he was special."

Jack nodded slowly. "He is, isn't he?"

"Yes." She gave his hand a gentle squeeze. "As my sister would say, he's a gift from God. Nothing less than a miracle."

"Your sister..." Jack chuckled. "She and Bill are about as dry as they come."

"Hey." Molly felt her defenses come to life. "Give them time. They just moved here a week ago."

"I know." Jack frowned. "But can't they talk about something besides God? 'God's will this' and 'God's will that'?"

"Jack...come on." Molly bristled. Beth was her best friend. The two were eighteen months apart, inseparable as kids: Beth, the younger but somehow more responsible sister, and Molly, the flighty one, always in need of Beth's ability to keep her grounded. For the past three years Molly had worked on Beth, trying to get her and Bill and their four kids to move to West Palm Beach. "Be fair." She was careful with her tone. "Give them a chance."

The lines around Jack's eyes relaxed. "I'm just saying..." He raised his brow at her. "They're uptight, Molly. If that's what church does to you"—he released her hand and brushed at the air—"count me out."

"The move's been hard on them."

"I guess."

"Hey, Daddy, know what?" Joey tapped both their shoulders and bounced in his booster seat. "The Great White is as long as four daddies. That's what the picture shows."

The sparkle instantly returned to Jack's expression. "Four daddies! Wow...how many little boys would that be?"

"Probly a million-jillion."

They turned in to the restaurant parking lot. "Here we are!" Jack took the first space available. "Pineapple pizza coming up."

"Jack..." Molly wasn't finished. She winced a little. "I forgot to mention—" She already knew the answer, but her sister made her promise to ask. "Beth and Bill want us to come to church with them Sunday. They're trying out the one down the street from the school."

Jack leaned over and kissed her cheek. He kept his face a few inches from hers. "When Bill says yes to one of my poker parties, I'll say yes to church."

"Okay." She hid her disappointment. "So that's a no?"

"That's a no." He patted the side of her face. The teasing left his eyes for a moment. "Unless you want me to. If it matters to you, I'll go."

Molly loved that about Jack. He had his opinions, but he was willing to do things her way, always ready to compromise. "No." She gave him a quick kiss. "We're going out on the boat this Sunday. That'll put us closer to God than a church service ever could."

Joey was already out of the car and up on the sidewalk, waiting for them. Jack opened his car door and chuckled. "Well said, my dear. Well said."

Not until they were inside the restaurant ordering their pizza did a strange ribbon of fear wrap itself around Molly's throat. Their attitude toward church was okay, wasn't it? They'd never been church people, even though Beth talked to her about it often.

"You need to take Joey," Beth would say. "All children need to be in church."

Molly looked at Joey now, golden-haired, his eyes adoringly on Jack as they considered the options at the pop machine. What they had was fine, wasn't it? They believed in God, in a distant sort of way. What harm was there in finding Him at a lake instead of in a pew? Besides, they already had everything they needed.

Jack's recent promotion had placed him in a dream job as vice president of sales for Reylco, one of the top three pharmaceutical companies in the world. He was making a healthy six-figure salary, overseeing top international accounts, and traveling half as often as before. They lived on a corner lot in Ashley Heights, one of West Palm Beach's finer upscale neighborhoods. The three of them took trips to Disney World and Sanibel Island and the Bahamas, and they fished at Lake Okeechobee once a month.

Every now and then they spent a Saturday afternoon serving lunch at a homeless mission in Miami, and then they'd take in a play in the city's art district. On weekdays, after dinner, they walked to Fuller Park with Joey and Gus, their friendly lab. There Jack and Molly stole kisses and laughter, watching sunsets while Gus ran circles around the playground and Joey raced to the top of the slide over and over and over again.

They kept an Air Nautique ski boat at Westmont Pier,

and on most Sundays they drove to the white sandy sea-shore and cruised to the bay, where water was smooth and deep blue and warm. They'd take turns skiing, and Joey would sit in the back, watching, pumping his fists in the air when one of them cleared the wake. This spring, for the first time, they'd bought a pair of training skis for Joey. More sunshine and laughter, day after day, year after year.

These thoughts chased away Molly's strange fear, and she found a window table where she could wait for her men. The uneasy feeling lifted. Why worry? The golden hue, the shining light, the pixie dust—all of it must be real. They were happy and healthy and they had everything they'd ever wanted. Most of all, they had Joey.

What more could God possibly give them?

TWO

Wendy Porter stared out the windshield and tried to slow her breathing. A cigarette. That's what she needed—a strong, no-filter cigarette. She reached over and rummaged through her purse, past the Wal-Mart receipts and old tubes of lipstick and the pink cracked mirror. Beneath her wallet and the smashed breakfast bar she'd kept there for the past month. Through the crumbs and loose change that had gathered at the bottom. *Where were they?* She took her eyes off the road and gave a quick look into the purse. She still had a few Camels, right? The good kind?

Then she remembered, and she put her hand back on the wheel.

The smoke would cling to her pretty pink blouse and black dress slacks. It would linger in her freshly washed hair and ruin her minty breath. Five years had passed since her husband, Rip, had been a free man. She didn't want to put him in a bad mood.

The news she had to tell him would take care of that.

Wendy tapped one slim fingernail on the steering wheel. So maybe it didn't matter if she had a cigarette. She tapped some more. No, better not.

"Dirty habit," Rip used to tell her before his arrest. Sometimes he'd snatch a cigarette from her lips and break it in half. "I hate when you smoke. It isn't sexy."

Not that Rip had ever been the picture of sex appeal. Last time they were together, he'd slugged her in the jaw while the two of them yelled at each other in the Kroger parking lot. The reason he was angry? She'd forgotten to clip the fifty-cent coupon for ground round. A police officer a dozen yards away saw everything and hauled Rip in for battery. With a list of priors, Rip was lucky to get six to eight in the Ohio State Penitentiary, out in just five for good behavior.

Wendy turned onto the interstate and pressed her high-heeled shoe hard against the gas pedal. It was four o'clock—almost rush hour. She had to make time while she could. A quick check in her rearview mirror and she switched to the fast lane. With any luck she'd reach the prison in half an hour. She and Rip had a lot to talk about. The last thing she wanted was to get things off to a bad start by being late.

She cracked her window and a burst of fresh air filled the car. Her mama had told her to leave Rip years ago. Way before the Kroger incident. And truth was, there'd been other guys in the past five years. A girl couldn't sit home year after year waiting for her man to get out of jail. Even a man she was crazy about. She hadn't been sure he'd even want to see her when he was released. Not until last week. The phone call came as she walked through the back door after church.

"Baby…" His voice was more gravelly than before. "It's me."

The call made her breath catch in her throat. She set down her Bible and the church bulletin and pressed the receiver hard against her ear. "Rip?"

"Yeah, baby." There was a tenderness in his voice, the tenderness that had attracted her so long ago. "Did you miss me?"

"It's...been a long time, Rip."

He rarely called, hated having a long-distance relationship. At Wendy's last visit, fourteen months earlier, he'd told her not to come again until he was released. Seeing her made the time pass too slowly, he said. So how was she supposed to take that? She was not for a minute expecting a call from Rip.

Of course, she'd drop everything if he was interested again. She'd given her heart to Rip a long time ago. He would own it until the day she died. She gathered herself. "You mean...you wanna see me?"

"See you? I'm crazy about you, baby. And get this...I'm out in a week. The thing I want more than anything in life is to walk out these doors and see you there. Waiting for me." He hesitated, and she could hear the voices of other prisoners in the background. "Be there, baby...please?"

"Oh, Rip." When she could breathe normally, she grabbed a piece of junk mail and a pen. "When are you getting out?"

He gave her the details, and then he exhaled, slow and tired. "I'm sorry, Wendy." His tone was broken. Maybe that's why his voice sounded strange at first. He sniffed hard. "What I did...it was wrong. You don't have to worry. It ain't gonna happen again."

Wendy felt a bubble of anxiety rise within her. He'd been sorry before, right? Why would this be different?

Every time Rip Porter walked back into her life, breathing apologies and lies, he left her with a broken heart and a few broken bones. Her mama said she'd be crazy if she took him back again, but that was just it. She was crazy. Crazy for Rip, in a way that didn't make sense. She loved him, that's all she knew. No matter his history, no matter the times when she was the target of what felt like a lifetime of rage, she loved him. There would never be anyone for her but Rip.

"I missed you, baby." His voice grew huskier as he breathed across the line. "I hope you kept my side of the bed open."

Fear poured into Wendy's veins. What if Rip found out about the other men? There hadn't been many, really. Four or five, maybe, and not for the past six months. That's why she was back at church. Trying to make a new go of things. Still, Rip hated other men. Hated when they looked at her, and hated it more when she looked back. If anyone from the pool hall ever told him about the other men, he'd...well...Wendy was sure whatever happened would make the incident at the Kroger look like horseplay.

But before she could think it all through, trying to imagine what life would be like with Rip back at home, she gave him the answer he wanted. "I'll be there."

"Okay, baby." His relief was tangible over the phone line. "I'll be counting the days."

Wendy settled back against the driver's seat and stared at the road ahead.

Since that phone call, her emotions had been all over the map. Excitement and the thrill of imagining herself in his arms gave way to a very real, very consuming fear. She hadn't told him about the boy. Now that he was getting out, she had no choice. He'd find out one way or another, and the longer she waited, the angrier he'd be. Rip couldn't really blame her for not telling him sooner. The two of them barely saw each other over the past five years, and as for her little boy—she tried not to think about him. Only on his birthday in September and a few other times each month when her heart raced ahead of her.

She reached over and rifled through her purse again. A piece of gum, that's what she needed. When she knew Rip was coming home, she'd hidden her smokes in a box in the garage. But now she was going crazy without them. Her fingers brushed against a sticky ballpoint pen and a wad of tissue paper, and then finally what she was looking for. A broken stick of peppermint Eclipse. She brushed off a layer of lint and popped the gum between her lips.

She hadn't planned to ever tell Rip about the boy. It wasn't any of his business. She'd had the baby at the beginning of his prison sentence, after all—a sentence that kept Rip in the slammer for five years. There were reasons why she gave the boy up, why she found a nice family and turned him over. But part of it was a matter of being practical. She had to work two jobs to pay the bills, right? How would she do all that and raise a baby by herself?

She found out about the baby the week after Rip was locked up. Rotten luck, nothing but rotten luck. She didn't visit Rip after her fifth month of pregnancy, not until she had her shape back and the baby was safe in his new home. Rip never suspected a thing. But the baby was his, that much she was sure about. The other men didn't come into the picture until the second year of his term.

The traffic grew heavier. She switched lanes again. The truth was, she'd almost done it, almost kept the boy. She didn't sign the paperwork until after she had him and held him and—

She blinked and the memory stopped short. There was no going back, no such thing as what might've been. What she did that day, she did for her baby, her son. He deserved more than round-the-clock day care and a father in prison for domestic violence. She picked the family, after all. They were perfect for her baby, willing to give him the life he could never have had with her and Rip.

But more than that, her decision was ultimately based on one simple fact. She couldn't tolerate seeing her little boy hurt. And if Rip got out and fell into one of his rages...Wendy shuddered and took tighter hold of the wheel. A man with a temper like Rip's had a heap of changing to do before he could be any kind of father. It didn't matter now. She'd signed both their names on the adoption papers and never looked back.

Almost never.

Tears stung her eyes and she cursed herself for being weak. The boy was better off, no question. What she'd done by giving him up made her the best mother in the world. Period. She drew a quick breath and dabbed her fingers along her upper cheeks. "Enough."

Her focus had to be on Rip now, and whether the two of them had anything left after five years of being apart. Had he gotten help for his temper, or maybe found Jesus? Or had the guys he ran with made him meaner? This was his second time in prison. Last time he came back showering apologies and sweet nothings, and he was hitting her again by the end of the week. Still, she loved him. Loved him and pined for him and wanted him back in the worst way.

So maybe this time would be different. Wendy worked her gum, demanding what was left of the peppermint. Rip had sounded nice enough on the phone. Maybe he really had changed, and this time things would be better between them. He'd come home and give up the anger and shouting and hitting, and turn into the kind gentleman she had always known was buried somewhere inside him. It would happen one day, she knew it. Deep inside he had a heart of gold, Rip Porter. She would give him another chance, same as always, and maybe this time love would win out over all the anger.

She eased her car back into the fast lane and picked up speed again. Yes, maybe everything would work out. Then when Rip's temper was under control and he had a steady job, they could have another child, maybe two or three. A light rain began to pepper the windshield, and traffic slowed. Great. Rip hated when she was late.

She flipped on the radio, gave each station three seconds to prove itself, and flipped it off again. Silence was better anyway. How was she going to bring up the subject, the idea that, hey, by the way, there was a baby and now he's living with another family? Before they could move ahead, she had to give him the truth about the boy. No way around it; she had to.

Brent and Bubba down at the pool hall both knew about her pregnancy. Brent lived a few blocks over. He and Bubba were on their way out one afternoon when she was at the curb getting the mail. She was days from delivering, and big as a house.

Brent stopped and rolled down his window. He gestured at her belly. "That Rip's kid in there?"

Wendy glared at the man and gave no thought to her answer. "Of course it's Rip's."

"Well, I'll be..." Brent cussed and chuckled all at the same time. "Poor kid. Future's already written with Rip as a daddy. Him sittin' in the pen and all."

In the seat next to him, Bubba slapped his knee and laughed out loud. "Got that right!"

Wendy waved them off, angry. "Ah, go off and get drunk," she shouted. "And mind your own business!"

Months could go by without seeing the rusty backside of Brent's beat-up Ford. Wendy didn't see Brent or Bubba again for almost a year. But just yesterday she was mowing the yard—getting things in order for Rip—when Brent drove up and once more rolled down his window. "Heard Rip was gettin' out." He stretched his head through the window, shouting to be heard over the roar of the mower.

"Yeah." Wendy killed the engine. Sweat dripped down the side of her face, and she dragged her hand across her forehead. "Good news travels fast."

Brent craned his neck, peering into her side yard. "What happened to the kid?"

Wendy was glad she was holding onto the lawn mower. Otherwise she would've fainted dead away, right there on the freshly cut grass. She had no family, no friends other than the people she'd met at church here and there. The baby was her deal, her decision. Not until that moment did it ever occur to her that just maybe the news might get back to Rip.

Brent was waiting for an answer.

"He, uh…we gave him up…to a family in Florida."
She tried to sound matter-of-fact, as if giving the baby up
for adoption was common knowledge. "Rip and I didn't
want a baby while he was in prison. You know?"

"Hmmm." Brent hesitated. "Doesn't sound like my main
man, Rip Porter. Guy always wanted a son." He shrugged.
"Not that it's any of my business." After a minute of small
talk, he flashed her a grin that showed his silver tooth.
"Tell Rip I got first game when he chalks up his cue stick."

"Yeah." Wendy rolled her eyes and gave the mower cord
a jerk. "Sure thing."

The man drove away in a cloud of exhaust fumes, but the
conversation stuck. Now, twenty-four hours later, she had a
knot in her stomach, thinking about the task that lay ahead.
She had to tell Rip the truth. Tonight. When she picked him
up. If she told him right up front, he wouldn't have to hear
the news from anyone else. That had to be better, right?

The Ohio State Penitentiary was outside the city limits.
Over the last few miles she picked up the time she'd lost.
She wheeled the car into the parking lot and hurried herself
toward the visitor area. The heel of her right shoe got stuck
in a warm patch of asphalt. "Come on," she whispered. Her
heart beat so hard she wondered if it would break through
her chest and race her to the front door. Once she was
inside, her steps clicked out a nervous rhythm. She checked
in, found a chair across the room from the prison door,
and waited.

At two minutes after five, Rip walked through the door
holding a brown paper bag. It took him a few seconds to
find her, but when he did, he lit up like a bar sign at sun-
down. "Wendy!"

Here we go. She stood and smoothed the wrinkles out of her dress slacks. Her knees felt weak at the sight of him. *What have I gotten myself into?* She found her smile. "Rip!" She mouthed his name. With a roomful of tired-looking visitors watching, this wasn't the place for dramatic reunions. But she didn't care. She had missed him more than she knew.

Rip looked at the guard who had accompanied him to the waiting room. The guard nodded. Rip was free; he could do as he pleased. Without another moment's hesitation, Rip took long strides toward Wendy. His grin took up his whole face. He wore a tight white T-shirt and jeans, his blond hair trimmed neatly to his head. He had filled out, probably from hours spent in the prison weight room.

She held her arms out toward him, and her heart fluttered as he came near. Something was different about Rip—his eyes, maybe. Whatever it was, Wendy felt herself drawn to him, taken by him. "You look great."

"Hey." He took gentle hold of her shoulders, drank her in like a man too long in the desert. Then he planted a long kiss smack on her lips. When he pulled back, he searched her eyes. "That's my line." His eyes drifted down the length of her and back up again. "You look like a million bucks, baby." He kissed her again. "I mean it."

Wendy could feel the eyes on them. She cleared her throat and took a step to the side. She could hardly wait to be alone with him. "Let's go, okay?"

Rip looked around the room at the dozen people watching them. "That's right!" he shouted, his tone full of laughter. "Eat your heart out. I'm going home!"

Wendy hung her head, her cheeks hot. Okay, so maybe

he hadn't changed. Rip was always loud this way, the center of attention. He thought he was funny, and when his behavior made people pull away or caused someone to ask him to be quiet, Rip would flip them the bird or snarl at them. "No one tells me what to do," he'd say. Then he'd go on being loud and obnoxious as ever.

Sometimes Wendy didn't mind when Rip acted up. He was just having fun, right? But once in a while Rip's public behavior had caused a private fight between the two of them, the kind that led to blows. That's why she wasn't saying anything tonight. Rip could stand on the roof of the car and sing the national anthem off key and she'd go along with it. Anything so she wouldn't make him mad. Not with the news she still had to tell him.

Rip raised his paper bag to the roomful of visitors, put his arm around Wendy's shoulders, and led her outside. The moment they were free of the building, he handed her the bag, took a few running steps, stopped, and raised both fists in the air. He let out the loudest whooping victory cry she'd ever heard. "I'm free!" A few more hoots, then he hurried to her and took her hands in his. The bag fell to the ground. "I'm a changed man, Wendy Porter. All my life's been leading up to this one single minute."

His excitement was contagious. She felt herself getting lost in his eyes. "Really?" She uttered a soft laugh and eased closer to him. Okay, maybe she was wrong. Something about him was different, definitely different. She was suddenly breathless, and she chided herself for worrying about his behavior. This was Rip Porter, the man she'd fallen for in high school. She was as in love with him now as she'd been the first time she saw him. "What happened to you in there, Rip?"

He spun her in a small circle before stopping and searching her face. "I got help, that's what." He caught his breath, and his smile faded. "I'm sorry, Wendy. It was all my fault."

Her heart was beating hard again. Was he serious? Wasn't this what she'd always wanted? Her hunky Rip, kind and gentlemanly? A ripple of nervous laughter slipped from her throat. "Really, you mean that?"

"Yes!" He raised one fist in the air and hooted so loud the sound filled the parking lot. "I love you, Wendy." He took her hand and began running toward the rows of cars. "Let's go home and celebrate."

The celebration started in the car and lasted long into the night. At two in the morning, still smiling, Rip finally fell asleep. Wendy hadn't dared ruin his joy and exhilaration in the hours after his release, but come morning she would have to tell him about the boy. Then she'd know whether Rip Porter had truly changed. Or whether the rage would find him again.

The way it had every other time.

THREE

The barbecue was Beth's idea.

Most of their boxes were unpacked, and though they'd been in town only three weeks, Beth knew where to find the can opener, and the ceramic serving platter with the watermelon slices painted around the edge, and the dehydrated onions. That and some hamburger meat and buns, and they were ready for company.

Not that Molly and Jack and Joey were company.

Beth took a handful of ground beef and pressed it between her palms. *God...let tonight work out....Let it be the beginning....* After all, this sort of thing—coming together for a Sunday evening barbecue—was what she and her older sister had dreamed about since they'd left home for college: the idea that one day they'd have families, and live a block from each other, and share meals on the weekend while they raised a passel of kids.

She and Bill had four: Cammie, twelve; Blain, ten; Braden, eight; and Jonah, five.

There had been speed bumps along the way, but here they were. Bill had taken a stable job at Pratt and Whitney, supervising the creative-design division of commercial jet-engine development. The position had more security than the one he left in Seattle, and best of all, she and Molly could be together. The whole move felt like an answer from God, a miracle in the making.

Bill came into the kitchen, dirt smudges on his cheek. "The garage isn't half done." He turned on the water, took a pumpful of soap, and rubbed his hands together. "When'll they be here?"

The clock on the microwave said 3:17 p.m. "Two hours." Molly rounded the edges of the meat patty and set it on a stack with four others. "They went boating this morning, remember?"

"Right. While we were at church."

Beth sucked the inside of her cheek. "They invited us."

"Knowing we wouldn't say yes because of church." He gave a sad chuckle. "You can see through that, right?" He leaned his hip against the kitchen counter and picked a piece of masking tape from the bottom of his shoe. "Besides, I'm not sure I'd do well out on the ocean."

"Bill..." Beth didn't want trouble—not now. "They'll invite us again." She rushed on. "You can keep working in the garage if you want."

"I wanted to work through the night." He gave her a wry smile. "Monday morning comes early."

"I know." Beth's tone was sheepish. "I guess I figured the garage could wait." She hesitated. "Right?"

Bill released a slow breath. The corners of his lips lifted, and the light in his eyes was genuine. "Right." He kissed the top of her head. "I'm glad they're coming."

"Even Jack?"

The smile faded. "Jack doesn't know me." He dried his

hands on a paper towel. "I guess the more we see each other, that could change."

Beth bit her lip. "Sorry. About Jack...about the garage."

"Don't worry about it." He kissed her cheek and looked out at the backyard. "I'll wipe down the patio furniture."

She watched him go. This was one of the speed bumps.

She and Molly hadn't attended church as kids. Their parents were nice people, good people. The sort of people who always had an extra plate at dinner, an extra pillow and blanket and spot on the sofa for someone who needed a place to stay. They believed in God, but they didn't pay Him much heed.

It was Bill who changed all that for Beth.

The two of them met at a jazz club a few blocks from Pike's Place in downtown Seattle. They snapped their fingers to the same songs and joined up at the coffee bar for espresso shots twice in the first hour. When the second hour started, Bill moved his coffee to her table. "Alone?"

She smiled at him over the edge of her cup. "I can think here."

"Me, too."

And that was that. They talked the rest of the evening. She loved bluesy jazz (especially in A-minor), fresh Alaskan salmon, hiking the shoreline at Depoe Bay, and jeans. She was a sophomore at the University of Washington studying nutrition, thousands of miles from her Central Florida home. Bill was a junior engineering major with a minor in accounting, a walk-on for the Husky swim team, and a Christian who was fascinated with the Bible.

On their first date, he showed up fifteen minutes early so they could read together from the New Testament. Bill read aloud from Philippians while Beth rolled her eyes and checked her watch. Once he put away his Bible, Bill was a fascinating date. But after three months of discussing Scripture, their discussions came to a head.

God wasn't a must-have, was He? She could live a good life without guidance from the Bible, couldn't she? Never mind that Bill was loyal and funny and that he had a standard of character that Beth hadn't seen in other guys. She was tired of talking about God. One afternoon when they were standing near Bill's car, Beth grabbed his leather-bound Bible and threw it on the ground, breaking the binding and scattering sections of the book across the road.

Bill didn't say anything. He just picked up the pieces, got into his car, and drove away without a fight.

That would've been the end of things, but there was a problem. Beth couldn't sleep. She couldn't eat or study or think, either. Not when every waking moment she kept replaying the scene in her head. How could she defend a life that was good and right by breaking a Bible? With her world spinning out of control, she went to the local bookstore and bought a Bible and an exhaustive concordance.

Between the reference tool and Scripture, days later Beth was convinced of two things. First, the Bible was full of sound wisdom, and second, the message might amount to more than head smarts. It might hold the difference between life and death.

She apologized to Bill and they never looked back, except when it came to Beth's family. Her parents were mildly tolerant of her newfound faith, but Molly thought her sister had been swallowed whole. A year went by before the two of them got together for lunch and laughed about the changes in Beth.

"I thought I'd lost you." Molly wrinkled her nose from across the table. "My little sister, Miss Bohemian Seattle, gobbled up by religion."

Beth downplayed the issue and the subject easily shifted to Molly and her own social life, mainly the relationship she'd found with Jack Campbell at Florida State University.

After that Molly never brought up Bill and Beth's faith except in passing—"Be careful what you say; Beth's in the room." Other than that kind of comment—usually born out of an attempt at sensitivity—the deep friendship and closeness between the two sisters remained.

The strain came because the men they'd married were so different. Jack was hip, with a winning personality, business savvy, and a light tan no matter what time of year. Jack smiled a lot. He was a walking picture of success and he'd done it all without God. If he were a movie star, Jack would be Brad Pitt. His self-sufficiency pervaded everything about him. Bill was more like Dustin Hoffman, serious and compassionate but with an underdeveloped fun gene. He was better in reports than in person. When the families got together once or twice a year at the home of Molly and Beth's parents, Jack kept his distance.

Both men were crazy about championship golf and Wimbledon tennis, and NASCAR. They liked Bill Murray comedies and scouring the business page for changes in their stocks. But none of that mattered. If Bill was in the TV room, Jack stayed in the kitchen. When Bill came in for a handful of Doritos or a cheeseburger off the grill, Jack would find his way outside to whatever relatives were smoking on the front porch. The distance between the two never translated to overt tension or trouble. But it was distance all the same.

"Jack can't get past the religion thing," Molly would say. Her tone always held the apology that never came. "Don't take it wrong, Beth. If they saw each other more often, it'd be different."

This was their chance. Now that their families lived so close they would finally find out if the guys could learn to be friends. Beth took another handful of raw hamburger. Yes, they were about to see. In this next season of their lives, they would certainly spend more time together, enjoy more barbecues like this one. It was the life they'd dreamed about.

She pressed the soft meat with her thumb until the edges were round; then she placed the patty on the platter with the others. Her candle set was still packed; otherwise this would be the time to light them—anything to add to the ambiance, the sense that she and Bill were warm and friendly and unthreatening.

Her cupboards were already full and fairly organized. Beth put her hands on her hips and surveyed her kitchen. Cinnamon sticks. That's what she needed. She found the spice cupboard, grabbed the cinnamon and filled a pan with water. It was a trick their mother had taught them. Boil cinnamon sticks in a pan of water and the house would smell good for days. When the water came to a boil, she turned down the heat, finished working with the hamburger, and moved on to the vegetable tray.

Everything would work out with their two families. Molly was her best friend, after all. They knew things about each other no one else would ever know. Not ever.

And on days when Beth didn't feel she had a friend in the world, there was Molly. It had been that way since they were little girls.

If only they shared their faith.

Bill was lighting the barbecue and Beth was giving the kitchen counter a final wipe-down when the doorbell rang. A surge of excitement bubbled up inside her. It was really happening. She and Molly, together again. Neighbors, even. As she reached the entryway, she had no doubt. Of course Bill and Jack would find a way around their differences.

Beth opened the door, held out her hands and squealed. "Can you believe it?"

"No." Molly rushed into her arms and the two of them hugged for a long time. When Molly drew back, they looked at each other. "I feel like our suitcases should be waiting out in the car."

Beth laughed. "Me, too."

Jack and Joey sidestepped them and Jack gave Beth a quick smile. "Hey." He held a tray of fruit with a can of whipped cream balanced on top. "I'll take this to the kitchen."

"Hi, Aunt Beth." Joey looked up at her and grinned. He was tanned, his blond hair lighter than usual. "We brought yummy fruit."

"I see that." Beth released her sister and put her hands on Joey's shoulders. "Mister Joey's been in the Florida sunshine."

He giggled. "Mommy bought me a swimming pool." He did a little jump and raised his fist in the air. "Me and Gus play there every day. Sometimes his tail hits me in the face and it tickles." His eyes caught Molly's. "I'm gonna help Daddy."

Molly smiled as he skipped off. "That child loves his father."

"Yes." Beth leaned against the wall and looked at her sister. "You let Joey *swim* with the dog?"

Molly shut the front door and let loose an exaggerated sigh. "It's a wading pool, Beth." She conjured up a mock look of concern. "Don't tell me! You read something online about dog germs and how they can spread through water." She raised her brow. "Right?"

Beth chided herself. She hated sounding like their mother, always finding something to correct about Molly. But she couldn't seem to stop herself. She shrugged one shoulder and led the way to the kitchen. "It's possible." Her tone was lighter than before. "All that hair and dirt in the same water as Joey. Yuck!"

"Lighten up." Molly set her purse down on the counter and rolled her eyes in a silly sort of way. "A little dog hair never hurt a growing boy."

"I guess." Beth took a plastic pitcher from a lower cupboard and filled it with water. "It's just…I wouldn't let George Brett swim with the kids."

"You might." Molly took one of the kitchen stools and leaned her forearms on the counter. "Wait 'til summer hits. Even George Brett will need a way to cool off." She grinned. "I still can't believe you named a female golden retriever George Brett."

Beth smiled. She felt her tension ease. "Not like I had a choice."

When Jonah was born, she and Bill disagreed over his name. Beth wanted Jonah; Bill wanted George Brett, after his favorite Major League baseball player. They compromised. Beth got to name Jonah, and Bill got naming rights for their next dog. When the dog turned out to be a female golden retriever, Bill didn't waver. "George Brett is a fine name for any dog," he still said. "Even a girl." The name stuck.

Across from Beth and Molly, Jack had Joey in his arms, and for a minute Beth was struck by the picture they made. Nose to nose, lost in a conversation all their own. Molly was right. Jack and Joey shared something very special. And whatever germs Gus carried, they didn't seem to be slowing Joey down. She reached into the freezer, took out a tray of ice cubes, and popped them into the water pitcher. "The kitchen's almost unpacked."

"I see that." Molly sat up straighter. "You're amazing, Beth. I'd be living out of boxes for the first month."

They heard the sound of the patio slider and immediately the shouting voices of Beth's kids. "Mom!" Cammie raced around the corner with a hula hoop in her hand. Blain and Braden were quick on her heels, with Jonah bringing up the rear. Cammie stomped her foot. "Tell Jonah it's mine."

"No!" Jonah caught up to her, his face a twist of anger. "It's my turn. Daddy said she has to share the hoop-a-hoop."

"Hula hoop." Beth caught both kids by the shoulders and stooped down to their level. She looked at Cammie. "And yes, you do have to share. That's what Jesus wants us to do, and it's the right thing." Beth thought she saw Jack shoot a look to Molly. It didn't matter. She wouldn't change the way she raised her kids just because Molly and Jack would be around more often. She leveled a smile at Cammie again and then at Jonah. "Besides, look who's here!"

The kids lifted their eyes and Jonah's face lit up. "Joey!"

"Why don't the three of you go out front and play? George Brett's out there and I think a few kick balls, too. You can take turns." She glanced at Molly. "I love the fence out front. Makes it so safe."

Before Beth could add that now would be a good time for Jack to join Bill out back at the barbecue, Jack eased Joey to the floor and took his hand. "I'll go, too." He gave the women a lopsided grin. "I was hula-hoop champ in fourth grade." He pointed at Molly. "Bet you didn't know that."

"Wow," Molly flashed flirty eyes at her husband. "Such a talented man I married."

"That's right." His look back at her was just short of suggestive. "Don't forget it."

Beth watched, amazed. Molly and Jack had been married almost ten years. Shouldn't the teasing and flirting have worn off by now? Maybe that's what she and Bill needed. More of whatever it was that came so easily to Molly and Jack.

Silence filled the kitchen as the group tromped off, Cammie still clinging to her prized toy. Molly stood, found a plastic tumbler and poured herself some water. "It's a hot one out there." She looked out the window at the sky overhead. "Looks like summer's here."

"I know." Beth pulled the vegetable tray from the refrigerator and peeled back the plastic wrap. "It's okay for the kids to be outside, right? I mean, it's not too humid?"

Molly laughed and the sound lightened Beth's mood. "This is nothing. Wait 'til August and we'll talk about whether it's safe to play outside."

"Right." Beth laughed, too, but it sounded forced. Why was it so hard for her to find that natural sister rhythm with Molly? *Come on,* she told herself. *Molly's right. Lighten up.* She popped a cucumber slice in her mouth and looked out the window. Bill was flipping burgers, not even aware that Molly and Jack and Joey had arrived. She turned back to Molly and crossed her arms. "Bill's adjusting at work."

"I figured." Molly took a baby carrot and dipped it into the ranch dressing at the center of the tray. "The guy's a brainiac." She finished the carrot. "Everything else falling into place?"

"Yep." Beth took another cucumber slice. "Took care of updating our driver's licenses and applied for new voter's registration cards."

Molly shook her head. A thoughtful smile played at the corners of her lips. "You never quit, do you?"

"Meaning what?"

"Meaning the licenses and the voter cards." She waved her hand in the air. "The unpacking thing, the organizing thing." A chuckle filled her throat. "Aren't there days you just want to go to the clubhouse and sit by the pool?"

"Well," Beth poured herself a cup of water and looked at her sister. "I guess I figure there'll be time for that." The clubhouse was five doors down, one of the benefits of buying in Ashley Heights. Other than a quick look around, Beth and Bill and the kids hadn't spent any real time there.

Molly took her place on the barstool again and let her shoulders slump a little. "Sorry we couldn't make church."

Beth worked to keep her tone even. "Maybe in a few weeks." She lifted her chin and met her sister's eyes, unblinking. "Sorry we couldn't make boating."

Molly smiled. "It was nice. This is my favorite time on the water. Maybe you can join us next Saturday."

"We'd like that." Beth felt it. Molly was trying. "Bill's never spent much time on the ocean." She giggled. "Might be fun to see him get a little green around the edges."

"Beth..." Molly snickered. "Be nice."

"I am." She ran her fingers through her bangs. "I guess we both need to lighten up a little."

"Right. Maybe." Molly angled her head. "Hey, what church is it again? Where you went this morning?"

"Bethel Bible. A mile from here." She hesitated, not sure how much to say. "We tried the Wednesday night group and—"

"Loved it." Molly reached for another carrot. "Right?"

Beth lowered her chin. "Why do I sense sarcasm?"

"Beth..." Molly was on her feet, her tone apologetic. She came close and slipped her arms around Beth's neck. "I'm sorry." She wrinkled her nose in the cutesy way she'd done since she was five. "I could never be you; that's all." Her mouth curved up into a sweet smile. "Come on, don't be mad."

"I'm not." Beth removed Molly's arms from around her neck. "I have to get dinner going." Even now when things didn't feel quite right between them, Molly was light-hearted. Like she'd spent the previous four hours at a spa and nothing could possibly ruffle her. It didn't make sense. Molly was the one who needed God. If anyone should've been at ease, it was Beth and Bill and their kids.

Instead, even George Brett was uptight.

Molly returned to the barstool. She sipped her water and peered at Beth over the edge of her cup. After a long drink she set the cup down. "Well? Am I right?"

"About what?"

"The Wednesday night meeting—the church?" She rested her elbows on the counter. "You loved it, right?"

"Fine." Beth tried to hold it in, but she couldn't. A quick burst of giggles came from her lips and she blew at a wisp of her bangs. She could never stay mad at Molly. Never. "Yes. It was perfect. All of it." She exhaled and felt the tension between them lift. "Maybe this Wednesday you and Jack and Joey could—"

Molly held up her hand, though her smile remained. "Stop."

Beth hung her head for a moment. "I'm sorry." Her eyes found Molly's. "It's just...the Wednesday program is so good for kids and..."

"I have friends there." Molly took another carrot. "It's a good church, Beth. I'm just not ready to go." She popped the carrot into her mouth as if to punctuate her statement. As she chewed, she grinned and when she swallowed she held out both hands, palms up. "I love you. Can't we agree to disagree on that one area?"

The dream—the one Beth had always nurtured—had the two sisters living in the same city and the same neighborhood, but also taking their kids to the same church, sharing in the same Sunday afternoon potluck suppers. Sharing the same faith, the same purpose for getting up in the morning. If Molly wasn't ready for that, well then at least they were neighbors, close enough for days like this.

Beth grinned. She parted her lips and pretended to bite her tongue—the sign the two sisters had always used to signal that, whatever the discussion, it wasn't worth fighting over. They both laughed, and Beth looked past the silliness to the deep layers of Molly's heart. "Yes. We can agree to disagree."

They heard the patio door again and Bill came in, both hands covered with oversized oven mitts. He grinned at Molly. "Barely off the moving van and already Beth has me at the barbecue grill."

"I see that." Molly slipped off the stool, walked to Bill and gave him a quick hug. "The oven mitts and everything." She patted Beth on the shoulder. "When I moved here, it was two months before I found my oven mitts."

Beth opened the refrigerator and pulled out the tray of meat patties. "Okay, so I mark the boxes." She handed the tray to Bill. "How hard is that?"

"That's my Beth." Bill gave her a kiss on the cheek. "Don't let your sister tease you, honey. I wouldn't change a thing." He stopped and looked around the kitchen. "Where's Jack and Joey?"

Beth jumped in. "Out front." She kept the concern from her voice. "Jack's keeping an eye on the kids."

"Oh." Bill raised the tray of meat a few inches and gave the two of them a quick shrug. "Guess I'm on my own, then."

The women watched him go, and Beth let her gaze fall to the floor. When she looked up, Molly was watching her. "Bill sees through it."

"I know. I'm sorry." Molly frowned. Her expression held no excuses. "We have to give the guys time."

It was a thought that hung over the entire evening. Jack kept himself busy with the kids, even leaving the dinner table early to get refills of strawberry Kool-Aid. When it was just Molly and Beth and Bill at the table, Molly tried to cover up for her husband, gushing about how he was such a hands-on dad, and how he rarely took time to sit and listen to anyone, even her.

"He loves that boy, I tell you." She found a bit of laughter. Then she looked at Bill and folded her hands beneath her chin. "Hey, Beth tells me the two of you like your new church."

Bill set his burger down and dabbed a blob of ketchup off the corner of his mouth. "Yeah. We do."

"It's active, that's for sure." Beth didn't want to push, but since Molly asked...

Bill lifted his hamburger bun and slipped a few potato chips on top of the cooked meat. "I was on their Web site last night. They have a summer adventure program, family activities almost every day for three weeks straight, mission trips and work trips...." He took another bite of his burger and raised his brow.

"Really?" Beth glanced at Molly. She was picking the sesame seeds from the top of her bun. "I'm not so sure about those trips. So much can go wrong."

"Like what?" Bill was ready to take a bite of his burger, but he froze. "I thought it sounded like fun."

"Fun? Parasites and malaria and terrorists and violent street gangs?" There was enough to worry about right here in West Palm Beach. Beth shook her head. "No mission trips."

"Well...maybe you could think about it." Bill worked

his napkin over his mouth again. "They're taking a work trip to Haiti at the end of summer. It's for families—even young kids." Bill set his burger down. "That sort of thing could be life-changing."

"In more ways than one." Beth stirred her fork through her fruit salad.

The conversation fell flat for a few seconds. Bill leaned back in his seat and looked at Molly. "Did Jack get enough to eat?"

"I think so. You know Jack." She gave another nervous laugh. "Can't sit still for fifteen minutes. Last time we went somewhere with Joey he was up pitching balls before..."

She ran on about Joey and baseball for another minute, but Beth stopped listening. Molly's excuses for Jack were limitless. No matter how much she tried to explain the situation, the truth was painfully obvious. Jack was uncomfortable around them, uneasy with their faith. Maybe worried that Beth and Bill would try to convert him. Whatever it was, it left a tension denser than the pound cake she served for dessert.

That night before they turned in, Beth had to wonder. The last thing she wanted was a strained relationship with her sister. When Molly lived across the country, the two sisters shared weekly phone calls and got along great. Maybe it wasn't such a good idea that they spend every weekend getting their families together.

The smell of cinnamon floated up to their bedroom, but any ambiance it might've created was lost. Bill was already snoring. Beth closed her eyes. *God, what about my sister? She needs You, but I don't know. Maybe I'm not the one to help her. Show me, God...please.* Even as her quick prayer came to an end, she had the sinking feeling they were headed for trouble. With the tension that had plagued her sister's visit that afternoon, not only were weekly visits likely to be a bad idea.

But maybe it would've been better if she and her family had never moved to Florida at all.

FOUR

Wendy Porter was stirring the scrambled eggs when Rip came up behind her and wrapped his hands around her waist. She squirmed and clicked off the heat beneath the frying pan. "Rip..." The frozen sausages were already heated in the microwave, the orange juice poured, toast buttered and on the table. She turned and faced him. "Mmmm." He was fresh from the shower, clean shaven. "You smell nice."

"Right back at ya." He nuzzled her neck. "Last night was amazing." He left a trail of kisses along her collarbone and then straightened to his full height. He wasn't a tall man—five-ten on a good day. But she was just over five feet in her slippers, and he towered over her. The look in his eyes made her knees tremble. "Talk about your welcome-home parties."

"Rip...you're getting me flustered." She smiled and sidestepped him. The heat in her face was from more than the stove. No matter how charming he was, no matter how much he wanted the celebration to continue, they needed to talk. If he heard about the boy from Brent or Bubba, Rip would never forgive her. She took the glasses of juice to the table. "Thought you'd like a real breakfast on your first morning out."

"That's my baby. The perfect homemaker." He grabbed the frying pan and scraped the eggs into an empty serving dish. "Can't believe I still know my way around the place."

Wendy looked back at the frying pan. Images of other men she'd entertained in this very kitchen flashed in her mind. If Rip found out about them, there'd be no reasoning with him. She already planned to deny any talk of cheating. But the boy...

Rip was saying something, and she tried to focus. "...when I woke up, and sure enough—I checked the classifieds first thing, and there it was! Manager Wanted, Cleveland Regal Cinemas!" He slid his chair up to the table and raised his hands. "Everything's falling into place."

Manager of a movie house? Rip had never held any manager jobs before, and him just out of prison? Wendy tried not to let her doubt show. It was possible, right? With Rip's charm and all? She smiled. "That's wonderful, Rip." She took a sip of orange juice. "You can call about it after breakfast."

"That wasn't the only one." He took a large scoop of eggs and slapped it on his plate. "They got a whole list of jobs in auto work. Right up my alley, and..."

Wendy stopped paying attention. She took some eggs, but after one bite she lost her appetite. In half a day she'd learned much about her husband's transformation. He'd found religion, or so he said, gotten himself into some sort of counseling, and taken classes for something the prison people called "rage management."

The training was about to be tested.

"Rip..." She looked up and met his eyes. His mouth hung open and he looked surprised. He was probably still talking. "Oh...sorry." She set her fork down. Her hand was shaking. "Go ahead."

Rip hesitated. "That's okay, baby." He flashed a quick grin. "Must be important." He set down his piece of toast. "What's on your mind?"

"Well," she remembered to smile, but she could feel it stop far short of her eyes. She breathed out. Her stomach hurt. It felt like someone was turning a wrench on her insides, making them tighter with every tick of the clock. "There's something you need to know." Her voice grew soft, timid. "Something I wanted to tell you first thing when you got out."

Rip grew stone-still. His smile was still stuck on his face, but his eyes changed. Fear and curiosity, the hint of anger, and then a deliberate patience. Each emotion took turns with him. Even so, the only obvious sign that something wasn't right was the way he held his glass of juice. He was squeezing it so tight his knuckles were white. Same way they were whenever Rip was about to hurl something across the room. "You, uh," he gave a short laugh and set his juice glass down. "You cheatin' on me, Wendy?"

"No! Rip it's nothing like that, nothing at all." She stumbled over her words. "There's no one else, I promise." Not for six months, anyway. She swallowed. He hadn't asked her to go on, but she had no choice. "That's not it." She picked up her fork and poked her sausage. Her eyes stayed on his. "Remember back when you first got sent away?"

"Yeah. Worst day of my life." Rip looked more relaxed. She wasn't seeing someone else, so what was there to worry about, right? He took another swig of juice. "What about it?"

"Okay, well—" She set her fork down again. Why was the room so stuffy? She stood, crossed the kitchen and slid open the window over the sink. "There. That's better." A few steps and she was back at the table.

Rip was taking another piece of toast from the serving plate. He took a bite and started to chew. "So what about it?" He chuckled. "Used to be I couldn't shut ya up. Now what—cat got your tongue?"

Wendy pressed her fists against her middle. Anything to ease the tightness there. "A few weeks after you left, I was late." She looked at him, waiting for him to understand.

"Late?" Rip slapped a forkful of eggs onto his toast, folded it over, and shoved half of it into his mouth. "Late for what?"

"Rip..." Her tone sounded painful now. He wasn't making this any easier. "My period was late."

Rip kept chewing, but his motions grew slower. "Meaning what?"

"Well..." She exhaled hard and covered her face with her hands. When she looked up, she shook her head. How could she have waited this long to tell him? "I took a test....I was pregnant."

For a moment, time seemed to stop. Rip stared at her, unblinking. "What?"

"I was pregnant, Rip." She lifted her hands and let them fall to the table. "You got me pregnant right before you left. I had a baby boy." Her voice fell off. "Eight months later."

"A boy?" Again Rip released a sound that was part

laugh, part confusion. "You're keeping a kid from me?" He glanced around the kitchen and peered beneath the table. "So where is he?"

Wendy moaned. Her head fell back a few inches. *You can do this.... Finish, already.* She looked at Rip. "I gave him up. To a family in Florida."

Rip dropped his piece of toast. The eggs that had balanced there splattered to the floor. "You *what*?"

The linoleum felt like liquid beneath her feet. "I...I gave him up, Rip." She raised her voice without meaning to. "What was I supposed to do?"

"Wait..." He pushed his chair back. For a moment he didn't move or breathe or speak. "You gave away..." His tone fell to a whisper, "You gave away my...*son*?"

"Rip!" Like a lead blanket, fear draped itself over Wendy and made it almost impossible to breathe. The rage was coming, she was sure of it. Like a barrage of bullets, like an air raid, he was about to unleash his anger, and this time maybe she wouldn't survive. She stood and took small steps backwards. "I had no choice! You were in prison and I—"

"Stop." He held up a single hand. This was the moment when he would normally explode, only instead of rage, his eyes held a strange mix of shock and anger and fear. He stared at his plate of half-eaten eggs and toast as if he were trying to put together pieces of a puzzle that wouldn't quite take shape. After a long time, he looked up, his eyes narrow. "Shouldn't I have signed something?" His words were quick and clipped, like the ticking of a time bomb. "Don't both parents have to sign when you give a kid away?"

Wendy took another few steps back until she hit the wall. She opened her mouth but no words came. This was the hardest part, the worst of it. She had to tell the truth, or Rip would find out for himself and then...then she'd never come out alive. She twisted her fingers together and looked down somewhere near her feet. *Why did I ever think I could pull this off?* She lifted her eyes to his. "I... I signed both our names."

The statement was like a lit fuse, and all at once Rip was on his feet. "You can't be serious." He took quick, menacing steps toward her, his eyes dark and flinty. He was a foot from her now. She could see the greasy toast crumbs on his lip. When he spoke again, his words came through clenched teeth. "You signed my name? So you could give my son to some family...in *Florida*?"

She nodded fast. "Yes, Rip." With every sentence he sounded angrier, more incredulous. Coffee percolated in the background, but the smell was too strong. It made her sick to her stomach. "I had no choice."

"That's it..." He raised his fist and she could feel it, feel his knuckles crashing down on her skull, feel herself being knocked to the floor. Except the blow never came. Instead he turned just enough and his fist smashed clean through the wall beside her, inches from her face.

She slid sideways, away from the damage, away from her husband. She was next, absolutely. She squinted, afraid to look. Her hands came up in front of her, shielding herself, creating a layer of defense between the two of them. But again the blow didn't come. After a few seconds she opened her eyes and looked at him.

He worked his hand free of the crumbling drywall, shook off the dust and debris. Almost in slow motion his shoulders hunched forward and his arms fell slack to his sides. He hung his head and his voice slipped to a mono-tone. "What am I doing?" The question was geared to himself, not her.

She moved a few more feet away from him.

"Wendy"—he twisted his brow and stared at her, deep at her—"I was never going to do that again. Never."

"I'm sorry." A good three feet separated them now. "I...you were in prison, Rip." She was shaking so hard her teeth chattered. "I didn't know what to do, and I couldn't handle raising a baby by myself, and I looked into adoption, and—"

Again he held up one hand. "I get it." The knuckles on his right hand were bloodied. He pulled his fist close and cradled it against his waist. She heard him exhale. He was trembling, the rage trying to find a peaceable way to leave his body. His face was pale and little drops of sweat dotted his forehead. His eyes found hers. "I'm so sorry..." He held up his bloodied hand. "I didn't mean it." He hid his face with his good hand and groaned. "I shouldn't have...I'm sorry."

Wendy felt herself relax. Maybe he wasn't going to hit her or knock her to the floor. She straightened some. Truth was *she'd* done wrong by Rip. She should've taken the paperwork to the prison and convinced him fair and square to give up the boy. But then... "I never should've signed your name."

"Wait..." Slowly, hope seemed to grab Rip by the shoulders and his expression changed. "You know what?" This time his eyes flashed with new life, new excitement. "Maybe it's not too late."

Not too late? Was he crazy? The child would be four

now. Five in the fall. He'd been with the nice couple from
Florida since he was a few days old. She and Rip couldn't
just call up and say, "Hey, we changed our minds. We're
back together and we want our boy."

She thought hard. *Could they?*

No, they couldn't. Of course not. She had to tell her husband before he got his hopes up. "Rip, they don't just give
'em back. The boy thinks *they're* his family now."

Rip pierced the air in front of himself with one finger.
The rage was gone, but the intensity of his tone, his words,
was still enough to take her breath away. "I never signed the
paper." He walked to the phone and picked up the receiver.
"You went through child welfare, right?" He looked at the
keypad. "If I call information, who do I ask for?"

"Rip!" Suddenly it dawned on her what he was doing.
"You can't call and tell them I forged your name. They'll
have police down here in ten minutes, and then it'll be my
turn in the slammer!"

He didn't say it would serve her right, but his eyes spoke
loud and clear. He put the receiver back on the base and
stroked his chin. "There has to be a way." He took a
few steps toward her and then turned and walked to the
phone again. "We need a plan...a story. Something they'll
believe."

In all her years knowing Rip, Wendy had seen only
two sides of the man: loving kindness and blazing rage.
But now he was almost frenzied with determination, looking for a way to bring home his son. Like a person driven,
the way a drowning man is driven to get his next breath.
She moved a little closer. "You're serious about this." She
gripped the counter.

Just for an instant, the rage flashed again. Then it was gone, his tone almost matter-of-fact. "Yes. I'm serious." He brought his face closer to hers. "My only son is some-where out there." He pointed sharply at the kitchen win-dow. "You gave him away without asking me, so yes...I'm serious about this."

He eased back and pulled out a tired smile. "I'm willing to forgive you." He strained his neck forward some, as if the task of forgiving was as easy as swallowing a turkey leg. He pointed at the telephone. "But I'm making the call, and yes, I want him back." He slumped against the kitchen counter, their elbows touching. "The sooner the better."

Rip raked his fingers through his hair, something he did when he was frustrated. What he'd never done, though, is back down from a fight—the way he'd just done with her. He looked at her, half grinned, and patted her arm. "I'm going for a walk." He winked. "Anger management."

Wendy watched him go. Her knees stopped knocking even before he shut the door. Tigger the cat brushed up against her ankles, but she barely noticed. Her eyes were still on the door, her mouth still open, unsure of what to do or say. Was he serious? Had he really just gotten what must've been the worst news of his life, smiled at her, and made the decision to take a walk?

A walk, of all things?

Rip Porter had made promises to her since she was a seventeen-year-old high school junior. Never once had he made good on his word, never stayed away from the easy girls, never quit the bottle for more than a few months, and never—never once—had he been able to keep his hands off her when he was mad.

Until now.

Sure, he'd punched the wall. But a lifetime of rage was bound to take some time to fix. Theirs wasn't a house with patched-up walls. She'd taken every one of the blows in the past. She blinked and her eyes found the hole, the one he'd just made. Yes, there it was. So, maybe Rip was right, maybe the prison classes had worked and now he could handle getting angry without hurting her.

His words played again—*I want him back . . . the sooner the better.*

For the first time, Wendy considered the possibility. Rip had a point. Since his name was forged, the paperwork was a lie. Fraudulent, right? Wasn't that the word? She gripped the countertop behind her. Could they really do it? Could they think up a story, a reason why Rip's name was forged, and keep her from getting handcuffed in the process?

She thought of the baby, the way he'd looked and felt and smelled in her arms all those years ago. And suddenly, in a rush of loss and regret and a love deeper than the ocean, it all came back. Every moment, every memory. She was no longer standing in the kitchen of their small two-bedroom ranch, smelling the mix of cooked sausage and thick coffee. She was in the hospital, doing the one thing the social worker had advised her not to do.

She was holding her newborn son.

FIVE

With Rip gone for a walk, the memories swirled in Wendy's head, drawing her back with a power she couldn't fight. In as many seconds, four and a half years disappeared and she was lying in a hospital bed, the day she delivered her baby.

He had the palest peach-fuzz hair and a perfectly round face. But it was his eyes she remembered most, the eyes she would never forget. They were light blue, almost transparent. And as she held him, as she snuggled his warm little body against her chest and stared at him, his eyes seemed to see straight into her heart.

If he could talk he would've said, *Mommy, don't give me away. I don't care if it's just me and you.*

She held her finger out to her son and he grabbed it, held tight as if he would do everything in his power to stay with her. But she had to give him up, didn't she? What sort of life could she offer a little boy? She was working two jobs to make ends meet. She'd almost never see him. And Rip? He was rotting away in prison.

Still...

A wild and reckless love began to take root in her heart,

working its way deep, to the outer layers of her very soul. It was a love so strong it took her breath away and brought tears to her eyes. Maybe love would be enough. If he could stir up these sorts of feelings in just one day, then there was no limit to how much she might love him. She could love him more in the few hours a day she might have with him than other mothers could love in twenty-four straight, right?

For three crazy hours, her feelings waged war within her. Several times a nurse came in to see if she wanted a break, but each time she only held up her hand and shook her head. She was with her son. No one would disturb them until she was ready.

Finally, just as the third hour came to a close, she remembered what had driven her to the social services office in the first place. Rip Porter's fists. She could still feel his knuckles crashing down on her, breaking her collarbone one time and fracturing her eye socket another. Rip hadn't even served time for those beatings. "Bad spells," Rip called them.

So what if he got out of prison and had a *bad spell* with the precious baby in her arms? Newspapers were full of stories about guys like Rip and babies like this one. They were the sorts of stories that took up just a few inches in a news column on the fifth page: *Baby Dies after Beating*. Nausea welled up in Wendy, and her tears came harder. If she kept Rip's baby, one day Rip would come home and she would take him back, because she always did. She didn't know how to not love Rip Porter. And then the baby would be just one more person to rage at. One more person at the wrong end of Rip's bad spells.

She clutched the baby more tightly and rocked him close. His eyes told her how he felt. He was hers; he wanted her to take him home and love him forever. But she couldn't, wouldn't. Not with Rip in her life. Her tears became sobs, deep and silent. "My little son, I'm sorry. I have to...have to let you go."

Then, before she could change her mind, she rang for the nurse. When the uniformed woman approached her, she gave her son one last kiss and held him out. "Take him. Please. The social worker is waiting down the hall."

The nurse hesitated, but Wendy waved her off. "Please. I have to do this."

Later that afternoon the social worker stepped into her hospital room with the paperwork. Allyson Bower was her name, a woman with deep eyes and a story she hinted at but never shared with Wendy. Like every other detail of that time in her life, the social worker's name was never more than a heartbeat away.

That day, after Wendy had said good-bye to her baby, Allyson took the chair next to her. She looked at her for a long moment. Then she sighed and spoke her question at the same time. "Your husband's still in prison, is that right?"

"Yes." Wendy felt dead, drained. Her arms ached to hold her baby again. Something told her they would always ache that way. "Outside Cleveland."

She pointed to a few marked places on the paperwork. "I'll need his signature in order to sever your rights as parents."

"Okay." Wendy squeezed her eyes shut. She crooked her finger and pressed it to her lip to keep from crying. "Thank you."

"Wendy..." The social worker hesitated. "Are you sure about this decision?"

"Yes." She looked straight at the woman and gritted her teeth. Should she tell her the truth, the real reason why she couldn't keep the beautiful baby in the other room? Then, before she could think it through, she pulled the top of her hospital gown down just enough to expose the bump on her collarbone, the place where she hadn't healed exactly right. "See this?"

When the social worker must've realized what she was seeing, her eyes hardened. "Your husband did that to you, didn't he?"

"Yes." She pulled her gown back into place. "The other scars have healed." Fresh tears clouded her eyes. "The ones you can see, anyway."

"Wendy..." Allyson took her hand, and for a moment she hung her head. When she looked up, new understanding filled her face. "Why didn't you tell me?"

Wendy lifted her hands as the tears splashed onto her cheeks. "He's in prison for domestic violence. What'd you think?"

"You said he pushed you in the Kroger parking lot." Allyson looked defeated. "Have you reported him?"

Wendy's voice cracked. "I can't." She bit her lip and shook her head. "I never could. I love him." In a distant room she could hear a baby crying and she wondered if it was hers. "But I can't...have my baby around that."

Concern added to the emotions on the social worker's face. "What about your husband?" She picked up her briefcase. "What if he won't sign?"

"He'll sign." Wendy's heart beat harder than before. *Rip would kill me if he knew what I was doing,* she thought. *He wouldn't sign the papers for a million dollars. He's always wanted a son, as long as I've known him.* She wiped the back of her hand across her cheeks. "He hates kids. I'll have the papers to you in a week."

Allyson filled her cheeks with air and released it slowly. She stood, righteous anger written in the lines on her forehead. "It's wrong, what he's done to you. I can get you counseling, someone to meet with every day. Whatever it takes to get him out of your life."

The ticks from the clock on the wall seemed to get louder. The right answer was obvious. Wendy would agree, of course. She would get help and she would put Rip Porter out of her mind forever. But as long as she'd known Rip, he'd always found his way back into her life.

"Well...?" Allyson touched her shoulder. "Can I make the call?"

Wendy looked down at her hands, at the way they had clenched into fists. She shook her head without looking up. "It's no use. I'll never be rid of him."

The social worker tried for a while longer, but Wendy wouldn't budge. She couldn't expose her baby to Rip, and she couldn't get counseling for a problem she would keep going back to. Finally there was nothing else Allyson could say. "I'm sorry, Wendy." She gathered her briefcase and gave a nod to the paperwork. "Get it signed and back to me as soon as possible. The couple will be here at the end of the week. We'll keep the baby in short-term foster care until the papers are in order."

The couple. Her son's new parents.

Wendy had picked them from a nationwide data bank. Their bios were the only ones that grabbed her heart.

She still had them now, on the top shelf in the linen

closet. She crossed the kitchen to the front door and looked out the living-room window. Rip wasn't in sight. Still, she needed to find the file. Now, so she'd have it ready when he got home. The folder held everything—pictures, the information on the couple, details about her baby's birth.

Even a copy of the forged paperwork.

She went to the linen closet and opened the door. Every September 22—her son's birthday—she'd pull the file from the top shelf and remind herself that she'd made the right choice. Once in a while she'd take a look on a random day in March or June or just before Christmas. When she missed Rip or when she wondered whether her little boy was walking or running or reciting his alphabet.

Now she reached up and carefully pulled down the file. It smelled like cigarette smoke, proof that she usually couldn't get through the papers inside without chain smoking over every page. The top of the folder read, "Porter Adoption File." Wendy read the words three times. Her mouth was dry, and her heart stuttered into an uncomfortable beat. She dropped to the floor cross-legged and opened the file.

And there they were. The faces of all three of them.

Clipped to the inside of the folder was a photo of her son, the only photo she had. Gently she slipped the picture from beneath the paper clip and held it closer. She could still hear his baby sounds, still feel the way he held tight to her finger. "What did they name you, little boy?" Softly, with great care, she brought the photo to her lips and kissed it. "Have they told you about me?"

At times like this, the ache was so great she could hardly

stand it. She eased the picture back beneath the clip and forced herself to look at the first pages in the file, the couple's bios. Back then he was thirty and she was twenty-eight. The woman was a dark-haired version of Kate Hudson, with laughing eyes and a carefree face. The man looked a little like Rip. Same rounded shoulders and dark blond hair.

They were successful, no question. He was an international businessman making more money a year than Wendy would ever see in ten. His smile had Rip's charm, but this man had obviously found a way to turn the charm into more than cheap one-night stands. Their house was a three-story on the edge of a lake in southwest Florida. They had a boat and nice cars and all the stuff rich people like to own. But it wasn't their looks or their success or even their stuff that sold Wendy on them. It was what they'd written about themselves. She moved her eyes halfway down the page and began to read.

Hi. This is Jack. I work for Reylco, Inc., as manager of international corporate accounts, overseeing sales of pharmaceuticals. Reylco is the world's largest supplier of cancer drugs. Okay, that's the boring stuff. Here's the rest. My work schedule's flexible. Sure, I travel a lot, but I take my wife with me half the time, and when we have children I'll take them, too.

Travel's great, but home's better. I love Saturday bike rides and Sunday afternoon football games and the smell of my wife's spaghetti sometime mid-week. Yes, she makes a lot of spaghetti and sometimes she burns the French bread, but I love her anyway. If I wanted gourmet dinners I wouldn't have married her.

Everyone thinks I'm safe and conservative, and I guess I am. I'm a stickler for seatbelts and helmets and life jackets. But here's a secret. Sometimes at night Molly and I take our speedboat out and open up the engine. Just open it up all the way, blazing through the darkness, wind in our hair, stars in our eyes. I know, I know. It's a little dangerous. But out there the corporate world falls away and it's just us, loving life, loving each other, living in the moment.

The guys at work know the other me. The boating thing would surprise them.

Anyway, I guess I should tell you I'm a romantic. I write music and play the guitar, and if I'm sure no one else is in the house, I sing at the top of my lungs. Sometimes I dream about walking away from the whole corporate game, the long hours and heavy demands, and taking my family far, far away. We'd set up on some deserted beach on an island out in the middle of the ocean and I'd drink raspberry iced tea and write songs all day.

But I'll probably save that for our vacations.

See? That's the romantic in me. One time I tricked my wife into coming out onto the porch when she thought I was in Berlin on business. I had a CD player ready, and when she walked out the door I held up a sign that read, "Wanna dance?" We laughed and looked into each other's eyes and waltzed on the porch that night. Fifteen minutes later I handed her the CD, gave her a kiss, and caught a late flight out to Germany.

That's how I like to live.

We stay fit, because it feels better to be healthy. But I have a confession. I hate exercise. I used the stair-step machine at the gym for a while, but now my wife and I wake up early and jog together, six days out of seven. I still hate it, but with her there, I laugh a lot. They say laughing burns calories and it's good for your liver. So I guess we'll keep jogging.

I almost forgot. We have a yellow Labrador retriever named Gus. He's part of the family, but he's willing to give up the crib when the baby comes.

That's about it. Oh, one more thing. I want children more than I want my next breath. And somewhere out there, I believe with everything I am, that you'll find this and know—absolutely know—that we're the couple you're looking for. Life is short and time is a thief. We would make every day something magical and marvelous for your baby. The place in our hearts and homes has been ready for years. I already wrote a song for our firstborn. Maybe I'll sing it for your baby one day.

Thanks for your time.

Wendy had goose bumps on her arms the first time she read the man's letter. She felt dreamy when he talked about taking his wife on their boat late at night and flying like the wind across the water, and she got tears in her eyes when she pictured him dancing with his wife on the front porch and catching a later flight for his business trip.

She giggled when he talked about hating exercise and she burst out laughing when he mentioned that Gus, the dog, would be willing to give up the crib when the baby came. The couple had the sort of marriage everyone wanted. Between their laughter and loving, they would give her son a dream life—the sort he could never have with her.

Guilt washed over Wendy as she finished reading it now. How could she even consider taking the boy away from a couple like that? But then...they'd been fine before adopting. They'd be fine if things didn't work out, wouldn't they? They'd still have the nice house and the fast boat, the laughter and love, right? They'd still have Gus.

Wendy sat back against the hallway wall and read the woman's bio. It was shorter, but it had been the icing on the cake.

> *I'm Molly, Jack's wife. I love theater and law and sunsets over the lake behind our house. I have a degree in political science and once, a long time ago, I wanted to spend my life putting away bad guys. That or work as a Broadway actress. Being a lawyer would've been a little of both, I guess.*
>
> *Jack and I met at Florida State University the fall of my sophomore year. We were both cast in "You're a Good Man, Charlie Brown." He was Charlie and I was The Little Red-Haired Girl—the one Charlie has a crush on. I guess the rest was history. Well, not really. But after a few bends in the road and broken hearts, it was history. He's always been the only man for me.*
>
> *Our social worker told us to write about things that were important to us. Top of the list is high morals and strong character. Both our families believe in God, and even though we're not big churchgoers, we believe in living right—doing unto others as you would have them do to you. That sort of thing.*
>
> *Jack and I always wanted a bunch of kids, but things didn't work out that way. We're hoping for a baby through adoption, the child we will love and raise and cherish all the days of our lives. We look forward to hearing from you.*

Wendy pulled her legs up and rested the file on her knees. Again Rip's words shouted at her. *I want him back . . . the sooner the better.* If that was true, she couldn't spend another minute thinking about the nice couple in Florida.

She flipped the page, and there it was. The place at the bottom where she'd signed Rip's name. How could she and Rip explain the forgeries any other way? A handwriting expert could tell, right? They could check and figure out that her signature and his were written by the same person. But if they had the right story, maybe no one would ever check.

She stared at the signatures. What had the social worker asked her to do? Take the papers to the prison and have Rip sign them, right? Her mind began to turn, creating lies, sorting through possibilities. What if she'd taken the paperwork to the prison and left it with a guard? And what if the guard gave them to the wrong prisoner? Maybe someone who didn't really care for Rip? Then that prisoner might've read the documents and thought, why not? Why not sign someone's papers?

By the time the paperwork was returned to the guard, the damage would've been done, right? And she would've dropped by the prison, picked up the documents, and never looked back. She hadn't talked to Rip much the whole time he was in, so it was possible the issue of the boy might never have come up.

The longer she played the story over in her mind, the more sure she became. The lie might just work. All they had to do was convince the social worker Rip was a victim, that he had no idea he was a father until he was released from prison, and that someone else—another inmate— had signed his papers.

She was perfecting the story when she heard the door open.

"Wendy . . . baby, I'm sorry." There was the sound of his footsteps, and then he found her, sitting in the hallway, the file on her lap. His face was dark with sorrow and remorse. He dropped to his knees beside her and framed her face with his hands. "I'm sorry. I'm not mad at you." He had never sounded more genuine, more loving. "I just want our boy back." He hesitated. "Help me find him, okay?"

And with that, the only real reason she'd given her son up faded entirely from the picture. Rip was a changed man, completely changed. He was kind and compassionate, and even when he was angry he wouldn't hit her. The hole in the wall was proof. The Florida couple would be all right one day. They could adopt another kid. What mattered was the boy, and the fact that he belonged with his real parents.

Suddenly she could almost see their lives laid out before her. Their son would come home, and whatever loss he felt, she and Rip would make up for it. He would be happy and well-cared-for, playing ball with his daddy on spring days and fishing all summer long. With Rip back to work at the movie theater or the local garage, they might move into a bigger house, in a nicer neighborhood. Their son would have other siblings one day, and the Porter family would live happily ever after.

She searched Rip's eyes. "I'll help you." The first bit of a smile lifted her lips. She handed him the file. "You need to read this."

He took it, his movements slower, gentler than before. After he looked at the cover he lowered himself the rest of the way to the floor and sat beside her. "The adoption file."

"Yes. And, Rip..." She drew a slow breath, "I think I have a story that'll work."

With that they set their plans in motion. Now it was only a matter of carrying them out and waiting for the day Wendy never thought she'd see.

The day her son would come home to stay.

SIX

By the time Molly picked Joey up at Cricket Preschool that Wednesday, she'd finished half her to-do list: an early workout with Jack in the weight room upstairs, an hour of unofficial secretarial duties—typing a letter and organizing his files on the Birmingham Remming account, the one that always drove him crazy. He had a secretary at the office, but Jack was ambitious. With his pace, he needed extra help, and she was happy to give it. Besides the work for Jack, she had her monthly phone meeting with their property manager to make sure all was well with their rental houses.

She still needed groceries and a phone call with Beth. Just to clear the air after their barbecue. The few times they'd talked since the weekend, Beth had seemed short, the way she always acted when her feelings were hurt.

Molly lined up with the other mothers outside Room 4, Mrs. Erickson's room. When Joey spotted her, his face came alive. He held up a small white teddy bear. "I won, Mommy. I did my best and I won!"

"Thatta boy!" She stooped down and held out her hands the way she always did when she picked him up from school.

He was only fifteen feet away, but he ran with all his might and jumped into her arms. He was getting bigger, and the lift up was harder all the time. But she was still able to swing him up into her arms. He wrapped his little legs around her waist, and they touched foreheads.

"Eskimo noses first, okay?" He hid his stuffed bear behind his back and waited for her response.

"Eskimo noses it is!" She brushed the tip of her nose against his.

"Butterfly kisses, too." He brushed his eyelashes against hers.

"Butterfly kisses." Her heart melted. She loved everything about being Joey's mother. "Okay." She drew back and grinned at him. "How'd you win the bear?"

"I knew my ABCs." He pulled out the stuffed toy and held it inches from her face. "He's the bestest bear ever, Mommy. Softy and furry and growly on the inside." Joey's brow lowered and he tried to make himself look mean. "I named him Mr. Growls. 'Cause bears aren't really that friendly with little boys and girls. That's what teacher said." He cocked his head. "But he'll get along with Mr. Monkey, right? 'Cause Mr. Monkey is my bestest animal friend."

"Right. They'll be pals, I'm sure." She hid her laugh and eased him back to the ground beside her. They walked outside and stopped on the sidewalk. "Okay, let's see this softy, furry, growly bear." She held out her hand.

Joey giggled and plopped the bear into her fingers. "See? Isn't he perfect?"

"Oh, my." Molly studied the toy, turning him sideways and upside down. She jumped back and held him out to Joey again. "He is growly. He scares me."

"Mommy!" He drew out her name the way he did when he thought she was being silly. Again Joey laughed, and the sound bathed the cloudy morning in warmth and sunshine. She took hold of his hand and they crossed the parking lot toward their SUV. "I have a surprise!" She looked down at him, at his bouncy way of tagging along beside her. She could feel her eyes dancing.

"What?" He stopped and faced her. He had Mr. Growls by the ear as he did a few jumps.

"Costco!" She raised her fists in the air as if this were the best possible surprise a mother could give her son.

He lowered his chin and gave her a pointed look that was all Jack's. "Ah, Mommy. You still have errands, you mean? I want to play give-and-go today. Me and you and Gus."

She wrinkled her nose. "Yeah." She clicked the locks open on the door and helped him into the back. He hopped up into his booster seat, and she buckled him in. "We'll play when we get home, okay, buddy?"

"Okay." He wasn't disappointed. His eyes shone with the same sweetness they'd had when he walked through the classroom door a few moments earlier.

"One more thing..." She kissed his cheek. "Don't forget about the samples."

A smile brought his dimples to life again. "Oh, yeah. They have the bestest samples, Mommy. Remember?"

"I know." She closed the door and climbed into the front seat. "That's why I saved that errand 'til you were with me."

"Okay." In the rear-view mirror she could see him studying Mr. Growls again. He scrunched up his face as mean as he could and growled at the bear. The scowl faded when he saw her eyes in the mirror. "I love samples."

Costco took longer than she wanted. Joey sampled enough teriyaki chicken and buttered bread to make up for lunch, so they decided to pass on the sandwiches. When they got home, Joey helped her carry in the groceries, managing the super-sized paper towels on one trip and the giant package of paper plates on another.

"That's almost bigger than you, buddy." Molly was trailing him. She wasn't sure he could see over the top of the package. "Want some help?"

"Nope." He heaved the plates a little higher, stumbled, and caught his balance. "Daddy says real men help out."

She sucked her cheeks so she wouldn't laugh out loud. He wasn't *trying* to be cute, after all. When she had her composure, she steadied the box in her own arms and leaned over him to open the garage door. "Well, no question about it. You're a real man, Joey. Definitely."

He puffed his chest out and carried the plates the rest of the way to the kitchen without any further stumbling. When the groceries were put away, they went out to the basketball hoop in the driveway. The clouds had parted and the afternoon promised to be nothing but blue skies and warmth.

"I love give-and-go, Mommy." Joey put one foot forward.

She bent over and tied his shoelaces. "I love it, too."

Give-and-go was something Joey had picked up watching basketball with Jack. During warm-ups, a player would pass the ball to a teammate at the free throw line. That player would then pop the ball right back to the first player as he cut to the basket, just in time for him to make an easy layup.

Molly finished tying his shoes and took up her position. She still needed to call Beth, though something about the pending conversation made her feel unsettled. She held out her hands. "Okay, I'm ready."

Joey dribbled the ball—a miniature replica of the kind used in the NBA—and pretended to pass it to a couple of invisible teammates. Then he did a sharp bounce pass to her and took off toward the basket.

In a single motion, she caught the ball and passed it back to him nice and easy. Jack had lowered the hoop so it was only nine feet high. Joey stopped as he reached it, and with impressive form, he sent the ball up and into the net. He pumped his fists into the air. "Yes! LeBron James scores again!"

"LeBron James?" Molly brushed a piece of hair back from her forehead. "I thought you were Shaq."

He shook his head. "Shaq's old, Mommy. Daddy says I shoot like LeBron James. He's the most amazing player ever. Maybe more amazing than Michael Jordan!"

"Oh...I see." She held out her hands. "Okay, LeBron. I'm ready for the next pass."

His giggles filled the air and soothed her soul. They played for an hour before Joey started yawning. At four years old he still took a nap. He made a few more shots, and they went inside. She read him *Yertle the Turtle*, his favorite Dr. Seuss book. Then she bent down and kissed the tip of his nose. "Have a nice nap."

The navy curtains were drawn, the baseballs and basketballs and footballs that decorated his wallpaper, cool and shadowy. She gave him Mr. Monkey, the well-loved stuffed animal he'd had since his first birthday, and then Mr. Growls. Joey tucked them in next to him. He looked at her longer than usual, straight to her heart. "Know what, Mommy?"

"What?" She studied him, her precious son.

"You're pretty." He grinned, his loose tooth hanging a little more crookedly.

Molly felt her heart light up. "Well, thank you, kind sir."

"Know what else?"

She smiled. These were the fractions of minutes—before he fell asleep—when he said the things that mattered most. When all talk of growly bears and basketball players faded and the deeper places in his soul came to life. She messed her fingers through his hair and smiled. "What?"

"You're my best friend." He thought for a second. "You and Daddy, o' course."

"Thanks, buddy." She felt a tug on her heart, the one that reminded her that he was her everything. "How come?"

He put his hand over hers and smiled. "'Cause you play with me. And that's what best friends do."

"Well." Molly kissed him on the cheek this time. "I guess that makes you my best friend, too." She tickled his stuffed bear. "And that leaves Mr. Growls with Mr. Monkey."

Joey laughed. "That's okay. Bears like monkeys."

She stood and waved good-bye. "See you in an hour."

He yawned and nodded. "'Kay, Mommy. Love you."

"Love you, too."

It was two-thirty when she walked down the hall and into the family room. Beth would be home, making sure Jonah was down for a nap. The older kids wouldn't be back from school yet. No time like now for a phone call. Molly clicked a button on the keypad at the corner of the room. The Steve Wingfield Band came to life, filling their home with the melodious background sounds of "I'll Be Seeing You." She smiled. Nothing like big-band slow songs.

She reached for the phone, but her eye caught something on the bottom shelf of the bookcase. It was an old photo album, the one Beth had made for her as a high school graduation present. She'd pulled it out the other day so she could take it to the barbecue at Beth's house, but she must've gotten distracted and forgotten it.

"Photographs and Memories," the cover read. Molly picked it up and took a seat on the sofa next to the phone. She picked up the receiver and dialed Beth's number. A busy signal sounded in her ear. Beth didn't believe in call-waiting. She said every caller deserved her full attention. Molly put the phone on the base again and turned back to the photo album.

She opened the cover. How long had it been since she'd taken a walk through their high school days? Beth had made the album for her. Beth, who was always doing thoughtful things, always so proud to be her little sister. On the inside cover she'd written something in neat, per-fect handwriting. It was faded some, but she could still make it out. *Molly... I can't believe you're graduating. What will I do next year without you? I made you this album so you won't ever forget the fun we've had these last three years. I love you so much. Beth.*

They grew up in Orlando, Molly and Beth, the two of them one year apart in school. They ran in different circles—Beth in the social crowd, Molly with the dancers and theater types. But they found common ground on the cheer squad. The first picture was of the two of them the year Beth entered West Ridge High. They had their arms around each other's necks, silly grins plastered on their faces.

What the photo didn't show was the reason they were hugging.

Molly squinted at the photo and the years fell away. The picture was taken after homecoming game that fall, hours after one of her worst moments in high school. It was half-time, and the squad had shared a cheer with the opposing team. They were heading back to their locker room to freshen up when all ten of the West Ridge High cheerleaders stopped in their tracks.

There was Molly's boyfriend of the past year, Connor Aiken, star wide receiver, fully making out with one of the seniors from the dance team. The two were so lost in the moment, neither of them looked up or even noticed the cheerleaders passing by. All of the girls knew Connor belonged to Molly. They whispered and stared and cast pitiful looks in her direction.

Right away Beth was at her side, looping her arm through Molly's. "The guy's a jerk. I knew he was a jerk."

When they had rounded the corner, Molly couldn't take the humiliation another minute. She was stunned, unable to speak or cry or scream. She dropped her pompoms and ran around another corner to the bike racks outside the athletic building, the darkest place she could find.

Molly looked at herself, the way she'd been back then. Even now she remembered the pain of that moment. She had loved Connor—at least she thought she did. She figured she'd stay there in the dark, crying her eyes out until the game was over. But she was alone in the darkness for only half a minute.

By the time the tears hit, Beth was by her side. "Molly . . . Oh, Molly, I'm so sorry." She put her arms around Molly's neck. "But he *is* a jerk. I always thought so."

Molly sniffed and peered at her in the darkness. "You did?"

"Yes." She made a sound that showed her level of disgust. Then she gave Molly a list of Connor's shortcomings. Ten minutes later she was still talking.

Tenderly, Molly put her hand over Beth's mouth. "Okay, little sister." She released a long sigh. "I'm going to be all right—is that what you're saying?"

"I'm saying you're the best girl in all the world, Molly." She pointed an angry finger toward the place where they'd witnessed the kissing scene. "You deserve better than that. And right now I think your life's just about to get very exciting." Beth handed Molly her pompoms. "Come on. Hold your head high. We have a game to finish."

Something about Beth, about the way she believed in her even when Molly felt ugly and worthless, gave her strength to pick up and go back onto the field. Whenever she found herself looking for Connor's number among the players, she would catch Beth's eye. Beth would shake her head and force a smile, reminding her to do the same.

After the game, Connor came looking for her. By then he'd heard the news that the entire cheer squad had caught him kissing another girl. He was panicked when he found Molly in the school parking lot. Beth was with her, but she walked a few yards ahead so the two of them could talk.

Connor's apology was only just underway when Molly held up her hand. "We're done, Connor." She caught up with Beth and grinned back at him. "My life's about to get very exciting."

Before she and Beth met up with their ride that night, one of the other cheerleaders snapped their picture. Beth and Molly. Sisters and best friends.

Molly turned the page. There were several layouts of Disney pictures. The cheerleaders competed at a sports complex outside Disney World and afterward they spent two days at the parks. Even though they were locals.

She and Beth walked through the gift store on the second day, taking pictures of all the things they couldn't buy. There was a photo of the two of them wearing pointed princess hats, and another with Beth dressed as a pirate, and Molly as Tinkerbell.

A few more pages and there was the beach trip they'd taken to Sanibel Island the summer before Molly's senior year. Their parents had invited another couple, so that left Molly and Beth by themselves much of the time. One of the pictures was of the two girls standing between two guys—locals they met the second day of the trip.

Again the photo didn't tell the whole story.

That night, the boys invited them to a bonfire half a mile down the beach. Beth hadn't liked the idea from the beginning, but Molly—always the sillier, more spontaneous one—had pushed until Beth agreed. Their parents were playing bridge that night with their friends, and gave their approval without asking many questions.

Molly and Beth and the boys walked to the party, and

at first their behavior seemed harmless. But then one of the boys brought them glasses of punch. Beth took a sip and spit it out on the sand. "Don't drink it, Molly. It's spiked."

The guys laughed. "Looks like your little sister's never had island punch."

"Island punch?" Molly sniffed it. "Is she right? Is there alcohol in it?"

"Of course not." One of the guys put his arm around her. "Your sister's just a worrier."

"Molly, don't!" Beth took hold of her free hand. "Let's go. We shouldn't be here."

But Molly didn't want her younger sister telling her what to do. She grinned at the boys and drank the cup of punch in a series of quick gulps. Fifteen minutes later she knew the truth. Beth was right. The drink had to have been mostly alcohol. Molly was so drunk she couldn't talk or walk straight.

There wasn't much she remembered about that night, but she found out later what happened. The guys tried to talk Molly into taking a walk with them down to the water, but Beth wouldn't let them. She took hold of Molly's arm and half-carried her all the way back to the hotel. When their parents wanted to know what had happened, Beth covered for her.

The pages of the photo album hinted at stories Molly had almost forgotten about. Near the end of the book came the saddest photo of all. Molly had a guy friend, Art Goldberg, someone she'd been close to since fifth grade. Though the two of them never dated, she could always call Art when she needed advice from a guy or just a fresh set of ears to tell her stories to.

Art hung out at the house, and Beth and her parents often teased Molly that the guy had a crush on her. Molly never saw it. She and Art were buddies, nothing more. But on the last day of Christmas break her senior year, Art's mother called with tragic news. Art and a few of his guy friends had gone up to Michigan for a snowmobile trip. Two days before his eighteenth birthday, a few of them took an afternoon run on a well-marked trail. Art was leading the way, but he took a turn too fast, flew off the machine and hit a tree.

He died at the scene. His mother was crying on the other end of the phone. "I...thought you should know."

Molly remembered her reaction. She was unable to tell Art's mother how sorry she was, unable to ask for details or even hang up the phone. The pain was so great, it was like someone had cut off her right arm. She collapsed to the floor in slow motion and from somewhere in the depths of her heart she let out a deep, gut-wrenching wail that rang in her heart to this day. Their parents were at work, but Beth was reading in the other room. She came running, and when Molly could finally explain what had happened, Beth held her and rocked her for almost an hour.

In the months that followed, when Molly wanted only to go to the room they shared, crawl under the covers and sleep away the afternoon, Beth wouldn't let her. The two of them started taking runs after school, and holding long conversations about Molly's memories of Art and how much she missed him.

Beth's perfect 4.0 grade point average slipped that semester, and she had little time for after-school activities. She devoted that much of herself to Molly, making sure Molly survived. No doubt, that's what happened. Molly had survived because Beth willed her to survive. Those were the days before Beth found God, so it wasn't about praying and reading Scripture. It was just one sister devoting herself to another so that healing could happen.

Tears filled Molly's eyes as she studied the pictures on that page. Throughout the album, there'd been shots of Art Goldberg and Molly. But this page was sort of a tribute, a collection of last moments. The first was of Art and Molly, sitting next to each other on her family's sofa, watching television. It was dated fall, her senior year—one of the last times they shared an afternoon that way. The next showed Art and her sitting in a single lounge chair near the pool in her family's backyard. This time the date was November— still plenty warm enough for parties around the pool, and probably the last time the two of them swam together.

There was a copy of Art's senior picture, and next to it Beth had written, "Art will live on, always, in the memories the two of you made together."

The last picture was taken at his memorial service. It showed Molly, dressed in her church clothes, standing at the podium, tears streaming down her face. She could never have said good-bye to Art without Beth's help. Never. Molly ran her finger over Art's senior photo. "I still miss you, friend. Why did you have to drive so fast, you big dummy?"

She wasn't quite ready to turn the page when the phone rang. It was Beth. She knew even before she glanced at Caller ID. She picked up the receiver and clicked the On button. "Hey, you."

"Hey." Beth let out an exaggerated breath. "I thought

I'd get an hour to myself, but Jonah was bouncing off the walls."

"I tried to call you earlier. It was busy."

"I know." Beth laughed. "Jonah was practicing his phone manners—something they're working on in Kindergarten, I guess. Only does he tell me he's got the phone off the hook? Of course not." She paused. "So what's happening at your house?"

"Well..." Molly could hear the sorrow in her voice. "I was looking at that old photo album, the one you made me when I graduated from high school."

Beth's laughter faded some from her voice. "Saddest day of my life." She made a sound that was more sigh than laugh. "I wasn't sure I'd ever forgive you."

"I was looking at the page about Art Goldberg."

Beth allowed a few seconds of silence. "He was a good guy, Art."

"I never would've gotten through losing him if it weren't for you." There were tears in her voice. "I guess I'd forgotten how much you were there that year."

"It made your leaving for college that much harder."

"Yes." Molly turned the page. Almost every photo was of the two of them, Molly and Beth, inseparable. "I left the last day of August. I cried all the way to my dorm room."

"I cried every night for a month." Beth groaned. "You weren't that far away, but all of a sudden everything was different. You might as well have been halfway around the world."

Molly sniffed, working hard to keep her tone light. "I was going to get there, turn right around and come home."

"I remember." Beth's voice was quieter, as if she too

were reliving that day. "You called that night and said it was too much—you could attend community college, stay at home."

"And you told me not to dare think of such a thing." Molly smiled, even as her tears clouded her eyes. "You reminded me of every reason I'd chosen Florida State and you told me that besides, you were looking forward to having your own room." Molly laughed. "Something about your speech gave me the strength to stay. By Christmas I was in love with the place."

"I have a confession." Beth sounded sheepish. "I didn't want my own room. It took me most of that year to figure out how to fall asleep without those talks we had every night."

"I know, Beth. I think I knew it then." Molly leaned her head back and held the phone a little tighter. "Ever notice how we weren't like normal sisters? I mean, I was the oldest and you, the youngest." She sat up and looked at another picture of the two of them. "But every time I turned around, you were looking out for me. You never, ever let me fall apart."

Beth sniffed and Molly wondered if the memories had stirred tears for her, as well. "That's because you needed me. And I needed you."

"Yes." Molly turned to the last page. There were photos of her high school graduation and the going-away party her family threw her before she left for college. "We were something else."

The sound of children's voices made it hard to hear Beth's response. Instead Molly heard questions about snacks and homework being fired at Beth from Cammie and Blain and Braden.

"Hey," Beth had to yell to be heard. "The Indians are home."

"And they're restless."

"Exactly." The noise in the background grew. "Can I call you later?"

"Sure." Molly hesitated. "Hey, Beth. I love you."

"Yep." She could hear the smile in her sister's voice. "I love you, too."

They hung up, and Molly read the words Beth had written on the final page of the photo album: *Life will take us far from here. But one day when we're all grown up, when all our questions are answered, maybe we'll be neighbors and raise our kids together. For now, I'll miss you. I'll never forget sharing a room with you. And a whole lot more. I love you, Beth.*

Molly closed the book and held it to her chest. Beth was right. Life did take them far from their Orlando home. Beth got a scholarship to the University of Washington, and both girls married in their early twenties. Molly and Jack moved to West Palm Beach, and Beth and Jack settled in Seattle. They never went longer than a week without a conversation, but nothing had compared to those first growing-up years, the days when she and Beth were inseparable.

Never for a minute had either of them really believed that one day they'd be neighbors. But here they were, a lifetime spread out before them, endless seasons raising the children they loved and living with the men of their dreams.

And she and Beth, together again, right in the middle of it all.

Molly wiped at an errant tear and put the photo album away. Life couldn't possibly get better than this. In fact, it was so good it almost frightened her. As if by recognizing the idyllic lives they lived, she might somehow jinx them. Molly blinked and headed down the hall to check on Joey. Her fears were completely unfounded. Life was amazing and getting better all the time.

It was as simple as that.

SEVEN

The office was in a brick building in the heart of downtown Cleveland. Department of Children's Welfare, the sign over the front door read. Wendy held tighter to Rip's hand. She hadn't slept at all the night before, replaying in her mind again and again details about the Florida couple. Were they wrong, coming here? What they were about to do *would* be for their son's best welfare, wouldn't it?

She stopped, her high heels unsteady on the wet sidewalk. Overhead another thunderstorm was rolling in. "We're doing the right thing, aren't we?"

"Of course." Rip smiled. He'd been mostly charming since their conversation on the hallway floor a week ago. He kissed her cheek. "Back then we weren't ready to be parents. Now we are."

"Right." She nodded, and he led her up the stairs and into the building. They had contacted the department the afternoon she showed Rip the file. Allyson Bower, the social worker, was still there.

They walked up to a window and Rip spoke into the small hole in the glass. "We have an appointment with

Allyson Bower. I'm Rip Porter." He touched Wendy's elbow. "This is my wife, Wendy."

The woman at the desk checked her computer. "It'll be a few minutes." She looked at Rip. "I'll tell her you're here."

Rip thanked the woman, and he led the two of them to a pair of open chairs. There were two other people in the waiting area: a sad-looking man in his thirties and a young girl, probably no more than eighteen. Wendy shivered and leaned into Rip's arm. "I'm nervous," she whispered near his ear. "What if they don't believe us?"

"They will." Rip's upbeat tone faded a little. "Remember what I told you? Act like it's true and this'll be a cinch."

"Okay."

Wendy didn't want to disappoint him. Not when this whole thing was her fault in the first place. In the past week, Rip had grown frustrated with her a few times when they'd rehearsed the story at the dining-room table. She would become flustered or miss a piece of the story and he'd snap at her. But right away he'd calm himself down and apologize. So far the anger management, or whatever they'd taught him in prison, was working.

Besides, there was no reason to be nervous. So far the social worker seemed to believe everything she'd said.

On their first phone call to her, the woman pulled her file and seemed to remember their case. "Your husband was in prison. You gave your baby up because you were concerned for his future." The social worker stopped short of saying whether she remembered the bump on Wendy's collarbone, or the fact that Wendy had feared for her son's life if Rip ever got out of prison.

"Yes." Wendy exhaled. Rip was watching her, desperate to know which way the conversation was going. She closed her eyes. "Anyway, there's a problem. My husband, Rip Porter, was released from prison this week." She forced herself to sound weak, victimized. "All this time I thought he had signed the paperwork, the release papers. But now he says he never knew about the baby at all." She hesitated. "He wants our son back, Allyson. We both do."

A long pause filled the telephone lines. There was the sound of shuffling papers and fingers tapping on a keyboard. Finally, Allyson sighed. "Let's arrange a meeting. This is the sort of thing we should discuss in person."

"Fine." She flashed the thumbs-up sign to Rip. "When can we meet?"

They scheduled the appointment, and every day for the past week, the idea became more exciting. Their son would've gotten a great start in life by now. Any healthy child would be able to make the adjustment from one home to another—especially if the move was handled right. They could tell him that his first family was sort of a foster family. Nice people who helped out for a few years. But now he was getting the chance to live with his real family.

Yes, that would take care of any issues the child might have. Wendy stared at her hands, folded in her lap. At least she hoped so. And if it took a little longer for their son to make the adjustment, then they'd all have to be patient. Because one day he'd understand. They were doing this because they loved him, because they truly thought he'd be better off with them.

His real parents.

A door opened and there was Allyson Bower. She looked

the same as she had five years ago. The woman was in her mid-forties, tall and thin with hazel eyes. She wore a no-nonsense look, one that said she wasn't there to make friends. She did her job strictly on behalf of the children.

"Wendy?" Allyson gave her a wary look, and then shifted her attention to Rip and back again. Her tone fell somewhere between anger and impatience. "I'm ready to talk with you and your husband."

Rip took the lead. He met Allyson in the doorway and pumped her hand like a used-car salesman. "I'm Rip Porter." He grinned, pouring on all the charm he was capable of. "Thanks for meeting with us."

"Allyson Bower." She stood eye-to-eye with Rip. She didn't smile. "Follow me."

The knots in Wendy's stomach tightened. Allyson hadn't seemed so intimidating before. Wendy held onto Rip's arm and tried to remember her story. Dropping off the papers with the guards, getting them back signed, the long silence between her and Rip, figuring out that another prisoner must've done the deed, maybe as a trick.

Allyson opened the door to a small office and directed them to two chairs opposite a large wooden desk. A single folder sat neatly on top. Allyson sat in her chair, folded her hands, and rested them on the file. Once Rip and Wendy were seated, she looked at each of them for a long while. Then she drew a tired breath. "You realize what you're asking me to do?"

Across from Allyson, Rip didn't blink. "There's been a mistake, Mrs. Bower. We're asking you to get our son back for us."

"At this point"—she opened the file—"he's spent nearly

five years as someone else's son." She looked at Wendy. "You picked the couple, remember?"

"I do." Wendy slid her chair closer to Rip's. "We never meant things to turn out this way."

Allyson studied the first page of the file for a while and shook her head. "Before we take this another step, I'm asking if you've considered the turmoil and devastation this could cause your son." She folded her hands again. Her eyes held a silent plea. "I've read the reports from the social worker in Florida. Your son is doing very well. Taking him from the only home he's known could cause him permanent damage."

Rip crossed his legs and leaned hard on the arm of his chair. He gave a brief, exaggerated laugh. "Making things right will be hard on everyone, Mrs. Bower." He lifted his hands and dropped them again. "But the boy's a child. A very young child." He looked at Wendy, nodded a few times, and turned his attention back to the social worker. "My wife and I think he'll be fine after he adjusts."

Allyson couldn't have looked more surprised if Rip had said he wanted to take their son to planet Mars. "The boy will not be fine, Mr. Porter. He is at an extremely impressionable age. He is excelling in every possible way." Her voice grew louder, and she brought it back down. "Removing him from his home is a decision I highly recommend against."

Rip must've seen that he had the edge. "You recommend against it." He pointed at her and then lowered his hand. "But it isn't up to you, isn't that right?" He nodded to the file on the desk. "If someone forged my name, then my rights were denied and the boy belongs to me."

A look of defeat washed over Allyson's face. She returned her attention to the file. Without looking up, she drew a slow breath. "So what you're saying is, if we can prove your name was forged on the paperwork, you want us to begin the process of having the boy removed from his adoptive home and placed into yours, with you and your wife." Her eyes lifted to Rip's. "Is that right?"

"Yes." Rip crossed his arms. "We're willing to deal with our son's adjustment."

The social worker tapped the file. "Fine. Let's look at the paperwork. Explain to me how your name might've been forged." She stared straight at Wendy. "Obviously if there is a forgery and we figure out who signed your name, this department will prosecute to the fullest extent of the law."

Wendy felt her palms get sweaty. She looked at Rip and back to Allyson. "That would be good. Prosecuting who-ever did this." She gave a serious nod. "This is a terrible thing."

"Right." Allyson never broke eye contact. "So tell me how this happened. I have in my notes that I instructed you to take the documents to the prison and have your hus-band sign them."

"Yes." Wendy looked at Rip. "That's what I did."

Allyson raised her brow and pulled a notepad close. She picked up a pen and waited.

"Go ahead, honey." Rip motioned to Allyson. There was a warning in his eyes that only Wendy could read. *This is it.... Don't mess up.*

"Okay." She cleared her throat and leaned forward. Her eyes were entirely focused on Allyson. She clenched her fists and kept them tight against her body, out of sight. "I did what you asked. I took the papers to the prison." She blinked. "My husband and I weren't exactly on speaking terms. I gave the guard at the desk the paperwork and a note explaining the situation. I was pregnant, and I was giving the baby up for adoption."

Across from her, Allyson scribbled something on the pad of paper. She glanced up. "Go ahead."

"I was very clear that the package was supposed to go to Rip Porter."

"See," Rip cut in. "It happened more than once where a guard would pass the mail to another guard and a few pieces would get delivered to the wrong inmate." He gave her a troubled smile. "We've talked about it, Wendy and me. That's all we can figure."

Allyson stopped writing. "So you think the guard gave the package to someone else."

Rip pointed at himself. "I know I didn't get it."

"And I know I gave it to the guard to give to Rip."

Allyson gave a long look, first to Wendy and then to Rip. "You're sure you never saw the paperwork."

"Never." Rip sounded convincing, because at least that part was the truth. He hadn't seen the papers.

Allyson studied her notepad and then wrote something else. "Okay, Wendy, what happened next?"

Wendy's palms grew even sweatier. She wiped at them with her fingertips. *This is it, make it sound good.* She steadied herself. "I went back a week later and the package was waiting for me at the guard desk. I checked the papers before I left." She shrugged one slim shoulder. "I didn't look real hard, but everything seemed right. How would I have known it wasn't Rip's signature I was looking at?"

"Most people recognize their spouse's signature." Allyson's answer was quick. "Wouldn't you agree?"

"Of course." She tried to sound indignant, as if she resented the social worker doubting her for any reason. "Rip's signature isn't real easy to read, and neither was this one. It looked close enough."

"So you turned in the paperwork." Allyson stared at her. "And until your husband was released from prison last week you believed that he'd signed off on the adoption."

"Yes." She felt her hands relax. *Was it that easy?* "That's what I believed."

They spent the next ten minutes helping Allyson understand that Rip and Wendy truly hadn't had more than a handful of awkward visits over the next four years, and that Wendy had been too disturbed by the adoption to bring up the baby when they were together.

"Out of sight, out of mind," Wendy finally said. "That's the way I figured it would always be. A mother would go crazy thinking all the time about a baby she gave up."

Rip reached over, took her hand and squeezed it. The hint of a smile on his lips told her she'd done well. He was pleased with her.

Finally Allyson had Rip sign several papers, swearing under penalty of law that he had known nothing about the adoption and that he hadn't signed the paperwork. There were other papers, and a sheet he had to sign several times so that a handwriting analyst could verify that the signature on the adoption documents truly wasn't his.

There was talk then about Rip's domestic violence charge and the counseling and rehabilitation he'd received in prison. "I'm a different man today, Mrs. Bower." He sat a little straighter. "I learned anger management. I'm ready to be a father."

"Yes." Allyson looked disgusted. "I'm sure."

When the meeting was over, Allyson stood and pointed them to the door. "As long as the handwriting analysis matches what you've told me, I'll have no choice. I'll conduct a home study with you and your wife at your house. Then I'll take the issue before a local judge, and most likely he will grant you custody, Mr. Porter." She sounded tired, defeated. "After that, I'll contact the social worker in Florida and we'll begin the process of removing the boy from his current home and placing him in yours."

"Hey, thanks for your time." Rip took hold of Wendy's hand and headed for the door. "We really appreciate your—"

"Don't." Allyson held up her hand. "I must say..." Her eyes were angrier than before. "I've never had a placement reversed because of a technicality. Almost always the system works on behalf of the child. But if you win custody of your son, Mr. Porter, I will be most certain that the system has failed." She clenched her teeth. "I wanted you to know that."

"Listen, that's none of your—" He stopped short.

Wendy held her breath. For a moment it looked like Rip might explode. "Honey..." She squeezed his hand, and suddenly he seemed to remember where he was and what was happening.

He frowned. "I'm sorry you feel that way, Mrs. Bower. Maybe when this is all over, you'll change your mind."

Allyson looked like she hadn't heard him. She picked up the folder, turned, and filed it in the top drawer of a cabinet.

Rip didn't make another attempt. He nodded to Wendy and led the way through the door and into the hallway. When the door closed behind them, Rip eased his arms around his wife. "You were perfect." He swung her in a full circle. "He's as good as ours. They know where he is, and he's doing great."

"I'm so glad it's over." Wendy felt faint, anxious for the fresh air outside. They walked to the end of the hall, far from Allyson's office. She stopped and faced Rip. "She knew we were lying, don't you think? I mean, I kept waiting for her to tell us to go home and never come back."

"She couldn't do that." Rip's smile stretched the full width of his face. "I didn't sign those papers, and she can tell. No matter what she believes, it was wrong that I lost custody of my son."

"Yeah." Wendy pulled a piece of gum from her purse and popped it in her mouth. "I need a drink."

"Me, too." He wiped his brow and led her through the waiting room and outside onto the front steps. "Let's stop and get a twelve-pack." He kissed her hard on her mouth. "We have a lot to celebrate." He skipped down the steps, turned and took her hand, making sure her high heels didn't cause her to fall. A dreamy look filled his eyes. "I'll bet he's something else, that boy of ours." They linked arms as they walked to the car. "Everything's going to work out."

Wendy smiled. He was right. The meeting had gone better than they hoped. But somewhere inside her there was just the tiniest seed of concern. Maybe it was because of the social worker's warning early in the meeting. Allyson didn't think the move would be good for their son.

She said he might never recover from it. And then there was the last thing she'd said—that if they got custody the system would've failed the boy. Whatever it was, it took the edge off the victory, and even that night when Wendy and Rip were halfway through the twelve-pack, the feeling most intense in her heart wasn't one of joy and excitement.

It was one of doubt.

Allyson Bower was tired.

She'd done everything she knew to get her mind off work. It was early summer—her favorite time of year—and the thunderstorms from earlier in the day had passed. As soon as she got home, she changed clothes and headed outside to her flower garden. Petunias and gardenias, roses and daffodils. All of them were thriving and would continue to thrive if she kept up on the weeds.

For the first hour after work, that's just what she did.

But with every weed, every flower, she could see the little boy's face, the pictures in his file. The ones she wouldn't show Rip and Wendy Porter until a judge ruled in their favor. Finally she tried something else to clear her mind. She went inside and checked her baking cupboard. Milk, cream, sugar, bananas. All the ingredients were there. Maybe if she made her famous banana pudding the boys would love it, and that would keep her too busy to think about the Porter case.

She pulled her recipe from the old box with the fading flowers. Each card was alphabetized, so she immediately found the one she was looking for. It took fifteen minutes to make the batter, and while the pudding was in the oven, she helped her boys with their homework. Travis, fifteen, had questions about lowest common denominators and factoring, and Taylor, seven, was trying to understand double-digit addition. More than enough to keep Allyson's mind distracted. Just before dinner, Tavia, her oldest, stopped by on her way home from work. She brought little Harley with her, Allyson's only grandchild. An hour of talk about Legos and dinosaurs and the chaos of fixing tortillas, beans, and rice with Harley underfoot, and Allyson wanted to think she'd put her work aside.

But it was impossible.

After the kids were in bed, she popped in a video of Alabama football highlights from the previous season, but even then she was distracted. Finally she clicked the Off button on the television, turned out the lights, and stared at the ceiling.

How could they do it?

The boy was absolutely perfect. He was ahead of his class in preschool, well-adjusted in every way possible. The latest report showed that relatives of the adoptive mother had recently moved to West Palm Beach. That meant the boy had an aunt and uncle and possibly cousins in the area.

She hadn't been lying to the Porters earlier that day. To tear him away from that environment truly would be devastating. She turned onto her side and stared through the sheer curtains to the streetlight outside. Something about their story didn't ring true. Even if a prison guard gave the packet of documents to the wrong prisoner, why would that prisoner forge Rip's name?

If it was a lie, it was a careful one. The way the story

went it, didn't matter why someone would do such a thing. The culprit was nameless, faceless. Short of interviewing every inmate at the prison four years ago, there was no way to find out who might've received the package and forged Rip's name.

Allyson suspected it wasn't a prisoner at all, but Wendy Porter herself. She'd documented the conversation she'd had with the woman in the hospital four years ago. And she'd read it several times that day, both before and after the meeting with the Porters.

Wendy Porter had been afraid of Rip. She hadn't wanted him to come home from prison and release his rage on her baby son. That's the reason she gave him up. At the time Allyson had asked the woman whether Rip would have a problem signing the papers, and Wendy's answer had been quick. Definitely not.

But did that really make sense?

The branches in the trees outside her window swayed gently, casting moving shadows on her bedroom floor. If the man was abusive, and if he followed the profile of most domestic-violence perpetrators, he would never have signed away his rights to a son. Abusers tend to have a strong sense of ownership. It was at the root of why they were abusive in the first place. They see people as objects to be owned and manipulated. When a person doesn't respond correctly, the abuser unleashes on that person as a way of keeping his possession in line. Abusive people are very aware of their possessions.

Especially their wives and children.

Allyson breathed out long and slow. She could put the pressure on Wendy, make her take a lie-detector test or have her handwriting scrutinized to see if it might be possible that she—and not an erroneous prisoner—forged Rip Porter's name.

But what was the point?

If her theory was correct, they could prosecute Wendy, maybe even send her to prison for a few years. But the boy would still belong to Rip. And that was the one part of the story that did ring true—until he'd been released from prison, Rip Porter knew nothing about having a son. The name on the paperwork did, indeed, look different from the signature he'd supplied them that morning.

So how would it help having Wendy sent away?

If Rip was going to get custody, if the boy had to leave his home and start a new life in another state with people he didn't know, then Wendy should be part of the formula. The boy would need a mother, wouldn't he? Someone to watch out for him if Rip's rage ever returned?

No wonder sleep wouldn't come.

By tomorrow afternoon she'd have her answer about Rip's handwriting, whether the county expert thought his name had been forged. Then the judge would follow the established protocol for a situation like this. He'd grant custody to Rip and Wendy. And in a very short time, the boy's idyllic life would come to a screeching halt.

She closed her eyes and pictured her own children. Tavia with little Harley...Travis...Taylor. How would they respond if someone called and said that life as they knew it was over? That they would have to leave and go live with another family, never to look back again?

Allyson did not cry often. She had seen too much, gotten too hard to get emotional over every case that didn't turn out right. Usually it was the temporary custody, the times when a child was making progress with a foster parent only to be placed once more with a natural parent—a drug user or rehabilitated convict. Heartache was part of the job.

But now tears spilled from her eyes and onto her pillow.

Something about this case made her think of her own father, the man she'd loved and lost to cancer so many years ago. A series of sobs shook her. "Daddy...I still miss you. Tell me what to do." It wasn't right. Somewhere in Florida, a little boy who had known from birth a very special relationship with his parents was likely going to lose them both. Not because of cancer. But because the system was about to fail him utterly.

And that—more than anything that had come across her clean desk in the past decade—was enough to make her weep.

EIGHT

Beth sat next to Molly on the bench that faced the park swings. Joey and Jonah were racing, seeing who could swing the highest.

"I love this." Beth breathed in through her nose and smiled. "Those two boys are going to be best friends." She glanced at Molly. "Can't you just feel it?"

"Yes." Molly leaned forward and put her elbows on her knees. "Every time they're together."

The older kids were riding their bikes on the path that circled the park. School was out, and it was the middle of June. Humidity had hit—but not to the point of being unbearable. Blue skies, eighty degrees, and a light breeze made the South Florida afternoon feel perfect. The heat from earlier in the month had eased, and they all looked forward to their twice weekly morning visits to the park. That morning Beth had called Molly, the way she'd done every Tuesday and Thursday since they unloaded the moving van. "Up for the park?"

Molly laughed. "Joey's been bugging me about it since he woke up. Let's bring a picnic."

Already the kids had been playing for almost an hour.

Beth leaned back. "Know what I was thinking?"

"Uh-oh." Molly looked over her shoulder at Beth and winced. "This isn't about church, is it?"

The question hurt. Beth hadn't brought up church since the barbecue; she'd made a promise to stay away from the topic. She felt her smile fade. "Thanks."

"What?" Molly was quick with an apologetic tone. She put her hand on Beth's shoulder. "Hey, don't get mad. I'm sorry." She giggled. "I'm just teasing. You've been very good about the whole church thing."

"Okay, then. Give me a little credit."

"I will." Molly angled herself so she was facing Beth. "What were you thinking?"

Beth took a minute to transition. When she spoke, some of her enthusiasm was gone. "I was thinking how the two of us were a lot like Joey and Jonah. When we were little, I mean."

Molly straightened and leaned back against the bench. She watched the boys, how Joey encouraged Jonah, spouting a series of pep talks and instructions. "Yeah. I can see that." She laughed. "Joey *is* sort of bossy."

"Not bossy." Beth angled her head, her eyes on the boys. "He cares about Jonah. Like he's personally responsible for Jonah's well-being."

Molly looked at her. "I was like that with you?"

"When we were little, yes." Beth crossed her ankles and stretched out her legs. "I can remember when we were learning to ride our bikes." She giggled, the hurt from Molly's earlier remark entirely gone. "Remember those burnt orange bikes with the white stripes on the sides?"

"And the white tassels flying from the handlebars?"

"Right." Beth looked up and watched a pair of blue jays land in a maple tree twenty yards away. "Anyway, you were seven and I was five, I think. You were learning to ride a bike, so I wanted to learn, too. It didn't matter if I was young."

"We had training wheels, right?"

"Right, but that summer Dad took them off." Beth could see them, scared to death about the prospect of riding two-wheelers. "Anyway, he worked with you first and then, I don't know, he must've gotten a phone call or something. He told you to keep practicing. He'd be out in a minute to teach me."

"Oh, yeah." Molly faced her again. "I remember now. As soon as he was in the house, I climbed off my bike and ran to you."

"Right. You said you didn't want to ride without me." Beth laughed and looked at the boys again. "Instead of practicing, you ran alongside me and after a few runs I was riding like a pro."

"But when I climbed back on my bike, I got about three wobbly feet and crashed to the ground."

Beth giggled. "Exactly." She watched the boys slow down, jump off the swings, and run for the merry-go-round. Joey was leading the way. "You weren't bossy. You were just looking out for me."

"The way you looked out for me when we were older."

"Yeah." Beth smiled at her. "Like that, I guess."

Just then the boys came running toward them, each shouting and pointing at the other. Jonah got his words out first. "He won't let me have a turn pushing the merry-go-round! He says I have to stay still and enjoy the ride."

"Joey... that's not very nice." Molly brushed her knuckles against her son's face. "What have we taught you about sharing?"

"Yeah, but I'm taller than him, Mommy." Joey pointed back at the merry-go-round. "I can push 'cause I'm a big boy. Jonah's a little boy."

"Am not!" Jonah stuck his tongue out at Joey. "I'm older than you! So you're a little boy, Joey!"

"Mom..." Joey held out his hands, pleading with Molly. "It's better to ride, anyway. I'm just trying to be nice."

"Why don't you boys take turns?" Beth patted Jonah on the back. "You're both big enough to push. Let's see how that works out."

They looked hesitant, but they ran off anyway. Halfway there, Joey tapped Jonah on the shoulder and stuck his tongue out. "There," they could hear him say. "That's a payback."

Both women laughed. "Of course, there was plenty of that between us, too." Beth sorted through her lunch bag for an apple. "I remember the time when the dog ate the head off your Barbie. We were maybe ten and twelve. Remember that?"

"How could I forget? I stole your Barbie head to replace mine and tried to pretend like nothing was wrong."

"Only my Barbie had a headband that matched her dress." Beth took a bite of her apple and chuckled. "Must have been pretty easy for Mom to solve that one."

"I never was a very good liar."

"No."

The clouds were gathering faster, darkening the sky. They'd had thunderstorms nearly every day since their family landed in West Palm Beach, and today's forecast was for more of the same. "Looks like a storm."

"Better move this picnic to my house." Molly stood and collected her things—the lunch bag and the mesh net with Joey's sand toys. She motioned to the older kids. "Want me to tell them?"

"Thanks." Beth grabbed her bag and peered at the sky. Lightning pierced the closest clouds. "We better hurry. I'll go start the car. The kids can throw their bikes in the back. "She cupped her hands around her mouth. "Come on, boys! Let's go—storm's coming."

Joey and Jonah hesitated, and for a moment it seemed they might complain about having to leave. But instead Joey jumped off the merry-go-round and tore across the sand for the grassy field adjacent to the play area. "Come on! Look at all the dandelions!"

"Just a minute." Molly jogged toward Beth's older kids and yelled for them to come to the car. Then she turned back to Joey. Just a month ago, the entire grassy field had been dotted with bright yellow dandelions. But now the ground looked like a million fuzz balls. When the boys raced across the field, they stirred up a cloud of seeds. Joey and Jonah giggled and ran back to Beth and Molly.

"There's a kabillion dandelions at this park, did you know that, Mommy?" Joey took Molly by the hand. "A super-kabillion."

"Yeah." Jonah skipped in alongside Beth. "They're fun to race through."

In the distance, another bolt of lightning flashed across the sky. "Okay, boys," Beth picked up her pace. "Time to run."

They piled into Beth's van just as the first raindrops hit the windshield. "Whew." Beth slid her key into the ignition. "That was close."

The older kids took the back seat. "I had the most laps." Cammie sounded proud of herself.

"Did not." Blain made a face at her. "I lapped you three times."

The debate continued. In the rear-view mirror Beth could see Joey staring wide-eyed out the window. "I love storms."

"Except at night." Molly gave Beth a wry look. "He's in bed with us as soon as the first clap of thunder hits."

Joey leaned forward. "Yeah, Mommy, but that's because storms are 'posed to be shared."

"Right." Jonah nodded, his expression serious. "I like sharing storms with my mommy and daddy, too."

The conversation remained comical all the way to Molly's house, through her garage, and into the kitchen. While they spread out their lunches on the dining room table, Beth savored how good life felt. Her sister was once again her best friend. And their little boys were on their way to the same sort of friendship.

Still, there was something missing, something Beth didn't dare bring up. And as Molly went to check the phone messages, Beth said a silent prayer. *God...please give Molly a reason to need You. I won't bring it up...so give her a reason, God. Please.*

❧

The kids were situated at the table, but the message light was flashing on the answering machine. Probably a salesperson. Jack would've called on her cell phone, and with school out there weren't many calls that needed her attention. Still...she wanted to check.

A burst of thunder rattled the windows, but Molly didn't mind. Lightning storms were a part of life in Florida. She'd grown up with them, and by now she rather liked them. They made her lakeside home feel safe and warm, like a cocoon against the elements.

She pressed the message button and waited.

"You have one new message," the automated voice announced. "First message, sent today at 10:31 a.m."

The message started. "Hello..." The caller hesitated. "This is Allyson Bower. I'm a social worker in Ohio, the one who handled the placement of your son."

Immediately Molly hit the volume button, bringing the sound down so that it was barely audible. Joey knew nothing about his adoption. Not yet. They were waiting until he started kindergarten to tell him something simple and straightforward.

Across the room, the message had caught Beth's attention. She stood and looked at Molly as if to say, "What's the problem?"

Molly waved her off and lowered her head so she could make out the rest of the woman's words. "I tried to contact the social worker in Florida who handled your case, but she's not with the department any longer." The woman released what sounded like a painful breath.

"Anyway," the message continued, "something's come up. I need to talk to you as soon as possible. I leave the office at two o'clock, so if you or your husband could call back this afternoon or tomorrow morning, I can update you about what's going on." The woman gave her name again and a number. Molly stopped the machine and saved the message.

Her heart slammed about in her chest like a frenzied pinball. What was the woman talking about? What could possibly have come up? The adoption file had been closed since Joey was six months old. The paperwork was signed, the courts had agreed, and that was all there was to it.

So who was this Allyson Bower, and how had she gotten their number?

Beth was at her side, her arm around Molly's shoulders. "Molly, you're white as a sheet." She led Molly to a bar-stool. "What is it?"

"Joey..." Molly couldn't finish her sentence. She pointed at the boys. "Joey."

"He's fine, Molly. I took out the sandwiches and got them set up. Don't worry about him."

Molly blinked, and her trance suddenly lifted. Why was she panicking? It was only a phone call, right? She straightened and looked at Beth. "That was a social worker...from Ohio. Something's come up. We have to...have to call her back."

"Okay." Beth didn't look worried. "There's probably some update they need for his file. Isn't that normal with state adoptions?"

"An update?" Molly's heartbeat found a more normal rhythm. "The social workers here in Florida do the updates. Once a year until Joey's five. After that, it's up to us to provide information for his file, for the...the birth parents."

"So maybe the Social Services in Ohio didn't get the

update this time." Beth still didn't look worried. "Isn't that possible?"

Molly closed her eyes. Yes, that had to be it. Something missing from the file. What else could a social worker from Ohio want with her and Jack? The adoption was as neat as it could be. No loose ends, wasn't that what her Florida social worker had told her? But a call like this could mean...

She looked at Joey, blond hair and laughing eyes, taking the top slice of bread off his sandwich and licking the strawberry jam. She felt her shoulders relax a little. He was fine; he was theirs. She wouldn't let herself think about it. She'd known very little about Joey's birth mother. The woman wasn't on drugs, and she hadn't been a drinker. The biggest problem was her husband, a man in prison for domestic violence. According to her social worker, the woman had given Joey up for his safety. She had picked Molly and Jack after looking through profiles from a dozen different states.

There couldn't possibly be a problem.

Beth was saying something, but Molly couldn't focus. "You're right. A technicality, something missing in the file." She forced a quiet laugh. "I panicked for nothing." She looked at Beth. "We made sure everything was right. No loose ends. That's what they told us. No loose ends. Nothing to make this a problem down the road when Joey was—"

"Molly!" Beth took hold of her arm and gave her a shake. "Shhh!" She looked behind her at the boys. "Joey'll hear you."

Molly held up her hands. "I'm fine." She lowered her voice. Had she been talking loud? She steadied herself against the back of a barstool. "Sorry. Everything's fine."

"Okay, then let it go." Beth's voice was urgent. "Come on."

She searched Beth's eyes, frantic for a reason to stave off the sudden, intense fear coming at her again. "Nobody would ever..." Her voice slipped to a whisper. "Ever try to take Joey from us." She faced her sister. "Would they?"

"No." Beth shook her head quickly. "Definitely not. The adoption was final years ago."

Yes, of course. Molly exhaled long and slow. All the reasons that had reassured her moments ago ran through her mind again. The adoption was final years ago. No one would question it after all this time. She ordered her heartbeat to slow down again.

"Mommy..." Suddenly Joey was at her side, tugging on her sleeve. "Are you sick?"

Molly let go of Beth and sat a little straighter. She looked down at Joey. "No, honey." She was still catching her breath. "Mommy's fine."

"How come you're not eating lunch with us?" He pointed back to the table. "It was a'posed to be a picnic for everyone. Even the moms."

"Right." Beth patted Joey's back and sent him in the direction of the table. "We'll be there in a minute."

"I'm on my second half, Mommy." Jonah held up his sandwich. "Hurry, okay?"

Another clap of thunder shook the house. Molly inhaled sharply and gave a quick shake of her head. "You're right." She stood and looked at Beth. "I won't worry about it."

"Good call." Beth spoke the words with certainty and confidence. "It's nothing—I'm sure."

"Right." She looked at the boys in the next room. Her

body felt unsteady, but her breathing was normal now. "I guess I just have a phobia of social workers."

"Yeah." Beth gave her the cuckoo sign. "I can see that."

Molly held out her arms and Beth did the same. They came together in a hug that righted Molly's world. When she pulled back, she grinned at her sister. "What would I do without you?"

Beth smiled, and in that single smile Molly could see a lifetime of moments like this one. "The good news is, we won't have to find out."

"You're right."

"Okay then..." Beth took Molly by the hand and led her to the kitchen table. "I think we have a picnic to attend." She slid in next to Jonah.

"Yeah." Joey patted the seat next to him, and when Molly sat down, he put his arms around her neck and kissed the tip of her nose. "Before it's all finished."

Her appetite wasn't what it might've been, but Molly put on a good act. While the lightning and thunder continued outside, they ate their peanut butter sandwiches and carrot sticks and drank their juice packs.

Jonah was impressed with the way Beth could take tiny bites from the carrot, leaving a toothpick-thin center before popping it in her mouth. "I think you're a champion, Mommy."

"Yes." Beth raised her hands in the air and took a bow. "When it comes to carrots, no one can eat 'em like me."

Joey laughed when Molly tried and the carrot cracked in half. "You're not very good at it, Mommy."

"I guess not." She giggled. For the first time since getting the message, she felt her fears subside. Gus had been sleeping by the door, but now he stretched and came to sit between the two of them. Molly tossed her broken carrot pieces onto her plate. "I think Gus could do a better job than me."

"Hey, Gus-boy...I'm almost done with my picnic; then I can play." Joey cooed at the dog. "Can he have a carrot, Mommy? Please?"

Gus loved it when Joey fed him carrots. Either that, or he just loved Joey. "Okay. But don't let him lick your fingers. Not while you're still eating."

The picnic came to an end, and Beth and her kids went home. Before she left, she shook her finger at Molly and gave her a look that said, *Don't think about it.* Everything was going to be okay.

Molly nodded. But after Beth was gone, she sat in the living room, watching Joey and Gus. The boy would sit on the floor next to the dog for hours, his head resting on Gus's back. Every now and then Gus would release a sigh and cast a look at Joey as if to say, *Hey, best friend, don't ever grow up.* Gus was eight years old and not as spry as he once was. But when the storm let up, he'd match Joey step for step in a race across the back yard.

Joey ran his hand along the dog's neck. "We went on the merry-go-round today, Gus."

The dog lifted his head and cast a slow look at Joey.

"I know." Joey's sing-song voice filled the house. "I wish you were there, too." He thought for a minute. "You couldn't have pushed very good, but I bet you could hold on tight. Know why?"

The dog yawned.

"That's right." He patted Gus's front paws. " 'Cause you've got good claws in your feet."

After a while, Gus put his head down and fell asleep. Joey lifted one furry ear. "You sleeping, Gus?"

When the dog didn't stir, Joey popped up and wandered toward Molly. Another clap of thunder made him hurry his steps. "Is it naptime?" He looked worried about the possibility.

"An hour ago." Molly lifted him into her lap and situated him so his legs stuck out to one side. "How 'bout we take a nap together on the couch today?"

"Yay! I like when we do that."

She stood him up, and stretched out on her side. There was still plenty of room for him, and he hopped up, cuddling against her as he closed his eyes. "Know why this is perfect, Mommy?"

"Why?" She kissed the side of his face. The social worker's message played in her mind again. It was nothing. A technicality. Something for his file. That's what Beth said.

"Because..." He opened his eyes so he could see her. He smelled like peanut butter and grass and Gus all at the same time. "Storms are 'posed to be shared."

"Yes, buddy." She held him a little closer. "They are."

This storm and any storm. As Joey fell asleep she hoped with all her heart that Beth was right. And that in the coming days the thunder and lightning outside would be the only type of storm they'd have to face.

⚜

NINE

J ack made the call early the next morning before work.

As soon as he'd gotten home from the office, Molly told him about the message from the social worker and he listened to it himself. He agreed with Beth. This Allyson Bower probably was missing a detail in Joey's file somewhere, a bit of information that was part of regularly updating the adoption files.

Still, the hour of wrestling on the floor with Joey and carrying him around on his shoulders like King Kong and reading him *Finding Nemo* before bed all took on extra significance. Joey's laughter filling the living room, the feel of his little-boy hands tucked safely in Jack's own, the smell of shampoo in his damp hair after bath-time. Jack was aware of every detail.

The boy was everything to them, the heartbeat of their home.

So even though he believed what Beth had told Molly, that the call wasn't important, that they'd laugh about it tomorrow, Jack had trouble sleeping. Couldn't the woman have left a more detailed message? Didn't she know how they'd take it if she told them something had come up?

By seven the next morning, Jack was ready to call the woman and be done with the situation. Joey was still asleep down the hall, and Molly sat on the bed beside him as he dialed the number. The radio played something soft and jazzy in the background. Molly gripped his knee with one hand and the bed with the other.

"It's nothing," he whispered to her as the ringing began on the other line. He checked his watch. Five minutes. That's all the call should take. Then they could wake up Joey, have cereal and bananas, and Jack would leave for work. Just like any other day.

On the second ring, a woman answered. "Allyson Bower, Child Welfare Department."

Jack's heart beat hard and then skipped a beat. "Hello." He used his business tone. "This is Jack Campbell, returning your call about our son, Joey." He paused. "You mentioned something had come up?"

On the other end, the woman hesitated. "Yes." She sounded tired or frustrated. He wasn't sure which. "Mr. Campbell, I'm afraid I have some bad news."

He didn't want to repeat what the woman said. Not with Molly sitting beside him, taking in every word. He pinched the bridge of his nose. "How's that?"

"Well, it's a long story. A few weeks ago I took a call from Joey's birth parents. Apparently his father was recently released from prison, and only then did he learn that his wife had given up their son for adoption. We had the paperwork examined, and the man's telling the truth. His name was forged on the release document. Which"— she paused—"I'm sorry to say means Joey's adoption documents are fraudulent."

His heart tripped over itself. What had she said? *No! No, it isn't possible—this isn't happening.* He made a fist and pressed it to his brow.

"What?" Molly's eyes were wide, terrified. "What's she saying?"

He shook his head and motioned for her to wait a minute. The woman's words were swirling in his brain. He closed his eyes tight. Never was he at a loss for words. He made his living as a smooth-talking salesman, after all. But here, now, even if he could think of something to say, he wouldn't be able to form the words. Nothing she was saying made sense. He reached over and hit the radio switch, killing the music. There. He needed silence.

The social worker was still trying to explain. "We're not sure who forged the birth father's signature, but I'm afraid it doesn't matter." She sounded beyond frustrated. "I'm so sorry, Mr. Campbell. I took the matter before a judge and the ruling was black and white." She paused. "Permanent custody of Joey has been reverted back to the boy's parents, with a shared custody arrangement that will play out over the next few months."

Jack clutched his throat, his eyes still shut. This time the words came despite his inability to think or reason. "Shared custody?" Next to him he could feel Molly losing control.

"There'll be a series of supervised visits, where Joey will spend part of a weekend with his birth parents and then return back to you and your wife." Every word sounded difficult for the woman. "This will happen every few weeks, and on the fourth visit custody of Joey will be turned over completely."

Jack was on his feet. He made a sound that was part anger, part disbelief. "Just like that? What about our attorney, our voice in the matter?"

Molly stood and began to pace. "No...no, this isn't happening." Her face was a pasty gray. She stopped and searched his eyes for answers, but he held his finger up and mouthed, "Wait!"

The social worker was going on. "Mr. Campbell, I'm sorry. In a case where adoption papers have been fraudulently signed, the law is clear-cut." She hesitated. "I was able to get just that one concession for you."

Concession? Concession about the custody of their son? Maybe this was the part where she'd tell him it was all a mistake and that the judge had changed his mind and tossed out the whole possibility of taking Joey away from them. Jack massaged his brow and tried to find a center of gravity. Everything was out of order, off balance. It was a nightmare, that was it. Joey had been theirs for almost five years. What judge in his right mind would grant custody of their son to someone else?

He forced himself to focus. "What...what concession?"

"The shared custody I told you about." She stopped, as if maybe he would express some sort of gratitude. He didn't, and she continued. "That's the best I could do."

Jack grabbed a deep breath and hung his head. Something inside him clicked, and he found center once again. "I'm sorry, what was your name?"

"Allyson Bower. I'm with the Child Welfare Department in Ohio."

"Yes, Mrs. Bower, well, I'm afraid your best isn't good enough in this case. I'll be contacting my attorney later this morning and we'll fight this as far and long as we have to fight it." He gathered his strength. Handling the social worker was nothing to the task that lay ahead—explaining the situation to Molly.

"Mr. Campbell, I'm afraid there's no further legal recourse in this matter, and that seeing your attorney would be a waste of—"

"Thank you, Mrs. Bower. My attorney will be in touch with you."

The minute he hung up, Molly grabbed his elbow, her eyes darting as she searched his face. "What is it? Tell me! Why do we have to call our attorney?" Her words came sharp and fast, saturated with a crazed fear. A fear he'd never heard in her voice before now.

Jack looked at the woman he loved more than life, and in that instant he would've given anything to make the entire situation go away. Somehow, by opening his mouth and answering her question, the sudden crisis they faced would be unquestionably real. But what choice did he have? He had to tell her; there was no way around it.

He faced her and put his hands on her shoulders. "Joey's birth father never signed the adoption papers." The words sounded like they belonged to someone else, as if any minute he should blink and apologize and none of what he was saying would be anything more than a bad joke.

"He never signed them?" Molly began to shake. Tears built up in her eyes. "So what does…what does that mean?"

"It means the adoption papers are fraudulent." He felt the tears welling in his own eyes, but at the same time a fierce anger began to build.

"Fraudulent?" The word was little more than a painful whisper. Her chest began working hard, her breaths coming twice as fast as before. "Meaning what, Jack? Just tell me!"

"Molly, calm down." His anger was taking the upper hand. This was all a mistake. He had access to some of the best attorneys in South Florida. Everything would work out fine in the end. He gritted his teeth. "A judge in Ohio has awarded permanent custody of Joey to his birth parents. The social worker said it was a black-and-white case. There's nothing more she can do."

"What?" Molly shrieked. She stood and stormed halfway to the door, and then back again. "Are they coming to get him? Right now?"

"No." He caught her arm and gently guided her back to the bed. "Don't panic." They sat down side by side, and he framed her cheek with his hand. "We'll hire an attorney." His reassurance was as much for him as for her. "Joey's not going anywhere."

She was shaking harder now. "W-w-when do they want him?"

"It won't happen." Jack didn't want to talk about the possibility.

"But if it does...how much time do we have?" Molly gripped his knee and leaned hard against him. She looked about to collapse.

"Molly, breathe....We're going to fight this; I promise you."

She jerked away from him and stood. "I don't want to breathe!" Her voice was loud, shrill, the voice of a crazy person. Her expression changed and she started to melt.

Slowly, she collapsed against him. Frightening sobs came over her and she looked like she might be sick. She lifted her eyes to his. "Jack...help me!"

"Molly..." He held her up by her shoulders, his arm around her. "No one's going to take him. I won't let it happen."

"I can't do this, Jack, I can't...let him go." Her sobs grew softer. But they were gut-wrenching, coming from a place so deep inside her even he didn't know his way around it. She squeezed her eyes shut, rocking and weeping. "He's my baby, my only baby. Please...don't let him go."

"Shhh..." He covered her with his arms, protecting her the only way he knew. "Joey's not leaving us. It won't happen." He talked to her that way for ten minutes, saying only what he could, what little bit made sense, until finally she lifted herself halfway up.

"I can't lose him." Her words were weak, childlike.

He stroked her back. "You won't have to, honey. Come on, pull yourself together."

Another sob washed over her, and then she drew a deep breath and faced him. "When do they want him? I have to know."

Jack understood. Worst case scenario, she had to hear the truth. He kept one arm around her shoulders. "She said something about a visit every few weeks." He could barely speak the words, as if doing so might somehow make them true. "On the fourth visit, Joey would move there permanently." Before she could respond, he rushed ahead. "But don't think about that. It won't happen. It won't."

She pushed herself to sit up the rest of the way, and after

a few seconds she worked her way to her feet. "I need to wake Joey up. We're going to the pool with Beth and the kids today."

"That can wait. We have a lot to figure out."

"No." Her eyes were swollen, and she rubbed them with her palms, drying what was left of her tears. "He needs a normal life, Jack. A day at the pool will be good for him." She gave him a pointed look. "Like you said, they won't take him away. You won't let them, and I won't either." Her eyes grew so hard she barely looked like herself. "They'd have to kill me first."

And those were the words that stayed with Jack all day, as he called his lawyer and got a recommendation for a high-powered family attorney in downtown Miami, as he drove south into the city, the adoption paperwork at his side. This wasn't a simple custody battle he was trying to ward off.

It was a fight for the heart and soul and breath of their family.

∞∽

The pool was wonderful.

Three hours of sunshine and splashing with Joey, and not for a minute did she allow her mind to venture to the unthinkable places of earlier that morning. Jack would take care of everything. She'd meant what she said. They'd have to kill her before she'd let her son go.

She and Beth were too busy at the pool to have more than a minute to talk, but afterward they went to Beth's house. Joey was asleep by the time they got there, and

Molly cradled him in her arms and laid him on the sofa. Beth walked Jonah to his room and laid him down, and the older kids put a movie on in the family room.

Molly found a pitcher of iced tea in the refrigerator and poured glasses for her and Beth. This wasn't happening. The phone call was the one thing she had feared since she and Jack first considered adoption. She had to talk to Beth now, before she imploded. All those other times—days represented in the photo album—came to mind. Beth was there when Molly's boyfriend publicly humiliated her, she was the strong voice of comfort and reason when Art Goldberg died, and she was the only one Molly could turn to now.

Jack would take care of the details, but still she needed to talk, needed to share the fears she'd been running from all day. The moment Beth returned to the kitchen, Molly looked at her and opened her mouth. But no words would come. Where could she start? The entire situation was like a scene from someone else's movie. She hadn't had time to put the details into words.

"Hey...what's wrong?" Beth met her near the kitchen island. Her voice was gentle, tender, the way it was with her children when one of them was hurt. But this time fear had a place in her tone, too. "Molly, talk to me, sweetie. What is it?"

"The call..." She felt her face twist up. Sobs choked out the rest of her sentence.

Beth searched her eyes, and then her expression changed. "The call? You mean the one from the social worker?"

"Yes." Molly took her tea and dropped to the nearest dining-room chair. Nothing made sense, not a bit of what she was about to say. "Joey's adoption paperwork was forged." She gripped the arms and stared at her sister. "His birth father never signed it."

"What?" Beth grabbed her glass and sat down beside her, facing her. Shock settled in the fine lines on her forehead. "Well, that's not your problem...is it?"

More tears, and Molly covered her face with her hands.

"Is it, Molly?" Beth put her arm around her shoulders. "I mean, that's something the social services people have to work out with the birth parents, right?"

"No." Molly dropped her hands and dabbed her fingertips beneath her eyes. She felt the fight rising up inside her. All morning at the pool, her feelings had warred within her. She'd be swimming next to Joey and she'd surface for air just as sharp terror made it impossible to draw a breath. Joey was everything to her—they wouldn't dare take him. Then she'd dive down to the floor of the pool and suddenly she'd be a mother bear, willing to do anything, all things, for the sake of her child.

Now she looked at Beth and grabbed a quick breath. "A judge in Ohio ruled earlier this week that custody will revert back to his birth parents in a few months. Because someone forged the father's name."

"It was probably the mother." Beth leaned her shoulder into the sofa. Her eyes never left Molly's. "Didn't you say the father was in prison for domestic violence when you adopted Joey?"

"Yes." She crossed her arms and pressed them to her waist. "He's out now."

"So if the mother forged his name, isn't that something the two of them have to work out?"

Molly narrowed her eyes, trying to remember. "The social worker said they didn't know who signed his name. So I guess they're ruling out his birth mother."

"That's crazy." Beth's voice rang with frustration. "What sort of protection does that give any adoptive parent?" She waved her hand in the air. "If birth parents can come back years later and complain about the paperwork, then no one's safe." She hurried on. "You're fighting it, of course."

"Jack's on his way to Miami right now. Our lawyer recommended some big shot in the city." Her shoulders had been tense, and she lowered them. *Relax, Molly. . . . Everything's going to be okay.* "Jack says not to worry; he'll take care of it."

"Good." Beth stood and put her hands on her hips. "The whole thing's insane. Imagine, taking a healthy child out of the only home he's known, the place where he's lived for nearly five years." She clenched her fists. "No one in their right mind would do that."

"Exactly." Molly savored the strength of Beth's words. Beth had always been more a fighter than a victim. "We should know something later today."

Beth's expression softened. "I know it's going to work out. It has to."

"It will." Molly repeated the words in her head for good measure. *It will work out; it will.* She drummed her fingers lightly on her knees. "Still, I wish there was something we could do today, this afternoon."

The fight left Beth. She sat down next to Molly. "There is." She held out her hands. "We can talk to God."

"I don't—" Molly started to bristle, but immediately she

changed her mind. Beth had a Bible verse for every occasion. Suddenly, Molly wanted to know. "What would the Bible say about this? About a child's future...or losing a child, fighting for a child?"

Beth didn't hesitate. "Well, Scripture has a lot to say about children and the battles we fight in life." She held out her thumb. "First and most important, there's a verse in Jeremiah that says God knows the plans He has for us, plans to give us a hope and a future and not to harm us."

Molly thought that over. If it was true, then God had plans for Joey. Good plans. The news settled some of her anxiety. "What else?"

"I could get you a Bible promise book. That way you could look at Scripture by topics."

"Okay. I'd like that." Molly could hardly believe this was her talking. But with Joey's future on the line, she was willing to try anything. She looked at her watch. "As long as Joey's sleeping, maybe you could show me some of the verses now."

Beth did exactly that. Until Joey woke up from his nap they looked at Bible verses, and before she left, they even held hands and Beth prayed. All her life, Molly hadn't paid God any heed whatsoever. It seemed unfair that she should wait until now—her most dire hour—to consider whether He was really there, whether He could help her. For that reason, their conversation about God felt strange and even awkward. But when they finished talking, Molly had something she hadn't gotten from Jack or from the knowledge that he was at the attorney's office, or even from Beth.

She had peace.

TEN

Wendy was giddy with the way things were working out. As long as she didn't think of her son's adoptive parents, as long as she didn't dwell on the loss they were about to experience, she went through each day happier than she'd ever been. Rip was home and handling himself carefully. He was looking for a job, and he'd already had two interviews at the movie theater. The manager position looked like a lock—which meant maybe in six months they could afford a bigger rental. But most of all, their son was coming home.

His name was Joey.

Allyson Bower had given them more information after the judge ruled in their favor. Now, in ten or fifteen minutes, Allyson would stop by to make sure their home was suitable for a child. After that, there'd be nothing left but the waiting. Joey would make his first visit to Ohio in two weeks.

Wendy grabbed a dishrag and washed down the kitchen counter one more time. Tigger, the cat, knew better than to walk up near the dishes, but sometimes he forgot. Cat hair on the counter wouldn't look good to a social worker.

Tigger rubbed up against her ankles and mewed loudly.

"Later, kitty." It was almost noon, Tigger's favorite time to eat. "Mama's busy."

She worked the sponge over each section, careful to leave the counter cleaner than ever before. When she finished, she looked around the kitchen again. Everything was spotless. Rip had bought a jar of putty, and while he was out looking for work she'd patched up the hole in the wall. Yes, everything was in order.

But maybe Allyson would be hungry. The smell of something cooking in the oven was bound to make the place feel more like home. She opened the freezer, pulled out a can of pop-up cinnamon rolls, and read the directions. Five minutes later they were in the oven. She washed her hands and dried them on the worn-out kitchen towel folded by the sink. The nice one, the one with the blue stripes, was hanging neatly on the oven door. Wendy leaned back against the counter and caught her breath. Life had been one continuous blur since their meeting with the social worker.

The first good news was the report from the handwriting expert. No question, Rip hadn't signed the adoption documents. She had held her breath when Allyson gave her the news over the phone. If the department suspected her of signing the papers, the accusation would've come then.

It didn't.

Instead, a few days later, Allyson called again and told them to be at a hearing the following morning. Judge Rye Evans would be looking at the case and making a decision. Rip and Wendy wore their best clothes, and Rip looked more handsome than he had when they got married.

The typing lady next to the judge couldn't keep her eyes off him.

Allyson did most of the talking. She told the judge that it had come to her attention that the adoption file involving the Porters contained a forged signature. She had no enthusiasm for the case; that much was obvious. At one point—after she presented the results from the handwriting expert—Allyson looked at the judge and said nothing for half a minute.

Finally she held up the file. "I have to say, Your Honor— this department does not believe it's in the best interest of the child to remove him from his adoptive home."

The judge nodded. He wore a scowl through most of the hearing, and he kept looking at a stack of papers on his desk. He asked about Rip's criminal background. Two assault convictions and a five-year sentence for domestic violence. Then he put Rip on the stand.

The questions were easy. Had Rip been through rehabilitation? Yes. Did he feel he'd learned his lesson? Of course. Was he a changed man? Definitely. Could he handle being a father? Yes, he was looking forward to it. Had he thought about how to discipline a child without resorting to rage? Yes, he would continue with counseling to make sure he was on the right track.

"Nothing more," the judge said. Rip stepped down. He smiled at the typing lady and took his place beside Wendy.

She was next. The judge asked even less of her. At one time she had wanted to give this child up for adoption, right? Yes, given the situation. But now she wanted to raise this boy with her husband? Right. She explained her motives. She hadn't thought he wanted the boy. Now she could only pray they'd have the chance they lost almost five years ago.

That was all.

Allyson sat at the front of the courtroom at a long table. Every now and then she looked at the file and shook her head. At one point she stood and asked the judge if he could postpone his decision until the adoptive parents had a chance to testify.

"Fraudulent paperwork is not of any consideration by the adoptive parents." The judge peered down from his elevated position. He looked almost sad. "If a birth parent's signature was forged, the adoption is no longer valid." He slumped a little. "You know that, Mrs. Bower."

She nodded and sat down.

The judge took half an hour to look over the paperwork and the information in the file. When he returned, his decision was quick. He used a lot of big words, lots that Wendy didn't understand. She held tightly to Rip's hand, waiting for the bottom line. Finally he said, "Therefore it is my duty under the laws of the state of Ohio to revert custody of this minor to his birth parents."

Allyson was on her feet again. She told the judge it wouldn't be fair to call the boy's adoptive parents and demand that they release him right away, with no warning. The judge agreed. He came up with a plan that Joey would have three visits over the next few months, and then he'd come to live with Rip and Wendy for good.

"Honey!" Rip's voice called from the bedroom, snapping her back to the present. "Where're my socks? I can't find a clean pair!"

"Oh, sorry." She jolted into action. How could she have

forgotten? She'd done all the laundry, but the last load was still in the dryer. "Just a minute."

"Hurry up," he snapped. His temper had been a little short lately. Probably the stress of the meeting they were about to have.

She would've run across broken glass to keep Rip from being upset today. The social worker wouldn't just be assessing whether they had enough bedrooms. She would look for signs that Rip's anger was still a problem. Both of them knew it.

The dryer door was open, the clothes inside still damp. She must've forgotten to start it. Fear seized her. Rip would never stand for wet socks, never. She slammed the door shut, added twenty minutes to the cycle, and pushed the Start button. She looked around, frantic. What to do next? How could she get a pair of clean dry socks for Rip in the next half a minute?

Then it hit her. She raced around the corner, into their bedroom and past Rip.

"What're you doing?" He twisted his face, frustrated. "Where's my socks?"

"The dryer's acting up." She pulled a pair of athletic socks from her own drawer, and hurried to him. "Here. Wear these. You can change later."

He jerked them from her hand. "I hate wearing your socks."

"I know. I'm sorry." She gave him a weak smile. "The dryer's working now."

"Fine." He huffed at her. "Is the house clean?"

"Perfectly."

"Good." He sat on the edge of the bed and slipped the

socks on. Then, as if it had just occurred to him that he wasn't acting very nice, he nodded at her. "Thanks for picking things up."

She felt herself light up inside. "You're welcome." She sat on the edge of the bed beside him. "I'd do anything to make this work."

"It will." Determination rang in his voice. "He's *our* little boy. I wish we were getting him back without all this visit garbage. As if we were some sort of strangers."

"Well..." She twisted her fingers together. She hated to go against him. "We sort of are strangers. For now, I mean." She uttered a nervous laugh. "He doesn't know us."

"He'll know us right off." Rip barked the words, but he kept his tone low. "Kids know their parents."

"Right." Wendy kept herself from saying that at this point Joey's parents were the nice couple in Florida. She understood what Rip meant. A child would know his birth parents simply because they were blood-related. She weighed the idea. Yeah, that might be true. Why not?

There was a knock on the door. "Get it." Rip gave her a quick shove. "I'll be right there."

"Okay." She hurried out of the room, straightening her beige slacks and patting her hair nice and neat. She opened the door and smiled at Allyson Bower. "Hello... come in."

"Hello." The social worker didn't look happy. "This shouldn't take long." She had a file in her hand and she stepped inside.

Only then did Wendy notice the curls of smoke coming from the oven. "Oh, no!" She gasped. "The cinnamon rolls!" She raced across the living room to the adjoining kitchen, grabbed a potholder, opened the oven door and yanked the tray out and onto the counter.

Allyson was a few steps behind. "Can I help?"

"No, it's okay." Wendy turned off the oven and shut the door. She'd let them cook four minutes longer than she was supposed to. Between the smoke and the blackened tops on every roll, the batch was a complete loss. She gave Allyson a quick smile over her shoulder. "My oven cooks a little hot lately."

At that moment, Rip came into the room. He smelled the smoke and frowned. "What happened?"

"I'm not sure." Another nervous laugh as she quickly dumped the burned rolls into the trash. "I guess the oven's cooking hotter than usual."

Allyson was getting situated at the kitchen table, so she didn't see the glare Rip gave Wendy. The minute the social worker looked up, Rip's expression changed to a smile. "Those electric ovens are touchy."

Wendy flipped on the exhaust fan over the stove and opened a window. She fanned at the smoke that still hung in the air. Then she pulled a few apples from the fridge, sliced them onto a plate, and brought them to the table. She took the seat between Rip and Allyson. "Okay." She smiled at her husband and then back at the social worker. "I guess we're ready."

The meeting didn't last long. There were questions about their daily schedules, and how available either of them would be for Joey. Wendy worked just one job now—a secretarial position at a local accounting firm. She explained that she'd be gone nine to five, but that she had eighteen sick days built up in case Joey needed her for something.

"Otherwise, what's the plan for the child?"

"Day care." Rip made the word sound like a reward, like Disneyland. "We've got a great little place a few blocks away. Clean and friendly. Affordable."

"What about you, Mr. Porter? What will your work hours be?"

He stuck out his chest just enough for Wendy to notice. "I'm waiting to hear from the movie theater in town. They're considering me for the manager position. I'll work nights, of course. Otherwise I'll watch Joey, and most days we won't have to worry about day care."

The look on Allyson's face said she wasn't sure that was a good thing. She wrote something in her file. "Okay." She looked up. "I'll take a look around." She pointed toward the hallway. "Two bedrooms, right? One for you, one for the boy?"

"Right." Again Rip took the lead down the hall. Allyson followed, and Wendy was last. The rooms were small, but clean and neat. The social worker said nothing as she looked through each bedroom door and then at the bathroom at the end of the hall. "Full bath?"

"Yes." Rip sounded proud. "There's another one off the living room." He hesitated. "Of course, after I get the manager position at the theater, we'll have much more money. We'd like to rent a bigger house, something near the nicer schools. For when our son starts kindergarten."

Allyson looked at him, but again she said nothing. When they finished the tour, she wrote something else in her file. This time she led the way into the kitchen, where she motioned to the refrigerator. "May I?"

"If you can stand the smoke." Rip chuckled, but as soon

as Allyson put her back to them, he scowled and shook his head.

The social worker gave the refrigerator a quick scan. Milk and eggs, cheese and vegetables. They'd gone shopping the night before and made sure the food was healthy and fresh. Allyson checked a few of the cupboards and asked about first aid. Wendy showed her a kit in one of the kitchen drawers.

After another few minutes she lowered the file to her side. "That's all I have." She nodded at them. "Thanks for opening up your house." She was heading out when she stopped and looked at the patched wall. Her brow lowered and she ran her finger over the patch. Then she turned and looked straight at Rip. "What's this?"

"My fault." Wendy took a step forward. She shrugged her shoulders and did a flustered laugh. "I was sweeping the other day, and pow! I poked the broom handle straight through the wall. Can you imagine?"

The look Allyson gave her said that no, she could not imagine any such thing causing a hole in the wall. She made a note in her file, nodded once more to the two of them, and told them she'd be in touch. Then she was gone.

As soon as the door closed behind her, Rip was in Wendy's face. "Burned rolls?" He forced the words through tight teeth. "Is that your idea of a good impression?" He groaned out loud and paced to the stove and back. The house was small, so his steps took only a few seconds.

"I thought they'd smell nice." She didn't want to fight with him. "Allyson didn't care. She even offered to help." Which was more than he had done. "Come on, Rip. Don't be mad."

"Mad?" His face was red now. His eyes bulged the way they did when he was about to lose it. "I'm beyond mad." He gave a sharp wave toward the laundry room. "First my socks." Another sharp wave toward the kitchen. "Then the rolls." He stormed over to the patched-up wall. He reared back and with a single ferocious blow he slammed his fist through the spot once more. He glared at her, plaster hanging from his knuckles the way it had before. "Then this." He took a few threatening steps toward her. "Your lousy repair job."

"Rip..." Was this it? The moment when it would be obvious to both of them that nothing had really changed, that they were crazy to be bringing a child into this environment? She held her breath. "Please..."

Suddenly, as if a switch had been flipped, he seemed to get a grip on his emotions. He exhaled hard and leaned against the back of the sofa. "I'm sorry." His anger faded, but he was a long way from happiness. He pointed to the hole in the wall. "Fix it right next time, will you?"

"Yes, Rip." Wendy took a few steps back. She would fix it right now, while he was watching. That way maybe he could offer a few hints so she wouldn't do such a bad job the second time around. "I'll get it right now so—"

He brushed his hand in the air over his head. "Never mind. It's my fault." He walked to the front door. "I'll fix it when I get back."

"Where are you going?"

"To cool down." He came to her and gave her a half-embrace. "I let the stress of that lady's visit get to me, that's all." His eyes met hers. "Forgive me?"

"Of course." She remembered to breathe. "Everything's going to be fine."

"Yes." His lips turned up just a little. "Thanks, Wendy. You're so good for me."

As soon as he was gone, the theater people called. "Have your husband contact us, please. He got the job."

Wendy kept her excitement down until she hung up. Then she ran out the door and down the sidewalk until she caught up with Rip. "You did it!" She took him by the shoulders. "You got the job!"

"I did?" His face lit up.

"Yes!" She squealed. Rip was right, things were all going their way.

Rip gave a victory shout. He picked her up and swung her around, the way he did when he was his happiest. And in that moment, Wendy knew she had nothing to worry about. Yes, it would be tough for the Florida couple to lose Joey, but they would be okay. The judge wouldn't have ruled for the change in custody if he was worried about them, right? And now that Rip had a job, he wouldn't be nearly so tense. They'd survived even the home study.

Now all they had to do was wait for Joey.

ELEVEN

Jack Campbell stayed in the slow lane all the way home from Miami. He was in no hurry to face Molly, to tell her that even the most high-powered attorney in all of Florida had nothing to offer them.

He wouldn't give up, of course. There had to be other attorneys, someone willing to take the case. But for now the news was horrible. It was shocking, the emergency conversation he'd had with the attorney completely hopeless.

"If the papers were forged, it's an open-and-shut case." The man was dressed to the nines, sitting behind an impressive desk in a corner office overlooking the city and the harbor beyond. At least he was kind. "Look, I cleared my calendar to meet with you. Your lawyer's a very good friend of mine." He slid his chair back and stretched out his legs. "If there was anything I could do to help you, I'd be on it."

Jack felt like a man slipping into quicksand. "Maybe I'm not making the facts clear." He sat on the edge of the chair, desperate to change the attorney's mind. "We were given signed and sealed adoption papers almost five years ago. The social worker promised us the birth parents could never come back looking for Joey." His voice had grown loud, and he lowered it again. "It was a closed adoption." He gripped the arms of the chair. "This was never supposed to happen."

The attorney stood and gazed out the window. "I realize that, Mr. Campbell." He turned around and faced Jack. "But those statements were made under the assumption that the documents were accurate, that the signatures truly belonged to the people who were supposed to sign them."

"Okay, so how often does something like this happen? What protection do adoptive parents really have?"

"Most departments are requiring notarized signatures now." He frowned. "That wasn't the case when your adoption was being handled."

Jack was stunned. "So you're saying that would've averted the problem? If we would've insisted on a notarized signature, even though the department didn't require it?"

Sunlight streamed in through the windows, but a shadow fell over the attorney's face. "The way I understand it, the birth father in this case wouldn't have signed the papers, Mr. Campbell. He had no idea his wife had given birth. So, yes, it would've solved the problem to ask for a notarization." He sat back down and leveled his gaze at Jack. "But you never would've gotten Joey in the first place."

They went round and round the situation for half an hour before the attorney looked at his watch. "I'm sorry, Mr. Campbell. I really wish there was something I could do to help you." He sighed. "Try to look at it from the position of the birth father. He gets out of jail and finds out his wife had a baby and gave it up for adoption without anyone telling him." The attorney pursed his lips. "Wouldn't you feel outraged?"

Jack didn't want to consider such a thing. He stood, shook the attorney's hand, and thanked him for his time. Somehow he made it down the elevator, out of the building, and back to his car, though he had no memory of any of it. Now he was on the freeway trying to imagine what he was going to tell Molly.

Traffic was heavy, but it was moving. He'd be home far too soon, and then what? He'd promised her he would take care of the situation, that no one would take their son from him. The idea was ludicrous. Only now, it wasn't so crazy after all. If the top family attorney in the state couldn't think of a single legal reason to fight the Ohio judge's order, then who would help them?

The air in the car was stuffy, and he couldn't grab a full breath. He hit a button and the passenger-side window lowered halfway. Warm air rushed at him, but even so he couldn't fully inhale. Was it really going to happen? In two weeks would they watch Joey leave for a visit to Ohio? And a few months after that, would he really be taken from their lives forever? Their only son?

His throat felt thick, and wetness clouded his eyes. Joey was theirs. He didn't belong with a couple in Ohio, with a father who just got of prison for domestic violence. Even a single visit could hurt Joey, right? Jack blew the air from his lungs and tried again for a full breath. He worked the muscles in his jaw. No one was taking Joey from them, no one. The courts might be crazy, the social workers and attorneys might be nuts, but at least he and Molly still had their common sense.

Joey was their son. Period.

He tightened his hold on the steering wheel, and as he did, a billboard on the side of the road caught his attention. "Go International in Less Than an Hour! Roundtrips to Haiti for Under $200!"

It was an American Airlines ad, and for a minute Jack forgot he was even on the freeway. His foot eased up off the gas, and behind him the driver of an eighteen-wheeler laid on the horn. Jack jerked back into motion and pressed hard on the pedal. International in less than an hour?

The wheels in his head began to turn. What if no one would listen to them? What if no attorney took the case? Were they supposed to help Joey pack his bag and then stand by and watch him disappear from their lives? Would they be good parents if they let Joey be placed in a home with a dangerous man?

A fierce determination welled up in Jack like a building tidal wave. He'd try a few more attorneys, of course. But if they couldn't do anything to help him, then he and Molly would have no choice. They could take Joey and leave the country, start a new life somewhere else. Maybe not Haiti, but on some island with miles of empty beach and no social services departments.

They could live off of the equity in their house and rental homes for several years, couldn't they? It would be only a matter of disconnecting from society and finding a way out of the country. What did they have that mattered more than Joey? His job? Their house? The friends they'd made? Family? No, nothing was worth losing their son.

As he got closer to home, the idea seemed more realistic. It could be done, couldn't it? They could get fake passports and make their way out of the country. Find a place to hide for a time, and then take Joey to Europe. They could continue living under their new identities, maybe in Sweden or Germany, send Joey to a private school, and no one would be the wiser. By then people would've stopped looking for them, maybe even assumed they'd died. Fleeing the country could work, couldn't it? He settled back into his seat and focused on the road ahead. If that's what it took to stop the courts from taking Joey, he would gladly move to the moon. Satisfaction welled up inside him. No one was going to paint him and his family into a corner. He would protect Joey with his life, whatever that meant.

Now it was just a matter of convincing Molly.

❧

The kids had grown restless after the movie and naps, and now Molly and Beth were playing with them on Fuller Park's jungle gym. Jack had called, so Molly wasn't surprised when she saw him pull into the parking lot, get out of his car, and walk toward them. His steps were determined. She climbed down the ladder and shaded her eyes. Yes, it was him. And he was certainly upbeat, wasn't he?

"Hey, Beth.... Jack's here."

Beth climbed down and stood next to her. "He looks okay."

"That's what I thought." She grabbed onto the metal structure. "It must be good news."

"See?" Beth gave her a quick hug. "That's what happens when you pray. God's will gets accomplished."

"God's will..." It was an idea Molly hadn't thought

much about. "You think He has a way He wants this to go, is that it? His will?"

"Definitely." The boys were laughing, giggling as they slid down the slide and rounded the corner. Beth leaned back against the ladder. "When you pray, God doesn't always answer with a yes. But you always get His will." She gave Molly a half-smile. "I can't imagine God's will is for Joey to be anywhere else but in your arms."

Molly felt her smile warm all the way to the most terrified places in her heart. "Thanks, Beth."

Joey spotted Jack. "Daddy!" He ran across the field of dandelions, stirring up clouds of seeds. "Daddy, you're here!"

"Mommy?" Jonah tugged on Beth's sleeve. "Where's our daddy?"

"He's at work, honey."

Molly squinted, taking in the sight of her husband and son. Jack swung Joey up into his arms and held him close. Longer than usual. When he eased him back down to the grass, the two held hands and kept walking closer.

Beth was watching. She grinned at Jonah. "Tell you what... Let's go get the big kids and get some ice cream."

"But, Mom"—Jonah whined her name—"I like playing with Joey's daddy. He's a good pirate."

"Well, today I think Joey's mommy and daddy need to talk." She pointed to the nearby swings. "Go get your sister and brothers."

Molly flashed Beth a silent thank-you.

"Ah, really, Mom?" Jonah bounced a little.

"That's right." Beth patted Jonah on the shoulder. "No pirates today."

"Ah, okay." Jonah kicked at the dirt. But after a few seconds his face brightened. "Can we have chocolate sprinkles?"

"Of course." Beth took Jonah to the bench and gathered their things. "What's an ice cream cone without chocolate sprinkles?"

"Can George Brett have some, too?"

"No...ice cream isn't good for doggies." Beth watched Jonah run for his siblings. When they were all gathered, Beth waved, and the group started toward the car. She held her hand to her ear. "Call me."

"I will." Molly turned her attention to Jack and Joey. They were twenty feet away, and she could make out Jack's expression better now. Maybe it wasn't exactly upbeat. But it wasn't defeated, either. She braced herself for whatever was about to come.

Beth and the kids waved to Jack and Joey as they passed on their way toward the parking lot. They stopped for a few seconds and then continued in opposite directions. Molly met Jack and Joey in a patch of dandelions. Jack dropped to Joey's level and kissed their son on the cheek. "I have an idea."

"Cops and robbers?"

"No." Jack worked his jaw, his eyes never leaving Joey's. "Not cops and robbers. Not today. Mommy and I have to talk." He pointed to the swings. "How about you pretend the swings are a great big airplane and you're the pilot?"

"The chief pilot?" Joey's eyes were wide and innocent, all of life as simple as a game of make-believe.

Jack smiled. But Molly could see that his eyes looked serious, almost frightened. "That's right, sport. The chief pilot." He stood up. "Show me how well you can fly that plane."

"Aye-aye, sir." Joey stood straight at attention and gave Jack a crooked salute. He ran toward the swings. "Just watch me fly!"

Jack still hadn't said anything to her, hadn't even acknowledged her. He stood stone-still, watching Joey climb onto the swing and start to pump his legs. Then he jolted into action. "Wait...I'll give you a push." Still in his dress shoes and slacks, Jack jogged through the few yards of weeds and grass, onto the sand, and to the place behind Joey's swing. He gave their son a couple strong pushes. "Now you're flying, okay, sport?"

Joey beamed. "Thanks, Dad. The skies are clear up here. You should fly with me."

"Maybe later." Jack looked at Molly, and only then did his smile fade. "Mommy and I will watch from the bench."

Molly realized she hadn't moved since she first saw him kiss Joey's cheek. Now her legs carried her to the bench, but she had the strangest sense that her body wasn't actually attached. That whatever was about to take place wasn't even happening to her, but to someone else. Someone in a movie scene, maybe, or a nightmare.

Jack sat down on the bench first, and she took the spot beside him. If she didn't ask him, they might never have to talk about it. The awful "it." They could sit here watching Joey fly his imaginary plane and bask in the Florida sunshine without ever giving a thought to something as insane as losing him.

Next to her, she felt Jack shift. He spoke without ever taking his eyes off Joey. "I met with the attorney."

"In Miami?"

"Yes." He narrowed his eyes and turned to face her. "I waited an hour to see him. It was a short meeting."

A short meeting? What did that mean? How was she supposed to read that? She felt sick to her stomach. "Jack, don't do this." Her words were breathy. "What's the bottom line?"

He drew a long breath and released it slowly. He faced Joey again. "There's nothing the guy can do. If the birth father's name was forged, the law is clear-cut. The judge has to assume that the birth father never intended to give his child up for adoption." He slid his hands into his pockets and stretched out his legs. "The birth father, in this case, becomes the victim, and the law works entirely on his behalf."

Molly wanted to scream or cover her ears, but neither action seemed appropriate. They were at a public park, after all. Two moms with strollers were heading toward another bench a dozen yards away. Anyway, it wasn't possible—the words Jack had just spoken couldn't be true. So she did the only thing she could do. She released a single bitter laugh. "I can't believe this."

"Me, neither." Jack took hold of her hand. "I asked him to take the case anyway. We need someone fighting for us."

"What did he say?" The feel of Jack's fingers between hers lent some sense of normalcy to the moment, as if maybe Jack had gotten off work an hour early and here they were, enjoying a late afternoon with their son. Rather than talking about how quickly they might lose him. She looked at Jack. "He'll do it, right?"

Slowly, with some of the shock that she, too, was feeling,

he shook his head. "He won't take the case." Jack's chin quivered. "He says it's not winnable."

The air around her suddenly became suffocating. She stood and slid her hand through her hair. Then she moaned and walked in little circles and figure-eights, dazed, unable to think or speak. "No. No—this isn't real." She felt off-balance, dizzy, and the entire park blurred around her. "This isn't happening."

"Molly..." He slid to the edge of the bench and patted the spot beside him.

"Daddy! Watch how high I am!" Joey called from the swings. "I'm the best pilot in the world!"

Jack turned to him. "Yes, sport. In the whole world."

"Wanna come fly with me?"

"Not yet...Mommy and I still need to talk."

The conversation echoed in her mind. *Wanna come fly with me?...Come fly with me....* Yes, that was it, wasn't it? She looked at her son, at his pale blond hair and tanned face, at the blue eyes, so gentle and trusting. That's all she wanted—to run from this horrible conversation and fly with him. High in the sky, hand in hand, and never ever come down. She and her son together forever and—

"Molly."

The sound of Jack's voice snapped her from the moment and she turned to him, startled. "What?"

"Come here." He patted the bench again. "I'm not done."

He wasn't done? Hope surged through her, like oxygen to a dying person. If he had more to tell her, then maybe that's why his step had seemed determined and upbeat. Maybe the attorney hadn't stopped there, and maybe he would take the case after all. *God...are you there? Do you see what's going on?*

She took shaky steps back to the bench, sat down, and faced Jack. "What?"

Jack's eyes were serious, more than she'd ever seen them. "I'm going to call a few more attorneys. But the guy I met with today says their answers will be the same. By law, Joey is no longer ours. He belongs to his birth father as long as the man won't give up his right. The attorney was surprised the judge allowed a period of shared custody for transition."

Molly was going to be sick. "I thought you weren't done."

"I'm not."

"Okay." Her heart was slamming against her chest. "How do we make the...the birth father give up his right?"

"Look, Mommy, no hands!"

"Joey!" Molly turned to him, frantic. "Don't let go."

The child had his hands straight out, but at her alarmed voice he grabbed hold of the chains again. "Sorry." He looked frightened. "I wanted to be a trick pilot."

"Be a passenger pilot, sport." Jack's voice was calmer than hers. "If you let go, it isn't safe for the passengers, okay?"

Joey grinned. "Okay."

A flock of birds circled and landed in the nearby maple tree. Molly wanted to shout at them to be quiet. Every breath depended on whatever Jack was trying to say. She pulled one leg up onto the bench and hugged it close to her chest. "Say it, Jack. If we can't get him to give up his rights, then what? What can we do?"

He turned so he was facing her straight on. For a while he only searched her face. The determination in his expression shifted to desperation. She had the feeling that whatever he was about to say, it was their only hope. He brought his hand to her face and with a tenderness that defied the moment, he touched her cheekbone. "We leave." He didn't for a single heartbeat break eye contact. "We take Joey and leave the country."

"Are you kidding?" She eased her foot back to the ground and slid a few feet away from him. She sucked in a fast breath, and then another. Her body had forgotten how to exhale. She shook her head and pulled at her hair. Was he crazy? "Everything was perfect just yesterday morning! This...this isn't real." She bent over, lowering her head between her knees. *Breathe out, Molly.... You're hyperventilating.... You'll pass out here on the sand.*

"Molly..." Jack slid close to her again.

"What's wrong with Mommy?" Joey's sing-song voice called out from the swings. He slowed himself and hopped off. "Is she sick? I think she was sick earlier at Aunt Beth's picnic."

"She's fine." Jack's voice was chipper—high-pitched and phony. "Mommy's just a little tired."

Breathe... You have to breathe! Molly forced the air from her lungs. There. That was better. She did it again and a third time before she allowed herself to sit up and look at Joey. He was running into the grassy field, into the sea of dandelions.

"I know how to make her feel better!" He stopped and squatted down for a few seconds. When he stood up he had a fistful of dandelions and a lopsided grin. He sheltered them with his other hand and ran, his hair flying in the wind, until he was standing breathless at her feet.

"Here, Mommy...watch!" He held out the bouquet of seedy flowers, then he brought them to his lips and blew with all his might. The fluffy white seeds came apart and filled the air.

Then they were gone.

"That's dandelion dust!" He tossed the green stems and held his hands out. "See? It disappears like magic!" He touched her cheek—the same way Jack did so often. "Isn't that fun? Doesn't that make you feel better?"

Molly blinked back the tears. A sound that was more cry than laugh came from her. "Yes, buddy." She wrapped her arms around him and held him close. He had the same summery smell he always had. Grass and little boy sweat and something sweet she couldn't quite identify.

He squirmed from her and looked at Jack. "Did you see the dandelion dust, Daddy?"

"I did." He held up his hands and dropped them. "You're right. It disappeared like magic."

"Yep." He turned and ran back toward the swings. "My plane needs me!"

When he was airborne again, Molly turned to Jack. She felt faint, completely lacking the energy she needed for this conversation, this nightmare. She wrinkled her nose. "Flee the country, Jack? Are you crazy?"

He looked at Joey for a long time. Then he turned back to her. "About my son, yes." His eyes grew wet and for a long moment he shielded his brow with his hand. Then he sniffed and sat up straight. The determination was back. "I won't let them take him away from us, Molly. I promised you that, and I meant it." He leaned closer. "What choice do we have?"

She pressed her palm to her forehead and a desperate stifled cry sounded on her lips. "How can this be happening?"

"You have to stop asking that." It was the first time Jack sounded frustrated with her. Immediately he leaned back and stared at the blue sky. "I'm sorry." He put his hand on her knee. "I guess I've had longer to think about the idea." He hesitated. "It's possible, you know. Like Joey's dandelion dust. Just . . . just disappear from everything."

"Disappear?" She could hardly believe the words were coming from her husband. Jack was the most upstanding citizen she knew. He was on the board of advisors for the YMCA and in charge of the Red Cross chapter at his office. He was the man who paid his taxes early and voted at every election. "You're serious? You'd consider leaving the country?"

He ground his teeth together, his chin trembling more than before. When he had regained his composure, he pointed an angry finger at Joey. "They will *not* take my son from me, Molly." A slight sob shook him, but he swallowed it. "No matter what we have to do."

"And I won't take up a life of crime." She stood and took a few steps in Joey's direction. "There has to be another way."

With that she began jogging toward her son. They were wasting time talking about leaving the country. That wasn't the answer. There had to be another attorney, someone who would take on this fight for them. Joey would be destroyed if someone took him away now. It would be the worst possible thing for him. "Mommy's coming, Joey!"

"Yippee! I'm the best pilot in the world." He grinned at her. "Hop on board!"

Just being near him gave her strength to keep moving, keep breathing. She lifted herself onto the swing next to his and began pumping her legs with all her might. Flee the country? Was Jack losing his mind? There had to be another way...had to be. She flashed a smile at Joey. "You're right, buddy. You are the best pilot in the whole world."

He giggled. "Where do you wanna go?"

She said the first thing that came to her mind. "Neverland."

"Neverland?" He hooted his approval. "That's the best place, Mommy."

"I know." Tears slid from her eyes and onto her cheeks, but the breeze dried them almost instantly. "Because in Neverland you never, ever have to grow up."

"That's right. We can stay just like this forever and ever."

For the next half hour, that's just what they did. With Jack watching silently from the bench, she and Joey flew and laughed and dreamed they were in Neverland. Where children never have to grow up, and people could stay just the way they were.

Forever and ever and ever.

TWELVE

Joey didn't want to cry. Babies cry, and he was a big boy. That's what the Cricket Preschool nurse said before summer came, when Joey tripped on Timmy's shoe and skinned his knee. So he didn't want to cry.

But he didn't want to go, either.

Mommy and Daddy told him a few days ago after dinner. He had to go on a trip with a nice lady to visit some people in Ohio. Another mommy and daddy.

"How come?" Joey called Gus and hugged his neck. He looked at them. "How come you're not coming, too?"

"Because we can't this time, sport." His daddy looked sad. Like maybe this wasn't the bestest thing.

"Then I'll stay here with you and Gus." He rubbed his face in the dog's furry neck. Gus turned around and gave him a big lick on the face. "Okay? That's what I'll do."

Only that's when Mommy told him that he didn't have any choices this time. He had to go for the visit and it would only last one single night and two single days. But that was too long, and now the lady would be there in the morning. Which meant he could sleep one more night with Gus and then he'd go far, far away.

Maybe a whole world away. He wasn't sure.

His mommy already helped him pack his bag, and a few times she wiped her eyes. "Are you sad, Mommy?"

"Yes. Very sad." She put her arm around him and held him for a long time. "But you'll be back on Saturday night. So we'll still have all day Sunday to play with Daddy before the next week starts."

Joey lay in bed and stared at the ceiling. He had a poster of Michael Jordan up there, even though Michael Jordan was really old. Still, he was a good player—at least that's what his daddy said. He turned on his side. Gus mostly slept on the floor, but tonight Mommy let him sleep up on the bed. Joey put his arm around Gus's furry middle. "How come, Gus? Why would I take a trip without Mommy and Daddy?"

Gus took a big breath through his nose. His eyes said he wasn't sure of an answer, either, but at least it would be a short trip.

"I know it'll be short, Gus." He gave the dog a kiss near his nose. "But short's still too long."

Gus nodded his head a little.

"Good doggie, Gus. You understand."

Joey looked up at the ceiling again. On his other side were Mr. Monkey and Mr. Growls, his other bestest friends. He picked up Mr. Monkey and talked straight to his face. Mr. Monkey's mouth was falling off, but that didn't matter—he could talk even when his mouth wasn't working. "What do you think this other mommy and daddy look like?"

Mr. Monkey thought for a minute. Maybe he didn't feel like talking, because he only gave Joey a look.

"And whose mommy and daddy are they, anyway?"

Mr. Monkey blinked. *Maybe you should take me with you,* he seemed to say.

"Okay, I'll do that." Joey had another question. "Why would a strange lady take me to see people I don't even know?"

This time Mr. Monkey yawned. *I don't have any answers,* he seemed to say. Joey laid him back down on the other side of his pillow. Mr. Growls said thank you because Mr. Monkey was his friend and he liked to stay next to him.

Joey asked himself the questions all over again. Who were the strange mommy and daddy, and why did he have to go see them? Mommy told him it was something the judge said. That was scary. Judges were on TV, sometimes with big black capes. Only not the kind of capes that Superman and Batman wore. The kind that stayed in close on their shoulders and made them sit higher up than everyone in the room.

If the judge said he had to go, then he had to go.

'Less they throw him in jail with the robbers. He put his face close to Gus again. "If they send me to jail, I'll slide through the bars, okay, Gus?"

Gus made a little whiny sound. He touched his nose to Joey's, and Joey giggled. Even with the scared in his tummy, Gus made him laugh. 'Cause Gus had a very wet nose, that's why.

Joey heard the room get quiet again. He needed to sleep. Mommy and Daddy would check on him pretty soon, and they wouldn't like it that he was still awake. But where was the strange lady taking him tomorrow? Daddy said it was

Ohio, but where was that? It sounded like an Indian place, maybe. If it was, then did the mommy and daddy he was gonna see live in a teepee?

Joey's head had a lot going on inside. So much that he saw little circles whenever he closed his eyes. Beside him he could hear Gus making little sleepy sounds. He needed someone else to talk to, but who? He tapped his fingers on his head. *Think, Joey. . . . Think of who to talk to.*

Then his eyes popped open and a big idea hit him right in the head. He could do what Jonah did! Once he spent the night at Jonah's house. He slept in a sleeping bag on Jonah's floor, and they talked and talked, even after lights out and Aunt Beth said no more talking. But when it was very late and they had nothing more to say, Jonah did a little yawn. "Time to say our prayers."

"What?" Joey didn't know about prayers. He'd heard of 'em, o' course. Maybe in the movies or something. He leaned up on his elbows. "Who do you say 'em to?"

Jonah peered over the edge of his bed. "God, silly. You say your prayers to God every night." He smiled. "Sometimes in the day, too."

"Oh." Joey felt a little funny, like maybe he should know about saying prayers to God. So he nodded and lay back down. That way it would seem like he said prayers to God every night just like Jonah.

That's when Jonah started talking out loud, just like there was someone standing right there to talk to. Only there wasn't anyone in the room but themselves.

"Dear God, it's me, Jonah. Thank You for this day and for my house and my mommy and my daddy and my cousin, Joey. But not really Cammie, because she told on me." He thought for a minute. "Okay, thank You for Cammie, too. But please make her turn into a nice sister tomorrow. Help us be safe, God. Gee this name, amen."

Joey waited a second. "Amen." It seemed like the thing to say. But Joey stayed awake for a long time that night thinking about the prayer. Jonah was lucky that he had someone as big as God to talk to. And every night! Joey was going to go home the next day and ask his mommy to teach him how to talk to God.

But the next day came, and he forgot.

Only now, maybe that's 'zactly what he should do. Jonah didn't use any special words when he talked to God. Joey looked out the window. He felt like crying again, but he didn't. "Dear God..." He breathed a few hard breaths. "Hi, this is Joey. I'm a'scared because tomorrow I'm getting on an airplane with a strange lady to see a strange mommy and daddy and I don't even know them." His words were little whispers, and they ran together like a long train. He blinked and waited, in case God wanted to say something back.

He didn't hear anything.

"God, I need someone to talk to 'cause I don't really want to go on the trip with the strange lady." He had an idea. One that made him feel just a little bit of happy inside. "How 'bout You go with me, God? You're invisible so no one would even care if You came, too." He thought some more. "Maybe You could even sit beside me. 'Cause that would make me get back home a little faster I think."

The scared in him seemed a little less. He yawned and remembered. "Oh, yeah. I forgot the last part. Gee this name, amen."

There. That was a real prayer, 'cause it sounded just like something Jonah would say. He yawned again. Sleep was coming. He still didn't want to go with the strange lady to the place called Ohio and maybe to a teepee. But if God would go with him, then maybe it wouldn't seem so bad.

One more thought came into his head.

"P.S. God...thank You for my mommy and daddy and Gus. Because they're the bestest family in the whole wide world." After that he felt a little smile on his face. He put his arm around Gus, and in a little bit of time he was sleepy.

Just like it was any other normal night.

THIRTEEN

At five o'clock that morning, Molly sat straight up in bed and gripped the down blanket close to her chest. Her sides heaved as if she were running a marathon. And she was. The marathon of surviving the past week, the race for a way to keep Joey home, to stop him from getting on a plane in just a few hours and leaving for Ohio.

But it was too late. All the running and striving and planning amounted to nothing. Joey was packed, ready to leave, and in five hours he would walk out their door. She relaxed her grip on the sheets and looked at Jack. He was sleeping still, though neither of them had more than a few hours' at a time before reality jolted them awake, forcing them to go through the possibilities one more time.

Molly crept out of bed and walked to the bathroom. She stared at herself in the mirror. Who would she be if she wasn't Joey's mommy? Her chest tightened and she banished the thought. It was one visit—just one night. He'd be home tomorrow. She showered and dressed, and at least six times a minute she wondered if she'd ever be able to draw a full breath again. She needed sleep, needed a good meal.

She needed Joey.

Her heart beat hard against her chest, so loud she wondered if it would wake Jack. She tiptoed down the hall. Joey's door was open. She took a few quiet steps inside and held her breath. Gus was stretched out along the wall, and Joey was curled up, soft little snoring sounds coming from his mouth. Mr. Monkey and Mr. Growls were tucked in close to his chest. Maybe it was her imagination, but in the shadowy early morning it looked like he was smiling. *Poor baby*... Chills came over her and she folded her arms. *You don't have any idea why you're leaving today.* How could he possibly understand?

For a moment she considered crawling into bed beside him, but there wasn't room. Besides, she didn't want to wake him. Morning would come soon enough. Instead she stood there, barely able to think, teeth chattering, and watched him. Every memory took a turn playing on the screen of her mind. He was big now, but the face was the same one she used to watch sleep when he was an infant, when he first came home to them.

She would wake up in the middle of the night and think she heard his cry. Then she'd creep into his room and look at him. Just watch him, watch his little chest moving up and down, up and down, up and down. Just in case, sometimes she'd hold her fingers a few inches from his nose. Only when she felt his warm damp breath would she take a step back and smile, relieved. He was a wonder boy, a sunbeam, and as long as he was sleeping down the hall, as long as he was okay, she, too, could sleep.

It was the same way all through his baby time and his toddler days. Some nights she wouldn't feel peace, couldn't find sleep, until she spent a few minutes watching him, listening to him breathe. Tears stung her eyes. It wasn't even possible that tonight he'd be sleeping in another state.

She moved closer, stooped down, and studied him some more. He was beautiful, a piece of stardust with a heart laced firmly to her own. Maybe if morning never came, if she could stop time and keep ten o'clock from ever crashing in on them...She leaned down and gave him the softest kiss on his cheek. "Don't wake up, baby. Not yet."

She straightened. What else could she do? Her fingers trembled, her heart pounding harder than before. Then it hit her. The baseboards needed cleaning. She left Joey's room, padded downstairs, flipped on the lights, and looked around. Twice a week a housekeeper put in three hours doing the tougher jobs, so there wasn't much mess to take care of.

But the baseboards...They hadn't been cleaned in six months at least.

She poured a bowl of warm soapy water, found a rag, and quietly moved to the far end of the house. She stooped down, dipped the rag into the water, and wrung it out. The house was still, silent. As if all of her existence were holding its breath in anticipation of the terror that lay ahead.

How could it have come to this? Jack had called every attorney in the state—everyone who might handle an adoption case—and all of them had said the same thing. Fraud in the original documents meant that those documents were nullified. As if they'd never been signed at all.

"Think of it this way," one attorney told Jack. "You were lucky to have the boy for four years."

Molly put her shoulders into the task and rubbed at

the first section of baseboard. Lucky to have him for four years? Was the world really that insane? Were people really that insensitive? Adoption didn't mean a lesser bond with a child. It was a bond she and Jack had chosen, and it was no different than if she'd birthed Joey herself. He was their son. Nothing could be more clear and obvious.

She scrubbed farther down the baseboard, all her fear and frustration and fury directed at whatever dirt had dared to accumulate there. She and Jack and Gus were all the family Joey had ever known. He was too young to understand about adoption, so when this came up—when it was clear that they had no choice about the impending first visit—they told him the only thing they could. A judge wanted him to take a trip, and so he had to take it.

He was scared to death.

They could both see that. Last night when they tucked him in, he hugged Molly's neck longer than usual. "How 'bout you go with me, Mommy? Would that be okay?" He looked at Jack. "Or you, Daddy. They wouldn't care if I brought you, would they?"

She and Jack were out of answers. How were they supposed to tell him that his birth parents wanted him back, that he had a biological father somewhere who was just released from prison, a guy who liked to hit people— especially his wife?

And now a judge was making him visit those same people.

It made no sense no matter how they looked at it. They could hardly expect Joey to make sense of it, or to find peace in their answers. Instead he tried to be brave. Jack sat on the edge of his bed and stroked his hair. "It'll be a short trip, sport."

Joey nodded. He sucked on his lower lip, probably trying not to cry. "Okay."

But what must he think about the whole thing? She put the rag back in the water, swished it around, and wrung it out again. What sort of parents let a stranger take their little boy to another state? Even if she was a social worker? Joey wouldn't understand that.

Molly scrubbed the next section of baseboard. She replayed the conversation she'd had with Jack in the park that day, the first time they were forced to realize the truth about the situation: that it was more than a slight wrinkle in their plans—it was a machete positioned directly over their family. *We can leave the country, Molly… disappear…* With every day that passed, she'd given his idea more thought. At first she'd figured he was delusional, crazy with fear and grief, the way she was. But he'd made it clear since then. He was absolutely serious.

The decision was Molly's. If she gave her okay, Jack would set the plan in motion, and sometime before Joey's fourth visit, the three of them would disappear. Like Joey's dandelion dust. She slid across the floor a few feet and rubbed out a dirt smudge on the shiny white wall. No smudges—not here and not in their life. Everything had been perfect, hadn't it? What happened to the pixie dust?

God…what about Beth's prayer? Molly barely spoke the words, and once she'd said them she blew at a stray piece of hair on her cheek. What had Beth said? People who prayed could at least be sure of God's will. Sometimes God gave people the answer they wanted and sometimes He didn't. But either way, if you talked to God about it, the outcome would be in line with His will.

At least that was the way Beth saw it.

Jack's take was entirely different. They'd had the conversation three nights ago. "God's will?" He laughed and raked his fingers through his hair. "Are you kidding? You want me to wait around for God's will when my son's future is at stake?"

Molly didn't know what to say. "It's not my idea, it's Beth's."

"Well." Jack rolled his eyes. "I think we both know about Beth and Bill. They're a couple of religious fanatics, Molly. We can't let them sway us now. We have to do something before we run out of time."

"But if God wants us to have Joey, Beth says everything'll work out somehow."

"Look, Beth is not the one about to lose her son." Jack lowered his voice. He took her hands and begged her with his eyes. "Please, Molly. Don't consider such a thing. Besides... what if God's will is for the Porters to have him?"

That was something Molly hadn't thought about. She figured that if God could see the big picture—the way Beth believed He could—then He would know implicitly that Joey belonged with them. Certainly the child didn't belong with a convicted felon, a man given to violence. Right?

The conversation about God died there. She and Jack had been on edge, but they'd agreed not to fight. There was no point. They needed each other now more than ever. Molly didn't push the issue, and last night after they tucked Joey in for bed, Jack gently pulled her into his arms. "Help me, Molly." His voice cracked as he spoke into her hair. He held her tighter than usual. "I'm out of options. I don't know what to do."

Neither did she. The tears had been nearly constant, and they came again now as she scrubbed the baseboards. She wiped her eyes with her sleeve since her hands were both wet with soapy water. Allyson Bower would be there in less than four hours, and their precious Joey would walk out the door with her. They could do nothing now to stop the visit from happening.

Molly kept cleaning, working the rag painstakingly over every inch of baseboard until it was cleaner than it had ever been. The project killed two hours. Just as she was finishing, she heard Joey's voice upstairs.

"Mommy! Mommy, where are you?"

Every morning he fell out of bed, and before he rubbed his eyes or took a first look at the world, he stumbled down the hall and crawled in bed between them. Gus was usually not far behind. It was their special way of waking up, with Joey snuggled in the middle, whispering good morning first to his daddy, then to her. She dropped the rag in the soapy water and turned toward the sound of his voice. He must've gone into their room and seen she wasn't there. Now he was wandering the hall looking for her.

She stood and felt a sudden pain in her knees. All that time kneeling without once taking a break—of course they hurt. "Joey...I'm down here."

"Mommy!" She heard his feet padding down the stairs. He came into sight, his eyes still only half open. He was wearing his basketball pajamas, one of the few pairs he owned that still had feet sewn into them. He held his arms out and took little running steps to her. "Mommy, there you are!"

She stooped back down and held him close, ignoring her

knees. With his little body tight against hers, she rocked him and whispered near his ear, "I'm here, baby. I didn't go anywhere."

"I thought the strange lady came and took you instead." He pulled back and looked at her. Confusion filled his expression, and he blinked a few times, trying to wake up. "But you're still here."

"Ah, Joey…" She hated having to hesitate, because the words she was about to say might not be true. But she spoke them anyway. "I'll always be here, buddy. No matter what."

Jack came down then, dressed in jeans and a T-shirt. Their eyes met, and she could see his were swollen. "Good morning." His tone was subdued, the desperation barely hidden.

"Morning." She stood up and found a smile for Joey. "Let's cook your favorite breakfast."

"Blueberry French toast?" He jumped up a few times. But the excitement in his face faded almost as soon as it appeared. "You mean a'cause I'm leaving on a trip?"

Molly picked up her bowl of dirty water. She wanted to throw it out the window, grab Joey's hand and Jack's, and run for their lives. And wasn't that all Jack wanted to do, anyway? Instead she took Joey's hand with her free one and nodded. "Yeah, I guess that's right. A good breakfast makes a trip go by more quickly."

"Okay." Joey followed her to the sink. "Should I get dressed first?"

The idea sent terrified chills down her arms. Get dressed? To leave the house with a social worker and start a process that would take him from their lives forever? She set the bowl of dirty water down in the sink and held on to keep from losing her balance.

Jack came up behind her and put his arm around both of them. "Yes, sport. Let's get you dressed."

"I'll do it." Molly was quick with her answer. What if something happened to him—a car accident or a plane crash? What if the social worker lost track of him at an airport or this Porter man harmed him in some way? What if the couple ran off with him and they never saw him again? The possibilities were frightening and endless. She gave Jack a look that said she was sorry for snapping. "I'll get him dressed, okay?"

"Okay." He smiled at Joey. "I'll make the French toast."

Molly led him up to his room and picked out the clothes: a pair of blue denim shorts and a white polo shirt. She dressed him and combed his hair, then found the right socks—white with blue basketballs. His favorites.

He steadied himself against her shoulder as she bent down and slipped the socks on his feet. "Thanks, Mommy. You picked good today."

"You're welcome." She smoothed his hair and kissed his forehead. "You have Mr. Monkey, right?"

"Yep. He's in the bag even though he's a'scared of the dark."

"He'll be all right."

"But not Mr. Growls." He shook his head. "He wanted to stay here with Gus."

"That's a good idea." The lump in Molly's throat wouldn't let her say more than that.

"Yeah." Big tears threatened to spill onto his cheeks again. His lip wobbled a little.

Molly took hold of him and held him. No matter how much she hurt, Joey was hurting more. Right now that's all she could think about. Making him feel better. "Listen, buddy. You'll be back tomorrow night, okay?" It was what she needed to hear, anything to keep from going over the list of possibilities again, the car accident or plane crash. The possible kidnapping. She held his shoulders and rubbed gentle circles into his small muscles. "Stay with Mrs. Bower, okay? When you're in the airport, there'll be lots of people. Make sure you hold her hand."

"Mrs. Bower?" Alarm filled his face, and in the corners of his eyes the pool of tears grew.

"The woman who's taking you, Joey." She hated this. How could she be Joey's mother and have no say in what was about to happen? She forced herself to speak calmly. "The woman's name is Mrs. Bower."

"Oh." He blinked, and two teardrops slid down his cheeks. He brushed at them quickly, as if maybe they embarrassed him. "Will she know?"

"About holding your hand?" Molly lifted herself to the edge of his toy chest, her eye contact even with his.

He nodded. "I don't want to get lost." Gus trotted into the room and took his place at Joey's side. "Maybe I should take Gus in case Mrs. Bower forgets about me."

Molly chided herself for making him worry. "No, sweetie. Mrs. Bower won't forget about you." She reached out and scratched Gus under his white floppy ear. He was big for a Lab. Big and friendly. If she could've sent him along with Joey, she would've. "You can't take Gus this time. Sorry. Just hold the lady's hand and everything'll be okay."

"All right."

They heard the sound of Jack coming up the stairs. "French toast is ready."

"Wow!" Again Joey's eyes lit up. "Daddy's fast."

They held hands as they went back down to the kitchen. Something about Joey's enthusiasm for breakfast made Molly even sadder than she'd been before. Kids were resilient. If Joey was taken from their home at this age, he'd struggle and miss them for a season. Maybe even for a year or two. But eventually he'd rebound. He'd get excited about basketball socks and swings and French toast. Same as now.

The thought brought with it a torrent of tears, but Molly stuffed them all. She could cry later. Joey needed her to be positive so he could walk out the door knowing that come tomorrow night everything would be okay. If she were crying, what would he think? Probably that his world was falling apart.

She swallowed back a few sobs and took a piece of French toast from the platter. Jack caught her eye and slipped his arm around her again. "You okay?"

"No." She looked at him. She imagined her eyes looked like those of someone about to die. They were headed straight for a cliff and there was nothing they could do to keep from plunging over the edge.

Joey was already at the table, setting the juice glasses out for the three of them.

"No juice for you, Gus." Joey bent down and kissed the dog on top of his head. "Not today." He framed his pudgy hands around the dog's face. "But maybe a leftover piece of French toast if Mommy says so."

Molly leaned into Jack and watched him. "He has no idea."

"No."

Breakfast flew by with conversation about why dogs snore and how fun it would be to go swimming on Sunday. Molly's stomach hurt more with every passing minute. She managed to eat just three bites of her French toast, and Jack did little better. Joey did most of the talking.

"Guess what?" He had syrup on his cheek and all ten fingers looked sticky. "I talked to God last night. Out loud, just like Jonah."

Jack looked at Molly. She shrugged and turned to Joey. "That's interesting." Her tone was kind, curious. "When did you start doing that?"

"Last night was the first time." Joey frowned a little. "I had Gus, but he fell asleep. I wanted someone to talk to, so I talked to God." He shrugged his shoulders a few times. "It made me feel sleepy."

Jack cleared his throat. He wiped his mouth with his napkin. "What did you talk to God about?"

Under the table Molly gave Jack's leg a quick squeeze. Her eyes told him to be careful. Their son could talk to God if he wanted to, no matter what they might think about it.

Joey took another bite of French toast. With his mouth still full, he began to answer. "I told him I was taking a trip with a strange lady." He finished chewing and swallowed. "I asked God to go with me, since my mommy and daddy and my Gus couldn't go."

Molly felt her eyebrows lift. "That's . . . very nice." She held back another rush of tears. Not once had they ever prayed with Joey or taken him to church or taught him how to talk to God. But now, all on his own, he'd done the very thing Beth would've told him to do. He'd asked God to go with him so he wouldn't be alone.

"Yes." Jack kept his tone light. He pushed back from the table and angled his head, curious. "Did Aunt Beth tell you to do that?"

A strange look crossed Joey's face. "No...Aunt Beth never tells me anything about God." He smiled. "I heard Jonah do it when I had a sleepover. If he can do it, I can do it."

Molly wanted to give Jack a look that said she told him so. Of course her sister would never consider going behind their backs and teaching their son to believe in God. Jack shouldn't have even suspected such a thing. But it was nine-thirty and there was no time for bickering or proving who was right.

Joey was about to leave.

They finished eating, brushed teeth, and brought Joey's little overnight roll-aboard suitcase downstairs. Jack went over some of the last minute things that had been on both their minds. They were standing near the door, and Jack swept Joey into his arms. "Mrs. Bower has our phone number. If you need to call us for any reason, you can ask her."

Joey nodded. The lighthearted look from earlier was gone. Now he had enormous tears at the corners of his eyes, but still he wouldn't cry. "What about at night? When Mrs. Bower isn't there?"

"Then you'll be with the Porters. They have a phone, too. Any time you want to call us, you just tell them and they'll let you call."

It was a detail they hadn't actually discussed with the
social worker, but it made sense. He should be able to call
home if he needed to. In preparation for this moment, she
and Jack had worked extensively with Joey so he'd have
his phone number and area code memorized. That way he
would always know how to reach them.

"Okay, one last time." Jack leaned Joey back enough so
he could see his face. "What's your phone number, sport?"

With ease, Joey rattled off all ten digits.

"And what do you have to dial first?"

"A one."

Molly stood next to them. She put her arm around Joey's
shoulders. "And you'll hold onto her hand at the airport.
When you're with Mrs. Bower, right?"

Before he could answer, the doorbell rang. Instantly, Joey
wrapped his arms tight around Jack's neck. "No, Daddy.
I don't want to go."

This was the worst part. Molly felt herself melting, but
she couldn't. She had to stay strong for him, otherwise
none of them would make it. She closed her eyes and leaned
her head on Jack's shoulder. "I can't do this," she said, her
voice meant for only him to hear. "How can we do this?"

Jack coughed twice, and Molly knew why. He, too, was
trying not to cry. He clung to Joey and rocked him a few
times. "I don't want you to go, either. But maybe it'll be
fun. Like an adventure."

The doorbell rang again, and again Joey tightened his grip
on Jack. "I don't want a 'venture. I want you and Mommy."

Molly pushed herself the few feet to the door and opened
it. A tall woman was standing on the other side. Molly
stood back and ushered her in. "Mrs. Bower."

"Yes." She held out a card identifying her as an employee with the Children's Welfare Department of Ohio. Her face was kind and troubled all at the same time. With Joey still clinging to Jack, she spoke only to Molly. "I'm so sorry." She looked down for a few seconds. When her eyes lifted, they were damp. "I want you to know I'm completely against this decision." She paused as if she were looking for some way around it. "Nevertheless, it's my job to carry it out."

"Is there any way?" Molly clung to the door. Her voice was a strained whisper, pinched with pain. She could feel the blood leaving her face. There had to be other options if even the social worker was against the idea. This was the first she'd heard of that. "We can't let them take him from us. Please, Mrs. Bower…"

Allyson closed her eyes and breathed out. When she opened them, she shook her head. "I'm sorry. I wish there was something I could tell you. The law's painfully clear on a case like this." She looked at Jack and Joey, the two of them still lost in their own private conversation. Joey was crying now, sobbing, his little face pressed against Jack's neck. The woman shifted her attention back to Molly. "Your husband tells me he's spoken with a number of attorneys. There's nothing anyone can do."

"What about the governor, or the President of the United States?" Molly had heard of cases like this one where the media helped create a great public outcry and the case gained the attention of top officials. "Should we start making phone calls?"

"I've looked into it." Allyson gave a sad shake of her head. "If I thought it would help I would've already suggested it. But in every case I looked into, where fraud was

the reason for restoring parental rights, the child always
went back to the birth parents. Even if the adoptive parents
contacted the White House." She took another step inside.
"Every time."

Molly was shaking. This was the part she couldn't let
herself think about, the part where a social worker took
hold of Joey's hand and led him out of their house. If it
were a movie, she'd take this moment to visit the restroom
or slip outside for a breath of fresh air. It terrified her even
to imagine such a scene, and now here they were.

The social worker looked at her watch. "I'm afraid we
have a plane to catch." She handed a packet of papers to
Molly. "This has his itinerary, the airline information, my
cell phone number, and the name and phone number of the
Porters, where Joey will be staying. Normally this information is not shared, but under the circumstances, the judge
authorized my giving it to you. Joey is very young. You
need to have a way to reach him in case of an emergency."

"An emergency?" Molly's heart leaped at the thought of
having the Porters' information. She could call Joey every
hour if she wanted to.

"Yes, Mrs. Campbell." Allyson's face was serious. "If you
make unnecessary calls to the Porters, the judge will frown
on it. He might decide to have the transfer take place sooner.
So that the process will be quicker, easier on everyone."

Jack closed the distance between them. He eased Joey's
arms from around his neck. There were tears on his face,
but Molly couldn't tell if they were his or Joey's. "Okay,
sport. Time to go."

"Please, Daddy, don't make me." Joey clung to Jack for
all he was worth.

Molly leaned against the wall so she wouldn't collapse. How was this happening? What were they doing, standing by and letting a stranger take him from his home? The room tilted and nothing made sense. "Joey, baby. Come here."

At the sound of her voice, Joey slid slowly down from Jack's arms and ran to her. He was heavy, but she could still sweep him up and hold him. He wrapped his legs around her waist and buried his head in her shoulder. "Come with me, Mommy. Please!"

She said the first thing that came to mind. "God's going with you, remember? You asked God to go."

For the first time in ten minutes, Joey's sobs let up. He was still sad, still crying. But he seemed more in control. He straightened himself and rubbed his nose against hers. "That's right, huh, Mommy? God'll be with me, 'cause I asked Him."

"Exactly." Molly wondered if God was right there with both of them, even in that very instant. Otherwise how was she standing or talking or doing anything but falling apart? Tears blurred her vision, but again she refused them. She smiled at him. "Eskimo noses, okay?"

In the background, she saw Jack turn and press his forehead against the wall. His shoulders were shaking.

Joey didn't notice. He rubbed Molly's nose with his. Then he blinked his eyelashes against hers. "And butterfly kisses."

"Yes." She pressed her cheek alongside his and held him, memorizing the feel of him in her arms. Then she brushed her eyelashes against his. "Butterfly kisses."

"Joey…" The social worker stepped up. "I'm Mrs. Bower."

Joey looked at her. He dragged his hands across his cheeks. "Hi."

"Hi." She smiled. "I'll take very good care of you and I'll bring you back before you know it. I promise."

Jack came to them then. He circled his arms around Molly and Joey, and they stayed that way for a full minute, none of them wanting to let go. Finally, Jack helped Joey to the floor. "Remember what we told you."

"I will." He was still holding Molly's hand. His eyes met hers. "Mommy?"

That was all he needed to say. In that single word he was asking her all the same questions again. Did he have to go? Couldn't she come with him? Why couldn't he stay with her and Jack and Gus?

Molly bent down and brought his hand to her lips. She kissed it and looked straight into his eyes, to his heart. "I love you. I could never love any little boy as much as I love you."

"I love you, too." He gave her one last hug.

When he pulled back, she held her breath. She had no idea how she was going to do this next part, but it had to be done. She pursed her lips and blew out. "Mrs. Bower will take good care of you, buddy." Then, slowly, she tucked his hand into the hand of the social worker. "Don't forget about God." She took a step back. Maybe she would have a heart attack or a stroke.... The pain was strong enough to kill her.

Again, peace eased the worry and fear in his precious features. "Yeah. God's going with me. I hafta remember that."

Jack stepped up and kissed him once more on the

forehead. "I love you, sport. Call us if you get lonely, okay?"

" 'Kay. Love you, too."

"Bye, Joey." Molly clung to Jack's arm, leaned on him so she wouldn't fall over.

"Everything will be okay. You'll come home tomorrow." Allyson Bower gave them a final look, as if she couldn't bear the words she was saying. Everything would hardly be okay. And though he'd come home this time, in a few short months they'd have to say good-bye forever.

The social worker took Joey's suitcase with one hand, and held onto Joey's fingers with the other. They walked through the entryway and down the sidewalk. Molly and Jack moved to the screen door and watched them go. Joey looked over his shoulder every few steps and waved at them.

He looked frightened still, but he wasn't crying. Mrs. Bower helped him with his suitcase, and then buckled him into a booster seat. Mrs. Bower said something Molly couldn't quite make out—something about getting ice cream at the airport. Joey gave her a weak smile, and a minute later, the social worker climbed into the driver's seat and the two of them drove away.

Molly had expected to collapse on the floor, screaming and wailing, frantic for her son. She'd been holding back the tears all morning, after all. Instead she only stood there, staring at the empty road outside their home, listening as the sound of the woman's car grew more and more distant and eventually faded altogether. When it did, Jack finally led her back inside and shut the door. She found her way to the sofa and sat down.

Neither of them spoke or cried or screamed. There was nothing they could do; Joey was gone. His entire next two days were completely out of their hands. Molly covered her face and wondered about herself. Where were her tears? Where was her heart in all the hurt and terror of the moment? How come she was still breathing?

And suddenly she knew.

Her body was carrying on in an auto-pilot sort of way. But her heart and soul and emotions...Everything else inside her was dead. She'd lost all connection with life the moment Joey walked out of their house. Yes, it could take a lifetime before her heart stopped beating, but without Joey she felt completely and wholly lifeless. Only one thing would breathe meaning back into her existence.

The moment Joey ran through the door and into her arms again.

FOURTEEN

The visit wasn't going all that well.

Wendy and Rip had everything all set when Allyson and Joey walked through the door that afternoon. She'd gotten the day off work, and even though Rip was scheduled to start work at the theater, they were letting him wait until Monday.

Ever since the day of the home study, she and Rip had gotten along fine. He was a little uptight now and then, but who wouldn't be? The changes in their lives were huge. He was out of prison, and now they were getting their son back. Neither of them had ever been a parent before, so sure, they were anxious.

Rip fixed the hole in the wall, like he'd promised, and for the most part he'd been a dream to be around. Even today. They baked chocolate-chip cookies, and Rip stayed with her the whole time.

"So they don't burn," he'd told her. But he wasn't mad; he winked at her and the job was actually fun. Something they could do together.

Joey's room was all made up, too. Rip had come home the day before with a stuffed bear. "Think he'll like it?" Rip arranged it just so, right at the center of Joey's pillow.

"Of course." She loved this side of Rip, the side that wanted to be a good father. "Do you like his new bed?"

"How much did it set us back?" Rip raised a wary eye.

"Not much. It was on sale."

"Three hundred?"

"Three-twenty." She winced. "But I charged it. Twenty dollars a month. We can afford that, right?"

He smiled and took her in his arms. "With my new job, we can." The pride in his face was contagious. "Everything's looking up for us, Wendy. I always knew it would happen this way one day. I just never thought we'd have a son so soon." He chuckled. "It's like all my dreams are coming true."

The trouble started when Joey arrived.

Mrs. Bower almost dragged him through the door. He looked tired and weepy, and Wendy's heart went out to him. This was her little baby, all grown up. The one she'd held in her arms all those years ago in that hospital bed. This was the boy who seemed to whisper to her, *Mommy...don't let me go. Don't give me up.* He was beautiful, all golden hair and pale blue eyes. She could see herself in the shape of his face, and Rip in the child's athletic build.

But the joy of seeing him for the first time was short-lived.

"No!" He turned and cried the word into the social worker's leg. "I wanna go home."

Allyson stopped and bent down. She said something they couldn't hear, but Joey shook his head. His tone wasn't rude, just very, very sad. Sad enough to break the

hearts of everyone in the room. Allyson whispered something else to him. Joey sniffed a few times. "No...I want
my mommy and daddy!"

Next to her, Wendy heard Rip chuckle. He sounded
nervous, the way he got right before his anger took over.
"Uh...this is awkward." Another chuckle. "Let's get the
boy inside. Maybe that'll calm him down."

The social worker managed to lead Joey into the house
and over to the kitchen table a few feet away, where he sat
close to her. Wendy took her place at the table, in the
chair on Joey's other side. Rip remained standing, leaning
against the nearest wall and shifting positions every few
seconds. He couldn't have looked more uncomfortable if
he'd been standing on a bed of nails.

"Please..." Joey folded his arms on the table and buried
his tearstained face. His words became muffled. "I wanna
go home."

Rip made a face and gave an exaggerated sigh. His lips
parted as if he might say something, but then he changed
his mind. He worked the muscles in his jaw, his anger
bubbling close to the surface. He moved into the kitchen,
grabbed a glass from the cupboard, and poured himself
some water.

Wendy prayed he'd keep his mouth shut. They'd been
warned about this, right? The social worker told them
not to say anything argumentative to the boy the first day.
They weren't to tell him that they were his real parents,
and they weren't to make him think their own house was
his home if he talked about wanting to go back to Florida.

Still, staying quiet looked like a struggle for Rip. She
gave him a stern look, the hardest look she'd given him

since he'd been out of prison. Normally he wouldn't have let her look at him that way, but here—with Allyson Bower in their kitchen—Rip knew better than to say anything.

Wendy put her hand on Joey's shoulder, and the sensation was like magic. This was her son, her baby. It was the first time she'd touched him since she handed him over to the nurse that terrible afternoon. She wasn't prepared for the feelings that stirred in her soul. "Honey..." She struggled to find her voice. "I baked you some cookies. Are you hungry?"

From across the room, Rip chimed in. "*We* baked 'em." He raised his water glass in their direction. "It was my idea."

Mrs. Bower shot him a strange look. But she quickly turned her attention back to Joey. "Did you hear what the mommy told you?" The judge had asked that Joey call them "the mommy" and "the daddy" from the beginning. That way it'd be easier on everyone when he came to live with them for good. And the social worker was clear about the wording. She didn't say, "your mommy." She said "*the* mommy."

Wendy was fine with that. The poor boy. He looked scared to death.

At the mention of cookies, Joey lifted his head. Even though his tears had stopped, he inhaled in sets of three quick breaths, as if the sobs were still cutting at him on the inside. That's when he looked at her, and for the first time since he was a newborn, their eyes met.

In that instant, Wendy knew she could never let him go. He'd found his way home by some strange miracle, because of a lie she'd told. What she'd done was wrong, yes. But now here he was looking straight to her soul, and the feeling was amazing beyond anything she could've imagined.

"Hi, Joey." She reached out and touched his fingers. He didn't pull away. "Can I get you a glass of milk?" She smiled. "Chocolate-chip cookies are really yummy with milk."

He narrowed his eyes, suspicious. Then he looked at Mrs. Bower and back to Wendy. "Yes, please." His words were so quiet she could barely make them out. But at least he wasn't crying. And he was so polite! Her little boy already had wonderful manners. The process would take time but everything would work out. Joey was amazing, so of course he would adjust.

"Okay, honey." She started to stand.

But a few feet away, Rip went after the milk before she could move. "I'll get it." He was acting like a spoiled child, jealous of every attempt she made to break the barriers between herself and Joey. He poured the milk and set it down, a little harder than necessary.

"Rip..." She kept her tone soft. "Be careful. You'll scare him."

That was all Rip needed to hear. His eyes grew dark, but before he might say something he'd regret, he seemed to remember the social worker. He smiled at her, but it fell just short of looking mean. "If you'll excuse me, I have some things to take care of out back."

"I think that might be best." Allyson looked at Joey. "Let's have your wife make peace with him first. Maybe he'll feel more comfortable."

Rip cast one more stern look at Wendy. Then he turned and hurried down the hall to their bedroom. He slammed the door behind him, leaving an uncomfortable silence hanging over the kitchen table.

"Sorry...Rip's a little nervous about..." Wendy looked at Joey. "Well, you know. This is our first time to..."

"I understand." Allyson slid her chair farther away, giving Wendy and Joey their own space.

Wendy took the cue and pulled the plate of chocolate-chip cookies closer to Joey. "Here, honey." She handed him one. "You can dip it into your milk."

Joey wiped his eyes again. His breathing was calmer than before. "Thank you." His voice was pitifully small, scared to death. He took the cookie and broke it in half. "It's easier in halfs."

"Yes." Wendy smiled. It was a victory. He'd talked to her! She felt her heart melt a little more. Never had she imagined this day, the chance to sit at the table with her son and share a moment like this.

He held out the other half to her. "Want some?"

She was about to say no thanks, but at the same time she considered something. Maybe he was reaching out, trying to make a connection the only way he knew how. She took the piece and smiled at him. "Thanks, Joey. You're a very nice boy."

He nodded and dipped his cookie. After one bite he cocked his head. "I go home tomorrow, right?"

Reality slapped her in the face. The child wasn't warming up; he was surviving. This wasn't his home, and she wasn't his mother. He was lonely and afraid, so many states away from everything he knew to be safe and good and true. She swallowed her disappointment. "Yes, tomorrow."

"Okay." He looked at the social worker. "You'll come with me, right?"

"Right." Allyson Bower clutched the file to her chest.

She glanced at Wendy. "If you don't need me, I think I'll let you two visit."

A lump of fear settled in Wendy's gut. Could she handle it, being alone with her son? What if he started crying? What if Rip came out and got angry? The boy wasn't reacting the way he wanted, that's for sure. Still...they would never know if they didn't try. She gave a quick nod. "Yes." She smiled at Joey again. "We'll be fine."

"I'll be nearby. I need to put in a few hours at the office, but I'll have my cell phone the whole time. Call me for any reason, day or night." She tapped the file. "Everything's in here. Joey knows that he can telephone me or his... parents if he needs to."

Wendy caught the way she hesitated on the word parents. Joey had no idea what was happening, that his understanding of "parents" was about to change. Allyson stood and put her hand on Joey's shoulder. "Remember what we talked about? You can call if you need anything."

"Thank you." He took another cookie and broke it in half. "See you tomorrow."

The social worker bid them good-bye, and then they were alone, Wendy and Joey, with Rip in the other room. She folded her arms and rested them on the table. "Did you like your plane ride?"

"Yes." He dipped the cookie and stuffed most of it in his mouth. When he could talk he gave her a crooked smile. "Sometimes I take plane rides with my mommy and daddy. Once we went to Mexico and watched the dolphins."

"Wow..." Wendy wasn't sure what to say. This was something else she hadn't thought of. Joey's adoptive parents were obviously rich people—taking Joey on trips to foreign beaches and giving him opportunities she and Rip could never afford. She straightened herself. Never mind all of that. A couple didn't need money to be good parents. They needed love, that's all. And who would love Joey more than his real parents, his biological parents?

"Also I took a plane ride to France once." He finished chewing and swallowed. There were cookie crumbs on his lips and cheeks, and he looked beyond adorable. "I saw the iceberg tower."

"The iceberg..." She squinted. "The Eiffel Tower, you mean?"

"Yeah, that one." He gulped the rest of the milk. When he set the cup down, he had a white creamy mustache that only added to his charm. He looked straight at her. "Do you have a dog here?"

"No." She looked around. The cat must've been in the back room with Rip. "We have a kitty named Tigger."

"Oh. I have a doggie named Gus."

The lump in her stomach grew. A doggie named Gus. One more reason it would be hard for Joey to make this transition. Harder than she'd ever thought. "Well...we might get a dog someday. I think dogs are nice."

He scrunched up his face. " 'Cept dogs eat cats."

"Oh, Joey...not always." She heard the alarm in her voice. "Sometimes they just chase cats."

"I guess." He looked around. "So where is he? The kitty?"

Before she could answer, Rip's voice sounded in the hallway. "Is she gone?"

"Yes." Wendy stood and met him halfway across the living room. She lowered her voice. "Joey's doing much better. Probably just needed time to get used to us."

Rip nodded, but he looked suspicious. "He doesn't like me." He peered over Wendy's shoulder to the table, and her eyes followed his. Joey was swirling his glass, playing with the last few drops of milk and cookie crumbs.

"That's ridiculous." She kept her tone hushed. "He doesn't even know you."

"Well, he'd better start." Rip thrust his shoulders back and stuck out his chest. "I'm his daddy, after all."

"Rip…" She held up her finger. "Don't go saying anything about that. Mrs. Bower told us, remember?" She peered at Joey. "He doesn't know yet."

"Okay, I get it." He made a mock show of putting his finger to his lips and zipping them closed. "I won't say a word."

Rip led the way back to the kitchen table. Wendy took her chair, and Rip sat on Joey's other side. "Hey, little man." He patted Joey's back, maybe a little too hard. "How'd you like the cookies?"

Joey lowered his chin. His eyes got big and he slid closer to Wendy. "Good, thanks."

"You don't need to be shy, kid." He stood and took Joey's hand. "How 'bout we show you to your room?"

"No, thank you." He leaned into Wendy and pulled his hand free. "I just wanna sit here."

Rip wore a look of disbelief, and Wendy wasn't surprised. People simply didn't tell Rip Porter no. He took Joey's hand again and this time gave him a tug that brought him to his feet. "We have to put your suitcase away, little man." His voice was stern. "Around here if I say we're doing something, well, then that's what we're doing."

Joey had no choice but to be pulled along. Rip grabbed

the boy's suitcase on the way, and Joey started to cry. He pointed back at Wendy. "I wanna sit with her."

"You can sit with her later." Rip tugged Joey again and this time the boy fell into step beside him.

Wendy understood what Rip was doing. He wanted to show Joey the bear, the stuffed animal he'd brought and so proudly set up on the child's pillow. But this was no way to do it. He should've waited until Joey was tired. Then they could've taken him back to his room together and the surprise might've been a good thing. She stood and followed them. *God...please let this go well.* "Rip...wait for me."

It was too late. By the time she reached the bedroom, Joey was sobbing and shaking his head, pointing back to the door. "I wanna be with her."

"Look!" Rip gave his arm a sudden jolt. Not enough to hurt him, but enough to make him stop crying. The fact seemed to please Rip. He relaxed a little and led Joey all the way to the bed. "See there." He nodded to the stuffed bear. "I bought you a gift."

Joey nodded. His shoulders still shook, but he wasn't making any noise now. "Th-th-thank you."

"Well..." Rip picked it up and handed it to Joey. "You can hold it if you want."

"I already...have Mr. Growls. He's b-b-back home." He pointed to his suitcase. "And Mr. M-m-monkey is in there." The child's words were quiet, but from the doorway Wendy understood them. Obviously he already had his favorite stuffed animals. He pulled free of Rip's hand, unzipped the top of his little suitcase, and brought out a well-worn stuffed monkey. "Th-th-this is Mr. Monkey."

"Fine." Rip's face showed his hurt. He fired the bear

back at the bed, and Joey jumped, dropping the monkey to the floor. Rip brought his face close to the boy's. "One day soon I'm gonna teach you some manners, little man."

Rip's tone and mean eyes must've scared Joey even more. He started crying and this time he dropped the monkey, ran around Rip and spread out, face down, on the bed. Wendy met Rip's eyes and Rip gave her a look that said, What? He glared at the weeping figure on the bed and then back at her. "I'm doing my best."

She shook her head, walked past him and sat on the edge of the mattress. If Rip was going to make a mess of things, then it would be up to her. She stroked Joey's back. "Honey, I'm sorry you're upset." She reached down to the floor, picked up the child's toy, and tucked it in near his shoulder. "Here, Joey. Here's Mr. Monkey."

He only cried harder. "I wanna go home! Please!" He lifted his tear-streaked face and gave her a look that broke her heart. "I want Mommy and Daddy."

"That's it." Rip slapped the wall and took two threatening steps toward them. He grabbed Joey's arm and jerked him into a sitting position. "Let's get one thing straight." He brought his face inches from Joey's. "As long as you're here, *this* is your home."

"Rip...don't!" Wendy tried to pull him from the boy, but he wouldn't budge. She knew better than to get in his way when he was at the start of a rage, but she wouldn't let him hurt Joey. Not even if it meant laying down her life. She snapped at him. "You're going to ruin everything."

"No." He put his arm hard around her shoulders. "I'm just clearing things up." He glared at Joey again. "Like I said, when you're here, this is your home." He jolted Wendy even closer to him. "This is your mommy." He grinned but it was the meanest look he could've given the boy. "And *I'm* your daddy." He shoved Joey back down on the bed. "Understand?"

"Y-y-yes." Joey's face was pale.

Wendy watched Rip's anger fade as quickly as it had come. He looked down for a moment and rubbed the back of his neck. Then he turned and left the room in a hurry, without looking at her or saying another word to the child.

The moment he was gone, Wendy instantly returned to Joey's side, stroking his back, sheltering him. She could've spat at Rip for what he'd just done. If the boy said anything, Allyson Bower would run to the judge, and that would be that. Joey would stay with his adoptive parents for sure.

"Honey, it's okay," she whispered near Joey's ear. "He's just a little uptight. He isn't always like that."

Joey was whimpering. "He...he's mean."

She cursed Rip under her breath. She'd told a few of the girls at church to pray for them, but nothing could make Rip behave the way he should all the time. Not when Rip had a will of his own. She smoothed Joey's hair. He rolled onto his side and looked at her. His breathing was uneven, his body still shaking with sobs. "Why is he...mad at me?"

"He's not." She sorted through her words, trying to find the right ones. "He just wanted you to like the little bear he bought you."

Joey nodded. He made his hands into fists and rubbed his eyes. "Maybe Mr. Monkey could be friends with t-t-two bears."

A ray of hope shone on Wendy's heart. "Yes, that's it. Maybe so."

"What time is it?"

"Almost dinner time." She rubbed his back some more. "Think you could come out of your room and have some pizza with us?"

"Yes." He sat up slowly and looked around the bed. He found the bear on the other side of the pillow and he picked it up. "It's a nice bear."

"It is." Wendy held her breath. If only Rip could see the child now...

Joey took the bear and placed it carefully on the pillow. Then he took the monkey and set it right next to the bear. Last, he took the bear's paw and the monkey's arm and crossed them so it looked like they were holding hands. "Listen, Mr. Monkey. This is your new friend—Mr. Bear. He's not Mr. Growls, but monkeys can have t-t-two bear friends. Okay?"

Wendy watched, fascinated. Just minutes ago Joey was cowering on the bed, falling apart under Rip's harsh words and hands. But now he was directing his attention to helping his toys get along with each other.

Dinner was less eventful. Joey asked Rip if he could have pineapple on his pizza.

"No." Rip snarled at him. He seemed to be making no effort to recover from the earlier disaster in Joey's room. "Pineapple's terrible on pizza."

"Okay. S-s-sorry." Joey didn't speak to him again the rest of the evening.

Rip spent most of the night watching a baseball game on television. Halfway through the pizza, Joey tugged on

Wendy's sleeve. He talked quietly, as if he was too nervous to speak up with Rip around. "Is he watching baseball?"

"Yes. The Indians." Wendy was still mad at Rip. He could've done so much better for Joey's first night. She smiled at the boy and put her arm around him. "The Indians are from around here." She looked at Rip. "He watches all their games."

Joey nodded, but he yawned at the same time. When dinner was over he helped Wendy clean up. Having him work at her side was amazing. All those years without him Wendy had wondered what it would be like to be a mother, to have the incredible privilege of raising the infant boy she'd cradled that day in the hospital. Today, for the first time, she had a chance to know the feeling for real.

As she tucked him in, she could only hope about the future, that this would be the first of countless nights of tucking him in, knowing that her son was asleep down the hall in the same house as herself.

Just as she thought he was falling asleep, he sat up, his eyes wide. "I need to call home. My mommy and daddy told me I could."

Wendy hesitated. She had hoped they could get through this first visit without his making any calls home. Otherwise how was he going to get used to them in just a handful of trips? She eased him back down onto the bed. "Let's call in a little while, okay?"

His eyelids were heavy. "Promise?"

"Promise." She rubbed his back until she heard little snores coming from him. Then, when she was sure he wouldn't hear her, she whispered close to his head, "Good night, Joey. Mama loves you."

As she left his room, a thought hit her. Rip had better figure out how to get along with Joey, how to treat him. Because now that she'd found Joey, one thing was sure.

She wasn't ever going to let him go.

꩜

Joey wasn't sure how late it was or how long until morning. His eyes opened and he sat straight up. He looked around. Where was he, and why was his bed different? He could feel his heart bumping inside him. Hard and fast. His fingers moved around his pillow. "Gus...Gus where are you?"

But there were no little dog noises, no furry tail wagging beside him.

Then he remembered.

He wasn't at home tonight. He was with the other mommy and daddy, sleeping in a strange bed. His hands reached around some more and...there he was. "Mr. Monkey!" He held the fuzzy friend close to his face. Then he whispered so only Mr. Monkey would hear him. "I wanna go home."

A light was coming in through his window, so he could see Mr. Monkey's face. *I wanna go home, too,* Mr. Monkey was saying. *But I like my new friend, Mr. Bear.*

"Yes, Mr. Bear is nice. I think Mr. Growls will like him." He patted his pillow and found the other stuffed friend. Then he held them both close and lay back down again.

The daddy at this house was very mean and mad. Not like his own daddy at all. Plus his arm hurt where the man grabbed him. He blinked in the dark. His heart was still bumping loud and fast. Then he thought about the mommy at this place. She was a nice lady. She made good chocolate-chip cookies, plus she had soft hands. Her eyes had nice in them, and that made him not so scared about the mean man.

He wasn't sleepy, but it might be a long time until morning. Mommy's words from a long time ago filled up his head. *Sleeping makes the nighttime go by a lot faster.* That's what she told him. He closed his eyes and tried. *Sleep. Sleep...sleep...sleep!*

It isn't working, Mr. Monkey told him.

"I know it isn't." He lay very still, but he opened his eyes and looked around. What did the mean man say? That as long as he was here, this was his home and they were his mommy and daddy? A scared feeling happened to him and his heart bumped even faster. Why would he say that? Maybe the nice lady would tell him tomorrow at breakfast.

He closed his eyes again, but still he couldn't sleep. He remembered the Indians. He knew Ohio was an Indian place, but how come no teepees? He shivered a little.

That's when he remembered about God. He smiled, and next to him Mr. Monkey and Mr. Bear smiled, too. This time he kept the words quiet, just in his heart. *Hi, God...It's me, Joey. Thanks for being with me on the plane today and at this house. Remember, God? A few times I was scared, only then I could feel You beside me.* He smiled again. *That's why I know You're real. Even though You're 'visible.*

He felt a little tired come over him. *Can You do something, God?...Can You please stay with me tomorrow and on the way home, too? 'Cause Mommy and Daddy and Gus aren't here, remember? And also can You tell my family something, 'cause I didn't get to call 'em? Tell them I love them and I can't wait to get home.* He tried to remember the ending, the way Jonah ended his prayer. He wasn't sure what it meant, but he said it in his heart anyway. *Gee this name, amen.*

Mr. Bear was already asleep, but Mr. Monkey tapped Joey's arm. *I like when you talk to God,* he said.

"Me, too." He was much more sleepy now. "I like it 'cause it means I'm not alone."

You're not alone, Mr. Monkey said. *You have me.*

"I know." He smiled a little, but he was almost asleep. He didn't want to tell Mr. Monkey, but he liked having God even better than his fuzzy friend. Because God was the strongest one in the whole universe. And that made him feel very safe. Safe enough to close his eyes and sleep. Because God was stronger than anyone.

Even the mean man who lived at this house.

FIFTEEN

Their plans came together at Fuller Park.

The place was quiet and close, and it gave them complete confidence that Joey wasn't listening to their conversation. Molly still couldn't believe it had come to this, but Jack was right. They were out of options. She settled in against the park bench and watched her husband, the man she trusted and loved with her whole life. He was pushing Joey on the swing, saying something about airplanes or pirates or reaching the sky. Molly appreciated the distraction.

Joey had been home just fifteen hours, and already she'd replayed his homecoming a dozen times in her head.

She'd been wearing out a path along the kitchen floor waiting for his return. When he walked through the door with Mrs. Bower, she rushed to him, dropped to her knees and held him close.

"Mommy! I missed you so much!"

"Me, too, buddy."

But even before she could ask questions or tell him hello, the social worker tapped her on the shoulder. "Can I speak with you...alone?"

Jack had been in the workout room upstairs. At the sound of Joey at the door, he hurried down and into the entryway. He, too, stooped down and pulled Joey into a hug. His words were tight with emotion when he could finally speak. "We missed you, sport. I'm so glad you're back."

Molly motioned to him that Allyson Bower wanted to talk to them. Gus was the perfect distraction. The dog trotted up and nearly knocked Joey down in his hurry to say hello. "Gus!" Joey sounded happy, healthy. Normal. Molly could finally draw a complete breath. Her son was out of danger. For now.

They followed the social worker into the kitchen where Joey couldn't hear them. She opened a file and took out a single sheet of paper. "You'll see four fingerprint bruises on Joey's left upper arm." Her face was shrouded in concern. "The Porters told me about it. Their story goes that Joey was falling or he needed help up." Her words dripped disgust. "Apparently, Mr. Porter took hold of Joey's arm to help him." She showed them the piece of paper. "It's all here in the report."

Once again, Molly felt the room start to spin. What was happening here? They were talking about documented bruises on their son's body? At the hands of a convicted felon? A domestic-violence offender? Had the whole world gone crazy? Joey would never be safe with a man like that—never! She tried to focus. Jack was talking now.

"What I'm saying is, did anyone ask Joey what happened?"

"The Porters told me the story in front of him." She shook her head as if to say that wasn't how things were supposed to work out. "I pulled Joey aside and asked him if the story was true, if that's how he got the bruises."

"What did he say?" Molly couldn't sort through her emotions fast enough. One moment she was furious, the next she wanted only to take Joey in her arms and rock him until he felt safe again.

The social worker gave a thoughtful nod. "He said it was true. What I didn't like was how he kept looking over his shoulder while I was talking to him." She hesitated. "I think he's afraid of Rip Porter, but I can't prove it."

"So, isn't that enough?" Jack's voice was a study in controlled fury. "The man's served time for domestic violence. He leaves bruises on my son's arm. Certainly the judge won't give the man custody now."

Mrs. Bower pressed her lips together. "If you and Joey were walking and he tripped, you'd reach out to catch him, too. And you might leave bruises on his arm." She lifted her shoulders. "I have no choice but to believe the story. Without Joey's testimony, no one would ever blame Rip Porter for a few little bruises."

Molly read more into the woman's statement. "Meaning what, exactly?"

"Meaning it'd take a lot more than that for anyone to accuse him of abusing his own biological son." She looked intently at them. "Children rarely testify against adults, Mrs. Campbell."

"But if the Porters are lying"—Jack's mind must've been headed in the same direction as Molly's—"and if we could get Joey to tell us that, then wouldn't the judge throw Porter back in prison and let us keep him?"

"No." Allyson was a strong woman from what they knew of her, a businesswoman. But in that moment she looked sad, even vulnerable. "The system doesn't work that way. The paperwork was forged, so by the court's standards, Joey's adoption was never completed, never official. If Rip Porter walked into a downtown bank and held it up at gunpoint with a dozen witnesses, they could send him to jail for the rest of his life, and still Joey would not belong to you." She tapped the file in her hand and looked from Molly to Jack. "Joey's adoption never took place. Not legally."

After Allyson left, Molly and Jack cuddled with Joey and Gus on the sofa. They watched Disney's *World's Greatest Athlete* and laughed when the coach's team was so bad, his football players didn't know which direction to run. When Nanu, the jungle boy, came with the coach to the United States to help the team, Joey sat on the edge of his seat. Clearly he was amazed at the way the jungle boy could run and jump and hit and throw. But near the end of the program, Joey cried quiet tears. "Nanu doesn't want to win. He just wants to be home."

"That's right, Joey." Molly kissed his head.

He looked up at her. " 'Cause home's the best place."

Jack and Molly exchanged a look. Then Molly said it was time to get Joey's pajamas on. They walked him up to his room and she took his T-shirt off. The bruises were easy to see. They couldn't have been made by anything but an intentional grab at their son's arm.

Molly ran her fingers over them. "Joey...what happened here?"

Joey stayed silent.

"It's okay, baby." Molly kissed his cheek. "You can tell us. You're not in trouble."

Joey bit his lip. Gus moved into the room and for a few seconds he was distracted, petting the dog.

Jack tried this time. "Joey, tell us about the bruises, sport. What happened?"

"You can't t-t-tell that other d-d-daddy, okay?"

Molly wanted to cry an ocean of tears. When had he started stuttering? Was he that afraid, that worried that somehow the "other daddy" would hurt him? In just one brief visit? What would a lifetime with a man like that mean for Joey?

"That other daddy is Mr. Porter." Jack's tone flowed with compassion, putting Joey at ease. "He won't find out. I promise."

Joey ran his other hand over the bruise and his eyes grew damp again. "That m-m-man was m-m-mad at me. I was laying d-d-down and he wanted to talk to me." The stuttering was worse with every sentence. "He grabbed me and made me sit up. Then he yelled at me. He t-t-told me pretty s-s-soon he would t-t-teach me a lesson."

Jack groaned and leaned against the wall.

Molly could only imagine the battle her husband was waging inside his head and heart, because the war inside hers was just as fierce. If Rip Porter were standing in front of her, she would punch him square in the face. How dare he lay a hand on her son? It didn't matter that Rip was Joey's biological father. The man was a stranger, and a bad guy at that.

She ran her fingers gently over the row of marks on Joey's arm. "Buddy, why didn't you tell that to Mrs. Bower?"

" 'C-c-cause...that mean daddy was watching us. If I t-t-told the t-t-truth he might hurt me again. M-m-mostly I talked to God. He stayed with me the whole trip."

Jack rolled his eyes. Molly understood. What was God

doing to help them? Joey had gone to Ohio despite her prayers and Beth's, and he had come home physically and emotionally damaged. Still, Molly refused to be cynical, at least where Joey was concerned. She leaned close to him. "I'm glad God was with you, buddy. I'm glad you weren't alone."

Jack took Joey into his bathroom to help him brush his teeth, and Molly unpacked his bag. Near the top she found the stuffed bear. She held it up. "Joey? What's this?"

"What?" Joey peered out from the bathroom. "Oh, that's Mr. B-b-bear. He's Mr. Monkey's new friend." Even ten minutes after talking about the bruising incident, Joey's stuttering was less than before. "The other daddy gave it to me."

In that moment, Molly knew what Mrs. Bower meant about children and abuse. Of course they didn't testify. Something inside children made them forget about traumatic events, like a safety mechanism in their hearts. One minute Joey had been terrified of Rip Porter. The next, he was happy about having received a stuffed animal from the man.

Half an hour later, when his bag had been unpacked and Mr. Monkey and Mr. Bear and Mr. Growls were tucked in on one side and Gus on the other, and when Joey was asleep, Molly and Jack stepped out into the hall. Molly stopped and faced him. She had just one thing to say.

"Jack . . ."

"I won't have it, Molly." He was fuming, pressing his hands against his temples and dropping them to his sides again. "I'd like to get my hands on him just for one minute! Grab a little boy who's already scared and alone and—"

"Jack…"

"No, I'm serious, Molly. This isn't right. There has to be a law in place that'll protect kids, because I'm not standing around and waiting until that man does something drastic to my son before—"

"Jack!"

He stopped. "What?"

She searched his eyes. When she had his full attention she opened her mouth and said the thing she never thought she'd say. "I'm ready for your plan."

That had happened just the previous night. Now here they sat in the park, ready to set the plan into motion—whatever the plan might be. A plan that would force them to cut ties with everything and everyone they knew in the United States and start life over again.

Molly felt as terrified and shocked about the idea as ever. No matter what they did, life was about to take a wild, frightening, uncontrollable turn. Jack's plan was worth pursuing because at least they would take that turn with Joey. Not without him. At the end of this very long, very dark tunnel, that was the only light whatsoever.

Jack walked back to Molly and took his seat on the bench. He turned to her, "I love you." His hands came up and he framed her face, studying her. With all the tenderness in the world, he kissed her lips. "Before we take this any further, I need you to know that. I've been in love with you since the day I met you."

She felt her throat grow thick. How had he known? This—his love for her—was exactly what she needed to hear right now. That whatever they faced, they'd face it as lovers and friends. She returned his kiss. "You're all I need,

Jack." She allowed herself to get lost in his eyes. "I trust you. Whatever we have to do, we can do it together."

They settled back against the bench and kept their eyes on Joey. "Okay, Molly." Jack put his arm around her and cradled her head against his shoulder. "What we're about to do, our plans, our conversations, all of it must never— not for a minute—be discussed with anyone else."

Molly was about to say that his warning was unnecessary. After all, they were making plans to leave the country, to create new identities for themselves.

But then he looked at her, his eyes full of sorrow. "That means Beth, too."

Everything around her faded. The sound of the birds, the subtle breeze, Joey on his swing, even the pounding of her own heartbeat.

Beth.

Why hadn't she thought about her sister? Molly sat back and looked straight ahead again. Her junior year of high school, she had played a pick-up game of basketball at lunch with some of the drama kids. None of them had much experience in sports, and one of the guys winged the ball at her when she wasn't ready. She had taken it right in the gut, and it was half a minute before she could breathe again.

She felt that way now.

Leaving Florida, leaving life as they knew it, leaving everything about Jack and Molly Campbell—she was ready for all of it. But leaving Beth? Forever? Molly bent at her waist and leaned over her knees. She was getting her wind back, but her heart was still spinning out of control. Beth had been her best friend all her life. She shared everything with her sister.

"Molly..." Jack put his hand on her lower back. "You hadn't thought about Beth?"

She squeezed her eyes shut for a few seconds, then slowly sat up. She turned to Jack and shook her head. "I guess not."

"You can't tell her any of this."

"No." The right answers were easy. Putting them into play would be another thing. She would be working through the most difficult, most painful time in her life, and she wouldn't be able to tell a word of it to Beth. Then, when all the plans came together, she would have to do the impossible. She would say good-bye to her sister and friend, knowing they would never see each other again.

Once more she faced forward and looked at Joey, at his pale blond hair dancing in the warm breeze as he pushed himself higher, higher. She had no choice about Beth. In a few months, Molly Campbell would be dead, and so would her relationship with her sister. Molly steeled herself against the pain that would come. She would do it all for Joey.

There was no other way.

She nodded. "I understand."

"All right." Jack sounded relieved. He angled himself so he could see her better. "I've been thinking of a plan."

"Okay." Her heart bounced around inside her. She felt like she was standing at the open door of an airplane, about to jump. Only she wasn't even sure she had a parachute. "We have to get out of the country, right?"

"Right." Jack's words picked up speed. "That's the hardest part, because we have to answer to Allyson Bower."

"Not for everything." Molly felt the fight finding its way

back to her. The energy felt wonderful, like she was less of a victim. "We share custody of Joey until that last visit. Isn't that what she said?"

"True." Jack thought for a moment. "In that case, it just might work." He tapped his knee a few times, something he only did when he was excited or nervous. "I went online and looked at work trips to Haiti. You know, the sort of trip Beth and Bill are taking with their church."

Molly felt a chill pass over her arms. Were they really doing this? Really having this conversation about how they could find their way out of the country? The temperature was over eighty degrees that afternoon, but she was suddenly cold. "Okay."

"Anyway, I was looking for a humanitarian group, the Red Cross or one of the international groups for humanity. Because it might look funny for two people who've stayed away from church to have a sudden interest in missions."

"True."

"Except here's the problem." He turned his hands over, baffled. "I couldn't find any in our area taking a trip in the next few months." He chuckled. "The only groups I could find were a handful of churches."

"Hmmm." Molly wasn't sure why, but she felt vindicated. At least on Beth's behalf. "Maybe we've been wrong about church." She thought about Joey's recent conversations with God. "About God, too."

"Maybe." Jack waved his hand, clearly anxious to move on. "We can talk about that later. The point is, most of the work trips won't let volunteers bring children younger than twelve."

Molly was confused. "So how is this going to help us?"

"One church in our area is doing a trip over Labor Day—it's an outreach to an orphanage." His eyes danced, and he lowered his voice. "People are encouraged to bring their whole families. That way the American children can play with the Haitian children while work is being done on the building."

Again Molly's heart beat harder than before. Jack had never looked more serious. "What church?"

He looked intently at her. "Bill and Beth's."

She froze for a moment. "You're kidding."

"No." He shook his head. "So first thing when we get home, you need to call Beth and tell her we'd like to come to church with them next Sunday." He covered her hand with his. "I know the two of you are close, but you have to do your part here, Molly. You can't give her a reason to suspect anything."

"Oh, sure." A sarcastic laugh came from her. "Just call her up and tell her we've changed our minds? After a decade of thinking they're weird for going to church and believing in the Bible, all of a sudden we're supposed to want to go to Sunday service?"

Twenty yards away, Joey waved at them. "Hey! Guess what?"

"What, sport?" Jack instantly turned his attention to their son.

"I'm gonna land this plane and go on that rocket ship." He pointed to the jungle gym, the one with two slides built into it.

"Sounds good!" Jack kept his tone cheerful. If anyone was watching them—even someone who knew them well—no one would have guessed they were making plans to leave the country, to run from the authorities and start life over again.

Joey slowed down, jumped from the swing, and ran to the jungle gym. He would be busy for another fifteen minutes at least.

"Yes, Molly." Jack turned back to her. His voice was quietly urgent. "That's exactly what you do. We're in the middle of the biggest crisis of our lives. People go to church when they're in crisis, right? Isn't that what they do?"

Molly thought about that. He was right. After September 11, record numbers of people filled churches for months. Tragedy, she remembered hearing a newscaster say, is the open door to finding faith. From the first day she'd learned about the fraudulent adoption papers, she'd discussed the matter with Beth. Her sister was praying for her and with her. Maybe she wouldn't think it was so strange that now they wanted to go to church.

"Okay, so I call Beth." She was still confused. "Then we become members and get involved in a work trip all in the same afternoon? We don't have a lot of time."

"I know." Jack didn't look worried. Whatever he had in mind, he'd thought through the details. "You said Beth's family is going, right?"

"Right. Last I heard."

"Okay...so let's just ask about it. It would be the last time our families could all be together before we had to give up Joey—barring some change by the judge." He sat back a little. "I don't think that's so strange. We could even say that we're thinking about adopting again—this time internationally. We'll say we want Joey to be part of the process."

"And the judge is going to let us go? Let us leave the country?"

"Work trips to Haiti happen all the time." He pinched his lips together, determined. "We've always been involved in civic groups, Molly. Of course we might want a trip to Haiti to be one of our final memories with Joey."

Molly had her doubts, but she didn't say anything.

"Besides, we won't be telling Allyson Bower." Jack leaned over and dug his elbows into his knees. "The social worker said nothing about leaving the country, no rules or mandates from the judge." He looked at the ground for a minute. "They aren't checking up on us, right? We haven't heard from Mrs. Bower since Joey's visit." He straightened again. "I say we just go. She and the judge won't figure out what happened until we're long gone."

She heard the bitterness in his voice, but his idea made sense. She and Jack were adventurous, and they loved taking on civic projects. They had helped raise funds for the YMCA building in West Palm Beach, and they'd taken part in several 5- and 10-K runs to raise money for a local homeless shelter. Taking a trip to Haiti to help repair an orphanage was something they would have done.

Beth and Bill wouldn't think that was strange, certainly.

It would be only natural that they'd want to get in on the work trip. The adventure would give them something to look forward to while they hammered away every day at the task of finding an attorney to fight for Joey's custody.

"Okay..." Molly was still shivering, but she was catching on, understanding what Jack was thinking. "Then what?"

"By the time we'd leave for the trip, we'd have to have all

the details in place. Our ultimate destination—at least for the first couple years—would be the Cayman Islands."

"Cayman?" Molly had to hold onto the edge of the bench. Again she felt like she was in some strange dream or acting out someone else's life. She'd been to Grand Cayman once with Jack. The place was beautiful, surrounded by gorgeous beaches and endless blue-green water. But could she spend two years there? She steadied herself. "Where would we live?"

"I'll take care of that." He was still composed, still anxious to tell her the rest of what he'd been thinking. "We'll need fake passports, but I made a few phone calls. There's a guy in Miami who'll work with me. He thinks we're missionaries."

"Why would missionaries need fake passports?" Molly's head was spinning faster than ever. It was all she could do to keep up with the conversation.

Jack made an effort to slow down. "Some missionaries visit countries that are hostile to the Christian teaching. If missionaries become targeted, they might need to flee the country under a different identity." He shrugged one shoulder. "The guy I talked to says he believes in freedom of speech. If we need fake passports to further freedom of speech, he'll do them half-price."

Molly pressed her hands to the sides of her face. "I can't believe this..."

"Hey, look at me!" Joey was standing straight up at the top of the highest slide. "I'm a fireman!" He slammed an invisible helmet onto his head and plopped down hard, sending himself flying down the slide. At the bottom he looked in a dozen different directions, spraying invisible water at what must've been ferocious invisible flames.

"You're a hero, Joey!" Jack paused for a few seconds. "Mommy and I are still talking, okay?"

"Okay!" He raced up the ladder on the opposite side of the structure. "Now I'm going to the moon!"

Another couple strolled by on the sidewalk that wound through the park. Jack waited until they had passed before starting in again. "So we have our fake passports, and the day before the trip, we transfer funds to an account in Cayman. It's the world's second largest offshore financial center. Then"—his voice grew more tense—"on, say, the third day of the trip, we'll take an excursion into town and we'll disappear. By the time they realize we're missing, we'll be on a plane with our new identities, headed for Europe. We'll stay there for a few weeks—just to make sure no one's onto us—then we'll fly to Cayman." He lifted his hands. "What do you think?"

What did she think? She had a thousand questions, all of them firing at her from different areas of her heart and brain. She opened her mouth and asked the first one that came. "Why *wouldn't* they be onto us?"

"We'll be using new identities. The authorities in Haiti won't have any trouble letting us through, and then we'll become part of the throng of millions of people in Europe. It's not like our faces will be plastered up in every police station in England. The authorities won't have a clue where to look for us." Jack's expression told her this was obvious. "See, we leave for a day trip, and we're never heard from again." He hesitated. "After awhile, they might even assume we were victims of foul play."

"We disappear a week before losing custody of Joey? The story'll make national news!"

"Yes. In time." His words were coming faster, as if he'd thought through even this detail. "By then we'll be in Europe with new identities. Tourists, mixing with other tourists. When the commotion in the press dies down, we'll fly to Grand Cayman."

The plan sounded plausible, but still she had more questions than answers. "Why would we take our four-year-old son into the streets of Haiti? Isn't it dangerous?"

"Yes, I've thought about that, too. These work trips include day excursions, trips to small villages to pass out food—that sort of thing." Jack wouldn't be swayed. "Don't worry, I'll find a reason to get us out on the streets. Then we'll find a ride to the airport. Once we get to Haiti, that'll be the least of our worries."

"All right." She would have to trust him. What else could she do? Another question hit her. Maybe she was wrong about her sister—maybe Beth would be suspicious after all. "What if Beth thinks it's strange, taking a trip out of the country right before Joey goes?"

He raised his brow. "You'll be in charge of that, of making her see things our way." He put his hand on her knee. "You can handle that, right?"

A man and his little boy came up along the sidewalk from the other direction, carrying a baseball and two gloves between them. Jack waited for them to pass. He dropped his voice another notch. "Of course it'll be suspicious, but Beth will believe what you tell her. Don't you think so?"

"Maybe." Fear built in her again, and the fight took a

backseat. "But maybe not. Maybe we'll do something that causes Allyson Bower to suspect what we're up to. Then we could get caught." She nodded in Joey's direction. "Our little boy could be turned over to the Porters and we could go straight to prison. Have you thought about that?"

"Of course." Jack's tone was just short of angry. "Listen, Molly. We won't be traveling under our own names. We'll have new identities, new passports. We'll leave Haiti under those names, arrive in Europe, and buy a few Eurail passes. We'll travel the region like a family on vacation, and at every hotel we'll check the news and the Internet. When the search dies down, we'll get over to the Cayman Islands."

"What about our money?" She was shaking now, trembling from her fingertips to her toes. "Couldn't they trace the money? You said we transfer it to Cayman, so once they find out, they'll put a lock on our funds and that'll be that." She hated that she was making this difficult for Jack, but if she didn't talk about her doubts now, she'd never feel right going through with the plan. "If they find the money, it'll just be a matter of time before they find us."

"I've got that figured out, too." He leaned forward again. His eyes were sharp and intelligent. "We'll move the money through a series of transfers. It's complicated, but when it's all said and done, the money will be in an account in Cayman under our new identities." He gave her a single nod. "Leave that part to me, Molly."

She felt weak, nauseous. Were they really going through with this? It was much more than she could handle or imagine. She looped her arm through his and leaned into his shoulder. "How much money?"

"That'll take some work." He kissed the side of her face. "But I've thought about that, too. We'll pull the equity from our rentals and from our own house. It should be more than a million."

"A million dollars?" The amount raised another list of questions, but she didn't have the strength to ask them.

"Yes." He put his arms around her and stroked her gently. "We'll be fine, Molly. We will. Once we're in Cayman for a few years, when the search for us has grown completely cold, we can travel under our new names. We could go anywhere, really. Just not back to the United States."

"And not back to Jack and Molly Campbell."

He gave a slow nod. "Right."

Molly closed her eyes and took a long breath through her nose. "Jack..." She clung to him. "I can't believe we're doing this."

"Me, neither." Jack held her tight, and for a long time they said nothing.

What was left to say? The judge had made his decision, and now they had made theirs. They would set the plan into motion, and they would have to hold discussions like this one often, making sure the details were coming together. They would say good-bye to everything they knew and loved about their lives as Jack and Molly Campbell, and they would start over again. If the courts wouldn't look out for the best interests of their child, then they'd have to take the matter into their own hands.

Whatever they had to pay in the process, the cost would be worth it.

All for the love of Joey.

SIXTEEN

Molly made the phone call that afternoon, when Beth and Bill would be home from church. She had practiced her part in her mind enough times that when Beth answered the phone, Molly kept her voice casual, normal.

The conversation started with talk about Joey and how he had handled his first visit.

"He's fine, but something has to be done." Molly sounded upset, the way she would've felt if they didn't have the plan to leave the country. "Tomorrow morning we're calling a list of politicians."

"That's a great idea." Beth was still ready to fight on their behalf. "I'll make calls, too. Whatever I can do to help." She exhaled hard. "This is ridiculous, Molly. That boy belongs with you."

"I know." She kept her tone sorrowful. At Jack's direction, she left out details of the bruises on Joey's arm. No reason to give Beth cause to suspect they were crazy with fear. She steadied her voice. "Jack's going through a new list of attorneys tomorrow, too. Someone will help us. I have to believe that."

"I'm so sorry, Molly. I can't even imagine going through

this." Beth hesitated. "It may not make you feel better, but everyone in our Sunday school class is praying for you. No one can believe a judge could order a child back to his biological parents almost five years later."

"That means a lot." This was her opening. "Hey, that reminds me. You won't believe this. Jack and I were talking today at the park." She pinched the bridge of her nose. She'd never lied to Beth before. Even now, everything in her wanted to share the details with her sister, but she couldn't. Not a word of them. "Anyway, Joey's been talking to God." She uttered a sad laugh. "I guess Jonah taught him."

"Really?" Beth sounded like her heart was melting. "That's so sweet."

"We thought so." She forced herself to take the next step. "Jack wanted me to tell you...we'd like to go to church with you next Sunday."

Beth's gasp was quiet, but it was a gasp all the same. "Are you serious?"

"Yes." Molly made a sound that was part laugh, part cry. "We need all the help we can get."

"Molly...I'm so glad." The happiness in Beth's voice was pure and complete. She had no suspicions whatsoever. "God has a plan for Joey, I mean that. No matter how things look now, if you seek God...if you really trust Him, I know He'll make those plans clear to you."

Molly hated this, hated lying to her sister. "That's what we're starting to believe."

"Well, let's not wait until Sunday. That's a week away. Bill and I can meet with you a few times this week so we can all pray. There's power in prayer, I tell you, Molly.

I'm just so glad you're seeing it now." Beth's words ran together, her excitement and fervor tangible. "Talk to Jack about that, okay?"

"Okay." The words felt like acid on Molly's tongue. And this was only the beginning. "Hey, Beth, I have to go. But thanks. I'm not sure we would've thought about turning to God without you."

"Oh, Molly." Beth's voice cracked. "I love you so much. It's only because I love you that I've always wanted your family to find faith."

"I know." Molly clenched her fists. She had to get off the phone, had to end the conversation before she burst into a confession about all she was doing. "I love you, too."

Beth went on a little longer about the benefits of having a strong faith. Molly wasn't really listening. Instead she did something Joey would do. She talked to God—just a little. *It's not a complete lie, God....I do want to know more about You, and I do think it's better if people are praying for us.*

Beth was winding up. "Okay...so talk to Jack and we'll figure out the details later."

"I will." They said their good-byes, and Molly hung up the phone.

The week played out just as they'd planned. Twice they met with Beth and Bill and talked about God, about His plan for all of them, His salvation. They looked at Bible verses, and Molly couldn't help but find herself really listening, really finding truth in the things Beth and Bill were sharing with them.

"It makes sense," Molly told Jack one night that week.

"It makes our plan work." Jack smiled at her. "That's all."

She didn't push the matter. Sunday came and Beth was sweet and tender. She gave Molly an envelope with her name written across the front. "It's a little card I found." Beth gave her a hug. "Don't open it until later today."

Molly didn't know what to say. With every heartbeat, she could hear a voice shouting at her, *Liar...Liar...Liar!* She returned her sister's hug. "It feels good to be here."

"It feels wonderful." Beth held onto her shoulders and studied her face. "I think God's about to work a miracle, Molly. I can feel it."

The four of them checked the kids into Sunday school classes and took seats together in a pew halfway back. Jack purposefully opened his bulletin and began reading it. Then, as if on cue, he leaned around Molly and spoke to Bill. "You and Beth and the kids taking this work trip to Haiti?"

"We are." Bill's expression was a mix of genuine friendliness and pure awe. Molly understood. Beth and Bill had probably prayed for this day ever since they became Christians. Bill opened his bulletin and pointed to the blurb about the trip. "There's an informational meeting about it today after service."

Jack gave Molly a pointed look. "Did you tell Beth?"

Beth was sitting between Molly and Bill. She looked curious. "Tell me what?"

It was Molly's turn. She plunged ahead, hoping the entire conversation didn't sound like a poorly acted script. "About the work trip." She looked at Bill and back to Beth. "We're thinking about going, too."

"You're kidding!" Beth said the words a little too loud. "I'm just getting used to the idea myself." She giggled and lowered her voice. She looked around, sheepish about being too noisy in church. Then, just as fast, her smile faded. "What about Joey?"

Jack squeezed Molly's knee. "We're believing that everything will work out. We have to believe that." He shot a sad smile at Bill. "But at this point in our lives, we need a distraction, something positive we can do with our son."

Bill nodded. "I understand."

"I went online a few nights ago and read about the work trip. It seems, well"—he looked at Molly—"like a good idea all the way around."

"It'd be a chance for our two families to be together." Beth sounded helpful. No question she liked the idea. She stopped short of saying that it would be their last time to travel together with Joey, if he were taken away. Instead she nodded. "We'd love it if you came."

"Do you think they'd let us—I mean, since we're new?" Jack kept his tone tentative.

"I think so." Bill looked at Beth, and then back to Jack. "You'd be with us. People bring friends or family on these trips all the time. It'd be different if it were a mission trip. But work trips aren't as regulated by the church staff."

"Right." Beth's eyes sparkled. "This trip's different. They'll run a background check on you, but other than that...if you can swing a hammer, you'll be welcome." She looked at Bill and then at Molly again. "Can you come to the meeting after church?"

"I think so." Molly met Jack's eyes. There wasn't a hint of duplicity there, and she was amazed. Maybe Jack had missed his calling. He was proving to be an amazing actor. "Do we have time?"

"Definitely." He directed his next question to Bill. "We can bring the kids on this trip, right? So we can bring Joey?"

"Yes." Concern slipped into his tone. "You think they'll let you take him? With all this custody stuff going on?"

Jack appeared as innocent as their son. He exchanged a look with Molly. "I don't see why not. We'll tell the social worker about it, of course." He breathed the lie as if he'd been telling lies all his life. "She'll have to give the okay."

Molly gave a look that confirmed their innocence. "We'll still have joint custody of him, no matter what."

Beth reached for Molly's hand and squeezed it. "Maybe by then it'll be permanent custody."

"Yes." They all settled back against the pew. A group of people were playing music up front. The service was about to begin.

"We'll talk more at the meeting after church." Beth whispered.

"Okay." Again Molly convinced herself it wasn't a lie, but still she hated herself for what they were doing. Beth and Bill believed their intentions completely. She smiled at Beth. "Thanks for everything."

Her sister slipped her arm around her and gave her a side hug. "I told you we'd be here. We'll do whatever you need us to do, Molly. I mean it."

During the service, Jack filled out a prayer card. Molly watched as he turned it over and scribbled, "Pray for our family." On the front he filled out their names and address and phone number. The church Bill and Beth attended was a large one—several services, six thousand members. Molly guessed no one was keeping close tabs on the infrequent attendees. At the bottom of the card, Jack had the choice to check "Visitor" or "Member." He checked the Member box, folded the card, and dropped it into the offering plate.

And just like that, the plan was in motion.

∼⌒∼

SEVENTEEN

The prop plane was just about to land in Grand Cayman. Jack could hardly wait.

The trip to the Cayman Islands was something Jack had to do every few years. He had a fairly large account there, and most of the time business could be handled by telephone. But every so often the company smiled on his decision to take a trip to the island, further goodwill, meet with the account executives, host some high-end dinners, and strengthen relationships.

Trips like that kept the competition at bay and the accounts loyal.

It had been fourteen months since his last trip to Cayman, so when Jack went to his boss and suggested a trip to the islands, there was no hesitation. The man looked at his calendar. "Great idea." He grinned at Jack. No question his boss saw him as the most-favored officer in the company. "You taking Molly and Joey with you?"

"No, sir. Not this time." He gave the man an easy smile. At least this part was honest. "Maybe next time."

No one at work knew about the custody battle Jack was facing. From the beginning, he'd thought it better if he said nothing. Now he was relieved he'd kept quiet. He didn't need people in every area of his life feeling sorry for him and wondering about the moves he was about to make.

The plans for the trip came together in a few days, and now Jack was minutes from landing in Grand Cayman. He looked out the window and let the scene wash over his weary conscience. Every now and then it occurred to him that what they were about to do was illegal. If for some reason they got caught, they would lose everything—their freedom, their reputation. Worst of all they would lose Joey.

Jack was careful not to let those thoughts come up often. It wasn't that he and Molly had accepted the idea of being criminals. In his gut, he believed that what he and Molly were about to do was wrong—people shouldn't take the law into their own hands. But if it meant saving Joey from a life of abuse, if it meant holding onto his son, Jack could justify it. He would do anything to keep his son safe. Absolutely anything.

It made him think about fathers who stole money to feed their families during the Depression. He'd never given much thought to the idea, never taken sides on the issue until now. In light of what was happening with Joey, he knew for certain what he would've done. If his family needed to eat, he'd find a way to feed them. Even if it turned him from an upright citizen into a common thief.

Whatever it took to save his family.

Below the plane, the ocean water grew pale where it splashed up against the land. The beaches in Cayman were beautiful, nothing short of paradise. He felt calmer just looking at them. He would buy an old guitar once they got settled and write songs on the beach. Just like he'd always dreamed of doing. Yes, he was taking the law into his own hands, and yes, it went against his nature. But the plan was a good one. It would work. And no one would be hurt in the process.

Joey's birth parents didn't deserve the child. His mother hadn't wanted him in the first place, and his father was a violent criminal. If they could figure out how to live a normal life, let them have more kids down the road.

Joey belonged to Molly and him. Period.

Jack pressed his forehead against the window and shifted in his cramped seat. No one was going to hurt Joey or take him away, not while Jack still had breath left in him. He closed his eyes and let the warmth of the sun calm his heart. His love for Joey was fierce, more intense than anything he'd ever known or experienced. It was proof that the judge was wrong. The Porters weren't the boy's parents.

He and Molly were.

After another few minutes, the plane circled and landed. Once he was off the plane, carrying his single bag across the tarmac, Jack took in his surroundings—the palm trees waving in the mild ocean breeze, the sky so blue it almost hurt to look at it, and the salty smell of the nearby ocean.

He pictured how life would be. Molly helping Joey with his lessons, making sure he was ready for school when it felt safe to move to Europe. Jack would be in charge of venturing into town for food and supplies, and on lazy summery afternoons, he would sit on the beach and play his guitar. They would take long ocean swims and run along the sand. At night there would be a million stars overhead, and endless hours of conversation and time together.

It wouldn't hurt Joey to live that sort of life for a few years. And when the search for them had blown over, they could start again in England or Ireland or Germany— enroll Joey in a private school so he would have the very best education and the chance to meet wonderful children in the process. Two years in the Cayman Islands wouldn't be a burden. If life as they'd known it had to end, there could be worse places to start over.

Jack picked up his pace. He had a busy three days ahead of him. Business meetings with account executives, and high-powered lunches and dinners for the first day and a half. After that he would hop a plane to Little Cayman, where remote rental properties were plentiful. If things went well, he would find a beach house for rent and make a deposit under his new name: Walt Sanders.

The first day went as planned, and over lunch and dinner, Jack resisted the urge to prod the locals for details about which beach was the most remote. He wouldn't do anything that could come back to hurt them. Once the authorities realized that they'd run, certainly his boss would be interviewed, and that could lead investigators to Grand Cayman. It was crucial that he did nothing to give himself away during this trip.

As far as the locals knew, he had business all three days.

The Cayman Islands were under the rule of the British government, but they lay smack in the middle of the Caribbean. They consisted of just three islands. Most commerce and tourism took place on the big island, Grand Cayman. Jack wanted to stay far from there. Too many people to avoid, too great a chance of being recognized.

He flew to Little Cayman early the next afternoon. There was a small account that operated off that island, which gave him a legitimate reason to be there. He spent half an hour with the client, then took a cab to the closest real estate office. The place was small and dusty, as if the Realtors spent most of their time on the beach—like everyone else on an island that remote.

"I'm looking for a long-term beach rental," he told the elderly woman who sat behind the desk. He and Molly had discussed this. They didn't want to buy a house. In fact, as soon as they arrived in Cayman, they planned to close their bank account and take the money in cash. Yes, it was a lot to be responsible for, but Jack could ask for large bills. With their new passports, they needed to be flexible and mobile. If for some reason people became suspicious of them, or authorities turned their search to the Cayman Islands, they would have a way to escape without leaving money tied up in an account or in real estate.

The woman smiled. "We have many places suitable for you." She had a thick British accent. "Would your schedule permit time to look?"

Jack was beside himself. This was exactly what he'd hoped for. "Yes." He glanced at his watch. "The rest of the afternoon."

They climbed into the woman's open-air Jeep, and she took him down a road she called Main Street, only it wasn't paved, and the further they went, the more it felt like a poorly-maintained footpath. After a short while, all signs of buildings or villages disappeared. The road wound through thick vegetation and palm trees. Occasionally, without warning, she would hang a sharp right turn and take them down an even narrower road that would put them out into a cluster of homes.

All of the homes were nice, but Jack didn't want other houses around them. Not for a mile. "Do you have something more private?"

"Yes." She gave him a look that said she didn't necessarily think more privacy was a good idea. "Farther out—farther in for food."

"Yes." He smiled. "That's fine."

The woman pulled her Jeep back onto the main road. For the next fifteen minutes, she drove without talking. When she finally made a right turn, Jack figured they were at the clear opposite end of the island. The driveway wasn't like the other ones she'd shown him. This one was two miles long, at least.

When they finally reached a clearing, the ocean spread out like a brilliant carpet in front of him. Up ahead, to the left, was a small white house with a screened-in lanai. It looked almost like something from one of the beaches in South Florida. The building was older and nondescript, so much so that it almost blended in with the white sandy beach.

"This is vacant, and very difficult to rent." The woman gave the house a look of disdain. "Most clients prefer higher quality amenities. This is not the finest Little Cayman can offer."

No, Jack thought. But it was perfect. He could tell already. They hopped out of the Jeep, and Jack walked toward the water.

"Would you care to see the interior first?" The woman looked confused.

"No...I mean, I want to take a look at the beach first."

"I'll never understand." The woman waved her hand at him. "Crazy Americans."

Jack laughed, but he picked up his pace. When he reached the water, the view was breathtaking. Like something from a magazine advertisement or a movie. They might as well have been the only people on earth for all the lack of activity around them. There were no other houses as far as he could see.

Someone had left an old picnic table in the sand a few feet from a small cluster of palm trees. Jack stared at it and he could see them—the way he and Molly and Joey would look there in just a few months. On that very picnic table they would sit and watch the brilliant sunsets. They would play cards and laugh about the things Joey would say and do. He jogged back up the beach to where the woman was waiting. "Yes..." He was breathless, his heart pounding, not so much from the run up the sand, but from the thrill of it all. The house was exactly what he was looking for. He pulled his digital camera from his pants pocket and snapped a dozen pictures.

"But your information is incomplete." She lowered her brow. He half-expected her to yell at him. "We must take a gander at the house."

Then he remembered what he was doing. He didn't want to seem strange or out of the ordinary. The odds of anyone ever questioning her about their time that afternoon were infinitesimally small. But still...

He chuckled, put his camera back in his pocket, and dusted his hands off on his pants. "Yes. Let's take a gander."

It had three bedrooms and a spacious living room. The lanai screen was ripped in a few places, but nothing he couldn't fix up. The kitchen was plain, simple. But it came with a refrigerator. The laundry room was smaller than Molly was used to, certainly. But again, the machines were part of the deal. He'd just have to pick up a few pieces of furniture now and then, some linens and necessities in the village, and they'd be set.

All the way back to the Realtor's office, Jack said very little. He was too busy taking in the scenery, the lush plants and trees, the tropical smell. It was hard to believe that in less than two months, this would be home. Yes, it would be an adjustment. For Molly, most of all. He wouldn't mind leaving the corporate world. And one day, when they moved to Europe for Joey's schooling, he could find another job. Get reconnected with pharmaceutical sales.

Molly, though—she would have to say good-bye to her friends, her social connections, and everything that made up their way of life. Worst of all, she would lose her relationship with Beth. Jack's throat grew thick at the thought, but he swallowed hard and his emotions eased. They had no choice. By doing this, at least they would have each other. Every time they talked about it, Molly said the same thing.

"You and Joey, baby...That's all I need."

By the time Jack boarded the plane for the flight home, he had the deal locked up. Using the name Walt Sanders, he filled out the rental agreement and gave the woman a deposit. He told her they'd be needing the house for at least a year, and that they'd check in with her middle of September sometime, when they landed on the island.

The last thing he did was open a bank account. Things were different on the Cayman Islands. For one, it was the largest offshore banking community in the world. On Grand Cayman alone—in a stretch of land just twenty-two miles long—there were more than five hundred banks or financial institutions. Hiding money would be easier there than just about any place south of Florida. A person could open a checking account and make a deposit with false identification, and as long as they didn't want to borrow money, the bank would never raise a question.

Jack opened an account under the names Walt and Tracy Sanders and deposited three thousand dollars. The bank representative made casual conversation, and Jack mentioned that he and his family would be coming there for a year while he worked on a project.

"Very good." The man was more than happy to take Jack's money. "Your account will be here for you when you come."

Now Jack settled back into his airplane seat and closed his eyes. He'd taken care of every last detail, even getting the names of the local grocer and a few furniture stores on Grand Cayman since Little Cayman Island was too small for more than just a basic food store. He could hardly wait to talk to Molly, hardly wait to show her the photographs of the place on Little Cayman. The few times fear tried to crash in on his satisfied feeling, he dismissed it. They were doing what they had to do.

The plan was coming together beautifully.

EIGHTEEN

It had been thirty minutes since Joey left with Allyson Bower for his second visit with the Porters, and Molly was in the midst of a full-blown panic attack. She and Jack were in the car with Jack driving, but he wasn't going fast enough. They were still fifteen minutes from the airport.

"Hurry!" She bit her finger, tapping her foot on the floorboard. Faster...they had to go faster. "We'll never get there in time."

They had to see Joey before he got on the plane. Yes, he'd been calmer this time when Allyson had picked him up. He had cried, but only a little. Allyson seemed just as frustrated as before. She told them that she'd made several calls to the judge, but still there was no bending. The boy would soon belong to the Porters.

Joey had used the bathroom one last time before he left. When he came out, he was drying his wet hands on his jean shorts. His cheeks were tear-stained but he wasn't sobbing, wasn't hysterically clinging to Jack.

Molly held her hands out to him and wondered, was this how change happened? Gradually, what had been horrific and terrifying became sad and uncomfortable, and then one day it became acceptable? A part of life?

Joey's stuttering had been bad for the first week after he'd been home from the Porters the first time. He'd wet the bed a few times that week, too—something he hadn't done in a year. But now he was talking fine and getting up at night to use the toilet, just like before.

She clung to Joey and whispered in his ear, "Call me, okay? Before you go to bed."

He leaned back, his fingers still linked around the back of her neck. "I asked God to go with me again."

"Good." Molly meant it. Her fears were still wild and daunting—that he would die in a plane crash or choke on a hotdog or get deathly sick and no one would notice. When she and Jack met with Beth and Bill the last time, Molly made a decision. Why fake something as simple as prayer? If Joey could talk to God, so could she. She kissed her son's nose. "I'll ask Him, too."

By then, Joey had already hugged and kissed Jack good-bye. Jack stood a few feet away, talking to Mrs. Bower. Joey rubbed his button nose against Molly's. "Eskimo noses."

She did the same. Then she brushed her eyelashes against his. "And butterfly kisses."

He returned the gesture, but he stopped partway through and let his forehead fall against hers. "I'm gonna miss you so much, Mommy."

"Joey..." Her heart might as well have spilled out onto the floor. It felt that broken. She tried to picture the little house in the Cayman Islands. This was only temporary, this good-bye business. Very soon they'd be together forever, and no one would ever take Joey from them again. She held him a little longer. "I'll miss you, too."

Gus was sitting nearby, and for some reason he chose that moment to whimper a few times. Joey let go of her and put his arms around his dog. "You don't like when I go away, right, Gus?"

Joey nuzzled his face into the dog's fur. "Did you hear him, Mommy?" He looked up. "Gus says, please, can I stay here?"

"Tell Gus that's what we all want." Molly stood back with Jack. They said another round of good-byes. Then Mrs. Bower was ready, and after they left, Molly did what she'd expected to do the first time he walked out the door, three weeks earlier. She collapsed in Jack's arms and wept. Fifteen minutes later they realized what he'd forgotten.

"We have to get it to him." Molly was antsy, moving from side to side in the passenger seat, checking her watch. "The plane leaves in an hour. They'll be boarding soon."

"I'm doing my best." Jack grimaced.

The whole nightmare was one insane day after another. That Joey was even out of their sight, ready to board a jet to Ohio with a social worker, was still more than either of them could believe. The Porters, the lack of help from attorneys, the stubborn judge, the ridiculous law. Their plan to leave the country. None of it seemed even remotely realistic. Not when life had been beyond idyllic just five weeks ago.

But even with all the insanity, this moment stuck out as being of utmost importance. "We have to reach him before he leaves."

"We will." Jack took the exit for the airport, and after

the curve he picked up speed. They were parked and running through the airport doors six minutes later. At the security checkpoint, they explained that their son, a minor, was on Flight 317 to Cleveland, and that he'd forgotten something.

"We have to get it to him."

The agent was happy to help. He wrote a temporary pass and ushered them toward security. The line was short that day, so within five minutes they were racing down the concourse toward the gate. They ran up just as Allyson and Joey stepped in line to board. Joey didn't look like he was crying, but even from twenty yards away his eyes were sadder than she'd ever seen them.

"Joey!" Molly barely recognized her own voice. She sounded like a lunatic, but she didn't care. "Joey, wait!"

He heard his name and turned around. "Mommy!" He broke free from Mrs. Bower and ran to them. "Daddy!"

The social worker stepped out of line. She didn't look altogether angry at them for coming to the airport, but the plane was boarding. She tapped her watch. If they were going to say something last minute to Joey, they'd better get it said.

Molly pulled the item out of her bag and held it out to her son.

"Mr. Monkey!" Joey's face lit up. "I forgot him on my bed this morning!"

"I know." Molly straightened, her eyes locked on her son's. "I saw it there after you left."

"We hurried here so you'd have him." Jack swept Joey into his arms and swung him around. " 'Cause we love you."

Joey giggled. "And you love Mr. Monkey, too, right, Daddy?"

"Right." It was a moment that shone among days of darkness. The three of them hugging and rocking and Joey holding Mr. Monkey tight against his chest.

In the distance, Allyson Bower shot them a silent apology, then tapped her watch again. Jack picked up on the gesture. He gave Joey one last hug and set him down. "Time for you to go, sport."

"Okay." Joey's eyes grew sad, but not as sad as before. "Know what?" He looked at Jack and then at her. "I always have God with me, 'cause God always comes with you if you ask Him." He held up the stuffed toy. "But it's nice to have Mr. Monkey, too. Because I can cuddle with Mr. Monkey." He made a silly face. "And you can't cuddle with God."

"True." Molly stooped down and kissed him. "Go, buddy. Mrs. Bower's waiting for you."

He waved good-bye, still clutching Mr. Monkey, and in a few short seconds he and the social worker walked through the Jetway and disappeared from sight. Molly felt satisfied. "I'm glad we got it to him."

"Me, too."

Jack took her hand and they walked—like normal people—out of the airport and to their car. Their son would sleep in a strange bed that night, in a house they'd never seen, with two people they'd never met. He was the subject of a custody case that could make national news if they chose to call the papers. He was about to be whisked from his South Florida home to a remote beach house in some island in the middle of nowhere. His name was about to go from Joey to Aaron. Aaron Sanders.

But at least for tonight, if nothing else, he'd have Mr. Monkey.

∝⊘

Wendy stood at the bathroom sink.

Her regular foundation should've been enough to cover the bruise on her cheek, but it wasn't working. The mark still shone through, and Joey and the social worker would be there any minute. Rip had given her orders.

"Cover the thing, or don't show your face. I'll tell the Bower lady you're out."

But that would never do. The agreement was very specific. Both Rip and Wendy had to be at the house to greet Joey, so they could go over any instructions with the social worker. Wendy couldn't be gone—that would raise red flags for sure.

But so would the bruise.

Wendy felt tears in the corners of her eyes, and she blinked them back. She couldn't cry, not now. Her tears would ruin what makeup she already had on her face. She sniffed. *Don't be sad. Joey'll be here any minute. Then everything will be okay.*

She dug through her makeup bag and found a jar of under-eye concealer. It was thick and pasty, but it would cover the bruise. She let out a shaky breath. No matter what she told herself, she wasn't doing well. Having Joey for a visit wouldn't solve the other trouble.

The trouble with Rip.

He had been doing so well until Joey's first visit. But when he didn't immediately connect with their son, something inside him seemed to change. He had grown short with Wendy, snapping all the time and finding reasons to be mad at her. Even that wouldn't be so bad, because his rehabilitation in prison had taught him how to handle his feelings.

But no program could teach an angry man how to drink well.

Some people fell asleep when they drank, and others got silly. Rip, well, as long as Wendy had known him, whenever he drank, Rip had gotten full-blown furious. That's why, when he got out of prison, when he found out they were going to get Joey and have a family, Rip had made her a promise.

He was finished with the bottle.

A few beers now and then, maybe. But no more hard liquor. Not if he was about to be a daddy.

He broke the promise the night Joey left after his first visit. Rip drove out to the liquor store, bought two bottles of Jack Daniels, and came home. The first one was already opened by the time he walked in the door. Wendy didn't say anything, of course. She knew better than to get in his way when he drank.

Instead, the next morning she brought the bottles to him—one half-empty and the other still unopened—and asked him to make a decision. "They could still change their minds about Joey, you know." She gave the bottles an angry shake. "They're watching us like hawks, making sure we don't take one wrong step to the left or right."

"I'll make my own decisions!" Rip talked big, but he

hadn't had any choice really. Later that morning he took the half-empty bottle and dumped what was left down the drain. On Monday afternoon, before he reported in for training at the theater, he took the other bottle back to the store, lied about it being a gift, and got his money back.

She wanted to think that was that.

Since then he'd had a few gentler weeks, working at the theater and feeling good about himself. Most nights he talked nicely to her and told her how important he was at his new job. "They see big things for me, Wendy."

"Good, Rip. I'm so happy." She meant every word. "I believe in you, baby. I always have."

That's when he began drinking beer. Serious beer—a few more bottles every evening. But no more hard liquor, until two nights ago.

It started with questions from him. "What if the kid doesn't like me again this time?"

"He will." She wanted it to work, wanted it with everything inside her. "Just give him time to get used to you, Rip."

After another hour of that sort of conversation, Rip grabbed his keys. "I need fresh air."

When he came back, he didn't have a bottle, but it was obvious he'd been drinking. That's when she did what she never should've done. She confronted him.

"Where is it?" She met him near the front door, her hands on her hips.

"What?" He reeked of more than beer, and his eyes refused to focus. He waved an angry hand at her. "Get outta my way."

"This is all about Joey, isn't it? You're afraid of your own son, Rip. Don't you see that?"

His features tightened, the familiar windup that would release only with a flood of rage. "Don't tell me..." He struck at her, but she dodged him.

"This is all your fault!" She was tired of walking on eggshells, tired of hoping he would stay nice, hoping he would stay sober. It was time she told him how she really felt. "What happened the last time Joey was here was because you were mean to him!" She leaned forward, speaking louder than she'd spoken to him since he'd come home from prison. Once more he swung, but his knuckles barely glanced her cheek.

She took a few steps backward. "What are you doing, Rip? It's the same thing you did to Joey. You think you can intimidate people and that'll make you bigger and better, is that right?"

"The brat doesn't have any manners." His words were slurred, and squished between his angry lips.

But she could make them out all the same. Wendy felt her own anger build. "Don't talk about Joey like that! He's a wonderful little boy." She backed up again. "You might try being kind, not grabbing his arm. Treat him like a father treats a son!" She was shouting, out of control. If Rip wanted to unleash on her, then she would have her turn first.

He took another step toward her. Surprise filled his face, and than an anger that scared her. The sort that meant whatever he did next, he would later claim he wasn't responsible for it. An anger that told her he'd slipped into one of his bad spells. He reared back and raised his fist at her.

This time when she tried to back up, she bumped into the wall. When Rip's fist came at her, she had time to turn her face, but not time to get of the way. The blow hit her square on the cheekbone, and the force knocked her to the floor.

The moment she hit the ground, Rip snapped out of his rage. He looked at her, horrified, and took small steps back. "What...what have I done?"

Bruised my face real nice, that's what. Now, struggling before the mirror, Wendy clucked her tongue, still angry at him. She dabbed the concealer over the spot and then worked another layer of foundation over it. There. She stood back and admired her work. It was impossible to see the bruise now. She brushed a light layer of blush over her cheeks.

Good as new.

Rip had been a perfect gentleman since hitting her. Several times he'd apologized, and until a few hours ago, he hadn't even been grouchy with her. Now, though, he wanted the bruise covered. No question about that. He was in the living room watching TV, and he'd made his orders clear.

The doorbell rang, and Wendy's heart danced inside her. Joey was here! The boy had warmed up to her real nice last time. Deep down he must've known that she was his mama, his real mother. She flipped off the light switch, ran lightly down the hall, and opened the door.

The first hour went much better this time. Joey didn't cry, and Rip pretty much kept to himself other than a few polite hellos and one-word answers. The Indians were playing again, and that had his attention. But before she left, Allyson Bower asked Wendy to come out onto the front stoop for a minute.

When they were outside, Allyson squinted suspiciously at her. "How's everything with Rip?"

"Rip?" Wendy laughed in a way that she hoped sounded more surprised than nervous. "He's fine. Anxious for Joey to be ours for good, that's all. This transition time is tough for everyone."

The social worker stared her straight in the face. "Is he hitting you, Wendy?"

"Of course not!" Without thinking, her hand came to her cheek. She dropped it to her side but it was too late.

"You're lying to me." She looked at Wendy's cheek again. "Under all that makeup, I'd bet money there's proof that Rip isn't doing well at all."

Wendy did her best to look outraged. It was none of the social worker's business. "Rip and I are getting along just fine. He took anger-management classes. I thought I told you that."

"Yeah." She frowned. "He took alcohol-recovery classes, too. I read that on his release papers." She nodded toward the house. "But I saw a six-pack of beer in the fridge."

"Now listen..." Wendy crossed her arms. "There's no law against having a few beers now and then. Everything's fine with Rip, and everything's great between the two of us." She straightened herself, doing her best to look put out. If the social worker suspected trouble, they might not get to keep Joey. She couldn't let that happen. "I don't appreciate your asking."

"Asking is my job, Wendy." Allyson looked at Wendy's cheek again. "You can take care of yourself. What you do with Rip is your business." She pointed at the door. "But that child is my business. If Rip starts acting out again, you need to tell me right away. Understand?"

"Yes. Fine."

The social worker went back inside and gave Joey the same speech about calling her or calling his parents any time he wanted. This time when she said "parents," she said it strong. So there wouldn't be any confusion about who she thought Joey's parents should be.

When she was gone, Wendy let out a long, heavy breath. That had been close. The social worker was wrong. Rip might hit her once in a while, but he'd never hit Joey. Not a child. Sure, he might grab his arm, but that was normal, right? If a child wasn't cooperating? But he'd never come unglued at Joey the way he did at her.

Would he?

Wendy took her place at the kitchen table next to Joey. Again she had cookies for him, and again he dipped them into a glass of milk. But something inside her refused to settle down. Allyson Bower's words haunted her all that afternoon and into the night.

Rip mostly kept his distance, but that didn't help. Wendy still couldn't find peace, and as she lay down to sleep that night, she finally figured out why. When she had told herself that Rip would never hit a child, never strike his own son, it wasn't a statement; it was a question. And the truth was, no matter what she wanted to believe, when it came to Rip, she didn't have the answer. That left her with another question, one that kept her awake most of the night.

What sort of mother would willingly place her son in danger?

NINETEEN

Beth couldn't quite put her finger on it, but something was wrong with Molly. They were at church, the second time Molly and Jack had come with them, and Beth was thrilled. Yes, the circumstances were dire, but what better place to get help than at church? God certainly did have a plan for Joey, and He would see it through. Beth was praying for that, so was Bill.

They were convinced.

The fact that Molly and Jack had decided to join them in praying for Joey's custody was a miracle, nothing less. But even with all that was going on in her sister's life—with the phone calls she'd been making to senators and congressmen and even to the Florida governor's office—Molly seemed different. Distant, maybe.

Always before, no matter what issue they were facing, Beth and Molly faced it together. That's why they'd stayed so close over the years.

Beth thought back to when she had suffered three miscarriages between Cammie and Blain. She had wondered if she'd survive. All those babies she would never know, never see until heaven. All those children who wouldn't grow up with her loving touch or Bill's kindness.

It would have been more than Beth could handle, except that she had Molly.

Molly had called her every night for a month after each miscarriage. Whatever else was going on for either of them, they would put it aside and make time to talk or laugh or cry together. And over the weeks, Beth found her way to daylight, found her way back to a strong faith and an understanding that God knew the number of their days. Even if the number was painfully short.

But now, in the midst of Molly's greatest trial, the two of them hardly talked at all. Sure they took the kids to the pool a few days each week, and they still visited the park. But Molly was distant and short. The way she'd been even at church that morning.

They were seated in the pew—Bill and Beth, then Molly and Jack. They'd made some small talk when they first sat down, mostly about the Haiti trip. The Campbells were all signed up, excited about taking Joey on his first work trip.

But Beth could sense something wasn't right, the rhythm of their conversation nowhere close to natural.

When Molly first got the news about the possibility of losing Joey, she'd been beside herself. She wept and shook and barely found the strength to breathe. Now, though she was still sad—always sad—she seemed less desperate. There was an emptiness in her voice, and her eyes held something Beth hadn't seen before, something she didn't know how to work with.

Beth sat back as the music started to play. She loved

worship, but today she couldn't stop thinking of Molly. Was there something else going on? Was she missing something? Was there more trouble than Molly would admit? Maybe her relationship with Jack? She glanced at her sister, inches from her on her right side. Molly was singing, keeping up with the words. It was hard to tell if her heart was in it, but at least she was here. In church. Facing what she was facing, there was no better place to be.

Maybe that was it. Maybe the distance was because of Molly's struggle with faith. Beth faced the words on the overhead screen. Then there was the other possibility, the one she hadn't wanted to talk about with anyone—not with Bill, and certainly not with Molly.

Though Molly reported nearly every day that she was making phone calls to officials, and Jack was contacting attorneys, they seemed to be making no progress. If someone were going to take away one of Beth's children, Beth would have the story on the news by now. There would be reporters hounding the judge, asking him why he'd allow such a terrible ruling to stand when it would only hurt the child involved.

Molly and Jack seemed almost passive. Maybe they were in shock, paralyzed from fear and grief and hoping for some last-minute miracle—the miracle Beth and everyone else was praying for. It could happen, of course. It *would* happen somehow. Beth believed that. What she didn't believe was that this was all the effort Molly and Jack were willing to make on Joey's behalf.

Miracle or not, she would've expected Molly to be going crazy by now, pulling out every stop, turning over every stone, willing to fight the judge herself if no attorney would take the case. Instead, her sister's conversations centered mostly on her latest phone calls to various politicians, and on the upcoming work trip.

"What type of clothes are you packing?" was her question last week. And, "Are you getting your kids immunized before you go?"

Beth wanted to scream at her, "Molly! Wake up! They're about to take your son away, and all you can think about is whether Joey should take long pants or shorts to Haiti?"

Beth squirmed in her seat. If her sister was riding out the journey in blind faith, then more power to her. God was Almighty, powerful enough to keep Joey at the Campbells' house if that was His will. But that's when the other possibility crept into Beth's conscience.

Maybe Molly and Jack weren't worried because they had a different plan, a more drastic one. Could that be why they were attending church and coming along on the trip to Haiti? Was it possible they were thinking of fleeing the country and taking Joey with them? Beth focused on the words to the song they were singing. No, Molly would never do that. Never. Beth hated when her mind took that path. It was an awful thing to think about her sister. Molly and Jack were law-abiding citizens. They wouldn't consider fleeing the country, living in hiding, and going against the authorities. They were fine, upstanding people, connected to their community and their neighborhood the way most people only hoped to be.

Beth sang another few lines.

Right? There was no way her sister and her brother-in-law would take Joey and leave, would they? Beth chided herself and dismissed the thought. Molly had a right to be distracted. Life probably felt like it was spinning out of control. Of course she wasn't acting like herself. She was in shock.

Still, when the service ended and they finished up with yet another meeting on the Haiti work trip, Beth pulled Molly aside. "You've cleared this trip with Joey's social worker, right? I mean, with the custody thing pending, I'm sure you'll need her okay before you take him out of the country."

For the briefest moment, Molly's expression became one of sheer panic. Maybe it was Beth's imagination, but she could've sworn Molly looked absolutely terrified at the idea of clearing this trip with the social worker. But just as quickly, she rebounded. The corners of her lips lifted in a gentle smile. "Of course, Beth. We've already gotten the okay."

"Good." Beth nodded. Relief filled her heart and soul. "Just wanted to make sure."

All the way home, Beth allowed herself to feel relieved. She must've been loopy to think her sister would take Joey and flee the law, flee the United States. She was probably just distracted with finding an attorney or a politician who could help them. And someone *would* help them. They would get their miracle.

Beth believed that with every breath she took.

⟨∾⟩

Allyson Bower hung up the phone and replayed the conversation in her mind. It was Tuesday afternoon, and she'd just spoken with Molly Campbell, calling with a special request. She and her husband wanted to take Joey on a work trip. They would go to Haiti with their church for five days, work on repairing an orphanage, and spend time with the children who lived there.

That would be okay, wouldn't it?

As a state-certified social worker, Allyson was trained to recognize red flags. Children were her business, and children did a poor job of knowing when they were in trouble. That's why in many cases they needed a state-appointed adult to help decide whether a situation was safe or not. A person working on their behalf.

Now this couple faced the loss of their only son after having him in their lives for nearly five years, and a week before they would lose custody permanently, they wanted permission to take the child out of the country?

Normally the answer would be an easy one.

No way.

Allyson couldn't open herself up to that sort of potential trouble, that sort of scrutiny if things went awry and the Campbells disappeared. Once the adoptive parents were out of the country, even if they bought a house in Port-au-Prince and posted their names on the front door, it would be difficult to get them back to the States.

Still, for some reason, the idea appealed to Allyson. A last vacation, a last time to bond with Joey and show him what was important to them. Besides, maybe Joey would make friends with one of the orphans, and maybe the Campbells would go on to adopt that child. A Haitian child.

It was possible.

The trouble was, Allyson hadn't seen any mention in the

Campbells' file about church or faith, about religion being important to them. She had asked Molly Campbell the name of the church, so now it was easy, really. She could do a little checking, and if their story held true—if they really were signed up with their church to go on a work trip—then Allyson would take the situation to the judge and recommend that permission be granted.

She didn't need a judge's order, not for this. At the time of the trip, the Campbells would have joint custody of Joey. Not until the Friday after the trip would they lose custody forever. If they wanted a farewell trip with their son, she wouldn't deny it.

As long as it checked out.

Allyson found the number for the Campbells' church. After being transferred to the secretary, she explained why she was calling, that she was a social worker and needed to verify the attendance of a few of their members.

The secretary was pleasant. "Go ahead."

"Their names are Jack and Molly Campbell. They tell me they've been attending regularly as members."

A series of clicking and tapping sounds filled the lines. "Just a minute, I'm checking the computer." She paused. "Yes, here they are. Jack and Molly Campbell."

"So they *are* members?"

"Let me see. Yes…their information chart says they're members."

"Which means they've been attending for how long?"

"Oh, well…that varies. We don't have specific requirements for membership." She thought for a few seconds. "But I'd say most people don't become members until they've been going here for at least a year."

Allyson smiled. Things were checking out. "Is there any record, any way of proving that the Campbells have been members for a year?"

"Well, we don't take attendance. But we do watch the pattern of giving. Our members tend to be regular contributors, as well."

"What about the Campbells? Have they been regular givers?"

"Let me scroll down here." Another pause. "Yes...why, it certainly looks like it. The Campbells gave regular donations every month for the past, let's see, thirteen months."

Allyson quickly jotted notes on everything the secretary told her. Then she asked about the work trip.

"It's a special time for our members. This particular trip is for families. It gives them a chance to make a special memory with their children while they're helping out at one of the six orphanages we support in and around Port-au-Prince. We've put together teams of twelve to fifteen people for each orphanage."

"What about supervision, someone from the church?"

"Yes, a church staff member will accompany each group."

Allyson smiled and added that information to the piece of paper in front of her. "Very good. Thank you for your time."

That afternoon she took the issue to the judge.

He read the file, looked over Allyson's notes, and frowned. "A work trip to Haiti?"

"You have to understand, Your Honor"—she was already passionate about getting approval for the Campbells—"work trips to Haiti happen all the time. They'll be with a group, and someone from the church will supervise."

He gave her a wary look. "So close to the transfer of custody..."

"Your Honor, the population of Haiti is almost entirely black. If the Campbells tried to get away on foot in the middle of the night, they'd be picked up at the airport for sure. They'll stand out, believe me." She sighed and waved her hand at the clock. "I'd like to call the Campbells with permission before the end of the day. Your Honor, this is very important to them. I feel good about it."

The judge tapped his finger on the paperwork in front of him. After another twenty seconds he took a slow breath. "Okay." He shot her a stern look. "I know how you feel about this case, Ms. Bower. But the law is the law."

"Yes, Your Honor."

"I'll grant permission." He narrowed his eyes. "But you'd better be right."

She could hardly wait to call Molly Campbell. "Thank you, Your Honor."

Fifteen minutes later she was back at her office and on the phone. "The judge granted you permission, Mrs. Campbell. Everything checked out." She tried to keep her tone professional, tried to keep the sound of victory from her voice. She was supposed to be a voice of the state, not someone who took sides. "You've been granted permission to take Joey on the work trip, so long as you stick to the dates you've provided this department."

"Thank you." Molly's relief poured from every syllable.

Allyson felt her throat choke up. "I hope you have a good time, Mrs. Campbell."

"Yes. It'll be very precious time for the three of us."

When the conversation was over, Allyson hung up the

phone. She was too street-smart not to have at least a little suspicion about the reason for the Campbells' trip. But she'd fought hard for the approval because of one single image: Wendy Porter's heavily made-up cheek. Rip Porter was being abusive again, and if she suspected one of the couples in this situation to be lying, no question she suspected the Porters first. Besides, she'd done her part by checking out Molly Campbell's story.

Anything else was out of her hands.

TWENTY

J ack had promised Molly he'd take care of the finances, and so far he was making good on his promise. The church thing had been nothing short of brilliant.

Their first plan was to keep the trip a secret from the social worker. It wasn't anyone's business if they wanted to take Joey on a work trip. But when Beth brought it up to Molly at church last Sunday, they had to revert to their second plan: calling Allyson Bower and asking permission. Before they could do that, they had to be sure to cover their trail. If they told the social worker they were members at Bethel Bible Church, then they had to be able to prove as much.

Thankfully, the church had virtually no requirements for members, and with thousands attending services every weekend, they had no real way to determine the actual attendance of any one member. Except by tracking whatever money people gave. That Sunday, after Molly's conversation with Beth, Jack went home and wrote a series of checks, each for two hundred dollars, and each dated the first of the month back some thirteen months. He put each check in an envelope, sealed it, and wrote the month on the front. Then he put all the envelopes in a larger manila envelope and hurried the package back to church.

Services were still going on—the last one had just started. He went to the church bookstore and explained that it was rather urgent, that he needed to see the church secretary. She wasn't there, he was told. Then he explained that he had checks to turn over, and in no time the book-store manager found someone who worked at the church office.

A college intern, as it turned out.

Jack saw how young she was, and he had to work to contain his excitement. "We've made a mistake, and I feel terrible about it," he told the young woman. She didn't look a day over twenty. He poured on the charm. "More than a year ago, my wife and I made a decision to give regularly—a set amount each month." He held up the envelope. "We wrote out the checks and placed them in here. And wouldn't you know it?" He made a silly face. "I thought she was turning them in each month, and she thought I was."

"I see." The girl looked completely baffled. "Why don't you drop them in the collection box at the back of the church? Anyone could make a mistake."

"Well, you see, it isn't that easy." He grimaced and looked over his shoulder. "My wife's mortified about this. She thinks people will see us as heathens for not giving all those months." He pointed to himself. "It's my fault, so I told her I'd make it right."

The girl shook her head and made a face. "Sir, how can I help?"

"If you could promise me you'll take these checks and enter them into your system by date, I'd be forever grateful." He gave her his famous smile, the one that had earned him sales bonuses every year since he'd been out of college. "What we want is for the record to show our intentions. That we planned to give this set amount every month. You understand, right? Rather than adding up all the checks and putting it in as one big donation in our file."

"For tax purposes, you mean?" She looked nervous. "We can't change records for tax purposes, I know that."

He shook his head and waved his hand. "No, no. Nothing about taxes." He grinned again. "This is July, ma'am. All I want is for my wife to feel good about our giving statement. You know, when it comes in the mail at the end of the year. I actually want it to be *less*, because half that money should've been given last year. See?"

"So you don't want a statement for last year? Even though some of the entries will be dated for last year?"

"That's right. Last year's taxes are over and done with. I'm not looking for a deduction, just a way to keep our heads high here at Bethel Bible."

She still seemed puzzled. "So you mean, just enter them by the date on each check?"

"Exactly."

Her frown deepened. "But if I do that, you won't get tax credit for the ones dated last calendar year."

"I know that." He gave her a lopsided grin. "We're not concerned with the tax break, ma'am. Seriously. This is about making my wife happy."

Those seemed to be the magic words. She smiled and nodded. "I wish more people were like you. We'll show it as one large donation for the church's budget. But on your records I guess we could enter each check by its date. I don't see why not."

"Thanks." He did his best to sound humble. "Do you think you could see that it gets done right away? My wife's worried about setting foot in church until it's taken care of."

"Tell you what." The girl smiled and checked the clock on the wall. "I'll do it right now. I have access to the computer." She gave Jack a knowing look. "But please tell your wife that no one would've looked down on her for not giving. Lots of people don't give. This is a church, not a club. Besides, only a few people ever even see those records." She took the envelope from him. "Just so you know."

"Thank you." Jack celebrated silently as he watched her go. One more step taken care of.

Now the memory of that day faded. Jack wasn't sure if Allyson Bower had asked the church secretary to check their giving record. But he was certain the social worker called to verify their membership. She said as much yesterday when she talked to Molly and passed on the judge's approval for the trip. The decision was based in part, she said, on the fact that her information about the church membership and the details of the trip to Haiti all checked out.

So far so good.

Now Jack was at the office of Paul Kerkar, one of the sharpest, most brilliant Realtors he knew. Paul dealt with high-end homes and commercial property. He had sold Jack and Molly their current home, and every now and then he called with investment opportunities.

This time Jack called him. "Look, I've come into some cash."

Music to Paul's ears. His tone was immediately cheerful. "How much cash?"

"More than a million, maybe a million and a half." He didn't skip a beat. "Molly and I talked about it, and we'd like to buy something commercial, something in old downtown West Palm Beach—the area where the renovation is taking place."

Jack heard the sound of buttons being pressed. Paul always had a calculator with him. "Okay, so you're looking for a property in the four-million to six-million range, is that right?"

"With 25 percent down, yes."

"That's how we'll work it. Twenty-five is minimum for commercial property, but with your excellent credit, that shouldn't be a problem."

Jack smiled. "I didn't think so."

Paul called him back an hour later with three possibilities. Jack took the day off from work, met Paul at his office, and toured all three. By the end of the day he was ready to make an offer on a medical office building, one that had a higher-than-usual vacancy rate, but was a better price per square foot than anything else downtown.

"This property has great potential," Paul kept saying. *Potential* was his favorite word. "The investment potential here is unmatched."

Jack was convinced. He called Molly and asked her to join them at Paul's office, where they spent nearly an hour going over the numbers and signing the offer. Jack wrote a check for ten thousand dollars earnest money. Before the end of the workday, he placed a call to his mortgage broker.

"How're my loans looking?"

"Great." The man chuckled. "It's not every day I have a client walk in and request an equity loan for more than a million dollars." Another chuckle. "Let me tell you how it's coming together."

The loan officer explained that he was drawing equity from each of the Campbells' three rental houses, still leaving at least 30 percent equity in each. "That's a safe cushion."

"Right." Jack was at his desk, the one in their home office. He tapped a pencil on a pad of paper. *Bottom line, buddy. That's what I need here—the bottom line.* "So what's the total you can get me on the rentals?"

"Just under a million." Pages shuffled in the background. "Here it is, the mid-nine hundreds. That's the best I can do."

"Good." He tapped faster. "What about our existing home?"

"The existing home…" More turning pages. "A comfortable amount takes us into the high four hundreds."

"More than four hundred thousand?" A thrill surged through Jack's veins. "That's higher than we thought."

"The appraisal came back high." The broker sounded proud of himself. "Property values are skyrocketing, Jack. It's a good time to be in real estate."

"I guess."

"Uh, Jack…" The man's tone changed. "You mind me asking what you need all this cash for?"

"I thought I told you."

"No…" The man let out an uncomfortable laugh. "I mean, it's none of my business. But one-and-a-half million? You and Molly starting a new business or what?"

Casual, Jack…Keep it casual. "Commercial real estate.

Found the perfect medical office building downtown, the area they're renovating."

"Really?" The man sounded impressed. "It's hard to find anything down there."

"I have connections." Jack chuckled. "It'll be a money-maker right off the bat."

"Great." He hesitated. "And by the looks of it, your income on the rentals will take care of your payment on the equity loan."

"Exactly." Jack leaned back in his chair and set the pencil down on the desk. "It's a win-win for everyone." He didn't want to sound anxious. "When can we expect funds from these loans?"

"We should sign papers in a week. Funds can be issued within a few days after that."

"Perfect."

They chatted for a few minutes more, and then the conversation ended. Jack could hardly believe it had all gone so well. He needed the real estate piece. Because if the social worker or the judge found out there were 1.4 million dollars sitting in the Campbells' savings account, they might be concerned, at least enough to watch them or deny them permission to leave the country.

But with a pending commercial real estate deal, it made perfect sense. That money was exactly what they would need to close the loan on the building. Of course they would have it sitting in their savings account. It was all perfectly explainable with the real estate deal in place.

The work trip was just one month away. Every time Jack thought about it, he was tempted to panic, to stay awake all night looking for loopholes, details he hadn't worked out. They had one chance to pull this off, just one. Anything short of perfection, and they would all lose.

But with those phone calls, the financial part of the plan was all but solved. There would be the last-minute transfer of the funds to a series of accounts, winding up eventually at their new account in the Cayman Islands. Jack had arranged for the money to arrive in Grand Cayman a few days before they did. Then almost immediately they'd withdraw all the money in cash. By the time the authorities figured out where the money had gone, the account would be closed. Another dead end for the officials.

Yes, everything was coming together. They would have to say good-bye to Joey just one more time, when he left for his next visit the second week of August.

Then, if the plan worked, they'd never have to say good-bye to him again.

❦

Beth hated herself for what she was feeling, but there was no way around it. She was worried about Molly and Jack, worried they might actually be planning something crazy. Molly had remained distant, even when Beth probed and prodded.

It was the first Wednesday in August, and they'd spent the day at the neighborhood pool. Now they were at Molly's house, the kids gathered around Molly's dining room table with grapes and string cheese.

Molly washed dishes while Beth stood beside her at the sink. "So you've heard nothing?" She kept her voice low. Joey still didn't understand what was happening to him.

"Nothing." Molly scrubbed at some dried egg on a breakfast plate. She flipped her dark hair over her shoulder and out of her face. "Every politician's office I've spoken with is writing a letter to the judge asking that he reconsider. We have to think that's going to make a difference."

Beth was baffled. "Make a difference when?" She leaned her hip into the edge of the counter and studied her sister. "Joey's final visit is next week. Then he's home for three weeks and gone for good."

"I know that." Molly stopped washing. She turned her head and stared at Beth. Her voice was laced with frustration. "That's why I haven't stopped trying." She began scrubbing the plate again.

"Okay." Beth held up her hands. "You don't want to talk about this. I get that." She let her hands fall to her sides. "But it feels like your house is on fire and you're throwing glasses of water at it."

Molly threw her scrub rag into the sink and frowned at Beth. "Are you saying I don't care about losing Joey? That I'm not trying hard enough?" She looked back at the kids in the dining room, and lowered her voice. "We're doing everything we can. We've asked for a hearing the third week of August. That's when the judge will look at the letters from political offices, and hear our reasons why we don't think Joey should be taken from us." She made a harsh grab at the rag again. "I go to bed crying and wake up crying, Beth." She paused. "You have no idea how much I care. I'd lay down my life to keep that child. What else do you want me to do?"

Beth was instantly sorry. She stayed still, silent for a moment, giving Molly a chance to calm down. Then she tentatively touched her sister's shoulder. "Molly...forgive me. I can't imagine being you, going through this."

"It's like..." Molly's hands went limp. Her eyes met Beth's and the pain there was so strong it was like a physical force. "It's like he's dying." Her lower lip trembled. "Like we're all dying." Her expression took on the bewildered look of a lost child. "I don't know how to act, Beth. I've never done this before."

The phone rang, and Beth held up her hand. "I'll get it." Molly kept her kitchen telephone on a small built-in desk adjacent to the pantry. Beth caught the phone on the third ring. "Hello?"

"Hey...I hoped I'd find you there. I got a message you called."

It was Bill. "Yes—" She motioned to Molly that the call was for her. "Hi, honey." She turned her back to Molly and stared absently at the clutter on the small desk. A few greeting cards, invitations to an upcoming wedding, and a baby announcement. Off to the side was a stack of papers from Bank of America. "Hey..." Beth looked a little closer. "Could you pick up a can of olives on the way home? I need them for the casserole."

"Sure. How was the pool?"

"Good." Beth tried to make small talk, but she was distracted. She leaned closer and read the first line on the Bank of America papers. *Congratulations! Your equity line of credit for $987,000 has been approved. As per our conversation you will sign papers next week, and the loan will be funded shortly after you...*

"Guess you have to go?"

"Sorry." Beth caught hold of the back of the desk chair

so she wouldn't lose her balance. Why in the world would Molly and Jack need nearly a million dollars? "Yeah..." She tried to concentrate. "Can I call you back?"

Bill laughed. "Sure. We can talk later."

She hung up and looked back at Molly. Had she noticed Beth snooping? Beth didn't think so. Molly was still washing dishes. Even though Beth was dying to ask her, she kept her questions about the loan papers to herself. But that night she shared every detail with Bill. By then she'd created a dozen scenarios in her head, reasons why Molly and Jack didn't seem to be scrambling to save Joey.

"Bill"—she put her hands on her hips—"I think they're going to run."

"Honey, you watch too much television."

They were in their bedroom, the kids asleep down the hall. Bill was watching ESPN. Beth positioned herself in front of the screen. "I'm not watching too much television, Bill. I'm serious. They're dragging their feet about getting someone to help them, and they're running out of time." She threw her hands up. "Molly hasn't even told Joey yet! And why would they need a million-dollar loan? It doesn't make sense."

"Maybe for attorney fees." Bill peered around her, determined to keep his eyes on the TV. "Maybe Jack's found a high-powered lawyer who knows how to win the case." He looked at Beth. "Isn't that possible?"

"A million dollars?" She frowned. "The guy better work a miracle for that kind of legal fee."

"What I'm saying"—he looked exasperated—"is that Molly doesn't have to tell you every last detail."

"She always did before." Beth walked to the window.

It was dark outside; only the sliver of a moon hung over the cluster of oak trees that separated their house from the neighbor's. She turned around and groaned. "Don't you see, Bill. I know my sister. Something isn't right. The loan papers are proof."

He held out his arms. "Come here."

She didn't want to. Bill was clearly dismissing her, making light of everything she was feeling. But she needed his hug, so she went. Slowly she crawled into bed and curled up beside him, her head on his shoulder.

"The only one who can work a miracle for Joey is God." He kissed the top of her head. "Remember?"

God. She thought about that for a minute. Bill was right. She drew a long, slow breath. "I'm praying for that." She relaxed and her shoulders dropped a few inches. "I guess I keep forgetting."

"I think Jack and Molly really believe in what God can do here." He looked thoughtful. "Otherwise they wouldn't be coming to church and praying with us."

"True." She looked down, searching for something she couldn't quite get her thoughts around. "I guess I can't make up my mind. On the one hand I'm asking Molly to trust God, to believe that God has a plan for Joey. Then I doubt her because she isn't panicking."

"Exactly." Bill turned off the television.

George Brett loped into the room and wagged his tail.

"Thanks for talking." Beth started for the door but did a double-take at the dog. "Who let you in here?" She clucked her tongue against the roof of her mouth. "Bad dog. Come on, let's go outside."

As she put George Brett outside, Beth closed her eyes and

tried to connect the pieces. Yes, Molly and Jack were trying to be proactive. They were making phone calls, asking for a hearing, begging God for a miracle. When she thought of it that way, her fears were completely unfounded. Molly and Jack weren't going to run; they were going to wait for God's will. Everything Bill had said made sense, except the obvious. And it was the obvious that kept Beth awake most of the night and into the morning.

Why, in the middle of all that was going on with Joey, would Molly and Jack need a million dollars? Even though she shouldn't have snooped, shouldn't have looked, it was a question that needed answering. By noon the next day, Beth made up her mind.

As soon as the moment seemed right—whether Molly got mad at her or not—she was going to ask.

TWENTY-ONE

The door closed and Molly let herself fall against it. She reached out and took hold of Jack's hands. Gus whimpered a few feet away.

"I hate this. . . . I can't do it again."

"I know."

Joey had just left for his third visit. This time he was less tearful, but more afraid. He had come home without any bruises after his second visit, but he was stuttering again, and he didn't want to talk about Rip Porter.

"He doesn't like me, Mommy," was all he'd say about the man. Then he'd change the subject.

"Does he hurt you, buddy?"

"No!" Joey shook his head fast. "He doesn't hurt me. P-p-promise."

Her son had never lied to her, not as far as she knew. But his quick answer and fearful eyes made her worry. Regardless of their plans, she would not let him go back to the Porters if the man was harming him. It had been hard enough to let him go back a second time after the bruises on his arm.

Now, her stomach knotted and her heart pounded against

her chest. "Every time I say good-bye to him, a piece of me goes dead until he comes home."

Jack rubbed the back of his neck. He looked exhausted. "Can you imagine having to let him go forever? In three weeks?"

"No." She came to him, put her arms around his neck. "I told Beth it was like knowing he was about to die, like we all were."

He studied her. "That's all you've told Beth?"

"Of course."

"And you're sure she didn't see the loan papers on the desk?" His words were slow, weary, as if he couldn't stop running through the possibilities.

"I'm pretty sure." She pressed her fist against her forehead. "That was so stupid of me. The mail came that morning.... I opened the stuff from the bank, and Joey needed sunscreen on his back. I set the mail down and made a mental note to put it away before we left." She lifted her hands. "I don't know how I forgot."

"But you don't think she saw it."

"No." She pictured that day. "Beth got a phone call from Bill, but it was quick. Besides, if she'd seen it, I think she would've asked. Beth and I don't keep secrets."

"Well…" He pulled her closer, tucked her head against his chest. His tone was sad. "You do now, love."

A pain pierced her heart and she closed her eyes. "Yes." She was counting down the days. They were down to fourteen. Fourteen days until the trip. Fourteen days until they would walk out of their home for the last time. Two weeks until she had to start wearing a blonde wig and going by the name Tracy Sanders. Worst of all, fourteen days until she had to say good-bye to Beth, her sister and best friend.

She survived most days by telling herself that some-how—someday—they might be able to find their way back. The Porters would die off, or the case would be forgotten. They could slip into the United States, spend a week with Beth and Bill and the kids, and be on their way again.

But the reality was something entirely different.

Jack nuzzled her. "You okay?"

"It's more than I can think about." She let herself melt into his arms. At times like these he seemed strong enough for both of them. "I wish I could be like Joey and talk to God whenever I'm scared."

She felt him stiffen. No matter how much time they spent meeting with Beth and Bill, no matter how many church services, Jack was no closer to a genuine faith. It was all simply a necessary part of the plan. "You can talk to God whenever you want." A hint of sarcasm crept into his voice. "Ask him to make the fake passports good enough to pass inspection."

"Jack…" She didn't like when he made light of God, or the idea of God. "It wouldn't hurt if you did a little talking to Him yourself."

He exhaled in a way that betrayed his frustration. "Maybe someday—when we're sitting on the beach in Cayman with too much time on our hands." He kissed her lips, slow and tender. "Right now I'm too busy making this happen to ask God about it."

Molly wanted to add something, remind him that Beth and Bill were praying for God's will, and that maybe she and Jack were going about this all the wrong way, and maybe they really should be calling politicians and lawyers and asking for hearings. But it was too late for any of that.

She leaned back. "How're the plans going?"

"Good. Money's taken care of, and I'm getting the passports next week." His tone sounded heavier than usual, full of sorrow. "But there's something we need to talk about."

"What?" Gus came up to them and sat against their legs. Molly pushed him back a little. "Go lay down, Gus."

Gus did as he was told and Molly looked up at Jack. "What do we need to talk about?"

"Him." Jack looked at Gus. "We can't take him, Molly. You know that."

"What?" She took a step back, horrified. "Why haven't we thought about that before? Jack, we have to take him. Joey would be crushed."

"I *have* thought about it, and there's just no way."

Molly let out an exasperated cry. She went to Gus and dropped to the floor beside him. "We're leaving him at the kennel, right? When we go to Haiti?"

"Right."

"So let's pay someone at the kennel to ship him over to the Cayman Islands at the end of the week."

Jack came to her. He eased himself down onto the floor and rubbed Gus behind the ear. "The whole state will be looking for us by then. Maybe the whole country." He tilted his head, doing everything he could to help her understand. "It'll be big news, Molly."

"But we've kept the story out of the news on purpose."

"Right. But the Porters will be talking to every reporter

who knocks on their door once they figure out we're not coming back."

Gus yawned and pressed his head against Jack's hand. "Good boy, Gus."

Molly looked at the ceiling for a few seconds. "So you're saying the people at the kennel could notify the authorities and tell them we left our dog with instructions that they ship him to the Cayman Islands?"

"Exactly. We can't risk everything for Gus, honey. We can't do it."

"If it makes the news like you think it will..." Her eyes found his again. "They'll be looking for Molly and Jack Campbell."

"Right."

"So let's use a new kennel. I'll wear my blonde wig and explain that we're moving to the Cayman Islands and we need someone to ship our dog to us in a week."

"I don't understand. How's that any different?"

Molly took hold of Jack's shoulders. "It's easy." She could feel her whole face glowing. "We'll register with the kennel as Walt and Tracy Sanders."

"Molly..." Jack's eyes welled up. He patted Gus and nuzzled his face against the dog's. When he looked at her, it was obvious that he wasn't going to change his mind. "I can't risk our future—our lives—just so we can keep him." He bit his lip. "We'll use the same kennel as always. That way when we don't come back for him, Beth and Bill will bring him home."

Beth and Bill? Gus didn't even know them. Suddenly the reality became clear for her, too. No matter what they did, what name they used, it wouldn't take more than an hour to call every kennel in town and ask if a yellow lab had been shipped out of the country. Jack was right.

They'd have to say good-bye to Gus, too.

Molly looped her arms around the dog's neck as the tears came. Gus was Joey's best friend. Why hadn't she thought about what would happen to him? It was a blow, one that took her breath away. Poor Gus…He would never be the same without his family—even if Beth and Bill did take him.

It was another blow, and with Joey gone to the Porters again, it was enough to do Molly in. The losses were so great, she could barely imagine them all happening at once. Sobs racked her body, and her tears spilled onto Gus's furry coat. He made a whimpering sound and looked up at her, his eyes gentle and trusting.

Next to her, Jack rubbed her shoulders. There was nothing either of them could say to fix the situation. They would say good-bye to everything they knew and everyone they loved, and they would do it all willingly for Joey. Then they would do the thing that would hurt Joey most of all, something he would never understand.

They would say good-bye to Gus.

❧

Joey was finally asleep, and Rip had left for the bar—same as nearly every night for a week. Wendy lingered on the edge of Joey's bed, watching his small sleeping body as it finally relaxed.

She was falling head over heels for her little boy, no question about it. This time he smiled when he walked through the door with Allyson Bower. Even though he didn't exactly run and jump into her arms, he wasn't crying, either, so that had to be a good sign.

He still talked about missing his mommy and daddy, and Wendy was puzzled. The Campbells should've explained things to the boy by now. That was part of the deal. By the third visit he was supposed to know that he was going to come and live with the Porters in Ohio. That they were his new family.

It didn't matter. Rip told Joey every chance he had. Tonight was no different. They were eating dinner—chicken nuggets and macaroni and cheese. Rip waved his fork in the air. "You can start calling me Daddy now. That's what the judge says."

Joey blinked. He looked both puzzled and frightened. "My d-d-daddy lives in Florida with me." He poked his fork into another bite of macaroni.

"Doesn't he know yet?" Rip looked at her. For once he wasn't angry, just curious.

"I guess not." Wendy wasn't hungry. She pushed her plate back and smiled at her husband. Anything to keep him calm. "It'll be obvious soon enough, Rip."

He looked back at Joey. "Here's the deal, little man." He waited until Joey's eyes were on him. "I'm your *real* daddy and this," he gestured to the small living area made up of the kitchen and living room, "this is your *real* home." He leaned over the table so his face was closer to Joey's. "The Campbells adopted you, only there was a mistake." He pointed at Wendy. "Me and her, we're your real parents and the judge says you're gonna come stay with us. Starting in three weeks."

Tears gathered in Joey's eyes and he shook his head. "My Mommy and D-d-daddy and Gus are in Florida." He dropped his fork. "That's my real f-f-family."

Rip was getting madder by the second. Just when it looked like he might throw a glass of milk at the boy, he jerked his chair back, stood, and grabbed his car keys. "I'll be at the bar."

That was that. It took Wendy an hour to calm Joey down, and she did it by agreeing with him. Yes, his real parents were in Florida. Yes, that was his real home. "But we're like your mama and daddy, too," she told him. Because if she didn't say so now, how would she explain the situation when he came to live with them in three weeks?

Joey looked confused. He didn't finish his dinner, and he talked to the Campbells on the phone longer than usual. He didn't really relax until Wendy led him into the TV room and turned on *SpongeBob SquarePants*. Halfway through the program, he even laughed a little. The sound of it made Wendy dream of the days ahead, days when the transition would be over and having Joey could be part of their regular routine.

When the program ended, Joey wanted to watch more cartoons. They found *Bear in the Big Blue House*, and after it got started, Wendy did something she'd been wanting to do since Joey's first visit. She reached out...careful not to startle her son...and she took hold of his fingers.

He looked at her and smiled. Then without hesitating, he tucked his hand the rest of the way into hers. The feeling of that single touch was so amazing, so right, it stayed with her the rest of the night. Even when he said his bedtime prayers.

"Please, God, bring me home safe and fast 'cause I miss Mommy and Daddy and Gus so so so much. Gee this name, amen."

Now Wendy looked at his sleeping form again and gently patted his back one more time. "Good night, Joey. Mama loves you."

She wandered down the hallway and back to the kitchen. Along the way she picked up her Bible. Actually it was her grandma's Bible, but lately she'd been reading it. Taking it with her to church on Sundays and trying to find meaning in it. Strength or peace or wisdom. Something to help her be the sort of mother Joey needed.

She'd been reading a part called First Kings, because that was where Solomon made a lot of decisions. That's what the pastor had said a few weeks ago. And no Old Testamant person was as wise as King Solomon. Of course, Rip didn't like her reading the Bible. Made him nervous, he said. But Rip wouldn't be home until well after midnight.

She looked out the window and sighed. Rip had hit her again the day before, this time on her back. She hadn't looked, but she was pretty sure she had a bruise. He was sorry, he told her so. When she looked at the big picture, he did seem to be doing better with his rage than he'd done before he went to prison.

But things weren't headed in a good direction. He'd quit his job at the theater. Too stressful, he'd told her—working nights when he was trying to learn how to be a father. Wendy wasn't sure how hanging out at the bars was helping, but she didn't ask.

She opened the Bible. She was on the third chapter, the part with the little heading that said, "A Wise Ruling."

The story was about two women who shared a house, and each of them had a newborn baby. It was fascinating and it caught her attention right away.

The story went on that one morning one of the babies was dead, and an argument broke out about which of the women was the mother of the living baby. The women took the baby to King Solomon and asked him to decide, so the king pulled out a long sword. He told the mothers he would cut the living baby in half and give them each a part since they couldn't agree about who the mother was.

The real mother stepped forward right away. "Give the baby to the other woman," she said.

But the other woman was defiant. She had no trouble allowing the king to cut the baby in half. The King then awarded the baby to the first woman. The reason was obvious—only the child's real mother loved him enough to give him up, rather than see him die.

Wendy finished the story and quickly shut the Bible. What had she just read? A story about two mothers, two women with a claim to the same child. Wasn't that just like her and Molly Campbell, Joey's adoptive mother? The two of them both loved Joey, and both of them wanted to have him for their own.

She pushed the Bible away. The story rubbed her the wrong way. What sort of wisdom did it have for her? In this case, she was the real mother, but she wasn't willing to give Joey up, not even if that was the best thing for him. She loved him too much. Especially now.

Enough Bible stories, she told herself. She put the big book away and turned on the television. Reruns of *American Idol* were on. That would help her forget the strange story in the Bible. At least in today's world, judges didn't decide custody issues by threatening to cut a baby in half. They handled it fair and square. Even if the decision seemed hard at the time. Wendy was beyond glad, too. She might've let Joey go once, back when she didn't know him. But now that she knew what it felt like to hold his hand and feed him dinner and sit beside him watching cartoons, one thing was certain.

She would never let him go again.

Never.

TWENTY-TWO

The office was as small as it was seedy. Jack sat in one of two available chairs. The other one was near the door, empty. Copier fluid and printer cartridges were stacked on two filing cabinets, and the place smelled of thick cigar smoke and ink. Angelo St. Pierre worked his machine in the back corner by the light of a pair of small, dusty table lamps. Jack guessed the place was maybe a hundred square feet altogether.

Angelo pushed a button on the machine and stood back. "Mr. Sanders?" He turned to Jack. The man was from the Dominican Republic, and his accent was almost too thick to understand. "You need these today, yes?"

"Yes." Jack folded his hands on the man's small desk. The legs were uneven and the desk wobbled hard to the right. "That would be best."

"Tell me your story again."

The man seemed to like stories. For the job Angelo was doing, Jack was willing to indulge him. "My wife and I are missionaries." He smiled, not his standard grin, but the humble smile he'd seen people at Bethel Bible Church use with each other. "We're taking our little boy to Indonesia." He frowned. "Very dangerous."

"Yes." Angelo St. Pierre punctuated the thought by jabbing his finger in Jack's direction. "I know that place. Very dangerous."

Jack had found Angelo's information in an Internet chat room. He did a search and wound up on a site where people with broken English wrote in what seemed like a code. It took Jack a few nights in the chat room before he realized that nearly everyone was—or claimed to be—an illegal alien. Fake passports were a hot topic, and when it came up, Jack joined in.

"I need documents fast. I live in Florida. Any suggestions?" "Fast" was the codeword for "illegal." Jack had picked up that much.

"AAA Copiers is a good place to start," someone wrote back. Two other people in the chat room agreed.

Jack looked it up the next day and had a phone conversation with Angelo St. Pierre. Again the conversation was in code. Jack talked about needing passports quickly, and Angelo said it wouldn't be a problem. He said he was in favor of American freedom. Whatever that meant.

"Just bring in your photos and we can do things very quickly." He paused. "There will be fee for very fast passports."

Jack agreed, and that was exactly how things had gone. When he got there, he filled out a piece of paper for each of the three of them, providing their new names and making up every other answer needed. Angelo didn't ask for identification; he merely looked at the papers, collected the small passport-size photos, and went to work.

Behind Angelo St. Pierre, the machines ground to a halt. He worked and folded and pressed the documents into another machine on the floor. He used a series of what looked like stamps and then a fine-point pen. After ten minutes he laid three passports on the desk and smiled. "There. You have your passports quickly."

Indeed.

Jack picked them up and looked them over. He'd used his own passport often enough to see that—at least to his eye—there was no difference here whatsoever. Angelo's work was brilliant. Certainly the passports would trick officials in Haiti. And once they did, once there were stamps in the back, it would be even easier to trick officials in Europe and Grand Cayman.

"You do good work, Angelo." Jack had already agreed to the price. Quick passports were expensive. Two hundred dollars each. Cash, nothing else. He paid the man.

Angelo smiled. "Angelo St. Pierre in favor of American freedom." He nodded. "Good day."

No need to wait for a receipt. Jack collected the passports, nodded one last time to the man, and left the building. Just as he stepped out, as he tucked the passports into his suit-coat pocket, a car approached from fifty yards away—one that looked an awful lot like the car belonging to Bill and Beth Petty.

Jack wanted to run or hide, but he didn't have time. It couldn't be them, not here in Miami in the middle of the week. Once in a while Bill did business in Miami, but the corporate offices were blocks away. Jack kept his pace normal, not too hurried. Angelo's shop was on a busy street, but it was smack in the middle of the worst part of town, the part run by drug lords and mafia and friendly swindlers from the Dominican Republic who believed in American freedom.

This section of town was no place the Pettys would come. But as the car approached, all doubt vanished. It was the Pettys' car, and Bill was driving. There were at least three other businessmen in the car with him. Jack kept his eyes straight ahead.

After the car passed, he allowed himself to breathe.

Ten more steps and Jack reached his car. Bill hadn't seen him—he was too busy making conversation with his passengers. But what could he possibly have been doing in that part of Miami? And what if he *had* spotted Jack? Wouldn't he have stopped and made casual conversation? Bill was driving, after all. He could've pulled over. Jack felt the adrenaline work its way through his body and out of his system. If Bill had seen him, he would've stopped. It was that simple. Jack put all thoughts of Bill and Angelo St. Pierre and what he'd just done by purchasing false passports out of his head, and focused instead on what was still left to do. He'd already done the unthinkable—lying and taking part in criminal activity. Every detail from here on out needed to be perfect.

The trip was in ten days; there was no room for error.

Beth and Molly were at the pool when Beth decided she'd had enough. They were leaving for Haiti in eight days. It was time to come straight out and ask the question.

The kids were in the pool, the boys gathered in the shallow end playing a wild game of water volleyball. Cammie sat with a few of her neighborhood friends at the far side of the deep end. All of them were out of earshot. Beth and

Molly sat on the edge of the pool, their feet in the water. Molly had her eyes on Joey, and Beth made little splashes with her toes. So far there hadn't been much conversation between them. Beth decided to start with the easy questions.

"When's your hearing?"

"What?" Molly didn't turn her head. She leaned back on her hands.

"The hearing. The one in Ohio to see if the judge will change his mind about Joey." She tried not to sound short. "That hearing."

"Oh. Right." Molly nodded. "Jack says it'll be Monday or Tuesday."

Beth hesitated. "So when are you leaving?"

"Leaving?" Molly blinked twice and turned to her. "Friday, same as you." She turned her focus back to Joey again.

This was ridiculous. If she didn't know better, she'd think Molly was on drugs. "Not for the work trip. When are you leaving for Ohio? I'm assuming you and Jack are going to be there."

Across the pool, Joey climbed out, dripping water, and waved at Molly. She waved back and then turned to Beth. "Jack found an attorney. He said we don't have to be there. He can get a continuance to buy time." She found Joey again. "I thought I told you."

Beth wasn't sure whether to feel relieved or to call her sister a liar. Bill had told her about seeing Jack in downtown Miami. He said he thought Jack recognized him, but since Jack looked away so quickly, he assumed whatever Jack was doing he didn't want to be caught. Even Bill was suspicious now. But Beth never got the chance to call Molly about it. Blain and Jonah had the stomach flu that day, and it had been all she could do to keep them hydrated between bathroom runs. Now, twenty-four hours later, the boys were well again and Beth was desperate for answers.

She swirled her feet in the water. "A continuance? You mean, you don't have to give Joey up the week after we get back from the trip?"

"Nope." Molly smiled, but something about it was flat. In the background, the sound of kids laughing and splashing water seemed to fade. "You were right, Beth. God worked a miracle for us. The attorney is buying us time—a month, maybe more. He says he can help us keep custody of Joey."

"So where's the hooting and hollering?" Beth laughed just once. "I would think you'd have called me with that news the minute it came in."

Molly looked at her, and her eyes were somehow deeper than before. "I can't call you with everything that happens in regards to Joey."

Beth had the strangest feeling. As if there was something Molly wanted to say, but she couldn't or wouldn't say it. "You always did before."

"I know." Sorrow welled up in Molly's eyes. "We're not out of the woods yet. That's the reason I didn't call."

It was time. If Beth didn't ask now, she would never have the courage. She angled her body and looked straight to her sister's heart, beyond whatever walls she'd put up in the past few months. "Can I ask you something?"

"If it's about Joey, there's not much else to say." Molly picked up the bottle of sunscreen beside her, and poured a small amount into her right hand. She rubbed it slowly onto her knees.

"Look at me, Molly. I have to see your eyes."

Her sister made a face that showed her surprise, but she did as Beth asked. "Okay."

"Why did you and Jack take out a loan for almost a million dollars?"

And there it was. The moment she asked the question, the walls in Molly's eyes fell and what remained was pure, terrifying fear. It was a deer-in-the-headlights sort of look. A look that said Beth had caught her.

But in just half a second it was gone. Molly raised her brow. "Nice. Snooping through our mail now, are you?"

"Of course not." Beth hissed the words. She didn't want to fight, but she couldn't stand by and do nothing. Not if Molly and Jack were really thinking of running. "It was out in the open."

"Right." Molly leaned closer. She was mad, and her tone didn't hide the fact. "Why do you think it was out in the open, Beth? Because Jack and I have nothing to hide, that's why." She straightened, indignant. "And if you must know, we're purchasing a medical office building in downtown West Palm. Okay? Any other questions?"

"In downtown..." Beth wanted to cry. The last thing she intended was to make Molly mad, but even with her sister's explanation, she still wasn't convinced. She swallowed and summoned her courage. "Yes. One more."

"Okay, shoot. Wanna know how much the building costs? Four million. Wanna know how we found it? Jack's real estate connections—Paul Kerkar, to be specific. He's listed. Look him up." She made a tight line with her lips. "Go ahead, Beth. What else do you want to know?"

The air around them grew still, the voices of the children

almost silent. Beth never broke eye contact with her sister. "I want to know... if you're going to run."

Molly's shock was genuine, or at least it seemed that way. "Beth Petty! Are you asking me if Jack and I are going to run away with Joey?"

"Yes." It was too late to back down now. "Bill told me he saw Jack in downtown Miami, near a place where they make phony passports." Tears blurred her vision. "I had to ask, because, Molly—you can't run. If they catch you, you'll spend the rest of your life in prison."

She didn't mention the other obvious consequence. That the two of them would be finished, their relationship over. It was the heartbreaking part of the possibility that Beth tried not to think about. It was one thing to want to protect Molly from herself, from doing something that might land her in prison. That sort of motivation was okay. But it was entirely different if she was concerned mainly for herself, because she loved Molly too much to lose her.

Molly lifted her legs out of the pool and pushed herself up onto her feet. She stared down at Beth, her face a mask of hurt. "I can't believe you'd think that."

Beth stood too, so they were eye-to-eye. "What was Jack doing in Miami?"

Then, as if something came over her, Molly's expression eased. "Beth..." She sounded kind, almost apologetic. "I'm so sorry. How long have you been thinking about this?"

"Since yesterday, for sure." Beth took a few steps back and sat on one of the pool lounge chairs.

Molly took the one next to her. "Jack was working with a document specialist, something about the deed to the building we're buying. He's done all his paperwork in Miami."

Beth wasn't convinced. Not then, and not later that afternoon when she was home mulling over everything Molly had said. Real estate transactions for property in West Palm Beach would take place here, not in Miami. Certainly whatever documents were needed, they could be picked up in town.

The evidence was still more than Beth could ignore. And she was running out of time to do something about it. The money, the phony passport place, the almost casual way Molly and Jack seemed to be handling what was happening with Joey. They were like pieces of a puzzle, and suddenly the picture seemed too great to ignore.

It was against God, against the law, against everything right and true for Molly and Jack to take Joey and run. They could get killed or arrested. They could lose both Joey and their freedom forever, all at the same time. With everything in her, Beth wanted to believe that her suspicions were outrageous, impossible. That her sister would never do such a thing.

But there was one detail Beth couldn't deny. Something Molly herself had said a few weeks ago. She said she'd lay down her life for Joey if she had to. And wouldn't she be doing exactly that if they ran? Giving up life as she knew it, everything about the old Molly Campbell, all so she could keep being Joey's mother?

There was only one way to make sure it wouldn't happen, to know for certain she'd done everything in her power to stop her sister from making the greatest mistake of her life. Beth knew the social worker's name. Molly had talked about the woman countless times in the past few months.

Allyson Bower.

She worked in Cleveland, Ohio, at the Child Welfare Department—Beth knew that, too. And with those two bits of information, in three quick minutes she was on the phone, being transferred to Allyson Bower's office.

On the fourth ring, a machine picked up. Beth took a deep breath, and when the recording asked the caller to leave a message, she waited for the beep and began to talk.

"Mrs. Bower, you don't know me. This is Beth Petty, Molly Campbell's sister." She paused. "This is a very hard phone call to make, but I think you should know I'm very concerned that my sister and her husband might be thinking of running, disappearing with Joey.

"As you know, we're leaving the country a week from today for a work trip to Haiti. I have a suspicion that the Campbells will take false passports with them on that trip. They also have access to an awful lot of money." Tears choked her throat. Her hands shook. Molly would never speak to her again if she knew about this call. She coughed a little. "Please, Mrs. Bower, if this concerns you, call me as soon as you get this message."

Beth left her number, and then hung up.

There. She'd done everything she could do. The social worker would get her message, and if Molly was lying to her, it was only a matter of time. Allyson Bower would stop them before they had the chance to do something stupid, something they would regret forever. They didn't have to give up Joey. There was still time for legal intervention, time for God to work a miracle on their behalf. But if

Molly and Jack ran, there would be no turning back, not ever.

Beth's head pounded. She took two Tylenol and stretched out on the sofa. The kids were playing in the kiddie pool out back, and dinner was an hour away. Not that she could bear the thought of eating. Her stomach was in knots. Making that call was the hardest thing Beth had ever done.

Now she could only pray that Molly never, ever found out. If she did, there would be no need to worry about whether her friendship with Molly would end because Molly would be in prison or living in some foreign country.

If Molly found out about the call, Beth would've killed the relationship herself.

TWENTY-THREE

They were in Joey's room, tucking him in and making sure his suitcase was packed for the morning. Molly's head was spinning so fast she could barely complete a sentence. They were just hours from setting their plan in motion.

"I won't see that other mommy and daddy on this trip, right?" Joey wore his dinosaur pajamas that night, the ones with the shorts and short sleeves. The Florida humidity was in full force, and even with their air conditioning, the room felt muggy.

"No, buddy." Molly sat on the edge of his bed and smoothed his sweaty bangs off his head. "This is a special trip with just us and Aunt Beth's family."

"What about Gus?" Over the past few months, Gus had made a regular habit of sleeping on Joey's bed. He was sitting on the floor now, patiently waiting for Molly to move so he could take his place.

Molly could feel her heart breaking. "Not Gus." She reached down and patted Gus near his ear. "He's going to a doggie day care."

Joey giggled. "I bet he has fun there, Mommy."

Molly wanted to weep. "Me, too."

Jack had gone down the hall to get something, and now he came back with his guitar. Before life had spun so wildly out of control, Jack had often come into Joey's room at night with his guitar. They'd turn off the lights and Jack would play something soft and melodic, something he'd made up or something retro from the Eagles or Boston.

Now Jack motioned to the suitcase. "All packed?"

"Yes." She leaned down and gave Joey butterfly kisses with her eyelashes. "Want a backrub, buddy?"

"Okay." He smiled at her. "The other mommy does that for me, too." He started to turn over, but he held her look a second longer. "She's nice to me."

Molly gulped. The other mommy was nice? She covered her surprise. "That's good, honey...I'm glad."

"But the man...he's still really mean."

"I'm sure." She looked at Jack. He'd heard every word, she could tell by his expression.

Jack played three songs, all lullabies he'd written. When Joey was asleep, they tiptoed out of the room. They had a lot to talk about and only a few hours left before they got on the plane.

After Jack put his guitar away, they met on the front porch. Even with the sticky night, it felt better being outside. It made the whirling thoughts in Molly's head somehow manageable.

They sat in the glider, the one that just perfectly fit the two of them. The crickets were louder than usual, and Jack leaned his head back, peering at the starry sky. "It's our last night here."

"Yes." Molly pulled her feet up onto the glider and

hugged her knees. "I have so many questions still. Tell me again what you did today."

Jack looked calm. "Everything's done." He put his arm around her shoulders. "I transferred the money. It went through half a dozen accounts all designed to break up any paper trail."

"And it'll be in our account in the Caymans the day before we get there?"

"Yep." He kicked his feet up on the porch railing. "I double-checked. The instructions I gave the banker in Sweden were very clear. Wait twelve days and send the money on."

"And you're sure the money made it to Sweden?"

"Before noon today."

"You made it look like it was going to an escrow account, right? From our savings?"

"Right. That way when the authorities interview Beth and she tells them we were purchasing a commercial building, everything will line up. At least for a little while."

"What about the Realtor?"

"He'll hear about our disappearance and assume the deal is cancelled." Jack was unruffled by her questions. "He'd have no reason to contact anyone about a broken real estate deal. Happens all the time."

"Okay, what else?" Her heart was going double-time. After all the talking and planning, she was suddenly scared to death. The way she'd felt since Beth asked her point-blank if they were running. "I've got our entire photo library on CDs and jump drives, all packed in the suitcase."

"Good."

The photos had been Molly's idea. She couldn't leave her past life without bringing photographs. At first she'd tried to imagine packing a dozen albums, but then she remembered. Since they'd adopted Joey, all their photos were taken digitally. All they needed were the CDs and a backup copy of the files on a jump drive. They could make new photos when they got situated in the Caymans.

Late at night when she couldn't sleep, she'd scanned special photos from before Joey's adoption into a file. Then she carefully put each photo back, so that when people went through their belongings, nothing would be out of place, no sign that they'd been planning this.

Molly packed only one photo album—the one Beth had made her when she graduated from high school. Also one small file of Joey's artwork. Otherwise everything was being left behind.

Jack leaned forward, elbows on his knees. "I cancelled our life insurance policies, effective today."

"Good. I like that." It was something they'd discussed a few weeks ago. If they didn't cancel the policies, and if eventually everyone presumed they'd drowned or been kidnapped or killed by a street gang in Port-au-Prince, disbursement on their policies would have to be made. Beth and Bill would wind up with at least half, since Molly's parents were both dead.

"I like it, too. We're not trying to get an illegal life insurance payout. We just want our son; that's all."

"Exactly." She hugged her legs a little tighter. "What else?"

"You'll take Gus to the kennel at seven in the morning. You've already called and set everything up, right?"

"Right. Last week." Molly started to shake. What were they doing? It still felt like something from a terrible off-Broadway production. People had kids taken away from them; it didn't happen often, but it happened. How many times did a couple run away with their child? And why hadn't she heard of anyone getting away with it? She clenched her teeth to keep them from chattering. "What else?"

"Beth hasn't asked you any weird questions lately, right?"

"Not since the pool." She'd already told Jack about that conversation. "I think she believes my answers."

"Okay. Then we're all set. The getaway is something we have to figure out once we're in Port-au-Prince." He stood and leaned on the railing.

Molly couldn't sit still another moment. She joined him, leaning against his shoulder and staring out at their front yard. The yard they wouldn't see again after tomorrow.

He laced his fingers with hers. "What are you thinking?"

"A lot." She let her head hang for a moment. Strange that she was shaking. It had to be almost ninety degrees out. She looked up and studied the stars. "I remembered something the other day, something Joey and I watched last Christmas."

"Mmm."

"It was a cartoon, a half-hour show on the birth of Jesus. The story of the Nativity."

"You thought of that the other day?" Jack gave her his most charming smile.

His look settled some anxious part of her heart. In her new life, the one that would start tomorrow, she would have Jack and Joey. Despite all the other losses, having them would be enough. Once they got through the next week, they'd find their way together. She nodded. "Yes. After Jesus was born, there was this evil king. He wanted to kill baby Jesus."

"Okay, an evil king..."

"Right, and an angel came to Mary and Joseph in a dream and warned them. They got up and left for another country. Then and there, no warning."

"Ah..." He looked at her, his eyes dancing in the star-light. "Sort of like us."

"Right."

They were quiet for a minute, listening to the sound of the crickets and croaking frogs in the marsh on the other side of the neighborhood. "I keep thinking about Joey's dandelion." He breathed in slow through his nose. "That day at the park all I knew was I couldn't let him go. I wanted to disappear."

"Like Joey's dandelion dust."

"Yes." They were quiet again.

Molly wondered if he could hear her heart beating. No matter how many times they went over the details, she was still terrified. They weren't the sort of people who did this kind of thing. They were good people, law-abiding people. What if they weren't good at being bad? She pressed her forearms against the railing. "What about God's will?"

Jack smiled at her, the sort of smile he gave Joey when Joey talked about Neverland. "God's will?"

"Beth said she's been praying for God's will. Bill, too. If God's will is for Joey to be with us, won't it happen anyway? Couldn't all of this be for nothing?" She didn't pause long enough for him to say anything. "But what if it's God's will for Joey to go to the Porters?"

"You mean, if it's God's will for him to leave us, then somehow he'll leave us no matter what we do? Is that what you're saying?"

"Yes." Her voice was quiet, sad. Beyond afraid. "What if that?"

Jack took a moment before he answered her. "I'm not sure about God's will, Molly. I told you, we can talk about that later." He put his arms around her and together they straightened and eased their way into each other's arms. "All I know is that my plan is going to work." He held onto her shoulders and looked intently into her eyes. "It is, Molly. Nothing's going to happen to us."

Through that night and as the sun started to come up, it was the only thought that made even breathing possible. Nothing was going to happen to them. Nothing. The plan was going to work.

It had to.

Joey wasn't quite asleep. He lay there petting Gus and staring at the ceiling. There was something he hadn't told his mommy and daddy, and he felt bad inside about it. Last time he was at that Ohio house, where the Indians played baseball, the mean man told him scary things.

He said Joey was really his little boy, and he was the real daddy. Joey told the man no, that his real family was here in Florida. Then there was something else even worse. The man came really close to his ear and he said, "If you say that again, little man, I'll give you a spanking you'll remember forever."

Then the man pushed Joey's head into the pillow for a long time. It was scary down there. His breaths were tight and small and he hoped the nice lady would come and make the man stop.

When she did come, she yelled at the man.

Joey looked at Gus. His eyes were open 'cause he was a good friend, that's why. "Hi, Gus...know what?"

What? Gus said with his eyes.

"I don't ever wanna see that mean man again. And maybe I won't have to. Know why?"

Why? Gus said.

"Because I asked God." Sometimes Gus forgot things even when he'd told him a hundred times. " 'Member, Gus? I asked God to go with me on the trips to Ohio and He did. So I asked God if I could please stop taking the trips so I could be home with Mommy and Daddy and you."

Don't forget Mr. Monkey and the bears.

"I know, Gus. I won't." He reached over and picked up Mr. Monkey. "But I can't be with Mr. Bear because I left him at the Ohio house. Under the bed. Know why?"

Why? Gus made a whining sound.

"Because he made me think of that mean man every time I saw him o' course."

Gus yawned and closed his eyes. He didn't like to talk much at night. That was okay. It gave Joey a reason to talk to God again, 'cause God never, ever fell asleep. He asked Jonah at the pool last time, and that's what Jonah said. God stays awake all the time. In case we need to talk to Him about something.

"God...it's me, Joey. I asked You before, but I think I'll ask You again. In case You were busy last time." He looked out the window. "God, please, could You tell the judge that I don't want to go back to Ohio? I just want to be here with my family. Mommy and Daddy and Gus and Mr. Monkey and Mr. Growls. And that's all."

He thought for a minute. "Oh, and Aunt Beth and Uncle Bill and the cousins. Especially Jonah." He closed his eyes. Sleep was easy after he talked to God. "Thank You, God.

"Gee this name, amen."

TWENTY-FOUR

Beth had never felt so sure of anything in all her life. The social worker never called her back, and now it was nine o'clock, the night before the mission trip. She hadn't confronted Molly again about the possibility that they might run, but even so, she felt the strain in her relationship with her sister.

In the past few days she asked Molly about the hearing—the one that was supposed to buy them more time with Joey. Even with the tension between them, Beth expected Molly to get excited about the hearing results. If they were good, anyway. Instead Molly only shook her head. "It was postponed until next week."

"Is that a bad thing?"

"The attorney still thinks he can get us more time. We're believing him, Beth. What else can we do?"

Nothing Molly had told Beth in the past few months could actually be verified. So Bill had snooped around and called Paul Kerkar, the Realtor. He mentioned his brother-in-law's purchase of a medical building and asked whether Paul knew of other similar properties.

"Perhaps." Paul was pleasant, not suspicious about the call.

"Jack tells me he's closing on the deal any time now—is that right?"

"In the next few weeks, for sure. The building inspection showed the need for a roof repair. That has to be done first."

Bill worked his way out of the conversation. Afterward he looked at Beth and held up his hands. "It's legit. Jack and Molly are buying a building in West Palm."

Still, Beth was worried. She hadn't seen one letter from a politician's office, or any reason why she should believe an attorney was really involved. Molly hadn't gone to any meetings, at least none that she'd mentioned. And even Jack never talked about the person he'd found, the guy's name or his law firm or how come he was able to help them when no one else could.

Now, with the plane leaving in twelve hours, Beth was still terrified that her sister was planning to disappear. She couldn't prove it, but she felt it deep in her bones. The way she had always known what Molly was going to do or how she was feeling or whether she was in trouble.

Because of that, earlier in the day she had called information and found the phone number for Wendy Porter in Cleveland, Ohio. Back when the social worker first contacted Molly and Jack, the details of the case were always a part of Molly's conversation. Though she hadn't mentioned the Ohio couple's name in recent weeks, Beth remembered.

Now, with Bill busy packing, she went upstairs and took a small piece of paper from the pocket of her jeans. The kids were asleep, packed and ready for the morning. She was pretty sure Bill wouldn't want her interfering this way. The conversation with the Realtor was enough to convince him that Molly and Jack weren't planning to run. But what if they were? What choice did she have? If she didn't make the call now, she wouldn't have another chance.

Her heart skipped a beat as she picked up the receiver and punched in the numbers. After a long pause, she heard a ring, and then another. Then the sound of someone answering and a woman's voice saying, "Hello?"

Beth held her breath, willing her heart to settle down so she could focus on what she needed to say. "Yes...hello." She shut her eyes. How could she be doing this, and what would it accomplish? She had no answers for herself, but she was out of options. She rushed on. "My name is Beth Petty. I'm the sister of Molly Campbell."

There was a hesitation on the other end. "You mean, Joey's adoptive mother?" The woman sounded baffled. Her words were breathy and laced with shock. "Why are you calling?"

Here goes.... Beth exhaled and plunged ahead. After this there would be no turning back. "Well, Mrs. Porter, here's the situation...."

❦

Wendy Porter was by herself when the call came in.

She pressed the receiver to her ear and tried to understand why the sister of Joey's adoptive mother would call. The woman was going on, talking about how much the Campbells loved Joey, and what sort of life he lived there in Florida.

"I don't understand." Wendy sat at the kitchen table and put her head in her hands. "I already know the Campbells have been wonderful for my son. But my husband and I are doing very well now, Mrs. Petty. We think it's right for us to have this chance at being Joey's parents—especially since my husband never knew about Joey until a few months ago."

"Right, well, that's why I'm calling." The woman on the other end sounded nervous. "See, something's come up and I think you should know about it."

At that moment, the door flung open and Rip walked in. He had a bag in his arms with a few liquor bottles peeking out the top. Wendy motioned at him to be quiet. She pointed at the phone and covered the speaker. "It's about Joey," she whispered.

He rolled his eyes, set the bag down on the kitchen counter, and pulled out a single bottle. A minute later he was pouring his second glass. He dropped a handful of ice into it and came to stand beside her. "Who is it?"

Wendy was trying to hear. Something about a trip to Haiti and this woman's thoughts that maybe the Campbells wouldn't ever come back to the United States.

"I said, who is it?" Rip's voice boomed at her. Wherever he'd been, he was already drunk. He could barely keep his eyes open.

She waved him off once more. With the phone pressed tight to one ear, she covered the other and tried to hear. "So they're leaving the country? How come I don't know about that?"

Rip made a face. He staggered a little and set his drink down on the table. "Who's leavin' the country?"

"Look." Wendy was sure the woman could hear Rip. The last thing she needed was Molly Campbell's sister knowing that things were out of control at the Porter house. "Can I call you back? I need to take care of something here first."

"Don't wait, please. I'm very concerned about this."

"Okay." Wendy got the woman's number. "Five minutes."

The second she hung up, Rip was on her. He grabbed her shoulder and jerked her to her feet. "What was that about?"

"Rip...please, give me some space." She tried to push him back, but he only dug his fingers into her arm and held on tighter.

She ignored the pain and lowered her voice, anything to help him be calm. "Look, everything's going to work out." Lying was the answer in this case. "No one's leaving the country. Let me take care of the phone call."

He gave her a shove and another glare. "You *make* me do it, you know that?"

This was the worst part of his drinking. He got sloppy and angry, and he started blaming her. "Don't, Rip."

He brushed her off, waving his hand in the air, almost losing his balance in the process. As he turned back to the kitchen, he grabbed his drink and downed it in seconds. A loud belch came from him as he finished. He chuckled and headed into the kitchen.

She watched him, the way she had to watch him when he was in this mood. In case he came at her swinging.

Rip held the liquor bottle up to the light and grinned. "Only the good stuff for me, baby." He poured a third glass and slammed the bottle down. That fast the rage was back and he glared at her. "It's all your fault." He was too unsteady to do much more than lean against the kitchen counter. "You deserve everything you get from me."

Wendy waited for the tirade to die down. There was nothing she could say to him, not now while he was drunk. Tomorrow they would have a talk and she'd encourage him to get back to counseling, back to the alcohol meetings. They were going to lose Joey if Rip didn't do something about his drinking—either that, or he was going to do something to wind up back in prison.

After a minute or so, Rip took his drink and staggered into the living room. He plopped into his recliner, flipped on the television and immediately got lost in some sports show.

This was her chance. Wendy picked up the phone and dialed the woman's number. Whatever she'd been trying to say, something about Haiti and leaving the country, the details sounded serious. Serious enough that the woman would call. Not just to say how much the Campbells loved Joey.

But maybe to warn Wendy of something the Campbells were about to do.

∽⊱

Allyson Bower had enjoyed every minute of her vacation. She and the kids loved taking a week each summer and heading south to Walton Beach in the Florida panhandle for sun and surf and relaxation. There was nowhere Allyson would rather be than sitting on a beach, staring at the water.

Never was the timing of the trip more perfect. The Campbell case had eaten at her all summer, but not for the past week. For most of the past seven days she'd been able to forget about work—at least long enough to enjoy her kids. Now, though, she was back, and her heart was heavy. It was Friday, the first day of Labor Day weekend. In just seven days the Campbells would lose their son forever.

The courts were wrong this time. No matter what the law said, Joey belonged with Molly and Jack Campbell. Allyson had no doubts. She couldn't prove that Rip was back to his violent ways—the little bruises where he'd grabbed Joey were explainable, and not enough to stop the transfer of custody.

But Wendy Porter could cover for her husband for only so long. The man was trouble, and Allyson worried about Joey, about his future once social workers and the system stopped looking in on him.

She surveyed her office. It was perfectly put together, as always. Every paper had its place, every file organized alphabetically. She had a dozen phone calls to make, but first she needed to listen to her messages. After a week away, there were bound to be dozens of them.

Halfway through the messages, a woman's voice rang out from the machine, one Allyson didn't recognize.

"Mrs. Bower, you don't know me. This is Beth Petty, Molly Campbell's sister."

What? Why would Molly Campbell's sister call? Allyson leaned in and turned up the volume.

"This is a very hard phone call to make, but I think you should know I'm concerned that my sister and her husband might be thinking of running, disappearing with Joey. As you know, we're leaving the country a week from today for a work trip to Haiti. I have a suspicion that the Campbells will take false passports with them on that trip. They also have access to an awful lot of money."

Allyson felt the floor beneath her give way. The Campbells' story had checked out; she had convinced the judge. Sure she'd had mild doubts, but never for a minute had she felt convinced that the couple would run. She looked at the calendar on her wall.

By now they would be halfway to Haiti.

The message continued to play. There was a coughing sound, as if maybe Molly's sister was choked up or crying. "Please, Mrs. Bower, if this concerns you, call me as soon as you get this message." The woman left her number, and the message came to an end.

Allyson pushed the stop button on the answering machine, gripped the armrests of her chair, and hung her head. Had she missed something? And how come this Beth Petty hadn't called someone else at the department if she was so worried her sister would leave the country and never come back? If the woman was right—if the Campbells had a plan to run—it would be all Allyson's fault.

The judge would demand to know why she had recommended in favor of the trip, and the Porters would have grounds to sue the department. Especially since they weren't notified. If Molly Campbell's sister was right, Allyson's career, her livelihood, and her future, were about to be destroyed.

Never mind that. She didn't blame the Campbells. It was her job to see that the law was followed, to make sure that whatever the system deemed best for a child was carried through. She pressed her knuckles to her brow. Who should she call first? The judge, probably. Yes, definitely. He could get things moving the fastest, contact authorities in Haiti and see that the Campbells were apprehended and brought back. Before they had time to commit a crime.

She went to pick up the phone, but just then it rang. She jumped, startled, then grabbed the receiver. Whoever it was, she needed to hurry. She didn't have time for other business until she contacted the judge. A quick tap on the right blinking light and she pressed the phone to her ear. "Hello?"

"Allyson Bower?" The woman on the other end was crying.

"Yes, this is she." Allyson looked at the clock on the wall. Every minute counted. She took a quick breath. "How can I help you?"

"This is Wendy Porter." The woman was definitely crying.

Allyson felt the blood rush from her face. "What's wrong, Wendy?"

For a long while, there was only the sound of the woman's sobs. Then, with a shaky voice she said, "There's something I need to tell you."

TWENTY-FIVE

The main road out of the airport and through Port-au-Prince was littered with potholes and broken-down cars. Molly and Jack sat in the third row of a rusty old van, Joey tucked safely between them. Molly's mind kept shouting the obvious at her. They were really here. They'd gotten out of the States, and in just a few days they'd be in Europe, pretending they were tourists—and a few weeks after that, they'd be in the Cayman Islands. It was working. The plan was working.

Her heart filled with equal amounts of joy and sorrow at the prospect.

Jesper, their driver, pointed to a building on their right. It was made of white, crumbling bricks, and it looked seriously damaged. "This is hospital." He smiled. "Hospital stay open even after hurricane."

Seated in front were Beth, Bill, and Jonah. The backseat was filled with the other Petty kids, most of whom were sleeping. In the van behind them were three college kids who would round out their group, and a leader from the college group at church. He would supervise their work at the orphanage.

Molly did everything she could to listen to Jesper. It took her mind off the details that still had to come together before they could leave Haiti.

Jesper was a gracious man with dark skin and bright eyes. He had a deep faith, that much was clear from the moment he met them.

"God give you a good trip, yes?" His smile lit up his face.

"Yes." Bill answered for them. "God gave us a great trip. Thank you."

Jesper went on about God's favor and God's mercy and God's providence, all while he was gathering their bags and leading the way back out to the van. He hadn't stopped talking since he picked them up.

At the moment he was talking about the faith of the Haitian people. "God is everything to people in my country. The people not committed to darkness." He gestured to the masses teeming on either side of the highway. "You see? You see how people live? God is everything."

Molly could hardly believe how the people lived.

Because of the broken-down cars and the occasional cyclist pulling a cart or the random person herding animals along in one of the lanes, travel was slow. It gave all of them a chance to take in the surroundings. Joey was sleeping between the two of them, but Jack was mesmerized by the sights, same as her.

They passed rows of dwellings that were little more than shanties, small shacks with dirt floors, some of them without even a roof. Very obviously most of them did not have electricity or running water. The people moving on the broken sidewalks carried large containers on their heads, and wove their way around what looked like one continuous flea market.

Jesper came to a grinding halt and slammed his hand on the horn. All the vehicles around him did the same thing. Up ahead, a pick-up truck had stopped in the middle of the road so six or seven guys could jump out the back and dodge through traffic to the side of the road.

The guys waved, friendly-like, but before traffic could pick up again, there was a thud and the van jolted.

"What was—" Bill and Beth spun around.

Molly and Jack did the same thing, and there, clinging to the back of the van, were two young men.

Jesper laughed. "Americans think strange that people take rides from each other." He rolled down his window and gave a thumbs-up sign to the men now hanging from the back of the van. "Bondye reme ou!"

Molly knew that one. *God loves you.* She smiled despite the absurdity of it all. Jesper picked up speed, and somehow the men clinging to the back held on. The next time traffic ground to a stop, they hopped off, waved, and went their way.

The stop gave Molly the chance to notice a village woman sitting in front of a dirty stone table. She looked haggard and weary, dressed in a rag skirt and blouse, her hair tied back. Before traffic eased enough for Jesper to move the van, the woman grabbed a chicken from a cage of squawking birds on the ground next to her.

She pressed the chicken's neck against the big dirty rock and grabbed a butcher knife. In seconds, the deed was done, and deftly the woman skinned and gutted the bird, tossing the meat into a bin behind her. A swarm of flies lifted as the meat fell into the container.

Molly felt a wave of nausea and looked at Jack. His face was pale and he nodded. He'd seen the same thing. Bill turned around and whispered, "Good thing we brought canned tuna."

"Definitely." Molly managed a smile. She tapped Beth on the shoulder. "Did you see that?" Her voice was barely audible, since Jesper was still talking up front.

"What?" Beth looked distracted. She'd been that way ever since they boarded the plane in West Palm Beach.

"The chicken, did you see the woman with the chicken?"

"No." Beth held her gaze for a moment. "I guess I have a lot on my mind."

Molly wanted to ask what, but she was afraid of her sister's answer. They had struggled since the day Beth asked if she and Jack were going to run. Molly guessed her sister was still worried about that fact. But Beth must know there was nothing she could do now.

An ache filled Molly's heart as Beth turned and faced the front of the van again. *My sweet sister...if only I could tell you, if only I could say good-bye the way I want to say it. Please...don't be mad at me forever.* She sighed and Jack looked at her. He put his arm along the back of the seat and stroked her shoulder. His look said not to worry. Everything would be okay.

She gave him a worried smile. It would have to be okay. They had no choice now.

Jesper was going on about the worship times. "Hours of singing, because the people know that God is everything. All we have, all we need."

Molly had a feeling that someday very soon, if she and Jack and Joey were going to survive their new life, they just might be saying the same thing.

❧

Beth wanted to focus on the trip, on the experience at hand, especially as they approached the orphanage. But every few minutes she found herself looking at her sister, trying to read her actions, her eyes, her tone. Was she wrong? Was everything really the way Molly had explained it? Could it be that she was only the victim of an overly active imagination—the way Bill suspected?

Jesper directed their attention to the buildings on their left. "The first is the orphanage, and next to it, the mission house."

Both sat behind thick brick walls, easily eight feet high. Along the top row of stone were loops of sharp razor wire. The windows in the van were open now, and they could hear the clamoring of children on the other side of the wall.

"Orphanage and mission house need security," Jesper said.

Beth assumed that most of Port-au-Prince must need security, since all the buildings on that street had similar walls and razor wire.

A guard with a rifle rolled open a heavy iron gate for them. He grinned at Jesper and tipped his worn baseball cap. The van pulled in and parked in the narrow driveway. "This is the mission house. We will walk to orphanage."

The Petty kids and Joey were all awake now, asking Jesper questions as quickly as he could answer them. They piled out through the side door, grabbing luggage from under the seats and trying to make sense of the chaos. The van with the three college kids and the young pastor pulled in and parked behind them.

"Who lives at the mission house?" Cammie climbed out of the backseat. Blain and Braden followed her.

"Volunteers and visiting Americans." Jesper smiled. "Today...you and your family!"

"What do people eat here?" Braden rubbed his eyes. "I'm hungry."

"Faun will have rice feast in one hour." Jesper's voice rang with pride. "We take good care American guests."

The questions continued as they pulled their suitcases into the house. "Were we supposed to bring pillows?" Bill uttered the question quietly as they made their way up the walk.

"I don't think so." Jack looked over his shoulder and smiled. "But I did, anyway. You never know."

Beth watched the men, not sure what to feel. This was something new, the way they got along and made small talk so easily. Was it genuine—something that had come from their prayer meeting? Or was this new camaraderie only Jack's way of getting along with Bill, keeping suspicions at bay until he and Molly and Joey made their break?

The men from the other van trailed them into the house. The leader said something about putting their suitcases away and heading over to the orphanage to meet the children. *Good,* Beth told herself. *Let them go.* It would take longer to get their two families settled at the mission house, and that meant Beth had more time to study her sister. Without the group leader interrupting.

She watched Molly, the easy way her sister smiled at Joey and Jack as one of the volunteers met them and directed them to a room off to the left. If they were planning a getaway, they didn't show it. They seemed surprisingly at ease. Beth was suddenly assaulted by doubt. What if she was wrong? How could she ever expect Molly to forgive her for the questions she'd asked, and the way she'd been acting?

Beth had no answers for herself. They were led to their rooms, and Bill nodded his approval. "Running water and electricity. I'd say they treat their guests very well."

"I hope they treat the orphans this nicely." Cammie grabbed her suitcase and flung it on her bunk bed. "I can't wait to meet them."

Again Beth was pulled back into the moment. They were here to take part in a work trip, after all. It was time to stop worrying about Molly and Jack and Joey. This was a once-in-a-lifetime experience for her own kids. She worked her bag beneath her bunk and sat on the edge of the mattress.

Suddenly tears blurred her vision, and she closed her eyes. For months she'd been preaching to Molly and Jack that the answer lay in praying for God's will. Trust God, she'd told them. He knows what's best for Joey, even if it doesn't seem best to you. But what had she, herself, been doing?

The whole time she'd been trying to teach Molly and Jack about faith, she'd been walking in her own strength entirely. Not once had she prayed about her doubts where Molly and Jack were concerned. Sure, she kept praying for Joey, that her sister would get to keep her son. But every time she felt doubts about what Molly and Jack might be planning, she turned into a detective, firing questions at her sister and snooping for clues.

Even the phone calls to the social worker and to Wendy Porter were done without so much as a single bit of communication with God. No wonder she'd been plagued by doubt and fear. She had no peace, because she hadn't taken her own advice.

Now she bowed her head and covered her face. The kids were distracted, heading out into the main room with Bill. Only Jonah remained, and he must've heard her crying.

"What're you doing, Mommy?" Jonah bounced down next to her. "Are you sad?"

"No, not really." She sniffed and put her arm around him. "Mommy needs a minute to pray."

"Is it okay if I play with Blain and Braden?"

"Yes, sweetie. Go ahead."

Jonah ran off, and Beth covered her face once more. Then she did what her soul had been crying for since she woke up that morning. *God...forgive me for my doubts and suspicions. I've tried so hard to be my sister's keeper, when You already know exactly what's going to happen. Help me remember the joy of my salvation and the certainty of Your truth, Father.* She wiped at her tears. They were meeting for the rice feast in just ten minutes. *And, God...I beg You that Your will be done for Molly and Jack and Joey. From this minute on I'll trust You—whatever happens.*

She opened her eyes and stood up. Without a doubt she knew what she was going to do the moment she saw Molly. She would sit beside her at the rice feast, and before another minute passed, she would do what she should've done a long time ago.

She would apologize.

~∞~

TWENTY-SIX

J ack could feel his heart changing.

On the inside where his existence had been all confidence and self-assurance, something was happening, a softening—a knowing that somehow all his life, just maybe he'd been wrong. He hadn't expected this kind of change to happen at this stage of the plan. The trip to Haiti, the work...It was all part of the guise to get them out of the country. But after a day of working with the Haitian people and the volunteers at the orphanage, Jack could see that Jesper was right.

God *was* everything to them.

It was their second full day in Haiti, and Jesper suggested a trip into the city. Day excursions were a scheduled part of the work trip, a way to take food and supplies to the people in the streets. For Jack, the day trips had been his guarantee that the plan would work. Once they were on the city streets, anything could happen. And he would make sure it did.

They'd spent that morning working with the children and the volunteers at the orphanage. Bill watched as Joey and the Petty kids mingled with the orphans. The children had only one small play room, a square area with a tile floor and no furniture. There were maybe four or five toys among more than forty boys and girls.

"I thought the church back home sent toys and clothes to these kids," Jack said to Jesper.

He smiled. "Kids get lots of toys and clothes. Much more than children on street." He motioned toward the front gate. "Volunteers box up things Americans send, give to family and friends on street who have nothing."

The answer was humbling.

They set to work repairing a collapsed wall on the south side of the orphanage, and at break time Jack found Joey with six little boys. He had a protein bar for his son, and a few others for the orphans. Hardly enough to go around.

He pulled Joey aside. "Hey, sport, I have a snack for you. Think you could share with the other boys?"

Joey's blue eyes shone with love. "O' course, Daddy." He took the bars and ran back to the circle of boys.

Joey broke the bars into small bits and gave each of the boys a piece. The children were overwhelmed with joy. They marveled and held up their snack, chattering in Creole, obviously excited. What Jack saw next only added to the strange feeling inside him. Each of the Haitian children took their piece and ran to a group of the other children. Still chattering and gesturing in sheer joy, they broke off piece after piece until every child in the orphanage had a small bite.

Jesper found Jack watching. The man put his arm around Jack's shoulders. "They understand God's teaching. Better to give than to receive."

Jack didn't know what to say. He could hardly wait to

tell Molly. What children back home would act that way, would think of others the way these kids did? Here they had nothing to their name, but when given a gift, they couldn't wait to share it. Back on the damaged wall, Jack took up his place with a hammer and a bag of nails alongside. Working next to him was an orphanage volunteer named Franz. Franz spoke broken English, and, like Jesper, he was talkative.

"God saved my family." Franz positioned a nail and sent it through a new piece of wood with a single blow from his hammer. He was built like Mike Tyson, but he had the tenderness of a child. "We have no food, dying on streets. Me and wife beg God for mercy, for help." He motioned to Jesper. "Next day Jesper come to us and ask work at orphanage for food and house." He pointed up to the hazy blue sky overhead. "Good God, our God. Very good."

"Yes." Jack would've had trouble denying the fact.

The day trips took place at three that afternoon, during naptime for the orphans. The college guys—including their group leader—were going to the roughest neighborhood in the area. The Petty family was headed for a busy street of townspeople a few blocks away, and the Campbells to another. They would take food bags and supplies to the people and distribute booklets written in Creole, explaining the message of hope in Christ and the path to salvation.

The pastor back at Bethel Bible Church had encouraged them that they didn't need to do anything more than smile at the people and be kind. "Anyone can do this; theological training isn't necessary. Remember...it's a *work* trip. The booklet says it all."

As they set out, Molly turned to Jack. "I'll be watching."

He nodded. They'd talked about it the night before. Being out on the street that afternoon would give them their only chance to make a plan. Then, the next day, they would ask to go to the same place, the same neighborhood. From there they would figure out their escape.

They had packed lightly for the trip, because there was no way to take their suitcases on a day trip into Port-au-Prince. Whatever they could fit in their backpacks and Molly's single roll-aboard would be all they could take. So that they wouldn't raise suspicions the following day, they brought the exact same bags with them for this current day trip.

"Why the suitcase?" Franz was their driver. He gave Molly a funny grin. "You Americans always take bags."

"I have allergies." Molly patted her bag. The lie tasted like rotten eggs on her tongue. "This has my food and medicine. In case we're gone for longer than we expect."

Franz gave an exaggerated shrug, but he never stopped smiling. "Fine with me. Throw in the back."

On the way to the neighborhood, Molly leaned around Joey and spoke low near Jack's ear. "I forgot to tell you. Beth apologized yesterday."

"Really?" He was surprised. "I sort of figured she still doubted us, like she'd be the first one on our trail when we go."

"She will be." Molly angled her head. "But I think she's done worrying about it. Almost like whatever her fears are, she's letting them go."

Jack let the notion settle into his heart. More proof that the faith Beth and Bill lived by was strong enough to change people. He looked out the window and studied the shacks and makeshift tables with wares for sale. There were so many people, all of them existing without any reason for hope.

The people who walked the streets were empty-eyed for the most part. Some sat on street corners, their heads in their hands, waiting for another day to pass. Others were hunched over in front of a table of dusty candy or bottled water, hoping to make a few dollars before evening came.

Only at the orphanage and in the mission house were the Haitian people alive and full of love and joy. Whatever Jack had thought about Christianity in the past, there was no denying its positive impact on their hosts.

Franz drove another ten minutes, then he turned down a narrow alleyway. At the other end, a village of people was gathered in what looked like a small courtyard. "We work here, yes?" Franz glowed at the possibility.

"Yes." Jack glanced around. Every eye was on them. He had thought once or twice about the possibility that this part of the trip could be dangerous for them, for Joey. He gave Molly a look. "Don't let go of his hand."

"I won't." He saw the fear in her eyes and he knew. She was afraid of more than the villagers.

Last night after everyone else was asleep, she had climbed into Jack's bunk and held onto him. "I'm so scared, Jack. What if we get caught?"

"We won't." He smoothed her hair and kissed her. "Have I told you lately how beautiful you are?"

She buried her head in his shoulder. "I'm serious, Jack. What if it doesn't work?"

"It will." The whispered conversation went on for nearly an hour before she fell asleep, her head still on his chest.

Now, her eyes were wide with the enormity of the task that lay ahead of them. They would have to greet people, pass out food and supplies and the church tracts, and somehow make contact with someone who would help them. That, or figure out a way to get lost, and then catch a ride to the airport before anyone found them.

Franz climbed out first. With his big voice and bigger smile, he announced something in Creole. Then he took the food and supply boxes from the back of the truck and set them on the ground. He said something else, and the people drew closer.

"I hope he told them we're friendly," Jack said, his voice low.

"Me, too." Molly clutched Joey.

"Is this the part where we tell people about God?" Joey was excited, but not the least bit worried. He had no idea of all that lay ahead.

"Yes, buddy." Molly kissed the top of his head. "This is that part."

They were waiting in the car for the signal from Franz, and at that moment he opened their door and motioned for them to climb out. "People are ready for their gifts."

Jack knew it was up to him. With Molly terrified and worried about Joey, the three of them wouldn't be friendly enough to attract the right type of people. His behavior would have to make up for theirs. While Molly and Joey stayed with Franz, Jack would mingle with the people.

The first half hour, they worked so hard filling the people's needs that they didn't have time to think of anything else. But after that the crowd started to break up. Somehow word must've gotten out, because carloads of people arrived, looking for a handout. The weather was much like South Florida, humid and tropical. Cumulus clouds gathered in the distance, and Jack checked his watch. It was four o'clock. They didn't have long.

Now and then he looked over the crowd to Molly and Joey and Franz. Once in a while Franz would see someone he knew and follow that person. Sometimes he was gone for three, even four minutes. Once he didn't return for fifteen. He had explained that he knew people in this area, and that sometimes he needed to visit someone at their house. "They need pray and visit," he said. "You be fine here."

The situation was working out perfectly. If Franz was given to brief disappearances, then tomorrow they could use a moment like that to run. But none of it would happen if Jack didn't figure out a contact. If not today, then tomorrow, when they were fleeing on foot. Someone who could get them to the airport.

"Bondye reme ou," Jack told each person. "Do you speak English?"

Most of them shook their heads. They took the food and supplies and tracts and didn't linger around the Americans. Jack began surveying the perimeter of the square. In the distance he saw several cars, each of them with a driver.

He made his way back to Franz and Molly and Joey. "What are they doing?" He pointed to the drivers. "Should I take them some gifts?"

"Why not?" Franz grinned. "They are drivers. Like... cabbies in America." His smile faded. "Most have no work, just sit. Some run drugs for drug lords."

Jack had wondered as much. In the distance there was a

light rumble, the first bit of thunder. "How much longer, Franz?"

"We stay until gifts gone." He squinted at the sky. It was still sunny where they were. "Or until big storm. Whatever first."

Molly cast him a nervous glance before turning her attention back to the people. The women and children were gathered around her and Joey—there seemed no shortage of them.

Jack scanned the cars again.

He filled his arms with gift bags and tracts and approached the drivers. Two looked uninterested, and a third was in a conversation with someone—a shady looking older man. But the fourth smiled at him and held out his hand. "Hello, American."

English! The man spoke English! Jack held up the gift bags and made his way to the man. "Hello! Bondye reme ou."

"God loves everyone!" The man chuckled. "I speak English, friend." He leaned out his car window. "What you bring me today?"

Jack gave the man several bags, some with food, some with supplies.

"You keep your book." He pointed up and winked. "I already know God. Good, good God."

"Yes." Jack felt a shiver pass over his spine. Indeed. He looked over his shoulder. Franz was deeply involved in a conversation, and Molly and Joey were still reaching into the supply box, handing out bags. He rested his elbow on the man's car. "You are a driver?"

"Yes." He gripped his steering wheel. "God gives Tancredo enough work." He motioned to the other men. "Others, dirty drivers." He lowered his voice. "Drugs...bad." His smile was back and he thumped his chest. "Tancredo drive for God."

Jack would've believed anything at that point. He took a breath and steadied himself. "My wife and son and I need a ride to the airport tomorrow. At this time."

Tancredo clapped his hands. "Yes, I do that. Tomorrow. Same time."

Jack took a few steps back. He didn't want to attract attention. "I will pay you a hundred dollars for the ride, okay?"

The man's mouth hung open. "One hundred?"

"Yes. But you say nothing. God has told us that we must escape tomorrow. For our boy's safety." He pointed down the alley. "You meet us at the end of this street. Okay?"

Tancredo looked slightly confused, but he nodded. "God tells you, I say nothing." He placed his hand over his mouth. "Tancredo drive, nothing more. I meet you in hidden place. End of alley, two streets to the left."

"End of alley, two streets to the left." Jack couldn't believe their luck. A driver who spoke English and understood their need for discretion. From the corner of his eye, he saw Franz walking toward them. Jack took another few steps backward and waved at Tancredo. "Bondye reme ou."

"Oui, Bondye reme ou!" The driver held up his gift bag and then leaned back against his headrest, resuming his wait for a customer.

"You did good, Jack." Franz fell in step beside Jack. "You make friends with Haitian people. God smiles at you."

Jack wasn't sure what to feel. How could God smile at him? He wasn't making friends, he was making plans to break the law, to run from his own country. He dismissed the thought and pointed at the supply box. "Are the bags gone?"

"All given out!" Franz held up his hands toward heaven. "God glorified this day, this place."

The ride back was quiet except for the occasional Bible reference or exclamation by Franz. Jack couldn't wait to tell Molly what had happened, but he didn't dare do it until they were alone. As they started back, he turned to Franz. "Can we come back here tomorrow—same place? I told one of the men to bring his friends because we'd be back."

"Yes, good plan." Franz grinned and stared at the sky. "Storm will be big tonight."

Halfway back to the orphanage, they stopped for gas. Rain had just started pelting the area. The station was a cacophony of chaos—fifteen or twenty people selling a hundred worn-out, tired-looking things, and large mounds of trash dotting the perimeter, each with a couple of skinny pigs rooting through them.

As soon as Franz left the car to find the attendant, Jack turned to Molly. "It's perfect. I met a driver."

"I saw." Their conversation was hushed, their words fast. Once more Joey was asleep between them, so there was no danger of him hearing. "What's the plan?"

"His name is Tancredo. We meet him there tomorrow. We'll keep your bag with us at all times, our backpacks on. When Franz goes off to meet with one of the villagers, we wander down the alley and run for it. The driver will be waiting."

He gave her arm a tender pat. "I have it all figured out, Molly. You can relax."

"I feel sick." She pulled Joey close and buried her face in his blond hair. Jack wasn't sure, but he thought she was crying. Tears stung his own eyes, too. They were doing what they had to do for their son, the only way they knew to protect him.

Jack would like to have left on the first or second day, but they needed to follow the schedule, needed a day in the village in order to make connections. And now they were just one day from seeing it all work out.

When they got back to the orphanage, they put Joey down for a short rest and made a plan to play cards with Beth and Bill in the common room before dinner. The college guys and the group leader had gathered with them that morning for breakfast and a briefing about the dangers of heading into the village. That night the group would split up so the guys could work with the orphans. Jack was glad for the sense of privacy. Before meeting with Beth and Bill, he led Molly to the corner of their room.

"Listen, I have an idea." He looked over his shoulder— no one was listening in on their conversation. His eyes met Molly's again, and he spoke quickly. "Tomorrow I'll take one of my T-shirts, rip it and get it dirty, and smear it with my blood."

"Jack!" The color drained from her face. "That sounds like a horror film."

"No, I'll just prick my finger. It won't be much blood, just enough that it'll look like something bad happened to us. I'll leave that on the street when we take off with the driver."

Molly still looked shocked. But gradually, as the information sank in, she nodded. "So it might throw them off the trail?"

"Yes, even for a few days." His mind ran ahead of him. "Because of the custody issue, it won't take them long to figure out we staged the shirt thing. But we can use every extra hour to get away."

"Okay. I get it."

"Anyway, by the time people realize what happened, we'll be on our way to Stockholm." They would buy tickets at the airport counter for a flight out to Europe. Jack had the schedule memorized. If there was room on the flight, they'd book one with Sweden as a final destination. Small enough that international police wouldn't yet have word of their disappearance, and with a local population blond enough that they'd fit right in.

"Molly?" It was Beth. She was standing at the doorway holding a deck of cards. "You guys ready?"

"Sure." Molly practically lurched from her spot. She took Jack's hand. "Come on, we can talk about this with Beth and Bill."

Jack was impressed. It was the best cover Molly had done since they'd gotten there. An hour later they were still gathered around the table playing cards and swapping stories of their day in the villages. The rice and bean dinner was almost ready, and like every other day, their hosts wouldn't think of letting them help with preparations.

A sense of euphoria and sorrow mingled and swept over Jack. This was their last night with Bill and Beth. Just when he was beginning to really like them. Their kids were all awake now, playing their own card game on the living room floor. Molly had mentioned several times that maybe someday—when the heat was off—they could return to the United States and reconnect with Bill and Beth.

Jack doubted it, but in that moment, it was a nice thought.

His eyes met Molly's and he knew. She was feeling the same thing, the nostalgia of the moment, the finality of it. Their last night of any sort of normalcy for what could be a very long time.

Molly laid down the final card in her hand. "Beth ... how could I forget?" She groaned. "I should've saved you a spade." She pressed her fist against her forehead. "And we were winning, too."

"It's okay." Beth leaned back and grinned. "We're still killing the guys. I can't really be—"

Before she could finish her sentence, the front door of the mission house burst open and five armed officers rushed in. "Police!" Their English pronunciation was better than most. "Everyone freeze!"

Jack's head began to spin. What was this? How could police get past the guard at the gate without at least a warning to the people in the mission house, and why were they there? All nine of them froze, and from the kitchen three volunteers rushed into the room, shouting at the police in Creole.

On the floor, the children didn't know what to do. Cammie and Blain lifted their hands slowly, as if they were under arrest. Braden and Jonah and Joey scampered to their parents. Jonah started to cry.

One of the mission-house workers took the lead. He stormed across the floor right up to the police, gesturing and talking in Creole. His tone was angry, offended. One of the policemen seemed to be in charge. He gestured back, and rattled off several lines of some sort of a response.

Across the table, Molly looked at Jack. She was pale, and he shot her a stern look. *Don't lose control now.* She swallowed and barely moved her head in a single nod. She wouldn't give them away.

"What in the—" Bill whispered to Beth, and she shook her head.

Only then did Jack see it, the look in Beth's eyes. It wasn't fear and shock like the rest of them. It was something unmistakable, a look Jack had never seen in Beth as long as he'd known her.

The look was guilt.

TWENTY-SEVEN

Molly couldn't breathe or speak or move. She didn't need anyone to tell her why the police had barged in shouting orders. She knew as certainly as she knew her heart was about to beat through her chest.

She looked at Beth. The guilt in her sister's eyes was so strong it might as well have been written on her face, and suddenly Molly could feel their plans unraveling. They were caught! They would be taken in and questioned and sent back to the United States. Law enforcement would be waiting for them, and Joey would be whisked away forever.

Black spots danced before her eyes, and she felt faint. That's when Jack fired another look at her. She couldn't fall apart, not now. Not with Joey clinging to her and the children watching. She turned away from Beth and saw the mission worker approach them. His face was troubled.

"The police have an order." He twisted his expression, confused. "This never happen before." He came closer, his steps slow. His eyes met Jack's. "You and your wife and son—police want all three. They have orders from embassy."

Molly clung tightly to Joey. There it was. She was right; they were caught. Only one person could've done this to them. She turned and looked at Beth. In a rush all the thousands of times she'd looked at her sister came back....

Beth was tugging on her arm, and they were three and five years old. "Wanna play dolls, Molly?"

And Molly was taking her sister's hand and finding a place on the floor beside her. And then they were a little older, and Beth was looking at her from her bicycle seat, Molly the hero for taking time to work with Beth while their dad was in the house. And they were in high school and Beth was holding her up, telling her that Connor Aiken was a jerk. And they were a year older, cheering at a basketball game and grinning at each other because no other two cheerleaders were ever as much in sync as they were. Then it was the middle of the afternoon, Christmas break, and Art Goldberg's mother was on the phone. "I have some bad news for you, Molly...." And Molly was in a heap on the floor, and through her tears, through her swollen eyes, there was Beth, promising her everything would be okay, someday, one day. And they were sitting next to each other at the park a few months ago, and Molly was saying how glad she was that they were neighbors, and Beth was hugging her and saying, "You'll always be my best friend."

Every one of those scenes flashed through her mind in the time it took her to look at her sister and say the only thing she could think to say. The question that would haunt her until the day she died. "How could you?" Her words were barely audible.

Jack and the mission worker were talking, trying to make sense of the police order. But the police had barked something else, filling the moment with urgency.

Beth shook her head, as if she might try to deny her

part in what was happening. Her lips parted but no words came.

The kids were crying now, all of them. The older ones hung on to each other, still sitting cross-legged in the middle of the floor. The younger boys still clung to their parents. Joey climbed up in Molly's lap. "Are the police taking us away?"

Molly was furious with herself, and with Beth. With Jack, too. What had they been thinking? Of course they couldn't get away with their crazy plan. Now Joey had to be exposed to more trauma, and worse—their chances at keeping custody of him were over. Forever.

She stared at Beth, unwilling to turn away. "You turned us in.... Beth, how could you?"

Beth opened her mouth again, but this time Jack interrupted. He stood and held his hand out to Molly. "Let's go. We need to see what they want. It's an order from the embassy."

Molly felt detached from her body. She shot a last look at Beth and Bill and the kids. Then she took Joey's hand and followed Jack. Halfway across the room, she stopped. "Our things."

Jack said something to the mission worker, and the man spoke Creole to the officer. After a brief exchange, he shook his head at Jack. "Police say you need nothing. Just yourself."

"M-M-Mommy...where are we g-g-going?" Joey clung to her. His eyes were wide, and though he had stopped crying, he looked beyond frightened.

"Stay with me, buddy. It'll be okay."

Her last glimpse of Beth was enough to stir a new level

of fury inside her. Beth had her head bowed, as if she was
praying. Of all things. Molly wanted to scream at her and
cry out to her all at the same time. It was too late for prayer
now. The damage was done, and it was done by one of the
people she loved most in the whole world.

The police led them out to a van, helped them inside,
and hurried off through the streets. It was just after six
o'clock—still daylight. Molly and Jack and Joey sat in a
compartment clearly designated for criminals. A plastic
shield separated them from the officers.

Molly reached for Jack, grabbed at his arm. "I...I can't
breathe."

"Mommy!" Joey jumped up onto his knees and looked
her right in the face. "Why can't you breathe?"

"Molly...don't!" Jack faced her, his eyes stern. "We
haven't done anything wrong."

She closed her eyes. *Come on, Molly, get a grip. Don't
panic.* She held her breath. Then she forced air from her
lips, once, twice, and a third time. After that a slight bit of
air made its way into her lungs. She opened her eyes and
somehow smiled at Joey. "Mommy's fine." Her words were
breathy, hardly okay. "Don't worry."

"Listen..." Jack took hold of her wrist and gave her a
light shake. "We've been caught, yes. But we haven't done
anything wrong, not yet." He changed places with Joey so
he could whisper to her without their son hearing.

Molly's head hurt. What was Jack talking about? Of
course they'd broken rules—they'd made a plan to leave the
country illegally under assumed identities. "Jack...think
of our plan. The false passports, the money. Of course
we've done something wrong."

"No, not yet. There's nothing illegal about buying a passport, or moving cash to a foreign account, or taking a work trip. The crime comes in *using* the passport or leaving Haiti under our new names." He was whispering, his words sharp and intense. "Being here doesn't make us criminals. We had permission from the judge, remember?"

Gradually, like the sun breaking a new morning, Jack's words started to make sense. He was right. They hadn't broken any law yet. "So what's this about?" She hissed, still terrified. In all her life she never dreamed she'd be here, in the back of a police van heading to the U.S. Embassy. They were in bigger trouble than they ever imagined.

Jack thought hard. "Ever since the police burst into the place, I've been asking myself the same thing. Was it the driver, Tancredo? Did he talk to Franz, maybe?"

"I didn't see them say anything to each other."

"Maybe it was Franz, maybe he heard something." Jack leaned his forehead against hers. "Baby, I'm so sorry. I can't believe this is happening."

"So you're saying..." She forced herself to breathe slower, to catch her breath before she started hyperventilating again. "We haven't done anything illegal, but someone found out about...about our plan?"

His eyes welled up with tears. "It looks that way."

"So...it had to be Beth." Molly raised one shoulder. "She was the only one who suspected anything..."

"Beth?" Jack gritted his teeth. "This better not be her doing." He pressed his fists into his knees. "How could she call herself a Christian if she turned us in for protecting our son? Can you tell me that?"

"Jack...please." Molly felt dizzy, unable to process

everything that was happening. This was their fault, not Beth's. She had only done what she must've thought was best, maybe thinking somehow that she was helping them. But they were to blame, she and Jack. They had mocked God, using the church as a means of breaking the law. If anything, this was happening as God's way of punishing them. "This isn't about Beth—it's about us. We never should've tried to escape. If we're caught, it's too late for anger."

"I know." His shoulders slumped a little. "It's too late for everything. But we had to try, Molly."

"Meaning they'll take Joey from us?" She felt panicked by the idea. She wasn't ready to say good-bye. "Jack, is that what you're saying?"

"Molly...I'm so sorry, baby." Jack put one arm around Joey and the other around her. Joey looked at them, wondering. But he didn't ask questions. Instead he buried his little blond head in Jack's side and the three of them said nothing else the rest of the ride.

The police took them to a two-story red brick building with a small sign that read U.S. Embassy.

This is it, Molly told herself. *They'll take Joey and we'll never see him again.* Some crazy part of her wanted to turn around and run, grab Joey and Jack by the hand and run until she felt the rip of bullets in her back. Life would be over, anyway. If Joey was taken from them, how would any of them survive?

"This way." One of the officers opened their door. His voice and face were equally stiff.

Dear God....No! Was this what Beth meant by God's

will? Had God wanted Joey with the Porters all along, the nice lady Joey had talked about? They walked across a bumpy street and the police officers led them up a narrow outdoor staircase. At the top of the stairs, the officer who seemed to be in charge opened the door and ushered them inside.

It was a holding room, a waiting area. The police formed a fortress that blocked the door. The one who spoke English pointed to the sofa. "You sit there."

Jack took her hand and the three of them did as they were told. Joey sat between them. Molly could feel him shaking, and she wasn't sure what to do. If these were their last moments together, then she had things to tell him, things that would take a year at best. But now they had only minutes, and she didn't know where to begin.

She put him on her lap and cradled his head close to her face. "Joey, Mommy loves you." The tears came then. They choked her voice, but she pressed on. If this was her only chance to tell him good-bye, then nothing was going to stop her. "Whatever happens, I want you to remember that, okay?"

He brushed up close to her ear. "I love you, too."

Jack seemed to sense what was going on. They exchanged a look, and the heartache between them was suffocating. Jack put his arm around Joey and leaned closer. "You know what? You're Daddy's special guy, sport. I love you so much." His voice cracked. He dropped it to a whisper. "You keep talking to God, okay?"

Molly hurt all over. When this nightmare came to an end, when she and Jack were left to pick up the pieces and start over again, maybe they would make the next attempt at living life the way Beth and Bill did. With God in the lead.

She was about to tell Joey that if someone ever took her away from him, she would love him all her life and always she would ask God to bring him back to her, but she didn't get the chance. The door beyond the officers opened, and two uniformed men entered the room.

One of them stayed near the officers, the other— clearly an American—stepped toward them. He had a piece of paper in his hands, and he looked at Jack. "Jack Campbell?"

"Yes, sir." Jack straightened. His voice wasn't afraid, but resigned.

Molly hung her head. They were caught; there was no getting around the fact.

"Molly Campbell?"

She looked at the man and nodded. "Yes, sir." This was the part where he would explain that the authorities knew about their plan. He would tell them they were being immediately deported because of their flight risk, and he would explain that Joey would be traveling with a police escort to Ohio, where his biological parents awaited custody.

Molly held her breath and waited.

The man came a few steps closer. "Mr. and Mrs. Campbell, I work for the U.S. Embassy here in Haiti. I've received urgent word from the United States. I was asked by order of a judge in Ohio to locate you and give you details of a message from"—he looked at the paper—"Social Worker Allyson Bower."

A message? What was the man talking about? Again

Molly's head was spinning. She held on to Joey so she wouldn't topple onto the floor.

Jack leaned forward. "Sir..." He looked equally confused. "I'm not sure I understand."

The man held up the paper. "Let me read the message. 'You are hereby notified that by order of Judge Randall Grove, Cleveland District Court, the case regarding custody of Joey Campbell has been dropped. From this point on, full and permanent custody is assigned to you, Jack and Molly Campbell.'"

"What?" Jack was on his feet. He looked at Molly and then at the man standing before them. "The case has been dropped?"

Relief washed over Molly immediately. Sobs tore at her, and she leaned back into the sofa, holding Joey close, rocking him. It wasn't possible. They were here to say good-bye, to be hauled back to the United States and reprimanded for ever thinking they could outsmart the system.

But God had worked a miracle, after all. Even when they had made a mockery of prayer and faith, church attendance and this work trip. Almighty God could've destroyed them for what they had tried to do. But instead He was showing Himself so clearly to them, she could hardly take it in.

Jack eased back down to the edge of the seat. He was crying openly, unable to talk. He motioned for the man to continue.

For the first time, the uniformed man smiled. "I take it this is good news."

"Yes," Jack managed. He wiped his eyes. "Very good. You have no idea."

The man cleared his throat. He looked back at the letter

and continued. " 'New adoption release papers have been signed by both biological parents, and notarized. You are required under conditions of the release papers to accompany Joey Campbell to one additional meeting at the Child Welfare Department in Cleveland, Ohio, in two weeks, after which time you will no longer be subject to any conditions by this department. Congratulations.' " The man grinned at them. "I have a copy of the paperwork for your records."

But Molly and Jack barely heard him.

They were too busy hugging Joey and each other, weeping and laughing and trying to believe what had happened.

"Mommy, Daddy...what is it? Do we have to get arrested?"

"No, baby." Molly kissed him again and again on his cheek, his forehead, his hands. "We get to finish our trip and go home with Aunt Beth and Uncle Bill and the cousins."

"And you never have to go on a trip without us again." Jack stood and swung Joey in a circle. Then he settled him on his hip. "How's that sound?"

Joey raised his fist in the air. "Great!"

The police escorted them back to the mission house, but everything about the ride was a blur. They had come so close to losing him. By now Joey could've been in custody, heading back to the United States never to be seen by them again. Molly was exhausted, drained, too giddy to do anything but try to somehow understand what had happened.

The Porters had changed their mind about Joey, obviously. But why? What had done it? And why the visit to the social services office in two weeks? Molly didn't care. She would've traveled around the world to meet the requirements of the adoption release papers.

And what about Beth? Obviously she'd been wrong about her sister. Beth hadn't turned them in, clearly not. Otherwise the meeting at the embassy would've gone very differently. Beth, her best friend, her closest ally. How could she have thought anything but good of her sister?

They reached the mission house before she had time to sort through her feelings. Somehow—as if they were floating on clouds—they made their way back inside. Beth and Bill and the kids sat around the living room, their faces tear-stained.

"Molly!" Beth stood. She looked at Jack and then Joey, and finally back at Molly. "What happened?"

Molly released Joey's hand and closed the gap between her and her sister. "He's ours, Beth. Joey is ours. The Porters changed their minds."

Beth's entire countenance changed. She started to cry and took Molly in her arms. They both apologized at the same time, and then they looked at each other and laughed.

"Beth, I'm sorry....I thought you turned us in." She kept her words quiet. Behind them Jack was explaining to Bill about the trip to the embassy while the Petty kids asked Joey about his adventure. "I figured you'd called the social worker."

"Wait..." Beth's smile faded. "I thought you were going to run. I mean, I really thought that."

"We were! I couldn't tell you, but you were right. Of course. I could never fool you, Beth." Molly let her head tip back. She had never felt so good in all her life. The nightmare they'd been living for the past few months was finally over. They had Joey back, and they had their lives back. It was more than she could take in. She looked at her sister again. "Really, I thought you turned us in. I'm so sorry, Beth."

"But..." Beth's face froze, confused and afraid all at once. Guilt covered her features once more. "I did, Molly." Her voice was so quiet it was almost soundless.

"You did?" Molly felt her own smile fade. "You called the social worker?"

"Yes." She hung her head for a moment. When she looked up, tears filled her eyes. "And Wendy Porter. I told her Joey belonged to you, that you loved him so much. But I told her I was afraid you were going to run."

Molly held her breath. Her head was spinning again. She wasn't sure what to say or do. Beth had indeed turned them in, but what did it matter? Here they were, and Joey was theirs. Forever and ever more. She found her smile again and hugged her sister. "I love you, Beth. I'm not mad at you."

"You're not?"

"No." She had never felt so good in all her life. "Don't you see? In the end it wasn't up to you or us." Her eyes were dancing, she could feel the glow deep within her. "It was up to God. We have Joey because that was His will— just like you prayed."

There was no other way to explain it.

While the party continued, while the rejoicing led to worship and the worship to rejoicing, a deep and abiding truth settled into the hearts of all of them. That night they had witnessed something very special. For reasons they might not ever understand, they'd been given the gift of their son for a second and final time. More than that, they'd gotten their lives back.

It was a miracle.

And before they turned in for the night, they made plans for an urgent morning call to a bank in Sweden. Jack grinned at her. "What about that medical building? It really is a good deal."

Molly laughed and pulled Joey onto her lap. "I don't care!" She kissed Joey's forehead. "Buy the whole block, as long as we have this little boy."

Before they turned in, Molly and Jack knelt near Joey's bunk bed. This time—for the first time—they talked to God together.

Jack went first. "God"—his voice broke—"I don't know what to say. I'm sorry.... I'm so sorry." He bowed his head. Then he motioned for Molly to pray.

Molly's heart went out to him. He was thankful, but he was sorry first. Sorry for going through the motions of faith, and not until now believing there was actual power in the name of God. She found her voice and began. "God...thank You. We have no words that can express how grateful we are. When we get home, everything will change. You worked out a miracle for us." She gave Joey a soft squeeze. "Now we'll give You our lives."

"Yes, God." Jack's voice was sure, strong.

It was Joey's turn. "Hi, God...it's me, Joey. 'Member I asked You if I could stay with my mommy and daddy and Gus and not have to go back to that other house in Ohio? I asked You two times, 'member?" He took a breath. "I knew You would do it for me, God. Thanks for this happy day. Gee this name, amen."

Her precious son. Molly kissed him and Jack did the same. As they left the room, a thought occurred to her. They wouldn't have far to go to learn how to talk to God, how to find a relationship with Him.

Their son was already showing them the way.

It was the middle of September, and still Allyson Bower couldn't believe the way the events had played out. She'd been seconds away from contacting the authorities when Wendy Porter called. Now, the meeting between Wendy and Molly Campbell and Joey was only minutes away.

Allyson sat back in her chair and tapped her pencil on the open folder in front of her. The final straw for Wendy Porter had been Rip, of course. The man had been drunk that Thursday night, the night before the Campbells' trip to Haiti. He had been angry that Wendy was on the phone, and when she hung up, he had ordered her to tell him everything.

When he wasn't satisfied with Wendy's answers, he came unglued.

Allyson saw her the next day, after Rip was in custody, after Wendy was released from the hospital. She had a broken arm, stitches near her ear, a bruised liver, and two black eyes. Still she'd found the strength to call the social worker.

"You're pressing charges, Wendy. You have to."

"I called the police." Wendy was crying. With careful

fingers she dabbed at her tears, but still she winced from the pain. "He's going back to prison."

"What about Joey?"

"I told Rip I'd testify that he didn't mean it, that it was just the alcohol making him crazy." She sucked in a few quick breaths. "As long as he'd sign the release papers."

Allyson hadn't known what to say. She wanted Joey to stay with the Campbells, she always had. But Wendy needed to understand the law completely. "You know that you can keep Joey if you want."

Wendy nodded. "His adoption wasn't valid, right? Because Rip never signed the papers?"

"Right." Allyson had held her breath. This was delicate territory. "Rip can go to prison and you can have sole custody of your son. It's up to you."

"I know." More tears slid down her face. Quiet tears, from a deep sorrow that had already counted the cost. "But one day Rip will get out and he'll find me again. He always does." She wiped at her eyes again. "When that happens, I'll take him back." She lifted her hands, helpless. "I always do." She looked at her lap, ashamed. "I gave Joey up once because I couldn't stand the thought of Rip hurting him. The reason's the same today."

The papers were signed and notarized over the next two days, and immediately Allyson set about getting word to the Campbells. They were a flight risk, and she wanted to get word to them before they fled. It had taken two painfully long days of red tape between her and Judge Groves and the embassy before the word finally came. Police were going to the orphanage to bring Jack and Molly and Joey to the embassy, where they would be informed of the change in custody. By some amazing set of circumstances, word reached the Campbells before they could pull off whatever they might've been planning.

Allyson smiled.

How she would've loved to have been in the room when the Campbells got word that the custody case had been dropped. Joey was theirs. It was a miracle—that's what Molly Campbell said. And maybe it was. Allyson had taken her kids to church each of the past two weeks—for the first time in years. If for no other reason than to thank God for pulling off what neither she nor the Campbells could've.

In the weeks since, the Campbells had filed all necessary paperwork. Joey was officially their son without any further question. Wendy Porter hadn't asked for any visitation rights, so none were granted.

Allyson looked at the clock on her wall. The meeting was scheduled to take place in two minutes. Molly Campbell and Joey were already in the child-care room, a private meeting area set up for comfort with sofas and overstuffed chairs and baskets of toys.

The phone on Allyson's desk rang. She pressed the flashing button and brought the receiver to her ear. "Hello?"

"Yes, Ms. Bower, Wendy Porter is here to see you."

"Thank you. I'll meet her in the waiting room."

Allyson released a heavy sigh as she stood and reached for the door. Wendy Porter's only request had been this: that the Campbells bring Joey to Ohio for one last visit at the Child Welfare Department.

So she could say good-bye.

❧

It felt like the longest drive in Wendy Porter's life.

The whole way to the Child Welfare Department, she replayed every event that had led to this moment. But especially her recent visits with Joey. Tears streamed down her face, and she looked in the rear-view mirror. *You've gotta stop, Wendy. Right now. Joey won't know what to think if you're crying.*

She exhaled and straightened her bangs.

Her hours with Joey had been the best in her life. In some ways, she wondered why she didn't take Allyson Bower up on her offer. She could keep Joey if she wanted to. All she'd have to do is find a way to never let Rip Porter back in her life. That was the problem.

Even now she loved him, sick as that was. He needed help; they both did. But she couldn't put Joey through that process—not for a minute. Rip would've beaten the child; she knew it as surely as she knew her name. He wouldn't have meant it, and when he was sober he would've been deeply sorry.

But she loved Joey too much to ever let that happen.

He was such a nice little boy, so handsome and kind. Even though he was scared to death, even though he missed his adoptive parents and his dog and his bedroom back in Florida, he'd still been kind to her. He liked her chocolate chip cookies.

Wendy climbed out of the car, and with heavy feet, she forced herself up the stairs and into the waiting room. Allyson Bower came for her in just a few minutes.

"Hello, Wendy. You look...better." She held out her hand.

Wendy shook it. She had been careful with her makeup

that morning. Other than the cast on her arm, it was impossible to tell what she'd been through just two weeks earlier. "Is Joey here?"

"Yes." Allyson studied her. "He came with Mrs. Campbell."

A sad smile tugged at her lips. "His mommy."

"Yes." The social worker gave a gentle nod. "His mommy." She took a step back. "Are you ready to see him?"

"Yes. I'd like to meet Mrs. Campbell, but then..." Her voice caught. She wasn't going to cry, not now. A quick breath and she found her voice again. "Then could I have a few minutes to say good-bye to Joey? Alone?"

"I'm sure that'll be fine." Allyson led her down a hall past three doors, and then into a room, and there they were.

A pretty woman with dark hair and a quick smile stood as they walked into the room. Joey was playing with Legos on the floor, but he looked up, confused at the sight of Wendy. He lifted his fingers and gave her a slow little wave. Then he went to Mrs. Campbell's side and pressed himself close to her. Like he was trying to hide.

Allyson took charge of the moment. "Molly, I'd like you to meet Wendy Porter."

The Campbell woman came toward her, and for a moment it looked like she wanted to shake hands. Then she held out her arms and pulled Wendy into a hug, one that lasted longer than she expected.

The social worker left the two women and went to sit with Joey on the sofa. She distracted him with a book from a nearby table.

"I...don't know what to say." Molly had tears in her eyes. She bit her lip to stop it from quivering. "Thank you for giving us Joey." She made a sound that was more cry than laugh. "A second time."

Wendy looked past the Campbell woman's shoulder to the place where her son was playing. Then her eyes met Molly's again. "Did you ever read the story of King Solomon, the one in the Bible?"

"No." Molly looked surprised. "But we're reading the Bible a lot these days." Her eyes glowed. "Last week Joey asked Jesus into his heart."

The news was bittersweet: one more step, one more milestone that Wendy had missed. She managed a smile. "Anyway...the story is in First Kings, chapter 3. It made me realize something."

Molly waited, never breaking eye contact.

"It made me know that any real mother would sooner walk away from her child than let him come to harm." Tears clouded her eyes again. "For any reason."

The Campbell woman didn't quite look like she understood. But she nodded anyway. "I'll read it later."

Wendy tried to focus. She didn't have long. Anything she might ever want to say to Joey's adoptive mother, she would have to say now. "Take good care of him, okay?" The tears spilled onto her cheeks, but she didn't try to stop them.

"I will." Molly was crying, too. They were both mothers now. Nothing about the moment was easy.

"And if...if he ever asks about me, tell him how much I love him. So much that I gave him to you."

"Okay." The Campbell woman brought her fingers to her lips, so she wouldn't cry out loud. "And if he ever wants to find you, I'll help him."

"Really?" The offer was more than Wendy would've asked for.

"Yes. Definitely." Molly pulled a tissue from her purse and handed it to Wendy. Then she took one for herself and pressed it beneath her eyes. "Anything else?"

Wendy looked at Joey again, at his towheaded hair and his earnest face, his precious smile. "That's all." She took a step back. "Can I have a few minutes with him?"

"Of course." Molly signaled to Allyson Bower, and then to Joey. "Mommy will be right outside, honey. Mrs. Porter wants to talk to you for a little bit, okay?"

"Okay." Joey looked less nervous than before. "Then we go home, right? To Gus and Daddy?"

"Right, buddy." Molly waved at him, and then she and the social worker left the room and closed the door behind them.

Wendy drew a slow breath. This was it. She crossed the room and sat on the sofa next to Joey. "Hi, honey."

"Hi." Joey still held the book, the one Allyson Bower had been reading to him. "Where's the other daddy?" Joey peered around her, his eyes suddenly fearful.

"He's not here. You won't see him again." She looked into his eyes, and suddenly she was back nearly five years ago, lying in a hospital bed, looking into those same eyes, her heart breaking. Trying to find a way to say good-bye. *I'm doing this for you, child of mine. Only for you.* She smiled at him. "You won't be coming to Ohio anymore, Joey. Do you know that?"

He nodded. "I asked God for that."

"Oh." She felt the cut in her heart go a little deeper, but she smiled anyway. "I'm glad. You keep talking to God, okay?"

"Okay."

She could still feel the way he felt in her arms that morning, hours after his birth, still smell his newborn smell and hear his little coos as she cradled him close. He was her son, her very own. She would only walk away now because she loved him—just like she'd told Molly Campbell.

Joey cocked his head and studied her. "How come you're sad?"

"Well—" She caught her breath. The tears came, but she kept her happy face. "See...today I have to say good-bye." She held up her good hand. "After today I won't see you again."

"You won't?" He was so young, so unaware of the battle that had been raging around him. It hadn't dawned on him that if he wasn't coming back to Ohio, then he wasn't coming back to her, either. He frowned, his eyes locked on hers. "Good-byes are sad."

"Yes." She wanted to hold him, hug him close and memorize the feel of him one last time. But that might scare him, especially with the Campbell woman out of the room. So instead she did what she'd done a few weeks ago when they sat on the couch and watched *Bear in the Big Blue House.*

She reached her hand out and took hold of his fingers.

He grinned and tucked his hand all the way into hers, the way he'd done before. "I like you." His smile fell off a little. "I told my mommy you were nice."

"We had a good time, didn't we?"

"You rubbed my back." He smacked his lips. "You told me, 'Mama loves you, Joey.'"

Wendy opened her eyes wider. "That's right, honey. I said that." He'd heard her? Those nights when she thought he was asleep, he'd heard her words of love. It was something she could hold onto, a last memory.

With all her heart, she wanted to think that somehow he'd remember her. The chocolate-chip cookies and holding hands on the couch and her voice whispering, "Mama loves you, Joey." But time wouldn't be that kind. A year from now he'd be five, almost six, and the nice lady in Ohio would be only a dim memory. One more year and she'd be forgotten altogether.

She gave Joey's hand a squeeze. *God...don't let him forget me. Please.* It would take a miracle, but that was God's territory. "I gotta go."

He seemed to sense the significance of the moment. For a long time he looked at her, then he stood up on his knees and put his arms around her neck. "I'll miss you."

"Ah, sweetie." She gathered his words to the most tender places in her soul. They weren't words of love, exactly, but they were close. And they were the most she would ever get from her precious little boy. "I'll miss you, too."

They stood up, and once more Joey tucked his hand in hers. She led him to the door, opened it, and nodded at Molly and Allyson a few feet away.

Molly hesitated. "Are you...are you ready?"

She would never be ready. "Yes." She closed the distance between them, and then she took Joey's hand and slipped it into Molly's. She bent down and kissed his cheek. Then, in a voice too pinched to be heard, she mouthed the word, "Bye."

She gave a final look to Allyson Bower, and through eyes blurred with fresh tears, she found her way to her car. She had lost so much because of Rip. Her youth and her ability to stand on her own, her health and most of all her golden-haired son. She would never see him off to kindergarten, never see him ride a bike or play with his dog, Gus. She would never watch him excel in school or graduate from high school or marry his college sweetheart.

The tears came in torrents now.

Wendy climbed into her car and let her head rest on the steering wheel. Saying good-bye to Joey was the hardest thing she'd ever done. This time more than right after his birth, because now she knew him. And she would never, ever forget him. Yes, she had lost more than she would ever be able to count. But the important thing was this.

Joey had won.

And because of that—in some sad, heartbreaking way—they had all won.

Even her.

❧

Molly spent another fifteen minutes visiting with Allyson and talking about Joey. The last few weeks had been an emotional rollercoaster—signing adoption papers for Joey, knowing he was theirs forever, but then realizing the sacrifice of Wendy Porter, the gut-wrenching sadness of her good-bye.

Allyson had brought all the pieces together, and now the woman looked happier than Molly had ever seen her.

"I need to say one thing before you go." Allyson crossed her legs and leveled her gaze. "I don't blame you for what you were going to do."

This was touchy territory. No question, she and Jack had

been planning to break the law. If they'd done it and been caught, they would've gone to prison for many years. Molly didn't want to admit to anything, even now, when the entire plan was nothing more than a bad memory. Instead of responding, she only nodded, the hint of a smile tugging at the corners of her mouth.

"I was prepared to go to the police, because that's my job." Allyson brought her lips together. She tapped the spot above her heart. "But in here I would've been cheering you on." She looked at Joey. "This case, the situation, it worked out like it was supposed to work out. That doesn't always happen."

Joey looked up at her. "That's 'cause God made it happen." He grinned. "I asked Him."

The women exchanged a look, and Allyson laughed. "Well, that settles it."

After a few more minutes, their visit ended. Allyson wished them well, and they set off in their rental car back to the airport. They had done the trip in one day, and Jack would be waiting for them back in West Palm Beach when their plane landed.

Somewhere, headed back to her house in Cleveland, Wendy Porter must still be crying, Molly had no doubt. Knowing Joey, spending time with him, would've made the sacrifice all but impossible. She thanked God every day that the woman had found the courage.

Wendy's broken arm told Molly pieces of the story the social worker wasn't able to tell. Rip must've gotten violent again, and that would've been enough to convince Wendy. She couldn't expose Joey to that sort of abuse. Never. Because she really did love him.

Molly and Joey walked hand in hand, and they were almost to the car when Joey gasped and pointed. Across the street was a field and something Molly hadn't noticed until now.

"Dandelions, Mommy!"

She stopped and looked. The field must've held a million dandelions—just like Fuller Park. How close had they come to making a crazy decision, to doing things that went against the law, and their consciences, and most important—against God Almighty? She shivered and held a little tighter to his hand. "Yes, buddy. Lots of dandelions."

They climbed into the car, and as Molly buckled Joey into his booster seat, she rubbed her nose against his. "Eskimo noses."

He did the same and giggled. Then he batted his eyelashes against hers. "Butterfly kisses."

"I love you, Joey Campbell."

He giggled louder. "Love you, too, Mommy Campbell."

Before she pulled away, she looked at him. "You know something, buddy? I can almost feel God with us right now, making everything work out."

"He is, Mommy." He gave her a silly smile, as if surely she must know this. "He's always with us now. I used to ask Him to go with me on trips 'cause I was scared. Now I ask Him to always go with us."

"Oh." She nodded. "No wonder."

She shut the door and climbed into the driver's seat. But before she started the car, he called to her.

"Mommy, can we talk to God? 'Afore we go?"

"Sure, buddy." She bowed her head and wondered what was on his mind.

"Hi, God...it's me, Joey. I'm happy that we're going home. But I'm sad for that nice lady. Jonah says since You're God, You can be with more than one person at a time." He stopped for a second. "I think that's true. So could You please be with that nice lady? 'Cause she was crying, and I think You would make her feel better."

Molly could hardly believe her ears. Here was her son, the one who had prayed without ever giving up—even when the adults around him were going about things their own way. And now—even though he was happy—he was worried about Wendy Porter. Because she'd been crying.

Thank You for this child, God.... Teach Jack and me to listen to him, that we might learn to have a faith like his.

In the backseat, Joey finished his prayer the way he always did.

"Gee this name, amen."

AUTHOR'S NOTE

Dear Friends,

Always at the end of a book, I stand back amazed. Awed that God would give me another story—one that grew first in the soil of my heart, and then on the pages of this book. But also amazed at the lessons I learned along the way.

I knew, of course, that *Like Dandelion Dust* would be the story of two mothers, and the love that both women had for a single child. But I wasn't prepared for the lessons of faith that would come by way of four-year-old Joey. I don't know why I was surprised. The lessons were there because they are also that vivid in the lives of my own six children.

The image of my eight-year-old Austin sleeping with his snow leopard under one arm and his Bible under the other.

My little EJ telling me that he slept great because, "I just remembered all my Bible verses and God gave me sleep."

My precious Sean coming up to me, all smiles, after his champion soccer team lost badly in the first round of the state playoffs. "Did you see me, Mom?"

"Yes, Sean," I told him. "You played very hard. I'm proud of you."

"No, not that." He pointed to the empty midfield. "Before the game I got everyone in a circle so we could pray."

The examples in my own life are without limit.

Big, strong Josh, taking half an hour to gather five packs of his own gum and write his sister and brothers each a note with a little cross on it. Josh taping the notes to the packs of gum, and secretly delivering one to the foot of each of his siblings' beds.

"I felt like God wanted me to share."

There's Tyler at thirteen years old, stringing a sign up on his bedroom door that reads, "I believe!" and telling me, "I just want everyone who comes here to know where I stand."

And finally Kelsey, who at sixteen is in the middle of strong peer pressure, finding her dad and me and saying, "You know what makes my day absolutely perfect? When I start out by reading my Bible."

Our kids come up with things like this, and my husband and I find ourselves wanting to memorize Scripture and strengthen our faith and wake up early enough to start our day right, too.

Like Dandelion Dust raises interesting questions, questions about what makes someone a mother, and what it means to truly love a child. You'll find more of these questions in the Reading Group Guide at the end of this book.

I realize that there are many true-life stories that start out like the Campbells'. But sadly, many do not have miracle endings—at least not the endings adoptive parents are praying for. In those cases, my heart and prayers are with you. I can only believe that we—like children—are in the backseat however long the journey lasts. God is driving, and we must trust that in the end, if we stay with Him, He'll get us safely home.

As always, I'd love to hear from you. You can contact me by visiting my Web site at www.KarenKingsbury.com. The site has a new look and many more reader features, including a running blog of my life as a wife, mom, and author, a section for book clubs, and a place where you can connect with other readers.

If you are part of a book club, take a minute and register your group. That way you can connect with another reader group—perhaps in your state or across the country. You can agree to read the same book, and swap e-mails in the process. It's a great way to make new friends!

I pray this finds you filled with joy and peace. May God always be at the center of your families, and may you learn from the children He has placed in your lives. Remember—we have much to gain by watching the faith of our children.

In His light and love. Until next time,

Karen Kingsbury

READING GROUP GUIDE

1. Have you ever known someone who adopted a child and then had that child taken away because the adoption fell through? Describe that situation. How did the adoptive parents handle the loss?

2. What did you think of Molly and Jack's decision to leave the country?

3. Is there any way to justify the decision Molly and Jack made?

4. Read the story of Mary and Joseph's escape to Egypt in Matthew, chapter 2. Did this give moral precedent for Molly and Jack to take Joey and flee the country? Why or why not?

5. What Molly and Jack wanted to do was illegal, no question about it. If you were Beth, would you have turned them in? Why or why not?

6. Molly and Beth shared a special relationship. What were some of the reasons they were close?

7. Describe a close relationship you have with a sister or a friend. What makes that relationship close?

8. Have there been times when you have had to make a difficult decision—like the one Beth made—for the good of someone you love? Describe that situation. What was the outcome?

9. How might God have blessed Molly and Jack if they hadn't tried to defy the law?

10. Why was Jack so closed to the possibility of God's help while he looked for a way to keep custody of Joey? Explain your answer.

11. What did Beth mean when she said that God's will is always accomplished if you ask Him? Can you give an example of this in your life?

12. Wendy Porter was a woman caught up in abuse. Do you know anyone in a similar situation? Why do people stay in harmful relationships?

13. Read 1 Kings, chapter 3. How does the story of the two mothers relate to the sacrifice Wendy made on behalf of her son? How is the Bible story different?

14. Who was your favorite character in *Like Dandelion Dust*? Why?

15. Which character are you most like? How?

16. Do you think Molly and Jack would've gotten away with their plan? Why or why not?

17. Do you think they would've been happy in their new life in the Cayman Islands? Why or why not?

18. What would you do if a judge ordered that one of your children had to be taken away?

19. If you could make any change to the adoption laws in this country, what change would you make? Do you think the current system protects children most of the time, some of the time, or all of the time?

20. What did you learn from reading this novel?

This Side *of* Heaven

To Donald, my Prince Charming

How I rejoice to see you coaching again, sharing your gift of teaching and your uncanny ability with basketball with another generation of kids. And best yet, now our boys are part of the mix. Isn't this what we always dreamed of, my love? I love sitting back this time and letting you and God figure it out. I'll always be here—cheering for you and the team from the bleachers. But God's taught me a thing or two about being a coach's wife. He's so good that way. It's fitting that you would find varsity coaching again now—after twenty years of marriage. Hard to believe that as you read this, our twentieth anniversary has come and gone. I look at you and I still see the blond, blue-eyed guy who would ride his bike to my house and read the Bible with me before a movie date. You stuck with me back then and you stand by me now, when I need you more than ever. I love you, my husband, my best friend, my Prince Charming. Stay with me, by my side, and let's watch our children take wing, savoring every memory and each day gone by. Always and always...The ride is breathtakingly beautiful, my love. I pray it lasts far into our twilight years. Until then, I'll enjoy not always knowing where I end and you begin. I love you always and forever.

To Kelsey, my precious daughter

You are nineteen now, a young woman, and my heart soars with joy when I see all that you are, all you've become. This year is a precious one for us, because you're still home, attending junior college and spending nearly every day in the dance studio. When you're not dancing, you're helping out with the business and ministry of Life-Changing Fiction™, so we have many precious hours together. I know this time is short and won't last, but I'm enjoying it so much—you, no longer the high school girl, a young woman and in every way my daughter, my friend. That part will always stay, but you, my sweet girl, will go where your dreams lead, soaring through the future doors God opens. Honey, you grow more beautiful—inside and out—every day. And always I treasure the way you talk to me, telling me your hopes and dreams and everything in between. I can almost sense the plans God has for you, the very good plans. I pray you keep holding on to His hand as He walks you toward them. I love you, sweetheart.

To Tyler, my lasting song

I can hardly wait to see what this school year will bring for you, my precious son. Last year you were one of Joseph's brothers, and you were Troy Bolton, and Captain Hook—becoming a stronger singer and stage actor with every role. This year you'll be at a new high school, where I believe God will continue to shape you as the leader He wants you to be. Your straight A's last year were a sign of things to come, and I couldn't be prouder, Ty. I know it was hard watching Kelsey graduate, knowing that your time with your best friend is running short. But you'll be fine, and no matter where God leads you in the future, the deep and lasting relationships you've begun here in your childhood will remain. Thank you for the hours of music and song. As you seize hold of your sophomore year, I am mindful that the time is rushing past, and I make a point to stop and listen a little longer when I hear you singing. I'm proud of you, Ty, of the young man you're becoming. I'm proud of your talent and your compassion for people and your place in our family. However your dreams unfold, I'll be in the front row to watch it happen. Hold on to Jesus, Ty. I love you.

To Sean, my happy sunshine

Today you came home from school, eyes sparkling, and showed me your science notebook—all your meticulous, neat sentences and careful drawings of red and white blood cells and various bones and bacteria. I was marveling over every page, remarking at the time you'd taken and the quality of your work, and together we laughed over the fact that neither of us really cares too much for science— but that it still matters that we do our best. You smiled that easy smile of yours and said, "Wait till you see Josh's—his blows mine away." You didn't know it at the time, but I was very touched by the tone in your voice. You weren't envious or defeated by the fact that Josh, in your same grade, might have managed to draw even-more-detailed pictures in his science journal. You were merely happy that you'd done your best, earned your A, and could move on from seventh-grade science proud of your effort. I love that about you, Sean. You could easily sulk in the shadow of your brother, a kid who excels in so many areas that the two of you share. But you also excel, my dear son. And one of the best ways you shine is in your happy heart, your great love for life and for people, and your constant joy. Sean, you have a way of bringing smiles into our family, even in the most mundane moment, and lately we are smiling very big about your grades. I pray that God will use your positive spirit to always make a difference in the lives around you. You're a precious gift, son. Keep smiling and keep seeking God's best for your life. I love you, honey.

To Josh, my tenderhearted perfectionist

So, you finally did it! You can beat me at Ping-Pong now, not that I'm surprised. God has given you great talents, Josh, and the ability to work at them with the sort of diligent determination that is rare in young teens. Whether in football or soccer, track or room inspections, you take the time to seek perfection. Along with that, there are bound to be struggles. Times when you need to understand again that the gifts and talents you bear are God's, not yours, and times when you must learn that perfection isn't possible for us, only for God. Even so, my heart almost bursts with pride over the young man you're becoming. After one of your recent soccer tournaments one of the parents said something I'll always remember. "Josh is such a leader," she told me. "Even when he doesn't know other parents are looking, he's always setting an example for his teammates." The best one, of course, is when you remind your teammates to pray before a game. What a legacy you and your brothers are creating here in Washington State! You have an unlimited future ahead of you, Josh. I'll be cheering on the sidelines always. Keep God first in your life. I love you always.

To EJ, my chosen one

Here you are in the early months of seventh grade, and I can barely recognize the student athlete you've become. Those two years of homeschooling with Dad continue to reap a harvest a hundred times what was sown, and we couldn't be more proud of you. But even beyond your grades, we are blessed to have you in our family for so many reasons. You are wonderful with our pets—always the first to feed them and pet them and look out for them—and you are a willing worker when it comes to chores. Besides all that you make us laugh, oftentimes right out loud. I've always believed that getting through life's little difficulties and challenges requires a lot of laughter—and I thank you for bringing that to our home. You're a wonderful boy, son, a child with such potential. Clearly that's what you showed the other day when you came out of nowhere in your soccer qualifiers and scored three goals. I'm amazed because you're so talented in so many ways, but all of it pales in comparison to your desire truly to live for the Lord. I'm so excited about the future, EJ, because God has great plans for you, and we want to be the first to congratulate you as you work to discover those. Thanks for your giving heart, EJ. I love you so.

To Austin, my miracle boy

I smile when I picture you hitting not one home run but three last baseball season—all of them for Papa—and I feel my heart swell with joy as I think of what happened after your second home run, when you had rounded the bases one at a time and accepted congratulations at home plate from your entire team. You headed into the dugout and a couple of your teammates tugged on your arm. "Tell us, Austin, how do you do it? How do you hit a home run like that?" That's when you smiled and shrugged your shoulders. "Easy. I asked God for the strength to hit the ball better than I could without Him." Papa must be loving every minute of this, Aus. I'm sure of it. What I'm not sure of is that missing him will ever go away. I can only tell you that our quiet times together are what I love most, too. That and our times of playing give-and-go out on the basketball court. You're my youngest, my last, Austin. I'm holding on to every moment, for sure. Thanks for giving me so many wonderful reasons to treasure today. I thank God for you, for the miracle of your life. I love you, Austin.

And to God Almighty, the Author of life,
who has—for now—blessed me with these.

ACKNOWLEDGMENTS

One night when I was putting the finishing touches on this book, Austin crawled up into bed next to me and stared at my laptop computer screen. "You know, Mom," he said, "I've been meaning to ask you about writing books. I have a couple questions." I smiled at him and asked him what he wanted to know. "Well," he said, "you know those beautiful covers on your books? They're so nice, with just the right colors and pictures, so do you do those? Do you make the covers?"

I shook my head. "No, buddy. I don't have anything to do with the covers, really. The publisher has these wonderful designers. They take care of coming up with a cover." He seemed a little disappointed for a few seconds. Then his eyes lit up. "I know, how about the design inside the book, the way the letters line up just so, and those little swirly things that make the first page of every chapter so nice." He scrunched up his face, slightly baffled. "Do you do that part?"

Again I shook my head. "No, honey. Actually there are designers at the publisher's offices who make sure the book looks nice on the inside." My smile turned a little sheepish. "They're the ones who do that."

His shoulders sank, and after a slight pause his brow rose, hopeful. "I know, how about the bookstores! Are you the one who gets all those books to the bookstores, so they can be there on the shelves for the people?"

Feeling the clear sense that I was disappointing him, I shook my head and managed a weak smile. "No, Aus, I don't do that, either. The publisher has a sales staff that handles getting the books to the bookstores. After that, other people at the bookstores open the boxes of books and put them on the shelves. I don't have anything to do with that."

"Wow." He climbed back down, but before he ran off he shrugged his shoulders. "You don't really do that much, do you?"

Austin has a point. No book comes together without a great and talented team of people making it happen. For that reason, a special thanks to my friends at FaithWords and Center Street who combined efforts to make *This Side of Heaven* all it could be. A special thanks to my dedicated editor, Anne Horch, who encouraged me often to stay with this story, however hard it was to write.

Also thanks to my amazing agent, Rick Christian, president of Alive Communications. Rick, you've always believed only the best for me. When we talk about the highest possible goals, you see them as doable, reachable. You are a brilliant manager of my career, and I thank God for you. But even with all you do for my ministry of writing, I am doubly grateful for your prayers. The fact that you and Debbie are praying for me and my family keeps me confident every morning that God will continue to breathe into life the stories in my heart. Thank you for being so much more than a brilliant agent.

A special thank-you to my husband, who puts up with me on deadline and doesn't mind driving through Taco Bell after a basketball game if I've been editing all day. This wild ride wouldn't be possible without you, Donald. Your love keeps me writing; your prayers keep me believing that God has a plan in this ministry of fiction. And thanks for the hours you put in working with the guest-book entries on my Web site. I look forward to that time every day when you read through them, sharing them with me and releasing them to the public, praying for the prayer requests. Thank you, honey, and thanks to all my kids, who pull together, bringing me iced green tea and understanding about my sometimes crazy schedule. I love that you know you're still first, before any deadline.

Thank you also to my mom, Anne Kingsbury, and to my sisters, Tricia, Sue, and Lynne. Mom, you are amazing as my assistant—working day and night sorting through the mail from my reader friends. I appreciate you more than you'll ever know. Tricia, you are the best executive assistant I could ever hope to have. I treasure your loyalty and honesty, the way you include me in every decision and exciting Web site change. My site has been a different place since you stepped in, and the hits have grown tenfold. Along the way the readers have so much more to help them in their faith, so much more than a story with this Life-Changing Fiction™. Please know that I pray for God's blessings on you always, for your dedication to helping me in this season of writing, and for your wonderful son, Andrew. And aren't we having such a good time, too? God works all things to the good!

Sue, I believe you should've been a counselor! From your

home far from mine, you get batches of reader letters every day, and you diligently answer them using God's wisdom and His Word. When readers get a response from "Karen's sister Susan," I hope they know how carefully you've prayed for them and for the response you give. Thank you for truly loving what you do, Sue. You're gifted with people, and I'm blessed to have you aboard.

A special thanks also to Will Montgomery, my road manager. I was terrified to venture into the business of selling my books at events for a couple of reasons. First, I never wanted to profit from selling my books at speaking events, and second, because I would never have the time to handle such details. Monty, you came in and helped me on both accounts. With a mission statement, "To love and serve the readers," you have helped me supply books and free gifts to tens of thousands of readers at events across the country. More than that, you've become my friend, a very valuable part of the ministry of Life-Changing Fiction™. You are loyal and kind and fiercely protective of me, my family, and the work God has me doing. Thank you for everything you're doing, and will continue to do.

Thanks, too, to Olga Kalachik, my office assistant, who helps prepare our home for the marketing events and research gatherings that take place there on a regular basis. I appreciate all you're doing to make sure I have time to write. You're wonderful, Olga, and I pray God continues to bless you and your precious family.

I also want to thank my friends with Extraordinary Women—Roy Morgan, Julie and Tim Clinton, Beth Cleveland, and the girls on the tour, along with so many others.

How wonderful to be a part of what God is doing through all of you! Thank you for making me part of your family.

Thanks also to my forever friends and family, the ones who rush to our side whenever we need you. Your love has been a tangible source of comfort, pulling us through the various seasons of life and making us know how very blessed we are to have you in our lives.

And the greatest thanks to God. The gift is Yours. I pray I might use it for years to come in a way that will bring You honor and glory.

…For Alyssa

"For I know the plans I have for you," declares the LORD, *"plans to prosper you and not to harm you, plans to give you hope and a future."*

—JEREMIAH 29:11

ONE

The pain was a living, breathing demon, pressing its claws deep into his flesh and promising never to let go, not until death had the final word. But even with every vertebra and tendon in his back aching and burning, even with how he felt prisoner to his own body, and despite the eternal relief that was bound to come with his last breath, Josh Warren was certain of one thing that cool autumn night.

He didn't want to die.

Josh braced himself against the kitchen counter in his cramped apartment and stared at the clock. Just after midnight, early by his recent standards. His eyes blurred and battled for a moment of clarity. The problem was the meds, and whether he'd taken a double dose at ten o'clock, or at six. He leaned over his hands and tried to work up a complete breath. He drew three quick gasps, but only a fraction of his lungs offered any assistance. He was twenty-eight, but his body made him feel twice that.

"God"—he clenched his teeth and the whispered word filled his small kitchen—"I can't take this. I can't."

Three years. That's how long it had been. A hero, they

labeled him. Saved the lives of two teenage girls. But where were the news crews and reporters and cameramen now? Now, when every hour was a struggle to survive.

He tightened his grip on the countertop, his arms trembling, his lungs holding steady, refusing to inhale in a futile effort to keep the demon at bay. Another quick gasp and he hung his head. For a long moment he stayed that way, willing the pain to subside. But before he felt any relief, a drop of tepid water hit his hand. A grimace tugged at his eyebrows, and for a heartbeat he wondered if a pipe had broken upstairs the way it had last month, when the fog of pain and OxyContin was so strong he didn't notice the problem until a small stream started oozing from the plaster ceiling.

Another drop. He brushed at it as a third drop hit him, and at the same time he figured it out. He lifted his fingers to his forehead and touched a layer of wetness. No surprise there. He was sweating, his body giving way to the pain, handling the fire the only way it knew how. He wiped the back of his hand across his head and looked around.

Never mind when he'd taken the last dose. He needed more. Needed it now. He tried to straighten, but the demon weighed heavy on his shoulders, slumping him over as he shuffled toward the cupboard. He grabbed the bottle and fumbled with the lid before sliding one single pill into his palm. One pill wouldn't be too much. He downed it with a swig of water straight from the faucet.

Sleep would come, the way it always did eventually.

But first he needed to find Cara Truman. Josh made his way to the computer, set up on a desk against the dining room wall. He pulled his chair into place and fell into it.

Even then there was no relief. Sitting only intensified the pain in his lower back. He narrowed his eyes, logged in to his Facebook, and opened the instant message window— the one where Cara lived. Josh would never meet her in person. He was almost certain of that.

If he ever found his way free of the pain, he would call Becky Wheaton first, Becky whom he had loved since he was fifteen. He'd heard from some of their old high school friends that her engagement had fallen through and she was single again. He thought about her constantly, but he couldn't call her. Not until he was healthy and whole and successful—the sort of guy she deserved.

Becky would have to wait, but when no amount of meds or sleep could take the edge off his constant pain, when concerned calls from his parents and his sister didn't bring relief, there was always Cara.

She knew him better than anyone, because she knew his story. The whole story. Even the part about his little girl on the other side of the country, the one no one else really thought was his. On late nights like this, across the invisible lines of cyberspace, he could share with Cara every crazy detail of the others, the stories that made up his life. And along the way Cara gave him a rare and priceless gift, one that kept him pushing through, battling the demon.

Cara believed him.

He studied the list of friends online, and she was there. He positioned his hands and tried to steady them as he tapped out the words. *Hey, it's me... you there?*

Half a minute passed and he saw that his neighbor Carl Joseph Gunner had tagged him in a few new photos. He clicked the album and for the first time that night he smiled.

Carl Joseph and his girlfriend, Daisy, both had Down syndrome. They lived with roommates in separate apartments in the adjacent building and both were very independent, with jobs and the ability to use the bus lines for errands.

The photos were taken by Carl Joseph last time he and Daisy stopped by the apartment. Carl Joseph had learned how to use the timer on his camera, so the pictures showed Carl Joseph, Daisy, and Josh standing in front of his TV, his refrigerator, and his patio slider—each one with the same cheeky smiles. Josh jotted a quick thank-you to Carl Joseph, and at the same time a response came from Cara.

I stepped away for a minute but I'm back.

Josh shifted positions, trying to find a more comfortable angle. *Can't sleep. I was hoping you were up.* Cara lived in Phoenix and she worked the swing shift at a data processing center. She usually didn't turn in until two in the morning.

Her next message appeared in the lower window on his computer screen. *I was thinking the other day about how we almost didn't meet. What would I have done without you?*

Josh smiled and moved his fingers over the keyboard. *Glad we'll never have to answer that. Just goes to show online poker's worth something. Even when you lose.*

The conversation came faster. *Lotta creeps play OP. You were like getting a royal flush, you know?*

Josh felt the compliment in the drafty corners of his heart. He leaned back against the vinyl chair and felt his body relax a little. *Thanks, sweetie. I'm just glad we found our way out of online poker and into this.*

Whatever this is.

Right. Josh chuckled. *Whatever it is. Hey, I talked to Keith yesterday. He's back with his wife . . . things are good.*

Really??? I'm so happy for him!! See, J . . . Where would he be without you?

Josh felt the warmth of her words deep to the center of his soul. Keith had been his best friend since grade school, but ten years ago he'd moved to Ohio. They still stayed in touch, and Keith sometimes joined him for online poker. That's how Cara knew him.

There was a pause in the conversation and then her next message appeared in the window.

How's your back?

Hurts like crazy . . . let's talk about something else. I go to court again next week.

To testify?

Yes. My lawyer says it should be the last time.

Yay! That means the settlement's coming! And then you can go after your daughter!

Josh read the line three times before his hands began moving across the keyboard. *That's why I wanted to talk to you tonight.*

Why?

Because you make her seem like a real person. My little girl.

She is real. Josh could hear Cara's indignant tone through the words of her message. *You're going to get custody of her one of these days, I just know it.*

The thrill of possibility sent tingles down Josh's arms. *Partial custody. But anything would be better than this.*

She's a lucky girl, J . . . I wish my kids had a daddy like you.

Josh stared at that part. Every time they had a conversation like this one, Josh wondered the same thing. Maybe he was wrong about never meeting her in person. Becky had probably moved on, anyway. If he and Cara got along so well, why not move their relationship from cyberspace to Phoenix? Or to Colorado Springs? Cara was a single mom of two kids—a boy and a girl. Her first husband had been abusive, and three years ago he'd moved out and found someone new. Cara found solace in online poker, and people who couldn't hit her, people who could pretend to be anyone they wanted to be.

Two years ago Josh was caught up in an online game with Cara—aka Miss Independent—when she said something that stayed with him still. In the comment section of the game, she wrote, *I play OP because my real life is on hold.*

That was exactly how Josh felt. Since the accident he'd been caught up in a web of depositions and hearings, meetings with lawyers, and waiting for workmen's comp checks in the mail. Since then, all of life had become a waiting game.

Waiting for the pain in his back to be healed.

Waiting for a decision in the trial against the drunk driver's insurance company.

Waiting for a chance at success so he could call Becky Wheaton and tell her he still loved her.

Waiting for his settlement money so he could pay back his parents and buy a house and take a paternity test so he could prove to all the world what he already knew: that Savannah was his daughter.

Another message appeared. *You're quiet. What are you thinking?*

Josh felt a tug on his heart. *How come you're there and I'm here?*

Yeah ... I wonder that too sometimes.

Usually when they flirted with the possibility of taking their relationship to another level, one of them would change the subject before the conversation became too serious. But sitting in his stuffy apartment alone at one in the morning with the trial and the settlement becoming more of a reality each day, Josh suddenly couldn't stop himself. His fingers flew across the keyboard. *Okay, seriously, Miss Independent. Why don't we stop all this typing and find a way to hang out in person?*

There was a hesitation, and Josh's heartbeat sped up. Maybe he shouldn't have said anything. Maybe this was all she'd ever be capable of, and if that was the case, then so be it. Besides, he would always love Becky, and he owed it to both of them to see if she might feel the same way about him—once he was successful. If not, if she'd moved on, then maybe Cara was someone he could love. *Come on, Cara. ...* He closed his eyes and remembered the words of the song he'd heard recently. "*I can only imagine ... what it will be like. ...*" God, please ... speak to her heart. If she's someone who could be in my life, then please ...

He opened his eyes just as the next message came across. *You're too good for me, J. You know that.*

Who are you kidding? ... I'm lucky just to be your friend.

Another pause, shorter this time. *Tell me again about God, about you and Him.*

Disappointment stabbed at him because he really wanted to talk about the two of them. He swallowed hard. If she was going to change the subject, at least she wanted to talk about his newfound faith. He was still in pain, still sitting alone in a cheap apartment, but in the last six weeks his life had changed. He loved that Cara wanted to talk about it.

He breathed in and began typing. *I don't know, it's weird. My family's been talking to me about God forever, but I guess I had to figure it out on my own.*

What did it feel like ... you know, when you heard that song and could tell God was talking to you?

Josh smiled again. He'd answered this question half a dozen times in the last six weeks, but Cara seemed to really need to understand.

He moved his hands across the keyboard faster this time. *I don't know, I mean ... it was like God was talking straight to my heart. Telling me that I wasn't waiting for a settlement or a chance to see Savannah or for the next stage of my life. What I was really waiting for was Him. It was like He was calling me, and if I wanted to really live I needed to finally answer. You know? Stop running from Him and tell Him yes.*

I love that. She hesitated. *Can I tell you a secret?*

Always. He longed to hug her, put his hands on her shoulders, and look deep into her blue eyes. In lieu of that he clicked on her name in the instant message window and was instantly on her Facebook page. She had short brown hair and a narrow face. Not too tall or athletic or strikingly beautiful. A few extra pounds that drove her crazy, but the part Josh loved most was her smile. Cara's smile had a way of staying with him.

Her message flashed into view. *I've been talking with God.*

Online? He grinned at his own joke.

No, silly. In my heart. When I'm looking out the window at the summer sky or when a monsoon sweeps over Phoenix and lightning dances across the street outside my apartment complex.

He read her message slowly. *You should be a writer.*

I'm serious, J. You've changed me, your story about God. I think He's calling me, too. I'm taking the kids to church this Sunday.

Josh raised his eyebrows. *Seriously?* In the time he'd known her, Cara had been opposed to faith and God and anything dealing with Scripture. She never quite came out and said why, but on her Facebook page she described herself as agnostic. *Not interested in faith,* she'd written. That had changed in the last few weeks, and the reason had to be Josh's story about Wynonna and hearing God and realizing he'd been running away all this time.

Very seriously. So maybe I'll go to church this Sunday and all the answers will suddenly fall into place...and you'll get your settlement and buy a house in Scottsdale and we'll become best friends...and then...well, and then who knows? Right, J...maybe all that.

His heart did a somersault. *Right.* He wasn't sure if he should push the issue, but he couldn't stop himself. *Maybe all that and more.*

So...are you feeling better? [[smile]]

He dropped his hands to his thighs and stared at the screen. He hadn't realized it until she asked, but he actually was feeling better. *You know what?* He typed the words quickly. *My back doesn't hurt like it did before.*

See, I knew it.

Knew what?

I'm good for you.

You are. Very good.

And you know what else, J?

He almost felt like she was sitting across from him. *What?*

You're very good for me, too. And that's enough for now.

Everything she'd said a moment ago suddenly felt like nothing more than wild-eyed dreams and make-believe. He wanted a cigarette so bad he would've walked three miles for one. *Yes,* he typed. *That's enough for now.*

They signed off, and Josh checked a few more profiles of his online friends before closing down the computer. He stood and the effort hurt, but it didn't slice through him the way it would've an hour ago. He wandered across the living room to the narrow wooden mantel above the electric fireplace. On it he had the photos that mattered. One of him and his family—back when he was in high school and all of life stretched out before him like a river of unlimited possibilities. Next to it was a picture of the two girls—the one that ran in the paper after the accident. And last was a photo of Savannah, taken three years ago when she was four. Maria sent it to him when she thought he was going to come through with thousands of dollars a month in child support.

But Josh didn't have that kind of money, not yet, and a few months after sending the photo she moved on—refusing his phone calls and never sending another photo.

Josh stared at the picture. *Please, God . . . keep her safe. I want so badly to be her dad.*

He heard no loud voice in response, no quiet whisper in the newly reclaimed territory of his soul. But a Bible verse played across his mind, one that the pastor had talked about last Sunday. He was going to church with Carl Joseph and Daisy, the same church where Carl Joseph's brother, Cody, and Cody's wife, Elle, attended. The sermon had been about holding on—even when there seemed to be no hope at all. The verse was from Psalm 119:50.

My comfort in my suffering is this: Your promise preserves my life.

Josh touched the frame surrounding Savannah's picture. *Thank You, God....I feel Your comfort.* In the last few weeks, no words could have spoken more clearly to Josh than the ones from that single Bible verse. He kept a journal for Savannah and in his last entry he'd written to her about the Scripture. Never mind his relentless back pain, or the fact that the doctors weren't sure surgery would ever heal him. Forget about the depositions in the coming weeks, where the attorneys for the insurance company would certainly try to rip his testimony to shreds.

God's Word was reviving him.

Josh took a final look at the pictures on the mantel, then turned and walked slowly down the short hallway to his bedroom. He could walk a little straighter than before. Amazing, the power of having a true friend. No amount of pain medication could fully relieve the spasms in his back or the burning along his spine. But an hour of conversation with Cara and he felt like life was possible again. Like he could tackle another day.

In the beginning, their talks left them both drained because when they were honest with each other it was obvious things hadn't been easy for either of them. But now—now she was full of hope and life and encouragement, and Josh realized there could be only one reason for that: His new hope was spilling over into her life. And that was something that made him feel useful, like he had a purpose.

As he finished brushing his teeth, Josh smiled at the memory of their talk. Tonight they had tiptoed out of the safe confines of an instant message and stood for a brief moment on the balcony where the view was far grander. As Josh lay down and tried to find that elusive comfortable spot, as he begged God to keep the demon of deep, excruciating pain at bay, and as sleep finally found him, he thought about Cara and realized something else. Along the way God's Word wasn't only reviving him.

It was reviving both of them.

TWO

Annie Warren pulled the chilled raspberry cheesecake from her built-in Sub-Zero refrigerator, set it on her granite countertop, and sliced it onto a dozen china plates. The cheesecake was the same kind she served at the last function two weeks ago, and it was a huge hit. This time, she had a backup in the fridge just in case. It took no time to line the plates on a tray and steady it in her hands.

"Need help?" Her husband, Nate, rounded the corner, two coffee cups in his hands. He dropped them off near the sink. "They're hungry out there."

"No, thanks." She could feel the weariness in her smile as she walked past him toward the dining room. She tossed a quick glance back over her shoulder. "Maybe check the coffee. This crowd keeps every Starbucks in Colorado Springs in business."

Nate's laugh was low and discreet, muffled by the sounds as he worked the coffeemaker, fiddling with the spring-form top, the metal against metal. Annie eased her shoulder through a pair of double doors and found her practiced smile, the one she used whenever they entertained—and with Nate a member of the Colorado State Board of

Education, the Warrens entertained this way at least once a month.

Tonight it was the public librarians. Nate was up for reelection in a year and whatever he did he wanted the public librarians on his side. The board made decisions at every monthly meeting that directly affected them, and Nate wanted to make himself very clear: He was a friend of the public libraries. Hence the cheesecake.

Annie set the tray down near two nearly empty silver carafes of hot coffee.

"I told you." Babette, a librarian from the north side of the Springs, led her coworker closer to the dessert table. She smiled at Annie. "This is the cheesecake from Marigolds, right?"

"It is." Annie took a step back from the table. Good thing she bought two. "It was Nate's idea. 'Only the best for the librarians.'" Even as she said the words she could hear herself saying them last week about the teachers union. "*Only the best...*"

Babette was rail thin, but Annie had never known her to attend a party and eat less than three desserts. She helped herself to the first piece. "Best cheesecake in town, that's what I say." The other librarians made their way to the table as Babette took a few steps closer to Annie. "So..." She turned her back to the others. "I was thinking the other day about Josh, and he's what, now, in his late twenties? Because I was doing the math and it seems like this past June it was ten years since he and Blake graduated."

"Right." Annie's stomach tightened. She stood a little straighter. "Ten years, same as Blake."

Babette took three quick bites and seemed to swallow

them whole. "Blake's an intern this fall, did I mention that? He ran into Becky Wheaton at the hospital the other day. She's a therapist now—beautiful girl. She was Josh's girlfriend way back when, wasn't she?"

"She was." Annie worked to keep her smile in place. "They haven't talked in a while."

"Blake says he might take her out for coffee. Just to reconnect." She waved her hand in the air, as if she'd forgotten her main point. "Anyway, Blake's the top intern in the program. I told you where he's at, right?"

"St. Anthony's in Denver."

"Yes." She picked up her fork and stabbed it in the air. "Boy's so driven he puts me to shame. Barely makes time for anything else. His instructors think he'll be a surgeon before he's thirty-two. Isn't that something?"

"Something."

"Becky Wheaton thought so. Blake said she was very impressed with how he was doing."

Becky Wheaton would never love anyone the way she'd loved Josh, Annie told herself. She poured a cup of coffee. She would need it to get through this night. Once she had it steadied on a saucer she looked at Babette again. "You must be proud."

"I am. I mean, my son was always driven, you know? Schoolwork, sports, the debate team. You name it."

"Definitely. That's Blake."

There was an uncomfortable pause. The familiar pause that told Annie exactly what was coming next. Babette consumed the rest of her cheesecake. "Like I said, I was thinking about Josh and . . . So, how's he doing, anyway? I mean, the whole recovery from the accident and everything?"

"Actually, he's doing very well." Annie didn't hesitate, didn't give the woman anything but her most practiced answer. "He's in rehab for his back, and making progress. He's talked about starting his own business once he gets his settlement from the accident."

The woman smiled in a way that fell just short of condescending. "That's the Josh I remember. Always resourceful. And that Lindsay of yours—she was a smart one. Saw one of her feature stories in the paper the other day and I told myself, 'That Lindsay, she'll have books in our library one day.' She's quite a writer." She paused just long enough to refuel. "But then sometimes girls are more ambitious than their brothers. I read that in a *Cosmopolitan* article, and I stopped right there and thought of all the cases where that was true. Girls more successful than their brothers and the brothers never really—"

"Babette, I'm sorry." Annie held up her hand. She couldn't take another minute. "I need to slice the second cheesecake. Nate doesn't want his librarian friends leaving here hungry." She turned toward the kitchen and sipped hard on her coffee. "If you'll excuse me."

"Definitely. Go ahead." Babette turned back toward the dessert platter. "If the rest of you haven't tried this cheesecake you better grab a piece now. Best cheesecake in the Springs."

Annie let the double doors swing shut behind her and she steadied herself against the kitchen island. Why did they have to ask? *Dear God, isn't it enough that everyone knows about Josh's failures? Do they have to make me talk about the details?*

Conversations like the one with Babette made her feel

like Josh was a piñata hanging high above the party while everyone took swings at him. Even her. Because the truth was she shouldn't work so hard to defend Josh. Just once, at one of these parties with people they'd known all their lives, Annie wished she had the courage to look a person like Babette in the eyes and say, "Josh is struggling. He moved here from Denver and he lives in a low-income, one-bedroom apartment. He's addicted to pain medication, he's trying to lose the last forty pounds of a significant weight gain, and his days are taken up waiting for a call from his lawyer saying that his settlement check is finally in the mail. But even then he'll probably spend the rest of his life in chronic pain."

Her heart hurt and she hung her head, blocking out the party chatter from the next room. He'd had so much potential, so many ways he could've succeeded. Her precious youngest child, her only son. The deeper truths Annie didn't want to admit to herself, let alone to a crowd of acquaintances. Josh had intentionally done things his way. He'd walked away from the faith he'd been raised with and made one poor choice after another.

And now he was paying for it with an existence that troubled Annie every waking hour.

She sensed someone behind her, and then felt a touch on her shoulder. "Annie?"

No need to find her happy hostess smile with Nate. She turned and let herself draw strength from his eyes. "Babette Long is driving me crazy."

"You?" He kissed her forehead. "I get e-mails from the woman every day, keeping me posted on the needs of the public libraries."

Exhaustion strained Annie's sense of control. "I don't envy you."

"What'd she do?"

Her eyes softened. "She asked about Josh."

Nate studied her for a few seconds, then he went to the fridge and pulled out the second cheesecake. "Not everyone who asks about Josh is trying to upset you." He set it on the counter next to the knife. "You know that, right?"

"How am I supposed to feel?" She kept her voice low. "The woman tells me about Blake, and 'Weren't Blake and Josh in the same graduating class?' and how Blake is breezing his way through med school."

A deeper pain flickered in Nate's expression, and for the slightest moment the last ten years of heartache showed in the lines around his eyes and the creases in his forehead. "You were smart to walk away." He sliced the cheesecake and grabbed another twelve plates. "Let's get this out there. They'll leave when the dessert's gone."

Nate was right, and not just about the dessert. Annie stayed away from Babette the rest of the evening, making her rounds and working the crowd—the way she was used to doing. This was their life, and Nate needed the support of every librarian in the Springs. That was the purpose of tonight, the reason she'd driven to Marigolds for two raspberry cheesecakes on a summer afternoon when she'd rather walk through their neighborhood or play tennis with Nate or sit on their spacious deck and watch the deer through the grove of trees that made up their backyard.

"The election isn't a sure thing," Nate reminded her often. "A position of influence comes with responsibility."

Annie knew the drill well. She worked her way around

the room telling each group of librarians the same thing.
"Nate's compelled to carry your needs before the board,"
or "Nate's always been passionate about public libraries."
Nate enjoyed his position on the school board, and when
she took a magnifying glass to her heart, she enjoyed it too.
Maybe not her husband's monthly trek to Denver, but the
sense of prestige that came with an elected position.

If people were busy looking at Nate and her, at their
efforts toward another winning election and their position
as part of Colorado Springs' social elite, then they were
less likely to notice the fact that Josh wasn't doing much
with his life. That's what Annie told herself, anyway.

The party ended and Annie moved into the kitchen.
Even over the kitchen tap water she could hear Nate saying
good-bye to the last librarians. "An increased budget for
new books," he was saying, "that's what I'll be bringing up
at the next meeting."

Annie rolled her eyes, and then felt bad for doing it.
Nate's promise wasn't an empty one. Her husband really
did care about librarians and public libraries, and whether
the Springs was competitive on a statewide and national
level with other progressive cities when it came to aca-
demic standards and testing.

It was just that on a night like this, when Josh was all she
could think about, every line felt practiced and forced—
like the plastic cheesecakes in the windows of Marigolds.

Finally, she heard the door shut, and silence. Wonderful,
delicious silence. Nate joined her in the kitchen, grabbed a
dish towel, and moved to Annie's left. She could feel him
unwinding, relaxing—releasing the extra bit of air he'd
kept in his lungs all night long. "That went well."

"Yes." She didn't look at him. She didn't want to spend another minute thinking about librarians. "Very well, dear." He dried a handful of silverware without saying anything. Then he turned toward her, the way he did when he had something profound to say. "Not every kid grows up to be a doctor or a lawyer or a writer." There was an edge to his voice. "Everybody doesn't make the all-stars, Annie. Not in Little League and not in life. That doesn't mean Josh is a failure."

"What are you saying?" She didn't want to get mad at him. They got nowhere when they let their frustrations about Josh come between them.

"I don't know, I feel guilty." He tossed his hands in the air and then leaned back against the counter. "What if he could hear us talking about him? How would he feel if he knew we were disappointed?"

"I'm not disappointed." She hated that word, hated the finality of it. She turned back to the sink full of dishes. "I'm *concerned* for him and sorry for him because he never asked to be hit by that car." A catch sounded in her voice. "Lindsay's off making a name for herself at the paper, and where's Josh? Hooked on pain meds, sitting around his apartment." She gritted her teeth. "I ache for that boy because if he hadn't been injured, who knows what he'd be doing right now." The futility of it surrounded her, suffocated her. She threw the sponge into the sink and grabbed hold of the edge of the counter. "That isn't *disappointment*, Nate. It's just...why did that woman have to make Josh sound like a failure when he's only twenty-eight?"

"Annie." Nate put his hand on her shoulder. His voice was calmer than before. "It's okay to be disappointed."

Before she could respond, he gave her a final look, picked up one of the clean pitchers, and began drying it. The conversation was over.

She studied him for a minute. In the past at a time like this she might've kept talking—just to make her point, or to get the last word in. But a long time ago she learned there was no point adding to a dialogue that had already ended. It was one of those understood aspects of their marriage—like how going out to dinner was assumed when he came home from work and found her curled in a chair reading a new novel or lost in the pages of her Bible study, or how a paper Nordstrom bag of his dress clothes left by the front door meant she was supposed to take them to the cleaners.

They finished the dishes in silence. Before Nate moved on to their bedroom, he leaned close and kissed her cheek. "I love you," he whispered near her ear. "Josh is going to be fine."

"I hope so." She responded to his touch, not angry with him. They needed each other more in this season of life than ever.

Nate slouched, his posture proof of what had to be an inner battle with defeat. "Josh is a good boy." His smile barely lifted his lips. "Some kids take longer, that's all."

Annie nodded and stared at the empty sink. "We'll keep praying for him."

"Yes." He touched her shoulder once more and then left.

She waited, listening to his feet leave the tiled floor and transition onto the carpet and up the stairs to their room. She dried her hands and went into the living room, to the bookcase next to the piano—the one with a dozen framed photos. She looked at them and then reached for the largest on the center shelf, the one of Lindsay and Josh in high school. By then Lindsay was shorter than her brother, but she was a senior, with confidence in her expression and the way she held herself.

Annie looked hard at Josh, at his eyes. He had that impish silly grin, the one he wore often in his early years at Black Forest High School. Like he didn't have a care in the world except one—his friendship with Lindsay. He looked up to her from the time he could crawl, chasing after her and beaming whenever she paid him attention.

Annie smiled at the picture, the way they had their arms around each other's necks. Their friendship had always been mutual—Lindsay adored Josh and saw him as her personal source of entertainment. While she was busy conquering one school year after another, Josh was less serious. He could make his sister laugh no matter what tests or projects she had pending. And up until his senior year in high school, Josh followed in Lindsay's footsteps, writing for the yearbook and newspaper and getting nearly straight A's in school.

But that was the year Lindsay fell in love with Larry, and after that she had less time for Josh. He had Becky Wheaton, of course, a bright, intelligent, beautiful girl who saw only the best in Josh. The two had been inseparable ever since they met at the beginning of their sophomore year. Josh loved her like he'd never loved anyone else in his life, and had even talked about marrying her after they finished college. But as she racked up one success after another, Josh began to flounder. He drank with his buddies on the baseball team and was kicked off the squad his senior year. They broke up, and though he tried junior college for a couple of years, he eventually lost interest in school. When he decided to tow cars in Denver instead of continuing at a university, Annie and Nate figured the job was only a phase. Give him a year, they agreed, and he'd be ready to get serious about his future again.

But that never happened.

Annie squinted hard at the photograph. Everything used to be so easy, so certain. Lindsay and Josh, best friends, with the whole world ahead of them. Becky, forever a part of Josh's life. Annie sighed. She had the ending all written, but somehow the story line changed.

Lindsay was busy now, married with two kids and a full-time job as a feature writer at the local *Gazette*. But even so, Lindsay was closer to Josh than she or Nate. Annie set the photo down, but her eyes lingered. Funny, she thought, how an entire lifetime can be summed up with one framed picture.

She let her eyes drift to other photos: Lindsay and Josh in an oversize raft catching white water on the Truckee River, Josh at age three dancing in six-year-old Lindsay's arms, the four of them at SeaWorld the summer before Lindsay started high school, Josh and Becky at their senior prom, a month before they broke up. The memories were like a balm to her soul, taking her back to a time when the questions were few and the answers easy.

A yawn caught her off guard and she checked her watch. It was after eleven, time to turn in. But she couldn't pull herself from the pictures. Her eyes fell on a photo of Josh standing beside his tow truck the week after he'd been hired in Denver. Heartbroken over the loss of Becky Wheaton, he took a trip to Las Vegas and came back with a confession. He'd met a young woman, inadvertently promised her a life of luxury, and been intimate with her. Eleven months later he drove to the Springs, sat both her and Nate down, and admitted something else.

The woman was married—though Josh hadn't known that at the time—and now she'd given birth to a baby girl. "She tells me the baby is mine. She wants child support." Josh looked devastated. "I don't know what to do."

Annie had been too stunned to speak, but Nate had calmly helped him sort through his options. "You need a paternity test." He worked to hide the pain in his voice, but it weighed heavy on his tone, anyway. "After that you can talk about the next step."

The paternity test never came. The woman found out Josh didn't have a hundred dollars in savings let alone money for child support. After that she wasn't willing to subject her daughter to the test, and Josh couldn't afford a lawyer. Over the years, though, Josh talked about the girl as if she were a very real part of his life. His daughter. He charted her birthdays and sent gifts to the woman without knowing whether they ever reached the child. And he talked about bringing her home one day, where she would become fast friends with Lindsay's kids—her cousins.

Only Lindsay listened. She would let him talk about the girl and always agreed that once Josh had his settlement money he should hire an attorney and force a paternity test. "What if she's really his?" Lindsay only asked the question a handful of times in the years since the family had learned about the child.

"Impossible." Annie always dismissed the possibility. "The dates don't line up—the woman didn't even tell Josh

about the baby until almost a year after the Las Vegas trip."
She hated even talking about the situation. The fact that
one of her children would be in such a quandary broke her
heart. The woman was married, after all. The child almost
certainly belonged to her husband.

"She wanted quick cash," Annie once told Josh when the
subject came up. "Let the matter go. Besides, what about
Becky?"

"Becky moved on." A deep pain filled Josh's eyes. "I
wasn't enough for her."

"I heard she broke up with that last guy." Annie always
thought Becky and Josh would get back together. "At least
give her a call."

"This isn't about Becky. It's about a little girl who belongs
to me. I'm a father now, Mom. I need help figuring out
how to connect with her."

"Don't be ridiculous, Josh. You have no way of knowing
whether that child is yours or not."

The conversation came up again several times, but
always Annie dismissed the idea and eventually Josh mentioned her less often. The child would be seven now, and
he sometimes voiced what he called his greatest fear—that
if his settlement didn't come soon he would miss her childhood entirely.

Another sigh filled the quiet room and Annie left the
room, turning the lights off as she went. Josh had compromised his faith, walked away from regular church attendance, and managed to ruin his credit rating with one bad
loan after another. He drove a beater pickup truck and
could barely afford rent each month. He didn't drink anymore, but he had no real friends and no girlfriend in the

picture. As if his entire life was wrapped up in his back pain, on hold for the day his settlement would arrive in the mail.

And then what? An expensive paternity fight? The sorrow of finally having to admit the truth—that the girl wasn't his in the first place? So what if he could finally buy a modest house somewhere in the Springs? The money wouldn't take away his back pain or make it easier for him to find a job.

She slowed her pace as she neared her room and all at once a reality dawned on her. She had no right getting angry at Nate for what he'd said earlier. Whatever she wanted to tell herself, Nate was right, and an image came to mind. A month ago she'd been caught in traffic on I-25 only to come across a disabled semitruck. The truck's trailer was extraordinarily high and hadn't cleared an overpass. There the truck sat, the overpass collapsed across the top of it.

That's how Annie felt now, like an entire overpass had given way and fallen around her shoulders. Because no matter how badly she wanted to believe otherwise, the truth wouldn't let her move out from beneath it. Yes, she was worried about Josh and frustrated for him and sad about his place in life. But there was no denying the other obvious truth.

She was disappointed in him.

THREE

S aturdays were tough because lawyers—for all the money they made—didn't work weekends. Josh understood. His attorney, Thomas Flynn, was one of the good guys. If the courts were open on the weekend, Flynn would be there fighting for him—Josh had no doubt.

But since he was still days away from his next deposition and moving his case one small step closer to settlement, Josh's plans for Saturday involved other jobs that needed tackling. He slept in and took the usual ten minutes to lie in bed, savoring that half-awake phase when the pain was still a spectator. His back hurt whether he was awake or sleeping, standing or lying down. But in the bliss of sleep, at least he wasn't aware of the pain. Not until ten minutes after he woke up.

Josh opened his eyes and, in as much time as it took him to look out the window and note the blue skies of another beautiful September day, the first deep ache tugged at his middle back. He shifted and winced and a crisscross of sharp, searing pains sliced one way and then another from his shoulder blades and hip bones across his spine.

You can do this, he told himself. *Please, God. . . . Help me get out of bed.* The getting out was the worst part—sometimes worse than any other pain he'd face all day. Something about moving around always made the pain lessen. He held his breath and swung his feet out over the edge of the mattress. The pain doubled and he cried out, panting, trying to find enough air to fill his lungs.

Please, God....

He remembered the pain pills at his bedside. Strange that it usually took trying to move before he remembered the OxyContin, maybe because in his mind he was still the same Josh Warren he'd been for the first twenty-five years of his life, limber and mobile and athletic, able to move without giving his body a second thought. But the limitations he lived with were a quick reminder each morning that he didn't dare try a single hour of life without the help of his medication. Not until something could be done for his back.

Using all his effort, he swung his legs back onto the bed and slid himself up toward the headboard. The bottle was open, and he tried to remember. Had he taken another pill sometime in the middle of the night? Eighty milligrams every twelve hours—those were his doctor's orders. But sometimes he had to count the pills before breakfast to make sure he wasn't taking too many. And if he did, well, then sometimes he had to admit to himself that he was doing the best he could. Too many pills or not.

He took hold of the plastic bottle and his fingers felt stiff as he tapped a single pill into the palm of his other hand. The glass of water he kept by his bedside looked stale. Josh didn't care. He downed the pill and set the glass back on his nightstand. *Work,* he ordered the little round pill. *Start working.*

Ever since his music video encounter with Wynonna Judd more than a month ago, he'd used this time to pray. Talking to God took the edge off the way his whole body screamed for relief, and he couldn't do anything else, anyway. He let his head drop back on the pillow and he closed his eyes.

Dear God, be with my parents. I know they're disappointed in me. He exhaled and tried to sink back into the mattress. He grabbed a quick breath and held it. *The thing is, they don't understand the pain. I can't look for a job until I feel better, so help them not to worry about me. Not to be disappointed.* He grabbed at a handful of his comforter and clenched his fist. "Work...start working already." He remembered his prayer. *Also, God, I pray for Cara and Carl Joseph and Daisy and Cody...for Ethel next door and Keith in Ohio. For Becky, that she's finding the happiness she wanted. And that maybe she might be ready to love me again when I'm the person I want to be. Also for all my friends, God. Be with them and draw them close the way*—he cried out again and rolled partially onto his side—*the way You drew me close with that music video.*

For Lindsay and Larry, and Ben and Bella—my sister's husband and kids; Lord, keep them safe. He felt the first wave of relief pass over him and he wiped the perspiration on his forehead. *And please, God, be with Savannah. One day I want to be healthy and whole and bring her home here where she belongs. Please, God, let her come home. I want her to know her grandparents and her aunt Lindsay and her cousins. I want her to know me.* He felt himself relax. *That's all, God. Thanks.*

He opened his eyes and swung his feet out over the edge of the bed once more. This time the pain was bearable and it didn't cause him to cry out. The pill was working. He clenched his teeth as he drew himself to a sitting position and put his feet on the floor. His head spun a little, the dizziness a regular part of his mornings—at least for the first few minutes after he sat up. A side effect from the medication, his doctor had told him.

He stared at the amber bottle of pills. One day soon he would have surgery and the doctor would fix his back, and then, with a lot of rehab and sweat, he would be his old self again. He'd seen the surgeon again last Wednesday and the report looked good.

"Another forty pounds," the doctor had told him. "You get that weight down and we'll do the operation."

He looked down at his gut, the way it hung over his sweatpants. Weight had never been a problem before, but sometime after high school the pounds piled up. He was seventy pounds overweight when the accident happened. After the accident, he ate out of frustration and boredom and added another thirty. Now he'd lost all but the last forty, but still the doctor wanted to wait.

"Some of your injury is still trying to heal itself," he explained more than once. "As you lose weight, your back is bound to work better and feel better. We can probably schedule the surgery sometime next month."

Josh rubbed the back of his neck. He grabbed a white T-shirt from his second dresser drawer and slid it over his head. At least he could fit into his old shirts now, and Cara had complimented him on a recent picture he'd sent her. "You're looking hot," she'd told him. "Now just get yourself well."

He used the bedpost to pull himself up onto his feet.

That was the goal. Get himself well again. He walked slowly into the kitchen, careful to keep his knees slightly bent so he wouldn't trigger a spasm. A single spasm in his back could lay him flat in bed for a couple hours or more, pain medication or not.

Josh was making himself a bowl of instant oatmeal—maple and brown sugar, his favorite—when there was a knock at the door. A quick survey told him the apartment wasn't as neat as it could be. Magazines were strewn on the couch and coffee table, and the blanket he kept along the back of the sofa had fallen onto the floor. Two half-full glasses of water sat on one of the end tables, on either side of a stack of unopened mail. When he got his settlement, after he started his own business and placed that first call to Becky Wheaton, he would have to make a habit of keeping things neat. Becky liked life to have an order about it, and Josh did, too. He only had to make time for that order. For now, this was usually how the place looked. Whoever was at the door, they weren't paying him a visit because of his clean apartment.

He moved as quickly as he could and opened the door. Bright sunshine met him on the other side, and standing on the front porch were his neighbors—Carl Joseph Gunner and Daisy Dalton. "Howdy, neighbor!" Carl Joseph grinned and pushed his thick dark glasses a little higher up the bridge of his nose.

"Howdy." Josh used the doorknob to steady himself. "Looks like a nice day out there."

"Another beautiful day in the Springs." Daisy looped her arm through Carl Joseph's. "Today's a bus trip to the movies. Saturday date day, right, CJ?"

"Right." Carl Joseph puffed out his chest. "Me and Daisy have a date day after a late breakfast."

Josh absently wondered if the two had come for a reason or just to say hello. They stopped by often—nearly every day—for one reason or another. "A late breakfast, huh?" He smiled, and the pain in his back dimmed in light of the distraction. "What's on the menu?"

Carl Joseph exchanged a frown with Daisy. "That's the problem." He shrugged big and shot a forlorn look at Josh. "The market trip was yesterday and we forgot."

"We forgot eggs." Daisy nodded. She pointed past Josh. "Can we borrow six eggs, Josh? Six eggs should be enough."

He chuckled quietly and the sensation felt wonderful. He stepped aside and motioned for them to come inside. "You bet. I can round up six eggs."

"Because, well"—Carl Joseph furrowed his brow, as if he was thinking very hard on the matter—"we could get by with five, but then maybe we'd be hungry at the movie."

"And hungry at the movie means too much popcorn." Daisy gave Carl Joseph a knowing look. "Not a very healthy choice."

"No." Josh patted his middle. "I know all about that."

Carl Joseph hesitated, but then he laughed out loud, as if Josh had just told the funniest joke ever. Again, Josh kept his own laughter quiet. The two were as guileless and transparent as any friends he had. He led them into the kitchen toward the refrigerator. "Let's see. We need something so you can carry them home."

"Not a basket." Daisy waved her finger, her concern genuine. "Mom says never to put all your eggs in one basket."

Carl Joseph's eyes lit up. "But maybe two baskets."

"Here." Josh pulled a square Tupperware container down from one of his cupboards. His back was loosening up, allowing him the ability to look almost normal as he moved about his kitchen. "This should hold all six eggs."

"I like that." Carl Joseph pushed his glasses up again and smiled at Daisy. "Plastic is good for eggs."

Josh placed six eggs carefully into the container and handed it to Carl Joseph. "What movie are you seeing?"

"It's an older one." A silly grin played across his face. "But Cody says what do you expect for three dollars on a Saturday."

"You expect a good time." Daisy cast a proud look at Carl Joseph. "Because that's a good use of money, CJ. It's a very good use."

The theater was an old one downtown, in a building that would have closed except for its decision to show old movies on the weekend at discount rates. Lindsay had written a piece on the theater for the *Gazette*. Low prices were filling the place and popcorn and candy sales were keeping it in business. Carl Joseph and Daisy were regulars.

"We're seeing *Flicka*. It's a movie about a horseback rider." Daisy must have realized that neither of them had answered Josh's question.

"A horse rider like my brother." Carl Joseph couldn't keep the pride from his tone. He thought the world of Cody, and Josh understood why. The guy came around all the time and Josh liked him. Back when they first met, Cody had shared with Josh his own story of heartache and pain. Somehow Cody's story gave Josh hope that maybe he'd come out happy in the end. The way Cody had.

"You can go with us if you want." Daisy took the container of eggs and held it to herself. She raised her eyebrows at Carl Joseph and her shoulders lifted a few times. "That's okay, right, CJ?"

"Sure." He tossed his hands. "Three people can take a movie date. Three or two, it doesn't matter."

For a few seconds Josh actually considered taking them up on the idea. He'd gone two or three times before, saving them a bus trip and spending the afternoon with them. But he needed to clean his apartment. "Not today, guys. I have plans."

Carl Joseph nodded. "Plans are good. Brother says a day with plans can't be half bad."

"Well..." Josh smiled. He thought about Cara and the plans they'd talked about just last night. "I'd say your brother's right. Planning is always good."

Josh was walking his neighbors to the door when Carl Joseph stopped and took a detour to the fireplace mantel. He squinted at the photos lined across it and pointed to the picture of the two girls. "Tell us the story again, okay?"

"Yeah, tell us." Daisy clapped her hands. "That's a very good story."

Josh didn't mind telling the story. Other than his neighbors, no one knew what really happened with the accident. The story hadn't been even a mention in the Springs paper. Josh gripped the mantel and leaned into it, buying a little added relief for his back. "Where should I start?"

"At the beginning." Carl Joseph took the photo down and held it close so he and Daisy could see it better. "I always like the beginning."

"Okay." Josh knew how to tell the story in a couple minutes. "It happened on New Year's Eve nearly three years ago."

"In Denver, right?" Daisy's eyes were wide with anticipation.

"Right. I was towing cars away from a no-parking area along one side of a busy street."

"Which is dangerous." Carl Joseph nodded his concern.

"Definitely dangerous." Josh hesitated, thinking back. "I was hooking up my sixth car of the night when those two girls came up and asked me a question."

"They were best friends." Daisy told the detail to Carl Joseph, as if she were the owner of that part of the story. "The very best."

"Right, and at that time there weren't any cars coming, so the girls were standing in the road. They were trying to find State Street and they needed directions."

"So you told them." Carl Joseph stared at the framed picture. "They seem like nice girls."

"They were. They hadn't been drinking, and they didn't want to get home too late. Too many bad drivers on the road on New Year's Eve." Josh ran his hand through his dark hair. He was feeling stronger than before so he released his hold on the mantel and crossed his arms. "I was giving them directions when I saw the drunk driver."

Fear lined Carl Joseph's forehead. "It's against the law to drive drunk."

"Yeah." Josh uttered a quietly sarcastic laugh. "I don't think the driver was very concerned about the law."

"Because he was passed out." Daisy nodded emphatically.

"He was." Josh could still picture the guy, his head

slumping forward onto the steering wheel as his car veered off the road. "And he was headed straight for the girls."

"This is the scariest part." Daisy partially closed her eyes, the way a person might in anticipation of a frightening scene in a horror movie. "I hate this part."

"Me, too." Josh imagined the accident all over again. "Everything happened so fast. The girls couldn't see the drunk driver, but he was headed straight for them. I pulled one of them out of danger, and as I reached for the other one the car slammed into us."

Carl Joseph and Daisy were silent, gripped by the story.

"I had time to throw the second girl onto the grass, out of harm's way, but at the same time the car hit my left shoulder and knocked me to the ground."

Daisy put her hand over her mouth. "That's terrible."

"He broke the law for sure." Carl Joseph's tone was hushed. "That was a very bad thing he did."

"Very bad." Josh felt the impact again the way he'd felt it that night, how the front grille of the Mercedes sedan had barreled into him, knocking the wind from him and leaving him in a heap on the ground. For the first few minutes he thought he was dead. He couldn't breathe, couldn't move, and as people surrounded him and sirens sounded in the distance he wanted only one more chance to tell his parents and Lindsay and Becky he loved them, to somehow get word to Savannah that he had tried to be her father, always he had tried.

Daisy allowed the hint of a smile. "The story has a happy ending, right?"

"It does." Josh had never told Carl Joseph or Daisy

about his back pain. They wouldn't understand, and it would only mar their visits with unnecessary concern. There was nothing they could do to help ease his pain or heal his back, so why complain to them about the way he hurt? Better to let them focus on the girls. He drew another breath and finished. "The car didn't kill me, and the two girls weren't hurt at all." He grinned at his friends.

"A happy ending for sure." Carl Joseph raised his fist high in the air. "I love that story." He smiled at the two girls in the photo and then at Josh. "That makes you a hero."

A hero. The words cast a ray of sunshine across his cloudy heart. All the pain was worth something, even if few people thought he was a hero. The girls did, certainly. And the people who read the article, and his neighbors. But he hadn't shared the story with his parents, not yet. He remembered the way his mother had received the news of his accident when he called her late that night.

"I was hit by a car," he told her, his voice flat. "I'm in the hospital, but I'm okay." He intended to go into the details, tell her how he'd pulled the girls to safety before taking the hit, but his mother was already talking.

"Josh, what happened? Are you hurt?" Then she called for his father. "We're on our way, son. We'll be there in an hour."

"Mom, wait." Josh was already on pain medication by then, and the scope of his injuries was still being realized. "I'm fine. I'm going home tonight and I'm coming down tomorrow."

"Oh, Josh." His mother's relief came in short breathy

gasps. "You scared me to death." She wasn't mad, just worried about him. Afraid because he could have been killed. But what she said next stayed with him still. "Now maybe you'll see why I want you to get your degree, do something with your brain for a change. Towing cars, Josh? Every day I worry about you, and now this. Why don't you take some time and think about getting back in school. Not one good thing comes from your work as a tow truck driver, son. Not one good thing."

So he hadn't told her or his father or Lindsay. Not because he wasn't proud of his role in saving the lives of the girls, but because it wasn't enough. He loved his family, and they loved him—their feelings for him were all that kept him going some days. But they hadn't spent more than a rare few minutes at his apartment, and none of them had noticed the small photographs on the mantel. One day he would explain it all. He would get his settlement—half a million dollars or more—and he would open his own garage, and then, when his back was healed and life was good, he would tell them the truth about how he was hurt.

Daisy took the photograph from Carl Joseph and set it back on the mantel. "I love hero stories." Adoration made her eyes sparkle as she looked at Josh. "You and CJ and Cody are the only heroes I know." She looked at her friend. "CJ because he protects me from the rain, and Cody because he made my sister, Elle, love again. And you, Josh, because you saved the lives of those two girls."

Josh liked being a hero for these two. It seemed to give them hope about the world in general, and if it did, well, then that was another good thing that had come from the accident. No matter what his mother thought about his job as a tow truck driver.

"What about this one?" Carl Joseph picked up the photo of Savannah and studied it. He pushed his glasses back into place again. "Can you tell us this story, Josh?"

"Not today." Josh kept his tone easy, his smile in place. "That one's not a happy story."

"Oh." Daisy frowned. "Then let's not talk about it. I only like the happy ones."

"Me, too." Josh could feel the OxyContin holding his pain at bay, making it bearable for him to be on his feet this long. "You two better get home for your late breakfast."

Daisy gasped and looked down at the eggs. She'd been holding them in one hand, clutching them to her chest. "I almost forgot about late breakfast."

"Yeah, we better go." Carl Joseph took charge and grabbed hold of Daisy's free hand. "We have our movie date." He waved to Josh as they reached the door. "Thanks for telling us the happy story."

"Anytime." Josh followed them and waited until they were down the walkway. "Have fun today."

They both turned around and waved one last time. When Josh closed the door and went into his living room, he took a minute to sit down and catch his breath. He hadn't stood that long at one time for a week at least. From where he sat, he looked at the photos on the mantel again and his eyes fell on the one of Savannah. Maybe one day their story would be a happy one, too. When he could finally prove that the reason her eyes looked like his was because she was his daughter. He stretched his back and tried to find a comfortable position. He agreed with Daisy. The happy stories were the best.

Even if he was the only one who knew how much the happy ending cost.

FOUR

Maria Cameron held tight to her daughter's hand and together they trudged down the cement steps to the subway that ran beneath the streets of Manhattan. She had panhandled her way through another Sunday afternoon and now she needed the red line north along Broadway to 145th Street in Harlem. She and Savannah rented a room from a guy she'd met in the park three months ago. Freddy B, he called himself.

She paid her rent one way or another—with the money from tourists in Central Park or by spending the night in his bed when he wanted her. He lived in a one-bedroom apartment in a brownstone in the part of Harlem that had yet to experience urban renewal. But it was a home, and it would do for now.

"I'm hungry, Mama." Savannah's strawberry-blond hair was pulled back in a ponytail, and her cheeks were smudged with dirt—the way Maria had smudged them earlier that morning.

"We'll eat when we get home." She gave the girl a look intended to quiet her. She didn't need people scrutinizing them on the subway. "Keep quiet, now."

Savannah nodded and bit her lip. She pushed the sleeves of her sweater up, but as she did she exposed a series of small bruises. Maria reached over, jerked her sleeves back in place, and gave the girl a look that told her to be more careful. Strangers didn't understand bruises on a seven-year-old. But sometimes Savannah walked too slowly, and she had to be pulled along. It wasn't Maria's fault the girl's skin was fair, or that she bruised easily.

She paid the fare and led Savannah to the first two open seats. The subway always smelled the same—a faint mix of sour milk and old urine. Maria took stock of the car. An old lady at the far end, half asleep. Otherwise they were alone. She pulled a wad of bills from her pocket and counted them. September was a good month. Lots of tourists around the zoo entrance, less heat and humidity. Everyone in a good mood. She sorted through the bills and came up with an amount that surprised her even for September. A hundred and forty-two dollars. Not bad for a day's work.

"How much?" Savannah crossed her ankles and put her hands on her knobby knees. "Enough for rent?"

"More than enough." She eyed her daughter. "Don't ask so many questions."

Maria tucked the money into the back pocket of her baggy jeans, leaned her head back against the window, and closed her eyes. Good day or not, this wasn't how life was supposed to turn out. She was so far from those days that sometimes on the long subway ride home she forced herself to go back. Otherwise she would forget where she'd come from, and that wouldn't be good. Because if she couldn't remember the past, how was she ever going to find her way back there.

She and Raul had married ten years ago with dreams of opening their own pizza shop on the Lower East Side. Raul had business partners who were shady, but Maria didn't ask a lot of questions. It wasn't her deal where Raul got his money or how he spent his time when he came home late at night.

The trip to Vegas was his idea. "Go meet a guy with money. Get yourself knocked up and we'll be set. Regular money coming in first of the month till the kid's eighteen."

Maria hadn't liked the idea, but the fact that Raul suggested it made her just mad enough that she decided to go. Could be fun, spending a week away from Raul, playing in the bed of a new man, someone rich and mysterious. She let Raul book her plane and hotel, and she took the trip two weeks later. Josh Warren was the first guy she met, sitting at a bar in the Mandalay Bay casino. He had dark hair and fair skin and blue eyes that caught her attention across the room. She had fifty dollars in her pocket and instructions to find the highest roller in the hotel. A nearby restroom gave her the chance to freshen her red lipstick and adjust her blouse so her cleavage was more prominent. Then she ambled up to the man and took the bar stool beside him.

"Hi, there." She played with a strand of her red-blond hair. "What's a pretty boy like you doing all alone in a place like this?"

He didn't seem interested at first. He pulled a cigarette from a pack of L&M lights and offered one to her. She took it and held it out while he lit both of them. "I came alone." He took a long drag from the cigarette. "Haven't had a vacation in a year."

"Me, either." She wasn't sure the guy had money, but

she was willing to take a few minutes to find out. "Buy me a drink?"

Josh studied her and exhaled a mouthful of smoke with a series of surprised laughs. "You're bold."

"Yes, sir." She crossed her legs and adjusted her short skirt in a phony show of modesty. "My mama taught me you get nothing in this world unless you ask for it."

"Touché." Josh held his cigarette up as if he were toasting her boldness. "Name's Josh Warren."

"Hello, Josh." The cigarette helped her voice sound velvety. She leaned over so he'd have a better view. "I'm Maria Cameron. Alone, same as you."

"Vacation?"

"Sort of." She willed herself to look the victim. "Old man used to beat me." She shrugged one dainty shoulder. "Finally left the jerk. Came here looking for a change in luck."

Josh didn't exactly look interested, but the glass of whiskey in front of him was half empty and he seemed pleasantly relaxed. "You a gambler, Maria Cameron?"

"Sometimes." She let her eyes move slowly down his frame. "Depends on the prize."

He laughed and they finished their cigarettes, flirting and making conversation. The part that caught her attention came just as he leaned across her to kill the cigarette in a nearby ashtray. Their shoulders brushed against each other and he whispered near her ear. "I got a million reasons why you should go out with me tonight."

"A million?" Maria's heart beat harder. What was he saying? That he was a millionaire? She leaned closer. "Tell me about it."

"I got plans." He ordered another whiskey for himself

and one for her. When the drinks came, he grinned at her in a way that sent chills down her arms.

"Tell me." Maybe she'd fall in love with this Josh Warren. That would serve Raul right for sending her here in search of a one-night stand.

"I work out of a garage in Denver, but in a year I'll own the place. Then I'll open a chain of garages up and down the state of Colorado. I'll be a millionaire in no time, baby." He clinked his glass against hers. "That's the plan."

Maria wasn't sure just how much money Josh had right now, but with plans like that she had to believe she'd found her guy. "I have plans, too." She looked over her shoulder and lowered her voice. "But I don't like talking about them in public." She felt the corners of her mouth curl up. "Know what I mean?"

Josh paid their tab and without asking what she meant he led her to the elevator and up sixteen floors to his room. They spent most of the next four days in bed, and she never even bothered to check in under her own name, never spent a dime. If Josh wasn't a high roller, he certainly played the role that week. He told her he was a Christian and that he'd never done anything like this, and he tried everything he could to sell her on Denver.

"We can get married and get a place together." He had stars in his eyes from the time he first brought her to his room. "We'll find a church and raise a family and I'll take care of you the rest of your life." As an afterthought he asked about her age.

She was a well-kept thirty-two, but he didn't need to know that. "I'm twenty-seven." She studied him across the table at breakfast one morning. "What about you?"

"Just turned twenty-one." He was smoking again. "But that's in style. Guys with older girls."

With every passing day Josh seemed to fall harder for her. He talked about his family, his sister, Lindsay, and how his parents wanted him to continue college. "But my plans don't need a degree," he told her. "Everything's falling into place just like I hoped it would."

Josh made her feel things Raul never made her feel, and after three days she was thinking about going home with him to Denver and never looking back. It wasn't until the last day that Maria made sense of the plans Josh had been talking about. Sure, he planned to own the garage at the end of the year, but right now he was living on a tow truck driver's salary.

They'd been in bed, and as the details fell into place, she climbed out and got dressed in a hurry. "You mean, you're not a millionaire?"

He leaned on his elbow and let out a nervous laugh. "Not yet. Not for a year, anyway."

She gathered her things. "This can't work, Josh." She was shaking by then, attracted to him but scared about Raul. He'd left her a message at the front desk asking her to call. If she left with Josh now, Raul would hunt her down. He had friends who frightened her, friends who could find her. And if Josh wasn't the high roller Raul had ordered her to find, then why would she go with him, anyway? More than that, when she got home he'd be furious with her. She shook her head. "Not yet, not now." She had his phone number and address, and she'd given him hers. She backed up until she hit the hotel room door. "Besides, I'm married,

Josh. I—I should've told you." She reached for the door handle. "I'll call you. Maybe then you'll have your plans worked out and I'll be single again and…and…"

Josh sat up. "You're married?" His cheeks lost their color. "How could you do this?"

Maria left without answering, angry and in tears. He shouldn't have exaggerated the truth. If he didn't have a million dollars coming, then why say so? Pretty boys with a tow truck driver's salary were a dime a dozen. Raul was better than that, after all. Josh followed her out into the hall, but she didn't look back. Once she exited the elevator she made her way to the front desk and called Raul.

"I found the high roller." She swallowed the lie and pressed forward. "I'm ready to come home."

Raul praised her and gave her instructions for catching a flight home to New York the next day. She spent the night with a stranger from Australia and flew home a few hours later.

"Think you're knocked up?" Raul asked her when he met her at LaGuardia.

Maria wanted to spit at him, but instead she glared with piercing eyes. "I had a good time. Let's just say that."

Her answer ticked him off. He beat her bad that night, punishing her for having a good time on a trip he had forced her to take. The bruises and screaming were the beginning of the end, and by the time she found out she was pregnant, her marriage was over. She moved in with a girlfriend and began a series of bad relationships, all the while waiting until the baby was born.

One look at Savannah and she was pretty sure who

the father was. The infant didn't have Raul's dark skin or the Australian's light blond hair. And by then Josh was the only person she knew who could help her financially. Raul's words came back to her.

"Get yourself knocked up and be set for life . . . a regular paycheck every month."

She made the call to Josh when Savannah was two months old. "How are those plans coming along?" That's how she started the conversation, and on her end she crossed her fingers. "You a millionaire, Josh Warren?"

"You gotta be kidding me." He sounded hurt, like he was still angry at her for walking out that day in his hotel room. "Listen, lady, if I were a millionaire you're the last person on earth I'd tell."

"Unless maybe I have news that might interest you." Lying on a blanket next to her, little Savannah began to cry. "You're a father, Josh. I had a baby girl and she looks just like you."

On the other end, he said nothing for half a minute. "You're serious? You had a baby?"

"I did. I want to share custody with you, Josh." She waited a deliberate amount of time. "But I'm out of money. I need monthly support."

Whatever emotion Josh had experienced with the news, he buried it quickly. "How do I know she's mine? You're married."

"Not anymore. The baby's yours. I'm positive."

Josh's voice softened a little. "How can I believe anything you say?"

Savannah's cry grew louder, loud enough that Maria was pretty sure Josh could hear her over the phone lines.

"That's your daughter, Josh. Send us some money and you can come see her for yourself."

"You're still in New York City?"

"Yes. I'm serious. Help me out and you can call her your own."

Josh paused. "What are you looking for?"

"Three thousand, maybe four. Enough for me and Savannah to get by."

Josh breathed in so loudly she could hear it. "Three or four thousand?" He released an angry laugh. "I'm still a tow truck driver, Maria. My plans haven't come together yet." He pushed ahead. "What if I come out there and meet you. For a weekend or so, something like that. If I could see her for myself then I'd know if she—"

"No." Maria was furious. "What are you saying? You have no money?"

"Not right now, but . . ." He sounded angry and shocked, not sure what to say or believe. "Let me book a ticket. I'll come in a few weeks and we can talk in person."

"Forget it." Maria raised her voice. She had a baby to feed and a life to figure out. The last thing she needed was a guy without money. "Call me when your plans come through. Otherwise, I'm not interested." She hung up the phone and didn't hear from him again for a year. He called with just one question. Did she still think he was the baby's father?

"Of course." She wasn't any kinder to him than she had been the last time they talked. "Did your money come through?"

"It will. I need you to do a paternity test, okay?"

"Not without money." Again she hung up on him.

Three summers passed, and he called again and this time he told her things were looking up. "My plans are working out. Tell me what you need."

Maria was still single, still trying to make things work out in the city. But she needed money more than ever. "Four thousand. Not a penny less."

"Okay." He sounded nervous. "I can do that. But I want something first."

"What?"

"A photo. I'll give you an address and you send me a picture of her. I won't write a check until then."

Maria agreed, and she kept her word. The next day she placed a picture of Savannah in the mail. She called Josh a week later. "I told you. She's your daughter."

"She—she has my eyes."

"Right, so when's the check coming?"

"As soon as I can pull the money together." Josh's tone took on a desperate quality. "I'll get you money, Maria, I will. Maybe not four thousand dollars, but something. I want to take responsibility. I want to meet her."

"Are you kidding?" Maria considered ripping the phone cord from the wall and throwing the receiver across the room. "You don't have the money? You lied to me?"

"Come on." He was pleading with her. "I needed to know. Now I only need to—"

Maria slammed the phone back on the base and cursed him for being a failure. A few weeks later she found a package from him in the mail. In it was a plastic-framed photograph of Josh, and a hundred-dollar bill. Tucked in the envelope was a note in which Josh promised to give more money, only if she would let him come for a visit. The hundred came in handy for a few days, but Maria tucked the package in a dresser drawer and when she moved a few months later she didn't give Josh her forwarding information. Since then, she hadn't talked to him, hadn't taken his phone calls. Once she could have sworn she saw him in Central Park, but she left before she had time to find out.

The subway ground to a stop and Maria opened her eyes. Savannah was still sitting beside her, still watching her with those big blue eyes. Josh's eyes. "We're almost home."

"I guess." She yawned and sat up a little straighter. Savannah's father never had any plans at all. He was like all the rest. The subway reached 145th Street and she took firm hold of Savannah's hand. They were home, and with this much money maybe she could get a good night's sleep in her own bed for a change and try to forget about the past and Savannah and a blue-eyed dreamer named Josh Warren. A guy who wasn't so much a high roller as he was like every other guy.

Just another loser.

◈

Savannah didn't really have her own room, just a corner halfway under a desk in the place where her mama sometimes slept. She wasn't allowed on the bed, in case her mama slept there. But even when Mama didn't, Savannah's place was on the floor. Her head beneath the desk, feet sticking out. She had a soft sleeping bag and a nice pillow, and anyway, she sort of liked sleeping beneath the desk because the little area was dark and private, like a tent or a fort.

Under the desk she kept all her treasures. There was a book called *Heidi* that some lady gave her when she was six and they were in Central Park, and a little plastic cross she got from her grandpa Ted before he died. Her grandpa told her about Jesus, but no one else ever talked about Him. It made her feel safe to think that someone like Jesus would care enough to listen.

But her favorite thing under the desk was the picture of her daddy. It wasn't very big and the black frame was cracked in two places. Savannah found it one morning in a box of things under her mother's bed. "Who's this?" She had held the picture up close to her mama's face.

Her mother smelled like beer, and her eyes didn't open very wide. "That?" She laughed, but the sound wasn't very funny. "That's your daddy. He's a real Prince Charming."

Later that day when her mama caught her looking at the photo, she grabbed it and threw it in the trash. But that night when Mama was drinking again, Savannah snuck outside and saved it. Mama didn't know she still had it, but she did. And it was her most favorite thing because someday she was going to find him and that would make everyone happy. Mama told her all the time that life would have been better if she didn't have Savannah.

"I'm not a very good mother," she would say.

Some nights—though Savannah wouldn't have told anyone but Jesus—she had to agree with Mama. Because some nights Mama grabbed her and shoved her under the desk earlier than her usual bedtime, and sometimes there was no dinner because there was no money from the people in Central Park. But the daddy in the picture gave her a reason to believe that Grandpa was right. Jesus had good plans for her.

After all, her daddy was a real Prince Charming, if only she could find him.

And what could possibly be better than that?

FIVE

Lindsay Warren Farrell was sorting through old magazines in a corner of her kitchen when the phone rang. The kids were at school and Larry was at work, so she didn't expect the call to be from one of them. She looked at the caller ID and smiled. Josh. She hadn't talked to him in a week, and she needed to catch up.

"Hello?"

In the background of wherever Josh was calling from, a familiar song was playing so loud Lindsay could hear it clearly. "Josh?" She could hear the words now, and she sat on the nearest kitchen bar stool. What was going on? Before she could ask whether it was really him or not, he spoke up.

"Do you hear that?"

"Yes." She managed a confused laugh. "It's loud."

"I know it is." Josh sounded happier than he had in years. "You won't believe what happened, Linds. Six weeks ago I found the greatest song. Wynonna Judd was performing something live on country videos, and—"

"Wynonna Judd?"

"Yes! She was singing this same song, 'I Can Only

Imagine.' So, I thought it was her song and I've been looking for it when I stop by the market—you know, in the CD section at the back. But then I had this idea to look online and sure enough ..."

"You found it by MercyMe?" Her smile spread down into her heart and soul.

"Just now!" He sounded amazed, almost breathless. "Today I can honestly say my back pain isn't the first thing on my mind. You know why?"

"You're too busy singing?"

"Sort of. I mean, I've been playing it all day." He rested for a few seconds, and when he started up again his pace was more controlled. "When I watched the video, I made a decision. Right then and there I gave my life back to Jesus and told Him I was sorry for every wrong decision I'd made without Him. I've been praying since then and, well, you know, just sort of thinking about how different my life should be at this point."

Lindsay could already feel the tears in her eyes. Sometimes Larry would see Josh's name on the caller ID and walk away from it. "He's always asking for money or needing some sort of handout," Larry told her once. "He's *your* brother, you deal with him."

But now Josh was proving why people could never, ever give up on someone they love. She'd prayed for Josh all her life—especially in the decade since he graduated from high school. Neither Josh's choices nor the circumstances that came with them had ever brought him closer to God, but now maybe he was finally ready to stop running his life on his own. "Josh ... I'm so happy."

"Me, too. It's like I finally get it about God, about Jesus

going to the cross and how He opened the gates of heaven for people like you and me. If we let Him, He'll give us life here and forever. So now this is my song, you know? 'I Can Only Imagine.'"

Lindsay's heart was so full she couldn't speak.

"Anyway, I called for a reason. Can I go with you and Larry and the kids to church this coming Saturday? Don't you go in the evening?"

"Six o'clock." Lindsay felt like one of the townspeople watching Ebenezer Scrooge run around handing out gifts on Christmas morning. "You're serious, right? You wanna go with us?"

"Definitely." He laughed and it was the laugh of a big kid, not a troubled young man in chronic pain. "Truthfully? I've been attending a Christian church with a few of my neighbors for the past five Sundays. I love it. Makes me not think about the pain so much, you know?"

"Yes." She felt hot tears on her cheeks and she dabbed at them. A picture came to mind: herself, Larry, Ben, Bella, and Josh sharing a pew near the front of their church on Saturday evening. "I'll save you a spot."

"Come on, Lindsay." He sounded like his old self, the way he was before the accident. "I know you better than that." Another laugh. "My sister, Lindsay, on time? I'll save *you* one."

The song was still blaring in the background, and Lindsay struggled to find her voice. "You know what this is, right?" She couldn't wait to tell her mom about this phone call. Her parents went to the more traditional Sunday morning service, but this was one Saturday evening they needed to attend.

"It's a miracle." Josh didn't hesitate. "I could feel God doing something in my heart, changing me. But finding this song today—it's like the whole world looks different."

A sound came from Lindsay, but she wasn't sure if it was a laugh or a cry. She put her fingers to her lips. "I've prayed for this moment for so long." She walked toward the kitchen window and stared out at Pikes Peak in the distance. "With all your pain and the accident and the struggles you've had, I knew only God could bring you relief. And now—now look at you."

"You're right. A week of days like this one and maybe my back will heal itself." He sounded beyond upbeat, like he actually believed such a thing was possible. "If not, then I'll wait for the surgery, but at least I won't be walking under a dark cloud. Not anymore. I remembered this afternoon what Mom and Dad always told us: God has great plans for His people." He laughed one more time. "Isn't that great, Lindsay, because guess what? I finally believe it."

Lindsay told him again how happy she was for him and how she'd prayed for him and how different he sounded now that his faith was back in place. "The kids have a lot going on the rest of this week—piano, dance, football practice. Then there's parents night at the elementary school. Bella won't let me miss it. But Friday's open." Lindsay walked to the family computer and pulled up her iCalendar. "Come for dinner?"

"I'm in court that day." He didn't sound weary or defeated the way he usually did when he talked about the hearings and depositions associated with his car accident. "Dinner would be perfect."

"Then on Saturday you can come to Ben's football game. Mom and Dad will be there and we can go to church after."

"You might even be on time."

"Yeah." She laughed at that. "Now that would be a miracle." She was about to hang up when a thought hit her. "Hey, I'm running out to do a few errands. I have to take a dish by Mom's house. Care if I come by? I'm not sure I can wait until Friday to hug you."

"I'll be here."

Lindsay ran a brush through her hair and checked herself in the mirror. She and Larry worked out nearly every morning, sometimes running the hills around their home. Her hours at the *Gazette* were manageable, eight to four with Sundays and Tuesdays off. If she needed more time at home, the editors were flexible, as long as her stories were in by Saturday at five. Life was good and healthy and it ran like clockwork.

Only Josh kept Lindsay awake at night, wondering how she could help her brother, and whether he would ever turn back to the faith they'd shared as kids. And now...She grabbed the baking dish from the kitchen, a bag of clothes for the cleaners, and a few packages for the mail and hurried to her Tahoe parked in the garage. Now Josh was finally having the turnaround they'd all wanted for him.

She stopped at his place first. She couldn't wait to see him. His eyes would tell her how deeply he was affected by this revelation that God was on his side, that He still had plans for Josh even if they'd been derailed for a season. Her brother's eyes.

The apartment complex where he lived wasn't the finest, and the few times Lindsay had been here she'd always looked over her shoulder to make sure no one was lurking in the shadows. She'd talked to one of the news reporters at the *Gazette* once about whether the Garden Terrace Apartments were involved in higher crime than usual, and she was surprised when his check came back negative. "It's in a questionable area," the guy told her. "But that complex houses some physically disadvantaged adults. Most of them have been there for years, and that kind of stability usually makes a place safer."

Lindsay walked quickly, anyway. Fresh graffiti was spray-painted on the garbage Dumpster at the center of the parking lot, and one apartment had a broken window. But whatever she thought of the complex, she would need to spend more time here. Usually Josh discouraged her from coming, complaining that he was too tired or not ready for company. He seemed to prefer their visits take place at their parents' house. But maybe that would be different now, too.

She knocked on the door and he opened it more quickly than usual. Was it her imagination or was he standing taller, straighter? "Josh..."

The song was still running from his stereo system, but it wasn't as loud as earlier. His eyes met hers and he held out both arms. "Everything's going to be okay, Linds." His voice was soft, full of the emotion he rarely showed. "It really is."

Her brother had been taller than her since her second year in high school, and at six foot four he had nine inches on her, easily. He'd lost a lot of weight, but he still hadn't found the svelte athletic build he'd had as a teenager. Lindsay didn't mind. She put her arms around him and pressed her head to his chest. He was a mountain of a man, and his extra padding made her feel small and safe in his arms.

When she pulled away, she let her eyes linger on his and she saw it, the sparkle that hadn't been there for three years. "You're really back, aren't you?"

He nodded. "Like I just woke up from a nightmare." He stepped aside and motioned for her to follow him into the apartment.

She had a little time. The two of them moved into his living room. She set her purse down on his cleaned and polished coffee table and as they sat on the couch facing his fireplace, he grinned. "See, Linds. Not a single dish or piece of mail." He gestured to the clean room. "Proud of me?"

"I'm trying not to pass out." She giggled. Her brother had always kept a messy room, even when they were kids. *"Life takes too much time,"* he used to say. But since his accident, the rest of the family worried that his dirty apartment was a symptom of his pain and possible depression. She surveyed the room, the way the furniture was in order, the clean windowsills, and she patted his knee. "I might have to hire you for mine."

They fell into an easy conversation and Lindsay turned the topic back to his renewed faith. "So you actually feel better today? I mean, your back doesn't hurt as much?"

Josh shifted, probably trying to find a comfortable position. "Before, I let the pain control everything I did, my entire day. Sometimes my back hurt so bad I could almost picture the pain like a living, breathing being, like the devil had me surrounded and there was no way out. You know?"

Lindsay reached for his hand. Her heart hurt to hear

her brother talk about his situation that way. So what if he hadn't wanted company. If he'd been that down and discouraged, if the pain had felt that overwhelming... "You should've said something. I could've come by after work more often and at least brought you dinner."

"No." Josh's forehead was damp, proof that he was still hurting even now as he talked with her. But the peace in his eyes went deeper than whatever he was feeling. "Don't worry about it, Linds. I was fine." He looked at the photos lined across his fireplace mantel. "I had to reach this place by myself. Just me and God."

She stood and moved closer to the three photographs. The one of the little girl caught her attention first and she took hold of it. "Were these here last time I came by?"

"Probably." He sounded sheepish. "It's not like I usually ask you to sit with me in the living room. Anytime you've been here I'm usually in a hurry to get you out."

"Why?" She still had the picture in her hand, but she looked back at him, hurt by his admission.

"Because." His expression begged her to understand. "I didn't want you to see me like this. My back...it can be a challenge getting around. When I'm here alone I don't have to act like everything's okay. I can lie down on the floor or stay in bed if that's what makes me feel better." He smiled. "But, I don't know. Today's been so weird. The pain's still there, but it's distant now. Like someone shouting at me from across a football field."

Her heart broke for him, her brother who had always been so happy and easygoing. To think he hadn't wanted her to stop by because he was embarrassed by his pain. The reality was awful. Lindsay sighed and turned her attention back to the photograph. She'd seen the picture just once before. "How old was she here? Four or five?"

"Four." Josh stood and walked to the spot beside Lindsay. "I keep thinking that a year from now I could have partial custody of her. I bet she's just perfect, you know?"

Lindsay smiled at him. "I can't wait to meet her." Never mind that their parents didn't think the girl was really Josh's daughter or that years had passed without any word from the girl's mother. The child honestly did bear a resemblance to Josh, so the possibility of her being Josh's daughter was a very real one as far as Lindsay was concerned. Besides, why argue the idea? Josh believed she was his daughter, and Lindsay believed in Josh.

She set the photograph down and looked at the one beside it. The picture showed two teenage girls dressed in jeans and sweaters, standing in front of the snow-covered front yard of a two-story home. "Who are they?"

"It's a long story." Josh's answer was quick. "They're best friends. I met them on a job."

Lindsay looked at the girls again and she knew without asking that her brother wasn't interested in either of them. They were ten years younger than him, at least. Whatever the story behind them, it must've mattered greatly to Josh for him to keep their photo where he could see it every day. "Did you take the picture?"

"No." Josh turned away and walked to the kitchen. "I'm not sure who took it." He pressed his hand to his lower back, but he didn't slow his pace. "It's no big deal, really. I just keep it there to remind me of the good that can come from towing cars." He reached for the cupboard near his sink. "Want some water?"

"Sure. Thanks." She was still thinking about the teenage girls. If Josh needed a reason to believe in his job, then whatever he had come up with, Lindsay was happy for him. Especially since his work had cost him his health, and, in the last three years, his employment.

Lindsay took a glass of water from him. "Tell me about these neighbors of yours, the ones you're going to church with."

"They're a great group. Carl Joseph and his girlfriend, Daisy, live in separate apartments in my building, and then there's Carl Joseph's brother, Cody, and his wife, Elle, who is Daisy's sister. The four of them go every week together, and ever since I told Carl Joseph about that Wynonna video and how I felt God calling me back to Him, they've included me in their group." Josh's eyes were full of light. "I really have a very rich life, Lindsay. The settlement has nothing to do with that."

She made a point to remember how he looked in that moment, sunshine streaming in through his small kitchen window, standing there in his tiny apartment, his back no doubt killing him, and believing with all his heart that no amount of money could make him any richer. Happy tears made her eyes damp. "I can't wait for Friday dinner. And Saturday, too." She hugged him one more time and held on longer than usual. When she eased back, she looked straight into his heart, the part that would always belong to her. "I think maybe you're just starting to live again."

"I am." He breathed in deep and stood straight again. "I can hardly wait to see what God has for me next."

"Me, too. I mean—I have my brother back." She took her purse from the coffee table and slipped it up onto her shoulder. Then she kissed her brother's cheek and headed for the front door. "Friday night."

"I'll be there." They were at the door and Josh leaned into the frame. "Oh, and that six hundred dollars you loaned me?" He pulled a check from his pocket and handed it to her. "You can cash it on Wednesday."

Lindsay hadn't thought about the loan since she gave him the money a few months ago when his doctor bills were too high for him to pay the rent. "Josh, you don't have to do that." She tried to hand the check back to him, but he wouldn't take it. "Consider it a gift."

"I can't." His tone was still light, but Lindsay knew he was serious about the money. "I told you I'd pay you back and I meant it. I have my bills figured out for next month." He smiled. "Thanks for being there. I didn't want to get behind, and because of you and Larry, I didn't."

"Well...you could've waited for your settlement."

"I owe Mom and Dad almost a year's wages." He gave her a funny look, the way he used to on a Saturday when they had just one afternoon to clean the entire garage. "That will definitely have to wait for the settlement." He touched her shoulder. "Yours I can repay now, so let me, okay?"

"Okay." She held his eyes a few seconds longer before she folded the check and put it in the pocket of her jeans. "I love you, Josh. I'm so happy you found your way back."

"Love you, too." His eyes danced. "Tell Ben to look for me in the stands."

With that Lindsay ran lightly to her car and as she pulled out of the complex she saw Josh standing on his porch watching her, his smile visible from across the parking lot. She waved one last time and then made a quick decision. She would do her other errands first, then go by her mother's house last. That way she wouldn't feel rushed. Today the two of them needed to talk about more than the schedule for the coming week, or who Ben's team was playing in Saturday's game.

She walked through her parents' front door an hour later and found her mother on the phone out back in the garden. Lindsay was practically bursting with the news about Josh, but her mom motioned to her to wait a minute. She had a pile of pulled weeds at her feet and a small box of gardening tools nearby. Lindsay leaned against the back wall of the house and looked beyond her mother to the acreage that made up the backyard. She and Josh used to play games out here every afternoon, and in summer their parents would set up an aboveground pool for them and their friends. So many happy memories.

"Like Nate always says, the election isn't a sure thing, so we have to be careful. We had the librarians here on Friday and this week it's another group of representatives from the teachers union. I think we're serving cheesecake again." She made a face in Lindsay's direction and drew small circles in the air with her free hand, as if to say she was trying to wrap up the call. "Right, well, maybe you should be here. You're a friend of ours and a friend of theirs. That's always good for Nate."

Lindsay worried about her mom. Before her dad ran for the Board of Education, her parents were involved with

a Bible study at church and bringing meals to the homebound. Now it seemed like nearly every hour of the day
was dedicated to helping her father get reelected. Maybe
the talk about Josh would help get her mind off the dinner parties and political posturing that took up so much of
their time.

Another two minutes and finally her mother's call ended.
She exhaled hard and made a mock show of exhaustion.
"That woman is more connected than anyone in the Springs,
but boy, can she talk." Her mom looked at her watch. "The
garden will have to wait. We have a dinner tonight with her
and three other people." She dusted her hands on her navy
cotton pants and smiled at Lindsay. "You brought back the
baking dish?"

"I did, but I was sort of hoping you might have a few
minutes."

"Oh, honey, I'm sorry. I need to get ready." Her mother
breezed past her. "Come into the kitchen for a minute. I
have to wash up."

Lindsay had no choice but to follow her. "I stopped by
Josh's apartment earlier. He was playing this song—"

Her mother flipped on the water, tapped a few squirts of
soap into her hands, and began rubbing them together. She
raised her eyebrows in Lindsay's direction as if to say she
was still listening. But over the sound of the water, Lindsay
knew her mother couldn't catch every word, so she waited.

After a minute, she turned off the water and reached for
a paper towel. "So he was playing Christian music, is that
what you're saying?" She dried her hands and tossed the
damp paper into the trash compactor. The sound of the

container opening and shutting added to the noise, and Lindsay waited.

Her mother seemed to understand that this conversation needed more of her attention, so she stopped short, her eyes on Lindsay. "Sorry, honey, go ahead."

"Anyway, yes. He was listening to 'I Can Only Imagine.' You know that song, right?"

"Hmmm." Her mother shook her head. "Doesn't sound familiar."

"It's a song about heaven, and when he called me this morning he was playing it so loud I could barely hear him over the phone, and he said it was like he finally—"

"He has to be careful of the neighbors. It's not like he has many friends, Lindsay." She looked at her watch again, and then folded her arms. "Loud music isn't going to endear him to anyone."

Lindsay stared at her mom. Why was she doing this, making it so hard for her to share the good news about Josh? *Be patient,* she told herself. *God, please give me patience. Mom doesn't know what's coming.*

"Anyway, the point wasn't the neighbors. It's that Josh seems changed by the song, by the message in it. He was talking about God today, and how he's going back to church, and...even his pain didn't seem as bad as usual."

Her mother took one of the oranges from the fruit bowl, grabbed another paper towel, spread it on the counter, and dug her fingernail into the fruit's skin. "You don't mind if I eat, do you? I completely forgot lunch, and breakfast was something small left over from yesterday."

Lindsay wanted to scream at her. This was outrageous.

"Did you hear what I said? About how he wants to go to church with us and how his pain seems more manageable?"

"I hate that pain medication he's on." She took a section of the orange, ripped it in half, and put one small piece into her mouth. With her free hand she dabbed at the corners of her lips and focused on her next bite. "That OxyContin can kill a person." She chewed and swallowed another piece. "I was on the Internet looking it up the other day and it actually said if you chew the tablets instead of swallowing them, the release of the drug could be strong enough to kill you." She waved another section of orange in the air. "The doctor has him on way too high a dose, and sure he might not feel any pain today, but what about when he's addicted to the stuff? Then we'll all wish he would've lived with a little more pain and not said yes every time the doctor increased his dose."

When Lindsay's frustration left her without a response, her mother continued. "And yes, dear, he talks about church and God once in a while. I'll believe something's changed when I see it. Otherwise it's just a lot of talk, and you know Josh. Always dreaming about his plans for this or that—even before the accident." She ate a few more sections of the orange, and then slipped what remained into a ziplock bag.

"Mom, are you even hearing me?" Lindsay wanted to cry. This was a big day for Josh, and their mother wasn't connecting with anything she was saying.

"Of course I'm hearing you, dear." She put the orange in the refrigerator. "It's just that if we're honest with ourselves we've heard these stories from Josh over and over again." Her look was bathed in discouragement. "I really worry about your brother. Ever since high school he's struggled to put his plans into action." She closed the distance between them and kissed Lindsay on the forehead. "Thanks for being such a good sister to him. It's important that all of us keep encouraging him. That's especially true for you." She began walking toward the stairs and her bedroom. "I have to get ready, but we'll talk more about it later, okay?"

If Lindsay hadn't been so mad at her mother, she would have yelled at her. She would have told her no, it wasn't okay, and that no dinner party was more important than the changes she'd seen in Josh that day. But if her mom didn't care to listen, then so be it. She wouldn't ruin the good feelings in her heart by fighting with her mother.

By the time Lindsay was back in her car, her anger had faded and in its place was the pity she felt more often for her mother. Pity because her mother's focus wasn't on her faith the way it once had been, and because she wasn't only worried about Josh, she was embarrassed by him. Their mom was frustrated that Josh hadn't become an educator like his father or a writer like Lindsay. As she turned onto the main road toward home, she thought again about her brother and his renewed excitement for God and life and his determination to find his way despite the pain.

If she was honest with herself, honest about the ugliest places in her heart, there had been times when she, too, had been embarrassed by Josh's career decisions. He'd been capable of so much more than driving a tow truck. But at least her embarrassment hadn't lasted long. If towing cars was what her brother loved to do, then she would be glad for him—no matter what else he might have done with his life.

She still didn't know the story behind the photograph of

the two teenage girls, but the next time they were together she would press him about it. Clearly, he kept the picture on the mantel for a reason—one that brought tears to her eyes as she pulled into her garage.

When no one in his family was proud of his work at the garage, when he couldn't find affirmation anywhere else, the photo probably gave him something that meant the world to her brother.

A reason to believe in himself.

SIX

Josh was about to pass out from the pain. He was on the witness stand, answering questions in a calm, deliberate tone, but on the inside his body was screaming for relief. *Where are You, God? I need You here....Please....*

The attorney for the insurance company was taking a minute with his associates, regrouping for the next round of biting questions. Josh closed his eyes for a few seconds and tried to adjust his position, tried to find even the slightest relief from the pain. The joy and hope and faith that had marked his world three days ago was still there, but it was harder to feel. That's all. *Please, God. Are You there?*

My child, I am with you always...even until the end....

The answer wasn't loud, but it resonated in his soul and brought with it a peace that reminded him of the truth. This deposition wasn't the end of the story—no matter what it netted. His life was changed now, and no amount of pain could undo that. He heard the attorney clear his voice as he stepped back up to the microphone.

Josh opened his eyes and tried to look relaxed and professional. Thomas Flynn, his attorney, had told him a number of times how important this day in court would be to his final settlement. The judge could still decide on an amount anywhere between a hundred thousand dollars and a million dollars.

The lead attorney for the insurance company was William R. Worthington, of Worthington and Associates in Denver. He was in his early fifties with a head of gray-flecked hair. Everything from his dark designer suit to the way he carried himself told those in the courtroom he was a force to be reckoned with. The insurance company was hoping Worthington would save them hundreds of thousands of dollars when the battle was over.

Worthington held a half-inch-thick document, and he flipped slowly through the first three pages. His actions gave the impression that he was carefully sorting through something important—a pile of damaging evidence, perhaps—and that he was putting great thought into his next question.

Josh knew differently.

"Everything an attorney does is part of the act," Flynn told him. "The confidence, the appearance that they've already won the case, the pauses—all of it."

Now the attorney leaned close to the microphone. "Mr. Warren, you've had trouble with your weight, is that true?"

"Objection." Flynn was on his feet. "Question is vague, Your Honor."

"Sustained." The judge was a wiry man who seemed bored with the proceedings. "Counsel will rephrase the question."

"Very well." Worthington nodded his head slightly. "Mr. Warren, you're overweight. Is that true?"

"Actually, over the past couple years, I—"

"Yes or no answers, Mr. Warren. Are you overweight?"

Josh pictured the doctor telling him he only needed to

lose another forty pounds. "Yes." He pulled a tissue from a box at the corner of the witness stand and dabbed it on his forehead. "Yes, I am."

Worthington flipped through another few pages. "More than one medical doctor has told you that your weight is a health risk, is that true?"

More than one doctor? Josh's mind raced through the possibilities, and then he remembered. The emergency room doctor who treated him in the hours after the accident told him he needed to deal with his weight. "However bad your injuries are, they'll be worse if you don't take care of your weight." Josh winced as a wall of pain slammed into his lower back. "Yes. Two doctors. That's true."

"Mr. Warren, do you need a break?" The judge's voice held more compassion than Josh had heard from him since the deposition began. "We can take a ten-minute break."

"No, thanks. My back hurts either way, and I'd like to get home. I have dinner plans with my sister tonight."

"Very well." The judge motioned to the attorney. "Carry on."

"Thank you, Your Honor." He looked at Josh. "I'm going to read a statement written by your current doctor, and you tell me if it's something you're familiar with. Do you understand?"

"Yes, sir." Josh hated how they talked to him, like he was a third-grader caught cheating on a math test. Did the guy really think Josh was making up the pain? That if he wanted to, he could drive down to the garage and start towing cars again tomorrow? He gripped the edge of the wooden desk in front of him and waited.

"Here's the statement: 'It is my opinion that my client,

Josh Warren, age twenty-eight, could experience dramatic improvement in the condition of his back injury if he would lose weight.'" Worthington paused for effect. "'It is nearly impossible to determine how much of his current pain and disability is caused by his excess weight, and how much is caused from being hit by the car.'"

Josh remained calm. Flynn had warned him the insurance company attorneys might take this angle, accusing him of destroying his own health and thereby calling into question whether the accident had really been that damaging. "Don't worry about it," Flynn had said to him that morning. "Even if you'd walked away without an injury, if the only reason you couldn't go back to work was an emotional one—like you're too afraid to drive a tow truck now—a settlement would still be in the works. The insurance company's client was drunk out of his mind. He drove off the road and hit you, nearly killing you. Your weight isn't going to factor into the judge's decision whatsoever."

Josh blinked. "Yes, I'm familiar with that statement." Why didn't the guy ask him about the weight he'd already lost? He was down sixty pounds from the time of the accident. He was exhausted and ready for his next pain pill. *God...please get me through this.*

"And is it true that you've been told by your doctor that surgery on your back isn't advisable until you lose another forty pounds?"

"Yes. I've been told that."

Worthington ran his thumb across a section of text at the middle of the page. "What was your weight when you graduated from high school, Mr. Warren?"

"One ninety."

"One hundred and ninety pounds, is that right?" He cast a knowing look at the judge.

"Yes, that's right."

"And your weight at the time of the accident?"

"Two ninety-five." Josh could hardly believe himself as he said the number. How had he let that much weight pile up over the years? More than a hundred pounds? No question the doctor was concerned about his weight. The fact that he'd already lost sixty made him determined to stay the course and get back under two hundred again.

Worthington raised his brow. "Two hundred and ninety-five pounds? That was your weight at the time of the accident?"

"Yes, sir." Josh felt the demons behind him again, poking a hundred pointy knives into his spine. *I need You, God. Make them go away.*

My strength is sufficient for you, My son. Trust in Me....

I'm trying, God.... I'm really trying.

Worthington turned the page and hesitated. "I have here"—he held the document up for the judge's sake—"a study done last year determining that people with morbid obesity—more than a hundred pounds over their ideal weight—are more prone to injuries on the job. I'd like to admit this document into evidence, Your Honor."

"Objection." Flynn was on his feet, his eyes blazing with indignation. "Unless that study involves my client personally, it's only hearsay and has nothing to do with my client's specific situation."

"Sustained. Relevance." He peered down at Worthington. "You should be familiar with the rules of evidence in a case like this."

"Yes, Your Honor." The attorney didn't look too upset. He probably expected the admonition, but either way, the information was out there. Heavy people were more prone to injuries.

Josh looked at his attorney, and he could almost read Flynn's eyes. The report about overweight people wasn't something he needed to worry about. Again, he didn't fall off a ladder or slip at the coffee counter. His weight had nothing to do with the fact that he'd been hit by the drunk driver. He took a few short breaths through his nose, expecting the pain to prevent him from inhaling fully. But the pain seemed slightly less intense than a few minutes ago. *Thank You, God.... You're holding me up. I can't do this without You.*

I am with you....

"You have no children, is that right? No dependents at all?"

Josh paused, but only briefly. "I have a daughter."

His answer seemed to catch Worthington off guard. Like Flynn had said, the insurance company preferred Josh to be single with no children. But Worthington covered his surprise well, barely hesitating to regroup.

He leveled his stare at Josh. "Were you considering a medical disability before the accident, Mr. Warren?"

The question seemed to come out of nowhere. "I'm not sure what..." He glanced at Thomas Flynn. "Could you restate the question?"

"At the time of the accident, were you planning to take medical disability?" His words were fast, rapid-fire, and aimed straight at his motives for filing suit.

"No, sir. I had no such plans."

"But your weight was making it difficult to keep working, right?"

"No, sir." He kept his voice in check, but his anger was rising. Flynn had warned him about this, too, and at previous depositions the insurance company's attorney had tried similar lines of questioning. Planting doubts, that's all the guy was doing. Josh steadied himself, forced himself to keep his answers free of emotion. "I had no plans for a medical disability."

"And because of your weight, you were struggling to keep up your production with the other tow truck drivers at the garage, isn't that right, Mr. Warren?"

"No, sir." He adjusted his feet, but the move brought no relief to his back. He was pretty sure if someone walked behind him they would see flames where his spine was supposed to be.

"And after the accident you were almost glad to have a reason to go out on medical disability, isn't that right?"

Josh hesitated, his eyes locked onto the attorney's. Before he could answer, Flynn was on his feet again. "Objection. Counsel is harassing the witness, Your Honor."

"Sustained." Again the judge gave Worthington a look that told him he was in danger of crossing a line. "Change your line of questioning, Counsel."

"Yes, Your Honor. I apologize."

"Carry on."

Worthington kept the questions coming for another ninety minutes. He asked Josh about his days at home and whether he was able to sit for an hour at a time, and if so was he aware that a majority of desk jobs didn't require more than an hour of sitting at a time, and had

Josh considered looking for a job, or was he content to sit
back and let an insurance company take care of his needs.
Thomas Flynn objected a handful of times, but at the end
of the questioning the damage was done. If Josh had been
a prizefighter, at the final bell he would've been bloodied
and battered on the ground in the middle of the ring—
victim of a knockout by decision.

One thing was sure. Whatever settlement this case netted, Josh would have earned every dollar several times over.

Flynn called a brief recess and he talked to Josh in the
hallway. "You look tired."

"I am." Josh's body was screaming for another pain pill,
something that would give him relief from the fire in his
back. But the pills could make him loopy, and he needed to
stay sharp just a little longer. "My sister's counting on me
for dinner."

Flynn was a family man, an attorney dedicated to seeing
justice done. He liked to gamble, but he also believed in
miracles. Both made him the perfect attorney as far as Josh
was concerned. Flynn looked at Josh with compassion.
"I'm sorry about your pain." He put his hand on Josh's
shoulder. "But I need a few minutes in cross. Something to
bring a little balance back."

"I thought you said the judge wouldn't consider that
stuff—my weight and whether I wanted a disability or not.
Which I didn't, by the way."

"I know, and I told you the truth. None of that should
matter." He folded his arms and released a frustrated sigh.
"But at the end of the day, the judge is as human as the
next guy. Deciding these cases isn't based on an exact
formula."

"Okay." Josh could no longer draw a full breath. He would exist on short gasps and forced exhalations, the way he had learned to do when the pain was this bad. "I can last another few minutes." He still had the hour-long drive back to the Springs, and it was almost five o'clock.

The break ended and Josh took the stand again. Flynn was deeply competitive when it came to law. Josh knew that from the private conversations they held in his attorney's office. Flynn had taught him every way to win the case from the witness stand, training him with more care and detail than any of Josh's baseball coaches ever had. Now he donned a look of kindness and empathy. "You doing okay, Mr. Warren?"

Josh almost smiled. The tone of the question, the wording, was intended to make one very clear point: that Worthington had all but whipped and beaten Josh in the earlier session. "Yes, sir. I'm okay."

"Is your back hurting?"

"Yes, sir."

"On a scale of one to ten, on the pain scale used by doctors, where's your back pain right now, Mr. Warren?"

Josh didn't hesitate. "A nine, sir." A ten happened when he could barely breathe at all. He was close, but for now he was still at a nine. Flynn let that detail sink in for a few seconds.

"Okay"—he looked at his notes—"you said your weight was two hundred and ninety-five pounds at the time of the accident. Is that right?"

"Yes, sir." Josh didn't worry about where Flynn was headed. His track record left no room for doubt, no matter what the line of questioning.

"Can you tell this court how many days of work you missed in the month leading up to your accident?"

They'd been over this a number of times, analyzing the actual employment records from the garage. "None, sir."

"Very well." He glanced down at the notepad in his hand. "How many days of work did you miss in the six months leading up to your accident?"

"None, sir."

Flynn looked impressed. "Okay, Mr. Warren, how many days of work did you miss in the year leading up to your accident?"

"Not one, sir."

"You were hired by the North County Police Garage four years and three months before your car accident, is that right?"

Flynn knew it was. Josh had worked at a smaller garage for a few months leading up to that move. Working for a police garage meant he had the chance to go out on police calls and tow cars from crime scenes and accident locations. The work was much harder than what he'd done before—towing stalled cars and parking violators from private strip-mall spaces—but it was more pay and more prestige. It hit him again, how much he'd lost because of the accident. "Yes, sir. I worked for North County for more than four years."

"And during that entire time were you morbidly obese—at least a hundred pounds overweight?"

The question no longer shamed him. He could do nothing to change the past. "Yes, sir, I was."

"And how many days did you miss work the entire time you were employed by North County Police Garage?"

"No days, sir."

"No days!" This time Flynn stepped just far enough out of his quiet, compassionate role that he could have won an Oscar for his show of surprise. Anyone in the courtroom would've guessed that this was new and shocking information to the veteran attorney. "Very well." He looked down at his notes.

Josh was ready to go. He felt his feet tense up from his effort to try to remain upright. *Help me survive this, God....I need You.* He shifted again and this time he found a small pocket of reserve stamina. Enough to survive. *Thank You, Lord. This is temporary, I can feel it. I'll get through this deposition, and the next, and one day soon I'll have that surgery. You'll see me through it, I know You will.*

I am with you always, My precious son.

Josh felt a peace push back the demon of pain.

"Now, about your weight." Flynn lowered his notes. "You were two hundred and ninety-five pounds at the time of the accident, though you missed no days because of health issues in the more than four years you worked for the North County Police Garage. Is that correct?"

"Objection." Worthington stood sedately, adjusting his cufflinks. "We've been over this, Your Honor."

"Sustained." The judge gestured for Flynn to move forward. "Counsel is correct. You've established the information about the plaintiff's work history."

"Yes, Your Honor. Thank you." Flynn looked contrite. He paused to gather his thoughts. "What is your weight now, Mr. Warren?"

"Around two-forty."

"Two hundred and forty pounds?"

"Yes, sir."

"So you've lost a great deal of weight since your injury, is that right?"

"Yes, sir, nearly sixty pounds."

"Are you on a diet to lose weight?"

"Yes, I am."

"Would you please tell this court why you're on a diet to lose weight?"

"Because"—Josh pressed his hand into his lower back—"I need surgery on my back and the doctor thinks it'll be more successful if I'm at a normal weight."

Flynn hesitated. He lowered his notes and shot a piercing look at Josh. "Did you enjoy your job as a tow truck driver, Mr. Warren?"

"Yes, I did."

"Tell us in your words what being a tow truck driver meant to you."

Josh hadn't been expecting this question, and he was surprised at the emotion that welled up in his throat. "I think—I think my family wanted me to be a teacher or a writer, maybe a doctor. They wanted me to go to college after high school. But I've always liked the idea of driving a truck." He shrugged, and the movement sent a different pain down the length of his back. "As a tow truck driver I could help people. They might've been in an accident or the victim of a crime, and, I don't know, I liked being there for them." He worked to keep his composure. "I loved being a tow truck driver, sir."

"But you'll never be able to drive a tow truck again, is that right?"

The detail wasn't something he liked to think about. "Yes, sir. My back—even after surgery—will be too unsteady for that sort of work."

Flynn nodded, his eyes deep with compassion. "I have one last question for you, Mr. Warren, and remember you are under oath." He looked at his notes again, letting the drama build. "You stand to win a large sum of money in this case. Right now, if you had to decide between going back to the day before your accident and being a tow truck driver for life or winning two million dollars in this lawsuit, which would you pick, Mr. Warren?"

Josh's throat felt scratchy and his eyes stung. "I would go back...to the day before the accident. I would have my health and my job, which is all I ever wanted, anyway."

Flynn nodded slowly. Then he turned a grief-stricken face to the judge. "No more questions, Your Honor."

The deposition was finally over. Josh didn't know a lot about the field of law, but he had a feeling that if this were a football game, Thomas Flynn had just scored the game-winning touchdown. Out in the hallway he shook his attorney's hand. "You're good."

"You're better. Sitting up there and taking that garbage from the other side."

He needed to understand one thing before he could leave. "Two million? I thought we were asking for one."

"I filed an amendment. With all they've put you through, and with the new information from the doctor about the impossibility of you returning to your preferred line of work, I changed the amount." They started walking down the hall. "And you know what?" He stopped and gave Josh a sad smile. "I think we'll get it."

Josh was in the car five minutes later, sorting through the center console of his old Mustang for a bottle of Oxy-Contin. It was six o'clock and he wasn't due for another pill until he turned in for bed. But if he wanted to breathe on the drive home from Denver, he would have to take the medication sooner than later.

He found what he was looking for and dug around the floor of his car through a stack of legal documents and an old McDonald's bag until he found a warm bottle of water. He opened it and downed the pill before he could give the move a second thought. One day he'd have to figure out a way off the pain meds, maybe with some of that two million dollars Flynn was going to get him. He held his breath and prayed the OxyContin would work quickly. He had a court case to win, a surgery to schedule, an old girlfriend to find, and his God to fully reconnect with. Most of all he had a little girl out there who needed her daddy.

For now, an addiction to OxyContin was hardly on his list of concerns.

SEVEN

Lindsay was putting the final touches on a spaghetti dinner, watching Larry toss a ball with Ben and Bella out back and listening for the doorbell when the phone rang. She checked the caller ID. "Josh," she groaned. "You're late." She answered the phone with one hand and with the other she stirred the spoon through a pan full of noodles. "Hey, Josh—where are you?"

"I can't make it, Linds. Sorry. Maybe nex' time."

"Josh?" Lindsay's heart skipped a beat. She turned off the stove and walked to the back door, her eyes on her family. "What's wrong? You sound funny."

In painstakingly slow and slurred speech he told her that he'd been on the freeway for only ten minutes and that he'd taken a pain pill. "I had to, Linds. It's so bad today. But...I feel sorta funny. I can breathe better but I'm a lil' dizzy."

"Josh, that's terrible. Get off the freeway and get to a doctor."

"Linds." Josh's laugh sounded easy and untroubled. "I'm fine. I would pull over if I thought I couldn't drive."

"How would you know? You don't sound right."

"I'm tired, tha's all. I'm fine. The deposition went longer than 'spected. I'll be fine with a lil' sleep."

"I'm staying on the phone with you." The way he was slurring his words terrified her. "Keep talking to me or I'll call nine-one-one." She didn't want to be angry with him, but if he was having trouble talking then he couldn't possibly be driving well.

"Don't worry about me, Linds. I've felt this way before. I've been driving under the influence of pain medication for almost three years."

He had a point. "Okay." She still felt worried. "Don't worry about dinner. Maybe Saturday night—after Ben's game and church. Larry could barbecue."

"Yeah, Sis...that'd be great."

"So the deposition...how did it go?"

"Flynn's a' best. With him and God, we'll win this thing yet, you know?"

"Good...but Josh, I still don't like how you sound. Maybe you should go to the hospital and make sure you're okay."

"I'm fine. I tol' you, Linds. Jus' need a lil' sleep."

"Okay. I'm staying on the phone until you get home."

"I love you, Linds, you know? You're my best friend."

She closed her eyes. What if he'd been killed in the accident? She couldn't imagine losing him—especially not now when he'd finally found his way back to the Lord. The years ahead would be their best yet. "I love you, too, Josh. Now we need to get you better."

"I can always count on you, Linds."

They talked about his faith and he told her about praying for God to get him through his time on the witness stand.

Flynn had doubled the amount he was asking for, but Josh didn't seem overly excited about the fact. "You know what?" He sounded a little better than he had earlier in the conversation. "I don't wanna get rich. I wanna get better."

"I know, and you will." She wished she could blink herself there, so she could take over at the wheel and get him home safely. "God has great plans for you, Josh. It's all just beginning for you."

"I'm gonna meet Savannah. That's the best part."

"Yes. You'll be able to afford a wonderful attorney."

"I already have him. Flynn can handle the custody case. It's next on his list as soon as the settlement comes through."

She stretched the call, talking about Ben's coach naming him the starting running back for tomorrow's game, and how Bella had designated herself as her brother's personal cheerleader. "She's three years older than him—just like you and me."

"I know. They're both lucky. Savannah will like having them as cousins."

Lindsay wasn't sure why, but tears filled her eyes. Her brother wanted so little from life, but somehow things had never quite fallen into place. Until now, anyway. If he could just get past his injury, get the surgery he needed, and be finished with the lawsuit. The best years for Josh really might be right around the corner. She was midway through telling him about a feature story on a local hiker whose hundredth birthday was next week when she heard him exhale loudly.

"I did it." He sounded relieved. "I'm home. Jus' pulled into the parking lot."

She breathed a silent prayer of thanks. "Okay, now go in and get some rest. Saturday's going to be a big day and you need to be feeling good."

"I will. Tell Ben and Bella I can't wait to see them." His voice broke, and she realized he was more emotional than he'd let on. "Thanks for talking me through that drive, Linds. I was a little scared."

"I love you. If you need anything, call. I'll be right there."

"Okay. Love you, too."

The call ended and Lindsay dabbed at her eyes. Why was she so sad now? Her brother was home safely, and after a good night's sleep he'd be the same cheerful guy he'd been a few days ago when MercyMe was blaring through his house. But she'd been looking forward to seeing him tonight, and without him her dinner plans suddenly seemed flat.

Lindsay sniffed and ordered her heart to change directions. She had no reason to be sad, nothing to be discouraged about. Josh was making his turnaround. Everything was going to be fine for him. Besides, they had Saturday to look forward to. Lindsay found her smile again as she finished dinner and called her family in to eat. That night at the table, six-year-old Ben said the blessing. He thanked God for the food and for family and for the football game tomorrow. And he asked God for a special favor.

"Please, God, be with Uncle Josh tonight. He's too tired to be here, so help him feel better. In Jesus' name, amen."

And as the meal began and the conversation shifted to Bella's fourth-grade reading assignment, Lindsay felt a peace she hadn't known since Josh's phone call. Because God had certainly heard the prayers of her little Ben and that could only mean one thing.

Josh would feel better in the morning.

❧

Annie called her daughter's house to find out how Josh's deposition went.

"He's not here." Lindsay was helping Larry with the dishes. "He was too tired. But he said it went well. I told him we'll do dinner Saturday night."

Too tired? Annie had talked to Josh that morning and he'd been full of energy, ready to face the attorney for the insurance company. "He was looking forward to having dinner with you." Immediately, Annie's concern turned to worry. Josh's medication was bound to have an effect on him. "Did he talk about the pain pills?"

"He said he took one before he drove home." Lindsay's voice fell. "Honestly, Mom, I was worried about him. He didn't sound right, like he was half asleep or drunk or something. I've never heard him like that."

"I have. It's not good. He has to be so careful with those drugs." Annie wrapped up the conversation quickly and immediately dialed Josh. It was just after eight o'clock, so even on a day when he was tired, he would normally still be awake. Annie stepped out onto their covered front porch and paced the length of it. The phone rang once... twice.... "Come on, Josh," she whispered. It was still in the seventies outside but a chill ran down her bare arms. "Pick up the phone, son."

He answered just after the fourth ring. "Hello?"

Annie pressed her hand to her chest. "Thank God." She dropped to the glider swing and sank back in the cushion. "Your sister said you were too tired for dinner."

"I was. But I'm feeling better now." He sounded tired, but sharp. None of his words were slurred as far as she could tell. "The deposition was terrible. The worst ever."

On days like this, when some hotshot lawyer had dragged her son through a day of emotional torture, when he'd been forced to drive an hour each way to give yet another round of answers in a game designed by a big insurance corporation to avoid paying Josh his settlement, Annie could only picture one thing: a trip they'd taken to Yellowstone National Park the summer before Josh started middle school.

They were about to leave their tent when they heard a barking dog. Annie was closest to the tent flap and she peered out in time to see the drama unfolding in a field across from the campground. A baby black bear had wandered away from his mother and now the barking terrier had backed him up against a tree. The baby bear looked one way and then the next, searching for an escape route, but the dog quickly closed off his options.

In a blur of motion, and with a bellow that rang through the campground, the mother bear tore into the clearing, picking up speed. The dog never knew what hit him. He was still barking at the bear cub when the mother reached him from behind and sent him ten feet in the air with one swipe of her massive paw. The dog flipped three times and landed on his back, but injured or not, he had the sense to run for his life.

The danger to her baby behind them, the mother went

to her cub and licked his face, nuzzling him and hovering over him until the two of them returned to the forest.

That's how Annie felt now, like the mother bear ready to tear into any attorney who would put her son through the rigors of demeaning questions, hearing after hearing after hearing. She thought about going to see Josh now, so she could hold him and will away his suffering.

"Mom?"

"I'm sorry." She leaned against the porch railing. "You shouldn't have to go through that." She breathed in slowly. *Positive,* she told herself. *You have to stay positive for him.* She pulled herself up a little straighter. "So tell me about it. Are they any closer to settling?"

"I think so." Josh was clear-minded and deliberate as he told her about the questions. "The insurance company wants the judge to think I was on the verge of a medical disability anyway, because of my weight."

"That's ridiculous. Besides, you're almost back to your normal size already." Annie pictured her son on the stand, the insurance company's attorney embarrassing him, humiliating him. "Is it worth it, son? I mean, what does Mr. Flynn say?"

"He thinks we'll have the judge's decision in a few weeks. The insurance company is running out of reasons to delay." Josh explained how his attorney had done a brilliant job at the end of the deposition, and how Flynn was asking for twice the settlement. He was still talking when Nate stepped out onto the porch and gave her a curious look.

"Josh," she mouthed.

Her husband nodded and hesitated. He must've seen her

concern because he came and stood beside her. He kept his voice low. "Is he okay?"

Annie nodded, but tempered that with a worried shrug.

"So, I'm almost finished with these hearings. Maybe one more, and Flynn says we'll be finished."

The news landed in Annie's gut like a bucket of rocks. One more deposition was like knowing her son would be exposed to one more beating. "Maybe I'll go with you next time."

"That's okay." He laughed lightly. "I'll get through it. Then I can pay you and Dad back, and move on with my life."

"And you're feeling better? Now that you've been home for a while?"

"Yes." Josh rarely complained about his pain, and tonight was no exception. "Hey"—his voice grew tender—"I talked to Flynn about helping me find Savannah. Once we have the settlement, you know?"

Annie opened her mouth to shoot down the idea. There were a hundred more important things Josh should take care of once he got his settlement—including his back surgery and figuring out whether he should go to college now or, if not, what line of work he was going to get into since driving a tow truck was no longer an option. Chasing after the child of a woman he'd spent a week with in Las Vegas couldn't possibly be good for him. Just another dead-end road.

But whether it was the concern in her husband's eyes or the whisper of God, she felt suddenly compelled to agree with him. "I'm sure Mr. Flynn would be a big help in whatever you need after the settlement comes."

"Yes." Josh seemed like he wanted to push the issue,

talk more about Savannah, but he exhaled instead and he sounded more tired than he had before. "You still don't believe she's mine, do you?"

Of course not, she wanted to say. "There's no proof. The woman—she wasn't reputable, Josh. The photo could've been of someone else's child for all you know."

Another slow sigh filtered across the lines. "I understand that. But when I look at her eyes I see my own. I have to find out the truth. At least pray for me about that."

"I will." She was grateful to have something they could agree on. She nodded at her husband. "Your father and I will both pray that when the time is right, you'll find your answers, okay?"

"Good enough." He must've been at his computer because she could hear the rapid click of his fingers on a keyboard. "Listen, I'm online but I'm going to turn in early. I'll see you tomorrow at Ben's game."

"All right." Annie couldn't explain it but she was almost desperate to keep the conversation going, to reassure Josh that she cared about him more than he could ever know.

Nate tapped Annie's hand. "Tell him I love him," he mouthed.

"Your father loves you. And I love you. You'll get through this."

"I know. I love you both."

She could hear the smile in his voice and it made her feel better. "Good night."

" 'Night."

Annie clicked the off button and set the receiver on the porch railing. What was the ache in her heart, the longing to drive across town and hold her son the way she'd done when he was a little boy? She went to Nate, leaned into him, and listened to the steady thud of his heartbeat. "I just want the whole court thing to be over."

"Long day?" Nate led her to the glider and they sat down together.

"I guess the deposition was very difficult. Intense questions from the insurance company's attorney. More harassment." She lifted her eyes to his. "I'd like to drive down to that man's office and tell him a thing or two."

"It won't be long now, right? A few more weeks?"

"I hope so. After three years it's hard to believe the case will ever be settled."

"It will." He kissed the top of her head and set the swing into a soft, subtle motion. "Josh will land on his feet and he'll find his way. I believe in him."

"I do, too." Her answer was quick, and she remembered her thoughts from last week, how she could do nothing but admit her disappointment where their son was concerned. She leaned her head on Nate's shoulder. "It was so much easier when he was little, when his bike was stolen from school or he didn't get a part in the middle school musical. I could hug him and pray with him and make him a plate of cookies." She blinked back the beginning of tears. "The world would always look brighter in the morning."

"He's still young, Annie. The accident was a big setback." Nate's voice was calm, full of the confidence Annie only wished she had when it came to their son. "Tell you what." He angled himself so he could see her better. "Let's pray for him right now. While he's so heavy on your heart."

Nate started and Annie finished, and after ten minutes of talking to God about her son, Annie felt better. Enough that she went inside and found the flour and sugar and chocolate chips and made Josh a plate of cookies. As she took them out of the oven, she smiled thinking about how happy he would be when she gave him the gift at Ben's game, and how good it would feel to hug him, to remind him he was loved, no matter what his circumstances. As she cleaned the kitchen that night she wanted to believe that hugging him, and praying for him, and baking him a plate of chocolate chip cookies could only mean one thing.

Tomorrow, the world would look brighter.

⌘

EIGHT

Josh had only been online with Cara for ten minutes and already he felt himself rebounding from the ugliness of the deposition. He was still exhausted and a little dizzy, but his pain was tolerable, at least. He leaned against the desktop and waited for Cara's next message. As he did, he remembered the strange way he'd felt in the car earlier. The trip home from Denver had been a little hairy, and Lindsay was right. He should've pulled over. But if he fell asleep in his car in some parking lot or on the side of the road, then what? The OxyContin could knock him out for eight hours or more and he would have been a target for anyone who happened by. Instead, he prayed constantly and took Lindsay up on her offer. Their conversation helped him stay focused and alert.

So...didn't you have a court thing today? Cara's message flashed in the box at the bottom of his screen.

Cara didn't know how much he stood to win in the settlement. Money had no place in their friendship, which was good. Especially after the mistakes he'd made with Savannah's mother. He clicked open his iTunes library and pulled up his list with the MercyMe songs. His fingers flew across the keyboard. *Yes. It's not worth talking about.... I came home, had dinner, and went back out to the grocery store.* He didn't tell her the part about picking up a bag of groceries for Ethel, the old widow in the apartment above his. It wasn't something he talked about, just a regular part of his week. Ethel was ninety-two and her hips hurt. No surgery would ever help at her age, so Josh saved her the trip to the market. It was the least he could do. He added to his last message, *Did I tell you my latest plan?*

Cara's answer was immediate. *Tell me.*

With all this healthy eating I've been doing, next summer I want to play football again.

Uh...on a real team, you mean?

No. LOL. At the park with my sister's son. The boy loves to play catch and since the accident I haven't touched a ball. All that's gonna change. And you know what else?

What?

I'm gonna play with my shirt off. I'll have my surgery and hit the gym the way I used to do, you know?

There was a slight pause before her next message. *If anyone can make that happen it's you, J. I mean, come on...you've lost almost sixty pounds. What's your secret, by the way? You never talk about it.*

No secret. Josh leaned back in his chair as a sudden searing pain shot through his lower spine. He winced and kept typing. *I cut out the junk, sugar and stuff. That's it. No more three-a-day root beer Big Gulps.*

LOL...good for you, J.

He yawned and wondered again whether Becky would ever want him back or if he should push things with Cara, talk to her about the future. The answers would come eventually, he had no doubt. He would call Becky and if she wasn't interested, he could fly out to see Cara once his health was right. He could stay at a nearby hotel and they'd have a few days to find out if what they shared online could translate into real life. *I have other plans,* he typed. *But if I tell you it'll spoil everything, so...they'll have to wait till later.*

[[smile]] *Now you've really got my interest.*

Let's just say I plan to keep it, you know? Your interest.

Ah...you're my best friend, J.

And you're mine. The pain in his back was intensifying. *Oh, and pray for Savannah, okay? I feel like she's not doing that great.*

I will, I'll pray....Hey, listen to me! A month ago the word "pray" wouldn't have been in my vocabulary. But you, J, you've changed me.

He had an answer as soon as he read her message. *God changed you. He changed me, too—isn't it great?*

Anyway...why do you feel funny about Savannah?

I don't know. He moved his mouse back to iTunes and double clicked the song that started him on the path back to God. The words filled the small spaces around him and he sang along. Cara must've been waiting for more of an explanation. He centered his hands on the keyboard and tried to get in touch with his feelings. Slowly, his fingers began to move. *Maybe it's because I haven't seen a photo of her in so long....Sometimes I wonder if she's still alive or if she knows about me at all.*

Cara's answer came slowly, one sentence at a time. *That's sad. And it's wrong. You've got to get your lawyer to help you find her.*

I will. And she's out there, I know it. I just feel like I'm supposed to pray for her. Until I meet her, it's the only thing I can actually do for her, you know?

The first time you meet that little girl, I want a front-row seat, J. It's like a movie or something. That's the kind of happy ending it'll be.

Josh thought about his conversation with Carl Joseph and Daisy last week, how the best stories were the ones with happy endings. He began typing. *That's what I'm asking God for…a happy ending for me and Savannah.* He moved forward in his chair and waited a few seconds, but the pain was gaining ground on him. At this rate he wouldn't last another few minutes at the computer. The song was ending and he started it over again. One more time through and he'd turn in for the night. *I need to turn in soon*, he typed. *Sorry.*

That's okay. I'm tired, too.

I might sleep a little longer tonight. I want to feel good for Ben's game tomorrow. We're all going to church after, and then to Lindsay's house for dinner.

Sounds wonderful. Wish I were there.

He smiled. *Me, too…you'd really like Lindsay.*

They talked about their siblings for a few minutes, but the fire in Josh's back was relentless. *Hey, gotta go. I'll check in with you tomorrow, okay?*

I'll be waiting. Sleep well, J.

Thanks. He flinched at another shot of pain. *Don't forget about Savannah.*

Josh powered down his computer and opened the top desk drawer. Inside was a picture of him and Becky from their senior prom. Was it all just a dream, the idea of contacting her after so many years, maybe asking her out for coffee, and seeing if there were still feelings there for both of them? Sometimes Becky seemed more like a fantasy, the perfect girl waiting for him to become the perfect guy.

But on nights like this he could still smell the shampoo in her hair, still feel her in his arms as he waltzed her across the prom dance floor. He could hear her laugh and feel the way his heart connected with hers. He doubled his determination as he set the picture back in his desk drawer. He would make something of himself and he would call her. God could take care of the rest.

Until then, he was grateful for Cara.

He yawned, and even that small action hurt his back. He wanted to head straight for bed, but lately he'd added a brief side trip to his bedtime routine. He pushed back from the desk, struggled to his feet, and then walked to his fireplace. Every step hurt worse than the last, and by the time he reached the mantel with the photographs, sweat was dripping down his forehead. *Dear Lord... I can't get through this without You. Please....* He closed his eyes and held his breath, looking for even a small window of relief. Two pain pills a day, those were the doctor's orders. But sometimes—when he'd been to Denver for another hearing, especially—he would take three. The increase wasn't much, not compared with the stories he'd seen online of some out-of-control people. Three was more than he liked to take, but it wouldn't kill him.

He exhaled and opened his eyes, opened them to the picture of Savannah. *I don't know where she is, Lord, but I know she's mine. I know it with everything inside me.*

He grabbed another excruciating breath and steadied himself against the mantel. *You can see her right this minute, so please...be with her and comfort her. Keep her safe, God, so that when I'm better I can have a chance to be her daddy. She's all that keeps me going sometimes.*

I am with her, My son...and I am with you...always.

The holy reminder seemed to come whenever he was at his lowest. Josh released his hold on the mantel, kissed his fingertips, and pressed them to Savannah's picture. *Thank You, God....Now, if You could please help me get some sleep.*

He gave his daughter a final look, turned, and shuffled to his room. The pain had become a spasm ricocheting from his shoulders to his lower back. He'd have the rest of the weight off by the end of February and then he could finally have the surgery.

He brushed his teeth, washed his face, and fell into bed. The haze of pain was making him nauseous, so he moved quickly for the bottle of pills on his nightstand and took one in the palm of his hand. His water glass wasn't even half full, but he didn't have the energy to get out of bed again. He'd have to down it quickly, making the best use of the water he did have.

For a moment he let himself imagine a life like the one he used to lead. Heavy or not, he could flop into bed and find instant sleep without so much as a thought of pain medication. He put the pill in his mouth and swigged the rest of the water, but the liquid slid down his throat leaving the pill behind. On impulse, he chewed the pill and swallowed it.

Not until he set the glass back on his nightstand did a thought flash in his mind. The doctor had said something about chewing the pills, right? How he had to be careful because a chewed pill could release the medication too quickly into his system or his bloodstream, or something like that. Panic flooded his veins and made him sit straight up despite the pain. His heart pounded hard, faster than usual. What if chewing the pill would hurt him? Maybe he should call 911, or at least contact his mother to ask for her advice.

But even as he sat upright sorting through his options, sleep came over him. Thick and heavy and sweet, the pain in his back faded and he felt his body relax. Slowly, he slid down until his head was partially on his pillow. In the farthest corner of his mind a nearly silent alarm was still sounding. He was okay, right? He had to be okay because God had great plans for him. *Lord…help me.* The sensation of sleep intensified and for the first time since the accident, Josh's pain all but subsided.

The relief felt wonderful, intoxicating. *Everything was going to be okay. You're with me, right, God?*

Until the end of the ages, My son…

Good. Josh smiled and let himself be dragged under, pulled into a sleep deeper and sweeter than any he'd ever known, even before the accident. God had great plans for him and for Savannah, so there was no reason to be afraid. And as he let the darkness close in around him, he released every care, every pain. The sensation of relief was so strong he felt like he was sleeping in the palm of the Lord's hand. The last thing Josh experienced was something he hadn't known for a very long time. Maybe not forever.

Complete and utter peace.

❧

Savannah didn't know the big man talking to her mama, but his dark eyes made little chill bumps up and down her arms. They were in Central Park begging money, that's what Mama called it—begging money—and a big man in nice clothes stopped and talked to them. Well, not to them, but to her mama. He had bushy dark hair and a little gold cross on a skinny chain and three big gold rings. At first her mama and the man laughed and talked loud about having a good time and what about plans for the night. But then Savannah saw the man show her mama some money. A lot of money, because there were zeroes on the dollar bills and Mama said zeroes were good.

That's when Mama told Savannah to sit on the bench and wait and she and the man walked toward the pond and their talking changed to quiet indoor voices. Savannah felt a little scared sitting there by herself, but she swung her feet and kept her eyes looking at the ground. Mama said it was always better to keep her eyes pointed to the ground so people wouldn't get the wrong idea. Savannah didn't know what that meant, but it sounded serious so she looked at the ground. Also she talked to Jesus, whom her grandpa Ted taught her about when she was five and they met for the first time in his hospital room. Grandpa Ted was her mama's daddy, but Mama said she didn't get along with him. She told Savannah they had to go to the hospital because Grandpa Ted was dying. That's the only reason.

"I don't have long, Savannah," he told her. Then he talked to her about Jesus—how He was God, but you couldn't see

Him, and how He made all things and even how He wanted
to be in her very own heart. Grandpa Ted took her hand
that day and smiled the nicest smile anyone had ever given
her. "If you love Jesus, if you talk to Him and trust Him,
then one day we'll be together forever."

"Where is that place?" Savannah liked Grandpa Ted.
She wished her mama had taken her to meet him before he
got so sick.

"It's called heaven, sweetie." Grandpa coughed a lot and
it took him a few ticks of the clock before he could talk
again. "Sometimes life isn't so good this side of heaven.
But, ah"—his eyes lit up and got a little bit of tears in
them—"heaven will be absolutely perfect, Savannah. Like
a birthday party that never, ever ends."

"A birthday party that never, ever ends."

Those words made the most beautiful picture in Savannah's head and that picture made her smile. She thought
about it again and again, especially after her grandpa Ted
went there a few days later. There were a lot of scary days
with Mama, so what Grandpa Ted told her sounded like a
good idea. Trusting in Jesus. Yes, it was a much better idea
than anything her mama had thought of.

*Jesus, I'm looking at the ground so no one gets the
wrong idea.* She held on to the edge of the bench, but it
was sticky, so she let go and folded her hands in her lap.
*I'm glad You're in my heart because I feel a little scared
about that man Mama's talking to. Maybe she knows him
from our room in Harlem. Or maybe not, and that means
he would be a stranger, so Mama shouldn't talk to him.*

She lifted her eyes for just a quick look, and finally her
mama and the man were coming back. They were laughing

and whispering and the man had his arm around her shoulders. Savannah felt a sick feeling in her stomach, because she didn't think her mama knew the man, which meant she was letting a stranger put his arm around her. Anytime that happened, her mama ended up hurt or crying or angry at the stranger.

Savannah sighed and looked at the ground again. Where was her daddy right now? *Do You know, Jesus? 'Cause if You do then could You tell me, please? He's a Prince Charming and he loves me, I just know it. So if You find out where he is, please ... tell me, okay?*

"Savannah?" Mama's voice was different, all sweet, like there was a song inside her. Not the way she usually sounded, which was sad and mostly angry and frustrated.

She looked up. "Yes?"

"This is Victor." She smiled at the man and blinked a few extra times. "He's going to take us to his house by the park today."

"For a sleepover." The man winked at Savannah's mama. Then he raised his hairy eyebrows at her. "Sound like fun?"

Savannah's heart beat harder, faster. Jesus didn't like lying, that's what Grandpa Ted told her. But just then her mama's look told her, *Listen, young lady, you better tell the stranger yes or else trouble for you!* She gulped at the man and answered him in her most quiet voice. "Yes, sir. But I like my own spot on the floor, thank you."

"That right?" The man laughed hard from deep in his round belly. "Don't worry, little one. We'll have a good time. All of us." He elbowed Savannah's mama. "I hope you have half her spunk."

"Spunk." People used words like that to talk about her. Spunky. Feisty. Spirited. Mama said it was because her hair was red and she had freckles. They all three started walking toward the pretty buildings on the edge of the park. Savannah couldn't read yet, because her mama said school could wait. But the building where the man took them had the letters R-I-T-Z, and a man in a fancy costume was waiting for them out front.

Victor took them through a pretty room to a restaurant and they ate dinner at a table with a white sheet over it and pretty glasses and plates and forks. Savannah didn't dare say anything, but she couldn't stop looking around. The people and the furniture and the carpet and the ceilings—none of it looked anything like their room back in Harlem. More like something from a movie. *This*, she thought, *is a place where my daddy would live.* She knew exactly what he looked like so she started checking to see if he was one of the people who walked by.

Victor talked mostly to Mama. They ordered steak and potatoes and Savannah got a hamburger and French fries with a tiny little bottle of ketchup. Savannah kept looking for her daddy while they ate, which took a long time because her mama and Victor had two bottles of wine.

After that Victor took them into an elevator up to his house. "His room," he called it. Savannah's mama and Victor were laughing loud and walking very crooked. But when they reached Victor's door, inside was a whole house with a living room and two TVs and big giant windows that showed the park across the street. Savannah had never seen anything so beautiful in all her life. Victor turned the TV on for Savannah and he found a show with kids

singing. "Wait here, little one. Your turn will come later."
He grinned at her, but the way his eyes looked made her
feel scared.

Then he and Mama went into another room and Savannah heard the click of a lock. They stayed in there a long
time until it was almost night. Savannah got tired of watching TV. She walked to the window and stared at the park
and the sidewalks that went along the edge. So many people. Sometimes she wondered if she would ever find her
Prince Charming daddy.

A thought, or maybe a wish, filled her heart. That
maybe right this minute, wherever he was, her daddy was
thinking about her, too. That made her feel safe and sleepy
inside. She went back to the couch and stretched out.

"Savannah?"

The voice belonged to a man and Savannah sucked in a
quick breath as she blinked her eyes open. She pushed herself into the corner of the couch. She must've fallen asleep.
This wasn't her place on the floor in their room in Harlem,
so where was she? From the window she could hear pour-
ing-down rain and a little bit of thunder. She blinked fast
and then she saw him. That strange man, standing close by
her. Light came into the room from the street outside and
she could see his grin. The same grin as before.

"No," she whispered. She tried to move farther into the
corner of the couch.

Please, Jesus.... Please keep me safe.

The man took a step closer, but just then Savannah's
mama stepped out of the room. "Victor, come back...."
She still sounded funny from the wine. "I wanna show you
something."

Victor looked once more at Savannah and touched a piece of her hair. "No loss." He spit a little when he said the word "loss." "I don't care for redheads, anyway." He did that belly laugh again. Then he winked at her and went back into the other room with Mama.

Once the door closed, Savannah breathed hard and fast, and her heart pounded like the rain against the windowsill. She wasn't sure what the man wanted or why he had come to her, but deep inside her she knew that God had heard her prayer, and that He had just rescued her from something very bad. *Thank You for my red hair,* she told Jesus before she fell asleep again. Because maybe that helped her be safe.

Two days later her mama and Victor got in a fight. He yelled and she yelled and then Savannah saw him slap her mama across the face. Savannah ran for the door and covered her face, but before Victor could do anything else bad, Savannah's mama took her by the hand and they left. In the elevator, Mama touched her hand to her cheek and she started crying.

Savannah thought it was because her cheek was red, and because Victor didn't want to be her friend anymore.

"Men are pigs." She closed her eyes. "How could I believe him?" She sniffed and then she rolled her eyes. "I'm a terrible mother, Savannah. I don't even like children. I should take you to CPS and drop you off. We'd probably both be better off."

"Is that where my daddy lives?"

Her mama looked at her with the strangest look. "Is that what you want? To live with your father?"

Savannah opened her eyes wide. "Yes, please. At least for a little while."

Her mama cried harder then. "Fine, Savannah. You'd be happier with him, anyway. And I could do whatever I wanted."

Mama said that all the time, that both of them would be better off if Savannah went to CPS or to live with her daddy and that then she could do what she wanted. But her mama never took her there. Savannah figured that was because her mama loved her, even though she said she didn't like children a lot. She probably just didn't know how to act around children. That's what Grandpa Ted whispered to her when they talked that time in his hospital room.

Savannah stayed quiet while they walked to the subway and climbed down the stairs. She wasn't sure where CPS was, or if her daddy was there, but she had a feeling that this time maybe her mama would really do it—take her to be with her daddy. Until then she would keep praying for that to happen, since her mama thought it would be better for both of them. As they got onto the subway and found two seats, Savannah pictured her daddy one more time. God had kept her safe and now God was going to let her find her wonderful Prince Charming daddy. She could feel it. And that must mean her daddy was doing more than just thinking about her. He must've been talking to Jesus about her, too.

And that thought made Savannah smile for the first time in two days.

NINE

Carl Joseph took one egg at a time from his new carton in the fridge and set them carefully in the same plastic container Josh had given them. Along the way he lost track of how many, so he counted them twice. When he was sure he had six eggs, he closed the fridge.

"A good neighbor returns things they borrow," he said out loud. "And so I'm a good neighbor." He held the eggs tight against his body, put his apartment key in his pocket, because an independent person always has his key in his pocket, and then he locked the door behind him and walked down to Daisy's apartment.

He knocked on the door two times fast, then two times slow. That was his special knock just for Daisy and only he used that knock, no one else. Not even Brother or Elle. He looked up at the sky and smiled. Blue skies meant Daisy would be happy all day long. He whistled a song about somewhere over the rainbow, and after the "dreams come true" part, Daisy opened the door.

"Hi, Daisy." He held the eggs with one hand and pointed to the sky. "Blue means dry, and dry means good."

Daisy smiled at him and her eyes were sparkly like sunshine on a lake. "Thank you, CJ. I love blue skies."

"Well." Carl Joseph pushed his toe around in a few shy circles. "Actually God gave 'em to you." He laughed at that joke. "But you already know that."

"Of course." She tapped him once lightly on the shoulder. "Silly, CJ. Of course I know blue skies are from God." She looked at the eggs in the plastic container and her eyebrows went up. "Good idea, CJ. We have to take the eggs back to Josh."

"Because that's what a good neighbor does."

"Right." She pointed her number one finger into the air, which she liked to do whenever Carl Joseph had a good idea. "Good job, CJ." She linked her arm through his, grabbed her big blue purse, and they walked across the parking lot toward Josh's apartment. "Remember Disneyland, CJ, and how I pretended to be Minnie Mouse?"

Carl Joseph pushed his glasses a little higher up on his nose. "And remember I bought you a pair of Minnie Mouse ears for that day?"

"Right." She walked a few steps without saying anything, which meant she was thinking. "I have an idea, CJ. How 'bout I wear my Minnie Mouse ears next time we have a date day?"

"We could go to the mall!" Carl Joseph could picture what a fun time that would be.

"To the Disney Store." Daisy pointed at Josh's apartment just ahead. "We could ask if Josh wants to come, too. Because maybe he could buy a Minnie Mouse dress to go with this...." She reached into her purse and pulled out a brand-new pair of Minnie Mouse ears. "Tammy and I stopped at the mall on the way home from work yesterday. I bought these for that little girl in the picture on his fireplace."

"That's very nice, Daisy." Carl Joseph smiled, but only halfway. "Except Josh said that story doesn't have a happy ending."

"But God gave us a happy ending at Disneyland, remember?"

He thought about that. "And Disneyland is the happiest place on earth...."

"Right." She pointed with her number one finger again. "So let's give these Minnie ears to Josh and ask if he should come with us next time and get that little girl a Minnie dress." Her smile got softer. "Maybe with these Minnie Mouse ears that story will have a happy ending, too."

"Yeah...maybe that, Daisy. Maybe that." They reached Josh's apartment. He had Daisy on one arm and the eggs in the other, so he used the tip of his foot to knock on Josh's door.

They looked at Josh's door, but Josh didn't come to open it. "Maybe your tennis shoe didn't knock loud enough."

The sunshine felt warm on Carl Joseph's shoulders. "Yeah, maybe." He put the eggs down carefully on the ground, because all his eggs were in one plastic container. Then he knocked real hard with his hand, the right way. He put his lips up close to the door. "Hi, Josh. It's your favorite neighbors!"

Daisy giggled beside him, and she twirled the new Minnie ears and they waited some more. A car pulled into the parking lot and dropped off two girls. A mom in the car told them good-bye and then she pulled away, and still... still Josh hadn't opened the apartment door.

"You think maybe he's sleeping?" Carl Joseph looked over his shoulder at Daisy.

"If he is, we should probably wake him up."

"Yeah, right." Carl Joseph pushed his glasses up on his nose again and tried the door handle. It wasn't locked, so the door opened right up. A nervous feeling came over him, but he tried to smile, anyway. "I guess he was expecting us."

Suddenly, Daisy's smile was gone and she shivered a little. "What if he isn't here? It might be breaking the law to go inside if he isn't here."

"He's here." Carl Joseph turned halfway around and pointed to the old Mustang in the parking lot. "See that, Daisy? That's his car, so he's here."

"Okay." Daisy didn't sound that sure of herself. "Let's go in together."

Carl Joseph picked up the eggs and went inside a few steps. He faced toward where Josh's bedroom was. "Josh... it's your favorite neighbors. Are you awake?"

"Josh?" Daisy put her hands around her mouth so her voice would be louder. "Josh, wake up, okay?"

The sounds in Josh's apartment were his refrigerator and his clock on the kitchen wall, and a buzzing fly near the sliding patio door. But not Josh's voice. A strange feeling started to grow in Carl Joseph's stomach. It was the same feeling he had when he took the bus one time before he graduated from Elle's class on independent living. That day he took the wrong bus and he almost got lost forever, except Brother and Elle found him. How he felt that day was how he was starting to feel now.

"Come on, Daisy." He walked into Josh's kitchen and Daisy followed him.

"I'm scared, CJ. Where is he?"

"I don't know." He thought about opening the fridge and putting the eggs away but then he remembered his manners. It wasn't his fridge, so probably only Josh should put the eggs away. He left them on the counter in their plastic container. "Daisy"—he put his hands on both her shoulders—"don't be afraid. Let's just go to his room and wake him up. Because that's what good neighbors should do."

Her eyebrows were all scrunched together. "Are you sure?"

"Yes." Carl Joseph didn't listen to the scared feeling inside him. He held out his hand to Daisy. "Come on."

Together they walked down the small hallway to Josh's room and Carl Joseph knocked again. Still no answer. "Josh?"

"He's asleep," Daisy whispered. "Go on, CJ...go in."

Carl Joseph opened the bedroom door and there was Josh, lying on his bed. "Josh?" He used a regular inside voice because he thought Josh would wake up if he heard his bedroom door open. "Wake up, Josh."

They walked up to his bed slowly, and halfway there Daisy stopped. "He—he doesn't look right, CJ."

"He's very sleepy." Carl Joseph didn't want Daisy to say that, because what if...He walked right up to the side of the bed and gave Josh's shoulder a little shake. "Josh!" This time he used his loudest voice because maybe that's what it would take to wake him. "Josh, wake up."

"CJ, I'm scared again."

"It's okay. Let's say his name at the same time really loud. Maybe that'll wake him up."

"All right." She was shaking very much, but at the same time they said the numbers.

"One...two...three." Then, they both yelled Josh's name and Carl Joseph gave his shoulder another shake. But Josh didn't blink or move or anything. He just lay there, frozen still.

That's when Carl Joseph thought that maybe Daisy was right. Maybe something was wrong with Josh, and he needed emergency help. On the wall of his apartment and Daisy's, too, there was an instruction sheet of paper that told about how to get emergency help. Carl Joseph pushed up his glasses and swallowed hard. "Daisy?" He took a step back and turned to her. "Maybe we should get emergency help for Josh. Maybe emergency help could wake him up."

"Oh, no!" Daisy put her hand with the Minnie ears to her mouth. "Emergency help is for very bad problems."

"But if he can't wake up"—Carl Joseph looked back at Josh—"then this is a very bad problem, right?"

"Right." Tears came to her eyes. "Hurry, CJ, call for emergency help!"

Carl Joseph felt his heart pumping hard against his chest because this was more scary than being lost on a bus. He picked up the phone next to Josh's bed and tried to remember the numbers. It was nine something—nine-nine-nine, was that it? He put the phone back down and closed his hands very tight. *Please, God....Help me remember the emergency help number. Please....*

"What are you doing?" Daisy was crying. "CJ, call emergency help!"

"I'm praying. Because that's the first emergency help for me." He didn't yell at her, but he said it in a certain way so she'd understand.

He saw in the corner of his eye that she was walking a few steps away from Josh and then back again, nervous and scared. "Hurry, CJ."

Just then God gave him the right number, because he could see it in his head. He picked up the phone and dialed just like he saw it. "Nine-one-one, that's how to get emergency help."

In no time a woman said, "Nine-one-one, what's your emergency?"

Carl Joseph looked at his favorite neighbor. "Josh won't wake up."

"Excuse me, sir?"

"Josh!" *Stay calm,* he told himself. Because he wasn't really feeling very calm. *Stay calm. Help me, Jesus. I need You.* The first rule in emergency situations was to stay calm and pray. "He lives in the apartment across the parking lot. He's our favorite neighbor and he won't wake up."

"Is he breathing?"

Was he breathing? Carl Joseph hadn't thought about that. His heart was running fast inside him now. "How can I tell?"

"Sir." The woman sounded a little impatient. "You check if his chest is moving and if air is coming out of his nose or mouth."

"Okay...okay, I'll check." Carl Joseph put the phone on the edge of the table next to the bed and he stared real hard at Josh's chest. But no matter how hard he stared Josh's chest wasn't moving anywhere. Then he put his hand up in front of Josh's nose, but no air was coming out. Behind him Daisy was crying harder, so when Carl Joseph picked the phone back up he had to talk loud so the lady could hear him. "His chest isn't moving and no air is coming out." He began to take fast breaths because that couldn't be good. No chest moves and no air. "Help us, please!"

"An ambulance is on the way, sir. Are you the only one there?"

"Me and my girlfriend, Daisy. We live in the independent living apartments, but we were here because good neighbors return things they borrow."

"Yes, sir. Wait there until the paramedics come, okay?"

"Yes, ma'am." He hung up and he looked at Josh. Maybe a person could stop having his chest move and air come out if he was very, very sleepy. So he tried one more time to wake him up. "Josh!" he yelled. "Wake up right now!"

Still nothing.

"He isn't okay, CJ. Let's go." Daisy sounded very scared now, like when the rain came and she was afraid she would melt. "Let's go outside."

"We have to wait for the paramedics." He put his arms around Daisy and rocked her one way and the other. "That's what emergency help told me."

So Daisy pressed her head against his chest and they waited that way until they heard sirens. *Please help us, God....Please help our neighbor.* Carl Joseph said the same prayer over and over and over again until he heard someone knock at the door.

"Paramedics. Anyone inside?"

"Carl Joseph and Daisy," he shouted. "We're back here in the bedroom."

Two men in blue uniforms hurried down the hall and into Josh's room. The first one looked at Josh and then at Carl Joseph. He was in a very big hurry. "Step out of the room, please." Then he yelled something to the other man about a cart and paddles.

Carl Joseph took one more look at Josh and then, together with Daisy, he left the room. He wasn't sure how far to step out, but he could hear more sirens, so he decided they should step all the way out to the sidewalk. He took the plastic container of eggs on the way, because he wanted to be sure Josh got them. Then he remembered that anytime he needed emergency help he was supposed to call Brother. He could hear loud sounds coming from Josh's apartment, and a horrible thought came to him.

What if Josh—what if he was dead?

"CJ, what's happening?" Daisy was still crying and some of her tears were falling on the new Minnie ears. She needed to be somewhere else, somewhere away from the sirens and police cars and the fire truck coming into the parking lot.

"Come on, Daisy. Let's go to my house." He took her there, and then he called Brother.

"Carl Joseph, how are you?" Brother sounded happy. "We're still on for dinner later, right?"

"Brother, something's very wrong with our favorite neighbor, Josh."

His brother's happy sound left right away. "What is it?"

"He won't wake up. We went there to take back six eggs because a good neighbor returns what he borrows, and Josh won't wake up." His words all ran together the way his breaths did. "He won't wake up and so I called emergency help and now paramedics and an ambulance and firemen and police are all here."

"Okay, buddy . . . don't worry. I'm on my way."

"Thank you, Brother." Carl Joseph held on to Daisy until Brother came through the front door. "Buddy, I'm going over to Josh's apartment. Do you want to come or stay here?"

"Come." Carl Joseph was still breathing too fast and he still felt sick, but he had to go back to Josh. Josh was his favorite neighbor. He released Daisy. "You, too? You wanna come?"

"No . . . yes." She held on tight to his arm. "Yes, if—if you stay with me."

"I will." They hurried out the door with Brother and by then there were other people in the parking lot looking at Josh's apartment, old Ethel from right upstairs over where Josh lived and the two teenage girls who had gotten out of the car earlier and some other people, too. No one was laughing or talking or doing anything but waiting and watching.

When they got as close as the police cars, Brother stopped and turned to him. "I'll be right back."

Carl Joseph felt like he might stop breathing. His face was wet across his forehead and his heart was still running hard inside him. "Brother," he tried to whisper so Daisy wouldn't hear him. "I'm very scared for Josh."

"Listen, buddy." His brother put his hands on either side of Carl Joseph's face. "Everything's going to be okay, no matter what happens to Josh." Brother sounded serious, but calm. "Josh loves Jesus, remember?"

"Yeah, I remember that now." Carl Joseph nodded a lot of times. "Josh loves Jesus." And for people who love Jesus, everything would be okay in the end. That was always true. His heart slowed down just a little. "Thanks for that, Brother."

Daisy was still holding the Minnie ears, but Brother's words seemed to make her feel better, too. He jogged from them to the front of Josh's apartment just as a police officer was coming out. Brother said something to the policeman and they talked back and forth for a minute. Then he looked down at the ground and rubbed the back of his neck and that made Carl Joseph feel bad all over again.

Because Brother only did that when something was very, very wrong.

❦

Cody had no idea how he was going to go back to his brother and Daisy and tell them the truth about their favorite neighbor.

Josh Warren was dead.

The officer stopped him at the door and told him the news. "How? What happened to him?" Cody could hardly believe it. Josh was only in his late twenties, healthy but for a few pounds and his injured back.

"Died in his sleep....I'm sure they'll do an autopsy." The officer had a cell phone in his hand. "This was in his room. Do you know the names of any of his family?"

"Not the names." Cody tried to think what Josh had told him. "His parents are in Black Forest, I think."

The officer was scrolling through the contact list in Josh's phone. "Mom and Dad." He sighed and gave Cody a sad glance. "If you'll excuse me."

Cody took a step back and then walked slowly toward his brother and Daisy. Somewhere across town Josh's parents were about to get the news no mother or father ever wants to hear. He stopped for a few seconds and stared into the blue sky. Death was never easy, but especially not the death of a young person. *I know You're in charge, God.... But I don't get it. Josh Warren? What did he ever have? What good ever happened to him?*

His thoughts weren't irreverent, just honest. The way he always was with God. When Ali had died, her loss shook him to his core, almost made him give up on living. But by some miracle, God had brought Elle into his life, and with her he'd found a way to live again, a way to believe.

But Josh? He hadn't found love or the settlement he was waiting for. And most of all he hadn't found his daughter. A heartsick feeling dragged at Cody's heart. That little girl would never know her dad, or what a nice guy he was. He swallowed hard against the lump in his throat.

Carl Joseph was waiting.

TEN

Annie was eating breakfast with Nate on the back porch, watching a pair of deer maneuver through a grove of pine trees when the phone rang. Lindsay, she figured, telling her exactly where they were supposed to meet for the football game and how excited Ben was that everyone was coming. Lindsay called often—at least once a day—so she smiled at Nate, excused herself from the patio table, and went inside.

Some people talk about having a premonition, how in the minutes or hours or days before a car accident or a drowning or before getting that certain report from a grim-faced doctor, there was a nudging, a small, slight certainty that something very bad was about to happen. Later, no matter how long the road of years or how many summers separated that event from current-day living, the premonition would remain. "I had a feeling," people would say as they looked back. "I just knew."

That wasn't the case for Annie.

As she walked into the house she noted that the sky was spilling rays of blue sunshine between the trees and the house smelled like the fresh, hot cinnamon rolls she'd just taken from the oven. Her only thought about the coming day was that God must have been happy with her for Him to allow a Saturday in early fall to feel this perfect. Her whole family was going to be together. A football game, a church service filling up nearly an entire pew, and dinner at Lindsay's. This would be the sort of day, she told herself, they would look back on years from now and relive over and over.

A smile was already on her lips as she answered the phone. "Hello?"

"Mrs. Warren?" The voice wasn't familiar.

"Yes?" A slight frustration buzzed at her. She glanced back out at the porch, at Nate eating by himself. The deer had moved on, and she had missed them. For a sales call.

"Mrs. Warren, this is Sergeant Daniel White with the Police Department."

He hesitated, and in that single hesitation, Annie felt her world turn upside down. Because why—why would a police officer call her at home on a Saturday morning? And at the same time, his tone of voice told her the answer. She braced herself against the kitchen counter.

"Ma'am, do you have a son named Joshua David Warren?"

"Yes." *Get on with it,* she wanted to yell. *Tell me why you're calling.* "Is something wrong?"

"Please come to his apartment as quickly as you can, ma'am. There's been a problem."

"There's been a problem?" Adrenaline screamed into her veins and her heart responded by trying to burst from her chest. "A problem?"

"We'll be here waiting for you, Mrs. Warren. Please hurry."

She hung up the phone and her feet somehow took her back through the house toward the porch. She hadn't said good-bye to the officer, or thank you, or any of the usual polite things. She hoped the police officer wouldn't think her rude, or assign the impolite behavior to her husband where it might hurt his reelection bid. She allowed the crazy, irrational thoughts because they held back the avalanche waiting to crash in around her.

"Nate." Her tone was flat. She stood in the doorway gripping the frame. "We have to go."

Immediate concern lowered his eyebrows. He pushed back from the table, his eyes locked on hers, still chewing his cinnamon roll. "Annie...you're white as a sheet." He came to her, put his hand on her shoulder. "What is it?"

The police officer wouldn't blame Nate. Not when he had the chance to meet them in person and see for himself that she wasn't rude or ungrateful or impolite. Not really. "The officer said to hurry." She turned and walked back into the house, grabbed her keys from the drawer near the refrigerator, and held them out to Nate.

"Annie...talk to me." He was following her, his face still frozen in alarm. "What officer? Who was on the phone?"

She blinked and her strange trance cracked just enough to let her say, "Something's wrong with Josh." The adrenaline kicked into another gear and she dropped the keys. Before they hit the floor she was in Nate's arms. "Dear God, no." Her words were wrapped in panic. "Not Josh...not my son."

Nate allowed the embrace for only a second or two, then he took firm hold of her arms. "A police officer called about Josh? Is that it?"

"Yes." Annie couldn't allow the first few rocks to tumble down the hillside of her heart, couldn't let her mind go where the events of the last minute wanted to take her. She locked eyes with her husband and implored him with her eyes. "He's fine. He has to be fine."

Nate grabbed the keys from the floor and took her hand. "I'll drive."

"Thank you." There. She'd remembered her manners. "We need to pray."

"I am. I won't stop." But he did three times along the ten-minute drive to ask the same question each time. "The officer didn't say what was wrong?"

"No." She took her eyes off the road only for a second or so each time. "Just keep praying." But each time she let her tongue hand out that answer, a voice in her soul shouted at her that maybe it was too late to pray. All of existence as she knew it was about to change, because this was how other people's lives changed. A phone call or a knock at the door, the mile marker of a life that would forever more be divided into two parts. Before that single moment and after it.

Her prayer was a cry for help and she silently uttered it with every few breaths. *Lord, be with Josh.... Comfort him and give him peace. Whatever's happened to him, don't leave his side, please, God.... I can't do this without You.*

Daughter, I am with you always....

The answer anchored itself within her and allowed her to draw her next breath. *Lord, be with Josh.... Comfort him and give him peace. Whatever's happened...*

Not until Josh's apartment parking lot came into view did Annie know for certain the gravity of the situation. An ambulance was parked at an angle not far from Josh's front door, and next to it a fire truck and two police cars. People stood in small groups and Annie wanted to yell at them. *Don't just stand there. Do something.... Help my son.*

"Please, God...." Nate spoke the words out loud as he slammed the car into park. This time there was no confusion or question mark in his voice because the answer was obvious. The emergency vehicles told them what the officer had not.

They climbed out of the car and then suddenly Annie had the most desperate feeling to be with her son, with her youngest. Her baby. She began to run toward his front door and she kept running, even when she tripped over the sprinkler head. A police officer appeared in the entryway, and he stopped and waited for her. But why wasn't he in a hurry? Why wasn't he helping her son?

She picked up her pace and behind her she could hear Nate running, too. Josh was in trouble, but they were there, so everything would be okay. *Please, God, let it be okay.* Josh had been through enough without this, but if she could reach him and take him in her arms and cradle him close the way she'd done when he was little, then he would be okay, because her love was that strong. Strong enough to change this trouble around.

"Excuse me." She motioned with her hand for the officer to step aside, but he moved right into her path. "I need to see my son!" Her voice was so filled with terror, she didn't recognize it.

"Ma'am, I'm Officer White."

"Thank you for calling." Her mouth was dry. "We need to see him."

Nate was a step ahead of her now, talking at the same time. "Is he inside?" He was breathing fast, and he barely glanced at the officer. "What happened to him?"

"Sir, I need you to stop." The officer held out both hands, partially blocking the doorway. "Please.... You can't go inside."

Annie opened her mouth to say something or scream or cry, but she felt suddenly paralyzed. Nate put his arm around her, and the officer's words mixed with the sound of a radio coming from one of the emergency vehicles behind her, and the traffic on Elm Street that ran alongside the apartments, and the fast, relentless beating of her heart. Every noise intensified so it was hard to hear what he was saying. Something about not knowing the cause of death and finding the open bottle of pain medication beside her son's bed and wondering if Josh ever took more OxyContin than the regular dose. And Nate was asking how long Josh had been dead and . . .

Annie's knees buckled and she grabbed on to her husband. Her son was dead? Her youngest child was gone and she hadn't said good-bye? It wasn't possible. She held her hand straight out, as if maybe she could touch him or reach him somehow. "Josh!" The cry that came from her was like that of a crazy person, a scream that begged God to turn back the clock, to give her a chance to come here and hold him the way she'd wanted to yesterday after his deposition. "Josh, no!" She screamed his name again and Nate pulled her into his arms.

"Please." He was shaking as he stared at the officer, his voice shrouded in fear and disbelief. "We need to see him."

The policeman hesitated. "You don't want to go in there."

He looked back into the apartment and then at Annie. "Remember him the way he was."

The way he was? This wasn't happening. She was just talking to him on the phone, telling him he should get some rest and making plans to see him at today's football game. If she could only go inside and see him, maybe the paramedics hadn't done a thorough check, maybe he was only sleeping hard, the way he sometimes did when he took an extra pain pill.

A paramedic came out, stopped at the doorway, and spoke in a low voice to Officer White. "The coroner is on his way."

And just like that, the avalanche gave. It caved in around her and buried her, in suffocating layers of pain and grief. "Not Josh, please, God!" The scream wasn't as loud as before but it was heavy with a fear Annie had never known.

Nate drew her close again and soothed his hand over her arm. "Shhhh, baby...it's okay. Hold on to me."

Annie wasn't sure how they walked from the front door back ten feet to a spot near the end of the sidewalk, or how long they stood there. But at about the same time, a white van pulled up and two men with a stretcher walked quietly past them. Annie stared at the ground, at a crack in the asphalt near her feet. She wanted to run back to the car and tell Nate to drive as fast and as far from here as possible, so the scene playing out before her wouldn't be real.

If she looked down long enough, she could convince herself she wasn't here in Josh's parking lot, but at the football game. Standing outside her car, walking to the bleachers, a blanket under one arm, a bag of water bottles on the other. None of this was real. She was at the football game and Ben was warming up on the field, and Lindsay and Josh and Nate were saving her a place in the bleachers. And she was thinking how just yesterday Josh was the one in the uniform, the one waving to them from the forty-yard line, and she and Nate were saying how with Josh's height and strength, maybe he'd play football in high school and even college. She blinked and she could see all of Josh, each first day of school, each long, endless summer, and every rushed morning trying to make it to the bus on time

Nate leaned his head against hers and a quiet groan came from some broken place inside him. "Not Josh," he muttered, and his grip on her grew tighter, more desperate.

She kept her eyes down, glued to the crack in the asphalt, until she felt something wet on the side of her neck. *Don't look up*, she told herself. The stretcher would have to come out eventually. *Don't look up*. But she wanted to see whether the tears on her neck were hers, so she lifted her gaze just enough to find Nate's. His anguished face a twist of sorrow and disbelief, tears streaming down his face. "He's gone, Annie...our boy is gone."

Annie shook her head. He wasn't gone. He was twenty-eight years old. He had his whole life ahead of him. She noticed the crowd of people. A handsome dark-eyed man standing next to a young couple with Down syndrome. A woman with two teenagers huddled close on either side of her. An old woman standing a few feet away by herself, arms crossed in front of her chest, squinting at Josh's front door.

Annie wondered if they were her son's friends, and a realization hit her at once. She didn't know any of Josh's neighbors. She wasn't sure if Josh knew them, for that matter. But since they were here and they cared enough to watch, she thought about introducing herself and thanking them for coming. The way she would if this were one of Nate's dessert parties.

But this wasn't...this wasn't...

She squeezed her eyes shut and pressed her cheek against Nate's. The police officer's voice was saying something about clearing the way for the stretcher, and all Annie could think was that someone was hurt. Josh. Yes, that was it. Josh was hurt and he was coming out of the apartment on a stretcher, and the people had to make way because he needed a doctor.

But for every ounce of effort she put into convincing herself of this, the real details screamed at her from all sides. The sound of wheels against concrete came from his front door and she did what she never should've done. She opened her eyes and looked straight at the sound, and that's when she saw it.

A memory flashed in her mind, of her and Nate reading the paper one morning a decade ago, and Nate sharing the story of a family hiking Pikes Peak when their teenage son slipped off the path and tumbled to his death. Paramedics were summoned, but they could do nothing to help, and the boy's parents and sisters were forced to watch while his body was retrieved and carried away.

"What a horrible thing," Annie had told Nate. "No mother should have to watch her son's dead body being taken away. I'm not sure I could bear it."

And now she was that mother.

With the two men from the coroner's office at either end, the stretcher came into view. The body was covered with a white sheet, and Annie knew without a doubt that the form on the stretcher was Josh. First, the feet nearly hung off the stretcher, the way Josh's feet could sometimes hang over the edge when he came for a visit and he stretched out on the living room sofa.

And second, because the sheet was part of a set Annie and Nate had given Josh last Christmas. White with a thin brown stripe near the top.

"Josh!" Her voice could barely be heard. "God, help him.... Please help him." She gripped Nate's arm tighter. "He can't breathe." She moved to take a step toward him, but Nate held her back.

"Annie, don't.... We need to call Lindsay."

Don't? She wanted to scream at them to stop, because Josh could hardly get medical help with a sheet over his face. But then someone was crying, and Annie looked over her shoulder. It was the young woman with Down syndrome. She was covering her eyes and sobbing, and her friend had his arm around her and he was saying, "Josh is in heaven now, Daisy. Heaven's a good place, remember?"

The reality hit her full force.

The phone call...the police officer...the coroner's van...the quietly grieving neighbors. All of it provided a truth that she could no longer deny. This wasn't a dinner party for Josh's neighbors, and no, her son wasn't sick or asleep or struggling to breathe beneath the Christmas bedsheets.

He was dead. Her baby was dead, and she hadn't had

the chance to tell him good-bye. She remembered something Josh had told her after his accident, how he was glad
he hadn't died that night because he would have been without family.

"Whatever happens to me, I don't want to die alone,"
he'd told her. "There's nothing more awful than that."

But that's just what had happened. Her only son had
died without any family at his side. "Josh...no! Not Josh,
God...please...." Annie started to cry again, and her cry
became a wail. Her Josh was gone, and she would never draw
another breath without feeling his loss, brushing against
her ribs and hurting her insides like a permanent injury. The
suffocating avalanche of pain shut out any glimmer of light,
and beneath the weight of it, Annie closed her eyes and felt
herself begin to fall.

Nate caught her. It had to be Nate. But she couldn't stop
the dizzy swirling in her brain or the way her arms and legs
and even her hands hurt from the loss. Josh was leaving
and she couldn't will herself to stand up and go to him,
to tell him a proper good-bye. Black spots mixed with the
blurred images in her mind, and around her the sounds
began to dim. *Josh...not Josh, God.*

She was fainting, and she couldn't stop herself no matter
how badly she wanted to move, to take the walk from where
she was standing to wherever Josh was. But he wasn't here
at all, because he was in heaven. She couldn't breathe right,
couldn't open her eyes. She had just witnessed two men
wheel her son's dead body out of his apartment and toward
a coroner's van. Nate was holding her, but she was falling
harder, losing control. The last thing she remembered was

the terrifying truth that Josh was dead, and the certainty that she would be next. She'd been right that day when Nate read her the article about the family on Pikes Peak. This was a pain she could never, ever bear.

Even if God Himself held her up.

ELEVEN

Thomas Flynn hung up the phone, pushed his chair back from his mahogany desk, and paced slowly to the oversize window in his office on the twenty-third floor of the Markham Professional Building. He stared out at downtown Denver and let the futility of the situation wash over him. Josh Warren was dead.

The message was waiting for him when he came in this morning. An urgent call from Josh's mother, Annie Warren. Somehow Thomas knew even before he placed the call that something was very wrong. Josh hadn't been himself at the deposition. His skin had paled to a sickly shade of gray and he shook from the pain. At the time, Thomas thought his client's appearance could actually be good for the case. Anyone in the room could see the damage the accident had caused him, because he wore it like a second set of skin, tight around his body without the possibility of ever taking it off.

He'd told Josh the truth—they were close to a settlement. A month, maybe two. Three at the absolute most. The judge was tired of the defense's attorneys, a trio of three overpaid suits who apparently made billing the insurance company something of a sport.

There were requests for delays due to scheduling conflicts and corporate meetings and the attorneys' inability to gather proper evidence. More delay requests came with the revelation of even the slightest new detail in the case— usually provided by Josh during a deposition. The idea that his doctor had asked him to lose weight before he could have back surgery, for instance. Something like that single detail could send the defense into a tailspin after which it would take four weeks to right itself.

The judge knew how the game was played. Deny a motion and the case could get thrown out on appeal. So he'd been patient, narrowing the window of extension as much as possible. If the defense asked for six weeks to examine and prepare for a response to some new detail, the judge would generally grant them three.

But the game was winding to a close—all parties could feel it, and Thomas had been through enough of these to know the signs. Already the defense had agreed that there was liability on the part of its client, the insurance company. The admission meant the judge would decide the settlement amount, which was far better for the defense than the alternative. No culpable deep-pocket client wanted a jury trial. Not when its insured was a drunk driver who hit a guy in the act of being a hero.

The determination that there would be no jury was, in theory, intended to make the process simpler. For that reason, the defense could only push the process so far without making a mockery of it and angering the judge. And the defense definitely didn't want an angry judge when it came time to determine the settlement amount.

Even so, on this Monday morning Thomas had expected

to find a copy of yet another motion on his desk. After all, Josh had revealed something fairly dramatic in Friday's deposition.

Josh had an heir, a daughter.

He raised his right arm over his head and leaned it against the cool glass window. Annie Warren didn't know how her son had died, just that he'd gone to sleep Friday night and never woken up. Some of his colleagues could hear this sort of news about one of their clients and be laughing over coffee and doughnuts in the break room ten minutes later.

Not Thomas.

Josh mattered to him, same as every client he ever represented. He handled personal injury cases because he enjoyed breaking stereotypes. Not all attorneys who looked for victim settlements were ambulance chasers. Some, like him, took on clients who really had been hurt by the misdeeds of someone else. Thomas liked to think of himself as a modern-day Robin Hood of sorts, taking money from the rich and guilty and putting it in the hands of the poor and damaged.

But now that would never happen for Josh, and Thomas asked his secretary to hold all calls. He would need a day to regroup, to figure out what to do next in Josh's case. Thomas squinted against the glare of the late September morning. If he'd known something was this wrong with Josh, he would have driven home with him or taken him to a hospital.

What happened to him, God? Josh's weight was down, and mentally he seemed more able to handle the deposition than on past trips to Denver. So how did he die in his sleep? Thomas turned and leaned against the windowsill.

As he did, his eyes fell on a small plaque that stood on his desk. His wife had given it to him because it contained one of his favorite Bible verses.

In all things God works for the good of those who love him, who have been called according to his purpose. Romans 8:28.

He read the words three times over, but still he wasn't sure. All things? He had loved God all his life, and Josh had come into a stronger faith in the last month or so. But how could his death now work to the good for anyone? Especially Josh's parents. Thomas sighed and the action slumped his shoulders some.

He returned to his desk and stared at the documents spread out before him. Josh's deposition from Friday's hearing. The page that troubled him in light of the news was toward the end, the place where Josh was asked whether he had an heir. The question wasn't a surprise to Thomas, of course. He had prepped his client that the topic was bound to come up the way it always did in a settlement case.

"You don't know the girl, and you can't be sure she's your daughter," Thomas had advised Josh every time the subject arose. "If they ask you about having an heir, I'm suggesting you tell them the truth—that as far as you know, you have none."

"But that isn't the truth." Josh had always seemed genuinely baffled by the recommendation. "I *have* a daughter, and most likely she lives somewhere in New York City."

"Just because you sleep with a woman and she has a baby doesn't make the baby yours." Thomas never wanted to sound cruel, only factual. "The woman wasn't trustworthy. She was married and she was looking for an affair.

Now, because there's a child involved, it's become an emotional issue for you. Take your feelings out of it and see the situation for what it is."

The reason Thomas was concerned, and he'd explained this to Josh, was because of his parents. Josh owed them just over twenty-five thousand dollars, and since the accident they had taken responsibility for him, sometimes driving him to appointments when he was in too much pain to move, following up with Thomas after a hearing or decision by the judge on one or another motion by the defense, and being his sole emotional support system.

If by some terrible series of events Josh were to die before the settlement came through, his parents deserved the money. Thomas even spelled that out for Josh, but he was still adamant. "If one of their attorneys asks me on the witness stand if I have a daughter, I'll tell them what Maria Cameron told me. Savannah is mine. That's what I believe, and so that's the only truth I can give."

Thomas read over that part of Josh's deposition again and the beginning of a headache started near his temples. He had no choice but to find the woman, to let her know about Josh's death and the pending settlement. If the search panned out, and if Savannah really did belong to Josh, then his parents would be repaid everything he owed them but not a penny more. The rest of what could be a two-million-dollar settlement would go to Savannah, by way of her mother.

Thomas pictured his client, the sincerity in his eyes. Kind, loyal Josh. For him, giving an answer in favor of Savannah was never about losing his settlement money to the girl's mother. Rather his testimony was a public validation of his love for the child, his determination to find her one day and share custody of her. In Josh's mind, he was Savannah's father. Period. He would do anything for her.

But what about Annie and Nate Warren?

The scenario raised the temperature in the room and made Thomas anxious to find out the truth. He stared at the deposition and shook his head slowly. The odds of Josh being the girl's father had to be slim. A woman like Maria Cameron could have slept with ten men that week and her husband, too. She wanted money, nothing more. That's why she'd called Josh looking for child support when the baby was a few months old. But she'd given up too easily, in Thomas's opinion. If Josh were really the girl's father, Maria would have checked in at least once a year to see if Josh had come into a better financial picture.

Thomas turned his chair so he was facing his computer. Josh's parents didn't know about this twist in the case yet, but eventually Thomas would have to tell them. Especially if somehow Josh's suspicions turned out to be true. Thomas remembered something Josh had told him about his parents and their opinion of Maria Cameron. "They don't believe I'm Savannah's father." Josh's disappointment had sounded with every word. "They'd like to forget I ever went to Las Vegas."

Thomas felt the same way. He signed in to an online service his law firm subscribed to, one that allowed access to information that could help locate a person of interest. In the search line he typed Maria Cameron, and for city and state he entered New York, NY. In almost no time the search turned up six women by that name. But the one that interested him was several years older than Josh, with a criminal record.

He double clicked that entry and a host of information appeared. Thomas scrolled through it slowly. The photo was taken during a booking for prostitution, and it showed a woman who might have been attractive at one time. Strawberry-blond overprocessed hair, pronounced cheekbones, and sunken eyes.

According to the file, she'd been arrested six times over the last several years for charges ranging from drugs to bad-check writing and sex for sale. He pulled up the most recent report, from over a year ago. At the bottom it showed the details of the woman's arrest.

```
Suspect is female Caucasian, age 38.
She was booked for suspicion of offering
sex for sale, and at the time of
arrest it was discovered that she had
a minor child with her, a six-year-old
daughter. Suspect was brought to the
precinct, booked and fingerprinted, and
held overnight pending formal charges.
Minor female child was turned over to
suspect's roommate, Freddy B. Johnson.
```

Below that the document listed Johnson's address and phone number—the only phone number the suspect gave, according to another paragraph written by the arresting officer. Thomas jotted down the number and did a quick check on the other five women named Maria Cameron. Each of them was married and without any sort of police record. Thomas had a strong hunch he'd found the right Maria Cameron with his first guess.

With everything in him he wanted to rip up the piece of paper with Freddy Johnson's phone number and explain that he'd tried to find the so-called heir of Josh Warren, with no luck. But all his life God had dictated his decisions, and that was especially true in his law practice. Josh claimed to have an heir, and it was the responsibility of Thomas and his staff to see that the claim was checked out, one way or another. Even if the news would be crushing to Josh's parents.

He picked up the receiver, dialed the number, and leaned on his elbows. After four rings an answering machine picked up. "Leave a message at the beep," was all the gruff voice said. The beep came quickly and Thomas hesitated. "Uh…This is Thomas Flynn, attorney for Josh Warren. I'm looking for a Maria Cameron and need her to call me back. Her daughter may be the sole heir and recipient of a settlement from a pending lawsuit." He rattled off his office and cell numbers twice, and then hung up. He'd done what he needed to do.

Now he could only pray that what happened next would fall in line with the Scripture on his desk, and that all things really would work out to the good of those who loved God.

Especially for the grieving parents of Josh Warren.

TWELVE

I t was a perfect day for a wedding, a beautiful fall Saturday bathed in cool blue sunshine and framed in green leaves with a hint of orange and yellow. That was the only thing Annie could think as she slipped into her dress and applied a second coat of mascara. Thoughts like that helped her stay sane, made it possible for her to get through the day without breaking down and never getting up again.

She repositioned a few loose strands of hair and lifted her gaze to the bathroom window and the blue skies far beyond. Back when Josh and Becky were serious, they had sometimes talked about wanting an early fall wedding. Annie could hear her son now, the timbre of his voice, the sparkle in his eyes when Becky was near.

"October," they used to say. "That's the perfect time for a wedding."

Annie had to agree. The dry heat was behind them and snow was still a month or more away. Resorts and cruises gave great deals in October and beaches were warm and empty, with schoolkids back in class. Annie spritzed hair spray on her long bangs. Becky Wheaton had arrived yesterday, still single and lovely, and she was staying in their downstairs guest room. Family had flown in from Maine and San Diego and Atlanta, and everyone was meeting at the church in an hour. Only this wasn't the wedding Josh had looked forward to.

It was his funeral.

Annie had survived the last week on God's strength alone, she had no doubt. But she did her part by keeping busy. Josh was her baby, her only son. She wasn't going to tell him good-bye without creating a movie of his life and a printed program that people could take home to remember him by. The program was first, and Annie got it off to the printer on Tuesday. The movie took longer.

Annie used the iMovie program on her Mac and mixed short video clips of Josh's life with still photos and occasional titles or bits of text until she had a seamless production nearly an hour long. Then she dubbed in music where it applied, using songs that spoke of a life gone too soon and the sadness of saying good-bye.

Late last night, Annie and Nate had previewed the movie through teary eyes and Annie found herself thinking of Babette and the others who had the nerve to look down on Josh. Whatever his situation at the time of his death, the movie had enough highlights to leave a stunning, poignant picture of Josh's life. His blue medal in the fifth-grade all-area track meet, the trophy for his Pinewood Derby car the year he was a Boy Scout, the time he emceed the talent show for the eighth-grade graduation party.

One memory after another combined to tell a story other people might've forgotten: that Josh had been a success at one time. Never mind the fact that there were only a few photos and no video after he began working as a tow truck driver. This was how Annie wanted to remember him, and it was how she hoped everyone at the funeral today remembered him. The way he was before he lost sight of his dreams.

Nate found her in the bathroom still messing with her hair. "You ready?"

She took a last look at herself in the mirror. Wasn't this how it felt when Lindsay got married, everyone in town for the occasion and the rush of getting ready for a meeting at the church? She swallowed back her tears. "I don't want to do this."

"Me, either." He put his arms around her. "I can't believe he's gone."

It was the sort of thing they'd been saying all week, even as they met with the funeral director and purchased a casket and made plans to bury Josh in a cemetery at the base of his favorite mountain. How could he be gone? What was this crazy chain of events they were caught up in, and why did it still feel like they could pick up the phone and call him or hear a knock at the door and find him standing there, looking for time with his family?

The walk to the car, the trip to the church—all of it passed in a blur. The service was set to start at eleven o'clock, and in the minutes before, Annie looked around and felt pierced with disappointment. The church was barely a quarter full, forty-five, maybe fifty people in attendance. Mostly family and a few of Josh's friends—Becky, Keith and his wife, and a handful of people Annie vaguely recognized from the horrific minutes spent in Josh's parking lot a week ago. Two more were signing the guest book at the back of the church.

Keith was a pallbearer as were Nate and Annie's two nephews, Josh's cousins from Maine. Again there was that uncanny similarity. The flowers marking the front of the church, the candles, the guest book. The dark suits for the pallbearers and the boutonnieres for the lapels of the men's jackets. It was the party Josh always hoped to have one day, with everything but the bride and groom.

Annie glanced over her shoulder again. There should have been more people than this, more lives touched by her only son. Where were the people they entertained? The ones whose kids had gone to school with Josh? Were they too busy to come, or had time created that much of a chasm between their lives and Josh's?

Tears stung Annie's eyes and she leaned closer to Nate. *I loved you, son. Your father and I loved you. Lindsay, too. That's all that matters. And God, You loved him, too, right? You loved Josh?* Annie suppressed a wave of panic, because what if Josh didn't love the Lord? He'd loved Him as a child and even as a high schooler. But lately? Annie wasn't so sure.

She dismissed the picture of Josh missing church and seeming distant from God in recent years. That wasn't the Josh she remembered, and now she had to believe with every breath that he wasn't the Josh God remembered, either. *Please, God. . . . Remember him the way he was. No one can snatch Your people from Your hand, right? Let that be true for Josh, please. . . .*

Her eyes fell on the casket at the front of the church. It was covered with a spray of red carnations and next to it, propped up on an easel, was a framed photo of Josh in hiking shorts and a white T-shirt, a picture taken by

Lindsay when the two of them climbed lower Pikes Peak a year before the accident.

The sound of quiet sobbing came from Lindsay, who was sitting on Annie's other side. Lindsay had her head on her husband's shoulder, and next to him, Ben and Bella sat quietly, with their eyes downcast. Lindsay tried to talk to her a few times this past week, something about a music video and Wynonna Judd, but the distraction of phone calls and the movie Annie had been making and the details of the service always stopped them from finishing the conversation.

Annie made a point to get the details later. For now she could only stare at her daughter. Her brother had been her best friend all her life. She would never be the same without him.

Music started, the haunting refrains of a pipe organ playing "Great Is Thy Faithfulness," and Annie tried to believe it. With everything inside her, she tried. But all she could think was if God was faithful, if there was no shadow of turning with Him, then how come Josh was in the wooden box and not in the pew with the rest of the family?

She closed her eyes and tried to imagine new mercies every morning, when every day for the rest of her life she would wake up and experience the same realization. Her only son was dead. *God...I can't do this. I can't live without him. Please, take me home so I can hug him one more time.*

The service was over quickly. A pastor from the college ministry shared a brief message because he was the last person Josh ever connected with at the church, back when it looked like he might finish college and become an educator and go the path of his parents.

"It's never easy when someone leaves us in the prime of their life," the pastor was saying. "At times like this we must lean on God more than ever before."

Annie leaned harder into Nate. She couldn't remember the pastor's name. Aaron or Andy...She opened the program and scanned the list of names at the front. The survived-by list and the pallbearers and there it was, Pastor Allen Reynolds. Of course. Pastor Allen had met with Josh several times the fall after he graduated from high school, trying to convince him to give higher education a chance and get more involved with the college group. But even during his two years of junior college, Josh had followed through on very little of what Pastor Allen suggested.

"God's ways are not our own." The pastor hesitated as he looked out over the congregation. "If they were, then what sort of God would we be serving?"

Annie blinked and two tears slid down her cheeks. *Good question,* she told herself. *What sort of God would take my only son before his life even had a chance to begin?* And why hadn't things worked out with Becky? The girl had spent all of high school in love with Josh, and the two of them talked about going to college together. So why didn't they? How come, like everything else about Josh's life, those plans had fallen apart?

One of her brothers read a section of Scripture from 1 Corinthians, but Annie wasn't really listening. She locked eyes on the casket and all she could think was that her baby was trapped inside that box. The newborn she had held in her arms in the hospital twenty-eight years ago, the one who at three months old smiled at her and captured her heart all in the same breath. The boy who toddled across the room in his daddy's shoes and who caught her a toad for her birthday the year he was four.

The child she had adored and dreamed about and planned a future for was in the casket and he wasn't ever coming out. Her body made a sudden move to stand, to cross the front of the church and close the distance between her and the wooden box. She might not be able to open it, but she could at least put her hand on it so Josh would know she was close by. But even as her legs tightened and she tried to stand, she ordered herself to stay seated. Pastor Allen was still talking. People didn't stand up in the middle of a funeral service, even if their only boy was trapped in a casket ten yards away.

After the Scripture reading there was another song. Finally, the pastor explained that people were welcome to follow the hearse to the cemetery and then back to the Warren house. His voice and the voices around her as the pastor dismissed the congregation sounded distant and small, like someone had turned down the volume on a distorted pair of speakers.

Somehow, she and Nate found their way back to the car, and Lindsay hugged her before she climbed inside. "It isn't fair." Lindsay was still crying just as hard as earlier. "I miss him so much."

Annie could hear the music coming from the church, another round of "Great Is Thy Faithfulness." She blocked it out and kissed her daughter on her cheek. "I miss him, too."

Nate hugged Lindsay. Then, they got into their separate cars and lined up behind the hearse. Again Annie was struck by the strangest, saddest thought. Since Josh stopped running track his junior year of high school, he hadn't been first at anything he did. Someone was always a little faster, a little stronger, a little more equipped for the right job or right break or right opportunity. But not here. Here he was in first place once again, the hearse leading the way in a procession that would cross town and end up at the cemetery.

When they arrived, Nate said a few words to the family and friends who followed them there. "We grieve the loss of our youngest child, our son, Josh. But we know we will see him again in heaven." The sincerity in Nate's expression was matched only by that in his voice. "Thank you for coming. We hope you'll come to the house when we're finished here."

There was little conversation as people quietly paid their respects and then made their way back to their cars parked along the private road that ran through the center of the cemetery. Becky was one of the last to leave. She walked up to the casket and touched her fingers to the wood. For what seemed like a long time, she stood there, her eyes closed, cheeks wet from her tears.

Maybe if you had stayed with him, Annie thought....But she couldn't harbor bad feelings, not toward the girl who had been the love of her son's life. Instead, all she felt was a great ocean of loss and sorrow. Because if they'd stayed together, this day could've been so very different.

After Becky left for their house, a finality settled over the moment because they were alone—just Annie, Nate, Lindsay, and her family. One at a time they took a few moments beside Josh's casket, until it was Annie's turn. She barely moved her feet through the fresh-cut grass until she was at his side. There she was struck by a sudden and profound thought. So many times when Josh was growing up, he'd brought her flowers. Her son was quick with a hug or a kind word, but often when he wanted to show his love he'd give her flowers. She could see him running through the door during the spring of his fourth-grade year, a handful of dandelions clutched in his fist. "Here, Mom. I picked these for you."

And she could remember holding them and smelling them and smiling at him and thinking, *I hope no one ever tells him they're weeds.*

There were flowers for her birthday each year and on the last few Mother's Days, a wild bouquet picked from a field not far from his apartment. She stared at the spray of carnations on top of the casket. Carefully, she eased three from the display and brought them close to her nose. They smelled of late summer and sweet sunshine, and Annie thought about where she'd dry them and how she'd save them forever.

Because these were the last flowers she would ever get from him.

✎

Only twenty people showed up back at the house for the late lunch spread Annie put together. The conversation was peppered with happy stories from Josh's childhood and wistful projections of what might have been if he hadn't had the accident. Becky stayed until the end, not saying much and keeping to herself. Before she left, she pulled Annie aside and hugged her, really held on to her. "I never stopped loving him." She whispered the words in a voice thick with tears. After another quick hug she was gone.

Annie still wasn't clear about what happened to end things between Josh and Becky years ago, but this wasn't the time to talk about it. Besides, it was too late to matter now. Josh had missed out on a life with Becky, and he'd missed out on the settlement he so badly deserved. He'd missed out on being a dad and having the life he dreamed about. His entire life seemed like one big missed opportunity.

When the last guest left, and after Nate turned in for the night, Annie went outside on the front porch and stared through the evergreen tops to the distant stars. Josh's funeral service had been like his life—small and insignificant. Just as well that Babette stayed away. The service would've given her one more way she could compare Josh with her son and find Josh lacking.

A breeze blew against Annie's brow and she thought of one more sad detail. The daughter Josh talked about, the one he was sure was his own, was also not at the funeral. She wasn't his daughter, definitely not. But still, something hurt deep inside her because the girl he'd thought about and prayed for and longed for didn't know he had died. But there was something even sadder than that. Whoever she belonged to, the girl hadn't only missed Josh's death.

She'd missed his life.

THIRTEEN

Freddy had saved the message for her, and by Sunday morning Maria had listened to it four times. Each time, the lawyer's words held a deeper reservoir of hope and potential. A settlement? From a big-time lawyer? So, maybe she *had* picked the right guy that night in Las Vegas. Josh hadn't been worth anything last time they'd talked, but he must have come into some kind of fortune, because now there was a settlement at stake.

And her Savannah was the guy's only heir. What kind of great luck was that?

The thought made her giddy with possibility. She had Savannah dress in her best jeans and T-shirt, the one with the flowers on it, and she took her downtown on the subway to Central Park. But this time Maria had no intention of begging money off people. Today was the turnaround Maria had been waiting for. They would walk the path through the park and talk about mother-daughter things, the way they always should have. And Maria would dream about all the ways she could spend the money.

Strange about the timing. On Friday night Maria had placed an anonymous call to Child Protective Services asking whether it was possible to turn a kid in if you couldn't handle raising her any longer. She wouldn't give her name, but the lady she talked to said it was definitely possible. First, they'd give the overwhelmed parent a class on child rearing and then they required the parent to take several counseling sessions and blah-blah-blah. But the bottom line was yes, CPS would take her. Maria was seriously thinking about taking Savannah this week and dropping her off for good.

Freddy was tired of sleeping with her, and a couple opportunities had come up with a pimp in the financial district. High rollers with big money and no one to spend it on. She could see herself in a penthouse suite, the kept woman of some bank manager or investment millionaire. But not with Savannah in tow, definitely not.

Late Friday she'd even told Savannah her plans. "My days as your mama might be just about over." She'd talked real nice, giving Savannah her most kind smile. "I care about you too much to let you live like this any longer. Plus, some big opportunities are showing up for your mama." Maria had drunk nearly a bottle of Freddy's burgundy wine, so she probably said more than she should've. "You understand, right?"

Savannah shook her head. "No, Mama. I don't wanna leave you."

But the girl had to know that her life was about to change. "Don't worry, Savannah. There's someone out there who wants you a whole lot more than me. Someone better for you."

"My daddy, you mean?"

Maria had only laughed. "Yeah, sure, baby. Maybe it'll

be your daddy." What mattered wasn't who took Savannah in, but that Maria could finally be free of her. At least that's how she felt Friday and Saturday. But all that changed the minute Maria listened to the message from the lawyer.

"Today's a celebration," she told Savannah when they stepped off the subway. She reached for her daughter's hand and realized how good it felt to connect with her this way. "Mama's ship has finally come in."

"What ship?" Savannah seemed confused, like she didn't know what to make of her mother's new attitude.

"The ship of good fortune."

"Is it in the harbor?"

"No." Maria laughed and she felt like other mothers for the first time, the ones she saw near the zoo and the playground and the fountain. The ones who were always walking and talking and laughing with their daughters. She smiled at Savannah. "This ship used to belong to your daddy, but now—now it belongs to me."

"To you?"

Maria suddenly worried about that answer. What if the attorney arranged a talk with Savannah and heard that Maria thought the money was her own? She cleared her throat and slowed her pace. "Actually, the ship belongs to—to both of us." She found her smile again. "Isn't that wonderful?"

Savannah shrugged one shoulder, but her eyes looked happier than they had in a long time. Maria could've burst into song. She still had a little money from her time with the high roller in Central Park, the one with the gold chains. At the hot dog cart, she pulled a ten from her pocket, bought chili dogs and pop for both of them, and together they sat on the nearest empty bench.

Maria savored every bite of her dinner and breathed in deep the air of change around her. She had been looking forward to the next chapter in her life, finishing her role as a mother and moving into the world of people with lots of money. But she could get used to this, being a mother without having to sleep with anyone just to survive. If the settlement was large enough, she wouldn't need to work her way into the world of the wealthy.

She was about to become one of them.

On Monday morning, Maria paced, checked her watch, and counted down hours until finally it was nine o'clock on the West Coast. At one minute after nine she placed the call to Thomas Flynn, attorney.

A woman answered on the first ring. "Flynn and Associates, how can I help you?"

Maria felt a little breathless. She stood straighter and leaned against the kitchen wall in Freddy's apartment. "This is Maria Cameron. I'm returning a phone call from Thomas Flynn."

"Just a moment, please."

Her heart beat hard, and she hoped this Flynn guy wouldn't hear it over the phone lines. Savannah was watching something on MTV, and Maria had turned the sound down so she could hear every detail of whatever good had come their way.

There was a click on the line. "Thomas Flynn here."

"Hello." Maria wasn't sure how formal she should be. "Mr. Flynn, my name is Maria Cameron. You left me a message on Friday."

"Yes." There was a pause and something changed in the man's voice. "I called about a client of mine—Josh Warren. Are you familiar with that name?"

"Yes, of course. We were—we were very close." Maria silently congratulated herself on her acting job. Besides, for those few days in Vegas, she and Josh truly were close. She would have moved in with him if he'd been honest about his financial status. She turned up the concern in her tone. "Has—has something happened to him?" Maria was pretty sure about the answer, otherwise there wouldn't be a need to discuss the fact that Savannah was his heir.

"Yes." The attorney let out a breath, as if the news was still difficult for him. "Mr. Warren passed away a week ago."

Maria allowed a soft gasp. "That's terrible. Was it an accident?"

"We aren't sure what happened. He died in his sleep."

"No." She pictured the virile young man who had shared a bed with her some eight years ago. His death truly was a shame. If he'd lived long enough to win the money coming to him, he would've been a great catch. She softened her voice. "That's just awful."

"Yes, well..." The attorney sounded disturbed by the fact, and maybe a little suspicious. "The reason I'm calling, Ms. Cameron, is because Mr. Warren was at the end of a major lawsuit when he died." He asked if Maria had a seven-year-old daughter named Savannah, and when Maria assured him that yes, she did, he went on. "His estate stands to receive a major settlement, and, well, he told the court that your daughter was his sole heir."

"That's true, at least as far as I know." Her contrite tone

hid the excitement starting to build within her. "Do you mind if I ask—how much is the settlement for?"

"That hasn't been determined." This time there was no doubt about Mr. Flynn's disgust toward her. "The point is, paternity needs to be determined before we can consider your daughter a rightful heir to Mr. Warren's estate. Would you be willing to subject your daughter to a paternity test?"

From the beginning Maria had known Savannah belonged to Josh. Her husband at the time rarely slept with her, and Maria suspected he was sterile because he'd never managed to get her pregnant. Not that she really wanted kids. She wanted the child support, and she'd figured a child wouldn't be too bad. Better than getting a job, anyway. When Savannah was born, she'd seen Josh in her from the beginning. The girl had his eyes and the shape of his face, and after a few months she was sure. Regardless of what people thought about her, she hadn't slept with more than a few men in the time frame when she'd gotten pregnant, and Savannah looked more like Josh than any of the others. She glanced at her daughter, sitting cross-legged in front of the TV. "Yes, sir, for sure. I don't have medical insurance, but if you set it up, I'll take her wherever you want for a paternity test."

"Very well." The man sounded tired. "I'll take care of the details and get back to you."

"Thank you, Mr. Flynn." She was still sounding the part of the grieving friend. "I'll share the news with Savannah."

"Let's wait. I think we should have test results first."

"Okay." Maria sounded hurt. "But I can assure you with my whole being that Savannah is Josh Warren's daughter.

If you want us to wait for the test to talk about it, I can do that."

"Thank you. I think it's the least we can do."

Maria hung up the phone and for a brief moment she felt sorry for Josh. He'd been a nice guy, a little heavy but good-looking. And in the few days they'd known each other he had fallen hard for her. There was something sad about the fact that he was dead—especially since he really was Savannah's father. But on the other hand...

For the first time in her life something good had come her way and she wasn't going to do a single thing to mess it up. Not this time. Once they had the results of the paternity test, she and Savannah would take the money and make the kind of life for themselves Maria had only dreamed about. The thought made her smile as she found a box of macaroni and cheese in Freddy's cupboard.

Poor Josh. He was just like any other guy until now. But once they had the paternity test, she and Savannah would ride this all the way to the bank, and in some ways that would mean Josh's death wasn't in vain.

All of which made Maria feel better about herself than she'd felt in a very long time.

❧

Thomas felt like he needed to take a shower after just five minutes on the phone with the woman. From the tone in her voice and her hurry to find out the amount of the settlement, he could sense that Maria Cameron was just like he'd imagined her to be. She couldn't care less about Josh Warren—only that by some good twist of fate she'd managed to trick him into fathering her child. If she was right, anyway, and Josh really was the girl's dad.

The paternity test would be the deciding factor, and he would set it up through a clinic in New York City. She had no insurance, so clearly Josh's estate would be footing the bill. He allowed a heavy sigh. With the certainty in the woman's voice, he had no choice but to give Josh's parents a warning.

He dialed Annie's cell phone, and when she answered, he heard the same thing he'd heard each time he'd talked to her since Josh's death: the hollow emptiness of someone whose heart had broken, someone who would never be the same again. "Hello, Thomas. How are you?"

"Hi, Annie. I'm fine." He wished he could tell her he was just checking in with her, and that he had no news on the lawsuit. He wished he could tell her anything but the truth. "There's, uh, there's some new information that's come to light in the court case."

She uttered a sad laugh. "It's been three years. How could there be anything new?"

"It's nothing for sure yet, but I wanted you to know I'm working on the case and I've come across a few speed bumps." His stomach churned with the possibilities. "When I have more information I'll call or come see you."

"Is this about the settlement?" The word "settlement" sounded bitter on her tongue.

"Well..." He was still standing at the window, still looking out over downtown Denver and wondering how he could find some good news for the woman. "It's more about Josh's estate, how the settlement will be disbursed." Thomas hated being evasive, but he had no choice. He had to raise the possibility of a problem, but there was nothing to tell her, not until the paternity test results were in.

"His estate?" Annie was a smart woman. Her voice told him that she suspected the news might not be good, even if she had no idea what the details involved.

"Yes." Thomas stood and paced to his window. How much heartache could the woman take? "I'll tell you when I know more, Annie. I promise."

There was a slight pause on the other end. "Can I tell you something?"

"Of course."

"My husband and I don't care about Josh's money, not in the way some people might care about a large settlement." Her voice sounded strained, like she was on the verge of crying. Each word was deliberate as she continued. "But my son lost his life because of that accident, because that driver drank himself into a stupor and got behind the wheel. Whatever this new information is, whatever's happening with Josh's estate, we're trusting you, Thomas, to see that justice is done." She hesitated. "The same way Josh trusted you."

Her words were like so many weights on his shoulders. "I appreciate that." He tried to imagine how she'd feel if the paternity test came back positive, and he put the possibility out of his mind. "Every day I ask God to give me the wisdom to do what's right by Josh's memory."

"Thank you." She sniffed softly. "Nate and I are doing the same, praying for you. No settlement will bring Josh back, but we have ideas about how to use the money he has coming to him. Charities and family members who can benefit from his legacy. A college fund for Josh's niece and nephew. That sort of thing."

"Right." Thomas swallowed hard. "Good. Well, like I said, I'll be in touch when I know more."

The call ended and Thomas lowered the phone to his side. He didn't know Maria Cameron but he could picture her, a single mom raising a lonely girl in New York City. What sort of married woman would go to Vegas alone and trap a man into sleeping with her? That's what she'd done, no question. He lifted his eyes to the hazy sky. He'd heard it said that when the haze didn't quite burn off over the city there was always sunshine just beyond the clouds.

But today he had to wonder.

Dear God... You know all things and I believe in You even when life doesn't make sense. But just know I'm struggling with this one. If the paternity test comes back positive, then everyone loses—even the little girl. She'll never see any of the money if her mother gets her hands on it. His head hurt again and he willed himself to trust. *If all things really work to the good of those who love You, then please work in this situation and let the right thing happen for Josh's family. Please.* As he finished the prayer, he didn't hear an answer or sense a Bible verse come to mind. But he had the undeniable assurance that he'd been heard by God Almighty—whatever lay ahead.

For now, that would have to be enough.

FOURTEEN

Lindsay was on her way to Josh's apartment and she couldn't shake the sick feeling surrounding her. She'd been in a fog since getting the news about her brother. Every hour of each day since his death, she'd walked through life like she was in some sort of trance, doing the next thing, breathing in and out and in again, but not sure whether she could make it through another day.

Her husband was being wonderful, taking care of the kids and giving her time to plan Josh's funeral with her parents. Now, this week, it was time to go through her brother's apartment and box up his things. Even the idea of such an action felt ludicrous. Her brother's life reduced to a few boxes of personal items?

Lindsay pulled into the apartment parking lot and took the spot closest to his front door. Her mother had given her one of the keys, and the apartment manager had told them to take the rest of the month to go through Josh's things. He'd already paid rent through the end of October. Lindsay wore jeans and a sweatshirt, and from the back of her Highlander she took out a stack of boxes and a dozen black Hefty bags.

She had no idea what she was about to encounter, but she had a feeling that over the next few weeks, they would learn more about Josh than they'd known before. The walk up to his front door felt strange, as though she were violating his privacy. Yes, she'd been here before—even recently— but to come here this way without him here...the whole trip made her uncomfortable.

Once she was inside, she was overcome by a rush of emotion. His cologne still filled the room, and there by the front door were his dress shoes, the ones he'd prob- ably worn to Denver for his deposition. She had the saddest urge to call out to him, just in case everyone was wrong and he was still here, still sleeping off the effects of the pain medication.

Her mom was meeting her here, and Lindsay hoped she'd be here soon. This wasn't a job Lindsay wanted to do by herself. She picked up her brother's shoes and brushed off a light layer of dust before setting them back down. His kitchen was neat, the way he'd left it, and his mantel still held the three photos—the family shot, the one of the little girl who might or might not have been his daughter, and the other of the two teenagers. A heavy coat of pain fell across her shoulders as she stepped closer to that third photograph. She had asked Josh about it last time she was here, but he hadn't gone into detail. Something about how the photo gave him a reason to believe that good could come from driving a tow truck.

Lindsay had told herself she'd get more details about the story later, when she wasn't in such a hurry. Only now that conversation would never take place. She gripped the mantel and hung her head. *Lord...I want to know why these girls mattered to my brother. Please help me find the reason.*

I am with you, My daughter.

The response whispered to the hurting places inside her, and Lindsay took them as a promise. Somehow she would know the story of the girls. She moved across the room to Josh's computer desk. Two oversize file drawers made up the right side of the place where the chair sat. Lindsay took the chair and opened the top drawer.

At first, the files showed little promise of being anything more than old utility bills and auto loan statements. One file showed Josh's bank records, and Lindsay pulled them out and studied them, feeling guilty. She still hadn't deposited the six-hundred-dollar check from him. Even then, what the statements showed stunned her—Josh was living on barely any money at all, averaging a balance sometimes less than a couple hundred dollars through an entire month. All this time she thought he'd been bringing home his same salary through workmen's comp, but apparently not. The amount going into his account every month was less than a thousand dollars. He had a balance of just over seven hundred now—barely enough to cover the check he'd written her.

No wonder he'd borrowed money from their parents once in a while.

She returned the bank records to the file, and there at the back of the drawer was a thick envelope marked with a single word: Accident. Lindsay picked it up and pulled it onto her lap. The details inside this envelope told about the event that changed everything for Josh. The event that killed him. Her eyes blurred with tears as she opened the envelope.

Inside was a set of letters paper-clipped together that looked like his initial correspondence with Thomas Flynn, his attorney. Beyond that were notices of hearings and details of his lawsuit against the drunk driver's insurance company. At the back of the envelope was a clipped-together file of letters and a newspaper article.

She carefully slid the bundle free from the envelope and studied the last page of a three-page letter. It was handwritten to Josh by a woman named Karla Fields. Before stopping to read the letter, Lindsay thumbed through the next letter and saw that it was from a man named Bill Sedwick. The newspaper article was at the back of the stack. Lindsay carefully pulled it free from the others and set it on top.

It was printed from an online newspaper, and Lindsay felt her pulse quicken as she stared at the photos that anchored the article. One was of her brother, a head shot, probably the one on his work badge. But what caught her attention was the other photo. It was a staff photo taken at what appeared to be the scene of Josh's accident.

The faces in the picture were the same as those in the photograph on Josh's mantel.

Lindsay knit her brow and read the headline above the story. *Tow Truck Driver Hailed as Local Hero*. Her hands began to tremble. Local hero? What was this, and why hadn't she and their parents ever seen the article? She began reading.

```
A local tow truck driver pulled two
teenage girls out of the path of a
drunk driver Saturday night, flinging
```

```
himself in harm's way and taking the
hit instead, according to police.
Josh Warren, 25, was giving the girls
directions when he saw the drunk driver
careen out of control and head straight
for them.
```

The article named the drunk driver, and the fact that
he'd been convicted three previous times for driving under
the influence.

```
"No question that the quick-thinking
brave actions of Mr. Warren saved the
lives of those two girls," one officer
at the scene reported. "Josh Warren is
a hero by every definition of the word."
  The girls, Sarah Fields and Susie
Sedwick, both seventeen, were unharmed
in the incident, but Warren was unable
to get completely out of the path of
the vehicle. The blow knocked him to
the ground and caused severe damage to
his back and neck. He remains in the
hospital in serious condition.
```

Lindsay stared at the words and tried to imagine again
why her brother hadn't told them these details. They knew
he'd been hit by a drunk driver, but not that he'd saved the
lives of two girls in the process. Why in the world would he
keep a thing like that from them? The story hadn't made
the Springs newspaper, and so without hearing about it

from Josh, there had been no way any of them might have found out.

She found her place and kept reading.

```
Witnesses at the scene said that the
driver was slumped completely over the
wheel when his car veered off course
and hit Warren. Police at the scene
determined that the driver's blood
alcohol level was nearly three times the
legal limit. Charges are pending against
the driver, who could stand to serve up
to five years in prison because of his
previous convictions.
```

Lindsay blinked and studied the photos once more. So that explained the picture on his fireplace mantel. He'd lost his health, his mobility, his career, and his ability to earn a living, but two girls were alive and well because of his actions. The drunk driver had been sentenced to four years, but Thomas Flynn thought he could be out anytime. No wonder the picture of the girls was a reminder. Lindsay could imagine that even on the most painful days, the photo gave Josh a reason to feel good about himself, about his actions.

Tears fell down the bridge of her nose onto the article and she set it on Josh's computer desk so it wouldn't get any wetter. The clipping was the first thing she was going to show her mother. She picked up the letter from Karla Fields. It was long and drawn out, but Lindsay read every word.

She wouldn't be alive today if it weren't for you, the woman wrote. *I pray God blesses you mightily for your sacrifice. I will continue to thank Him for your act of service all the days of my life.*

The letter from the other girl's father was very similar. One paragraph read, *In our culture of self-serving, self-seeking young people, you give me reason to hope for our future. I've enclosed a photograph of the girls so you'll always remember what your act of heroism meant to all of us. Thank you will never be enough.*

Lindsay cried through the reading of both letters, touched to the core and yet not surprised that her brother would do such a thing. Hadn't he looked out for her through high school and the years afterward, even though she was older? He was always putting more care into the lives of the people around him than worrying about himself.

Of course he kept the girls' photo on his mantel.

She sat back in his computer chair and remembered a few conversations she'd had with her brother—especially the year after he started working as a tow truck driver.

"Mom and Dad aren't happy about it," he'd told her once when they met in Denver for dinner. "They want me to finish college and teach somewhere."

Lindsay had wanted to stick up for him, help him so he didn't walk away from the conversation feeling lesser because of his job. "They think you're going through a phase. You'll get back to school eventually."

"What if I don't?"

"Then they'll live with it." Lindsay covered his hand with hers. "Besides, you look great in a tow truck."

But the conversation came up a number of times, and always Josh couldn't be convinced that his parents were proud of his work towing cars, even for one of Denver's official police garages. His concern for what they thought only grew after the accident. Not only had the job failed to become something lucrative or successful, it had cost him his health.

Something else he'd said came back to her. It was after the accident, maybe six months or so. "After the settlement comes through I'll open my own business, something Mom and Dad can get behind."

Lindsay always felt sorry for him when the topic of his job came up, so she agreed with him, even tried to get excited for him. But it hurt her that Josh lived in the shadow of his parents' silent disapproval. Now the reason he hadn't shared about rescuing the girls seemed obvious. The act of pulling the girls from the path of the drunk driver wouldn't be enough to gain their respect for his job. That would have to wait until he found another line of work—at least by Josh's estimation.

The possibility that Josh was too embarrassed to tell his family about his rescue brought with it a fresh wave of tears. Her poor brother, suffering every day with his back pain and not feeling good enough about his heroism to share the details. Before she could look at the bottom file drawer, her mom walked in. She held on to the door frame and looked like she was being hit by a wave of the same emotions that had hit Lindsay half an hour ago.

"It's wrong, being here without him." Lindsay stacked the article and the two letters together and held them on her lap.

"I had the strangest thought that if I walked into his apartment he'd still be here." Her mother came in and took the seat closest to the computer. "Like it wasn't possible to be here without him."

"Exactly." Lindsay was about to hand her the information about Josh's rescue when there was a strong knock at the door. Lindsay set the stack of documents on the desk and answered it. Standing on the front step were Josh's neighbors, the couple with Down syndrome.

"Hi." The young man pushed his glasses up on the bridge of his nose. He had a plastic bowl of eggs and he held them out to Lindsay. "I saw your car." He leaned in and looked at Lindsay's mother. "Yours, too." He did a half bow. "I'm Carl Joseph. This is Daisy."

"Hello." Lindsay took a step back and welcomed the pair into the apartment. "You knew Josh?"

"He was our very best neighbor." Carl Joseph's eyes teared up.

Lindsay could see that her mother wasn't sure what to say, so she took the lead. "Carl Joseph...Daisy...I'm Lindsay, Josh's sister."

"Yes." Daisy had a bright orange beach bag over one arm. She looped the other through Carl Joseph's. "Josh said you were his best friend."

The ache in Lindsay's heart doubled. "He was my best friend, too." She pointed to the plastic container. "You brought some eggs?"

"Josh loaned them to us before"—he looked at Daisy, his chin quivering—"before he died."

"We wanted to be good neighbors, and good neighbors

return what they borrow." Daisy took the eggs from Carl Joseph and handed them over. "You're Josh's family, so you can have them."

"Okay." Lindsay wanted to keep from crying, but she was losing the struggle. She set the eggs on the kitchen counter. "Thank you."

Daisy rocked back and forth on her feet a few times, and she looked at Carl Joseph, then at Lindsay. "You know the story about the little girl?"

"The little girl?"

"On the fireplace." Carl Joseph pointed past them to Josh's living room. "That little girl."

"When we came over here"—Daisy thought for a second—"because good neighbors visit each other"—she nodded at Carl Joseph—"every time, Josh would tell us a story about the two older girls."

"Because he's a hero." Carl Joseph was emphatic about the point.

"And I only know three heroes altogether." Daisy looked at Lindsay's mother. "Your son is one of them."

Lindsay shot a look at her mother and saw her confusion softened by a new tenderness in her expression. Her mom blinked twice. "He was a hero?"

"Because of the two girls and the dangerous story." Admiration filled Daisy's tone.

"Josh only told us the story when we asked." Carl Joseph stepped cautiously past Lindsay and her mother and over to the fireplace. He picked up the photo of the teenage girls. "That was our best Saturday morning story, right, Daisy?"

"Yeah, because of the happy ending."

Lindsay was starting to understand. These two must've come over on occasional Saturday mornings, and when they did, they would ask Josh to tell the story about the two girls—a story Lindsay only found out about a few minutes ago.

"What...story did he tell you?" Her mom followed Carl Joseph and stood beside him. Daisy and Lindsay came, too, and filled in the places on his other side.

"It happened on New Year's Eve three years ago." Carl Joseph pushed his glasses higher up on his nose again.

"In Denver." Daisy gave a definitive nod. "Josh was towing cars and two girls had a question. They were two best friends."

"Yeah, they were nice girls and they were trying to find the United States, I think, right, Daisy?" Carl Joseph cocked his head. "I think it was the United States."

"No." Daisy smiled and patted Carl Joseph on the shoulder. "Not the United States. They were trying to find State Street." She looked at Lindsay. "Definitely State Street."

"So it's against the law to drive drunk but that's what the other guy was doing." He thought for a few beats. "And he had his head down, which is not the best way to drive."

"Passed out." Daisy shook her head.

"Yeah, passed out. And Josh pulled the girls out of the way so they were safe."

"And Josh got hit on the shoulder, but he wasn't too hurt and the girls were safe." Daisy's smile was wistful as she remembered these last details. "So there's a happy ending." She raised her eyebrows at Lindsay's mother. "That's one reason why Josh was a hero. Because God used him to make a happy ending."

Lindsay spotted a box of tissues on a nearby table. She gave one to her mom, who was holding the photo now, tears streaming down her face. "Why didn't he tell us?" she whispered. The words were meant for Lindsay, not Josh's neighbors.

But Daisy answered, anyway. "He only told us because we asked."

Lindsay pressed her tissue first to one eye and then the other. These two kind strangers had asked Josh about the picture of the teenage girls, but no one in his family had taken the time to learn about his heroism or the deeper details surrounding the accident. She held the tissue to her nose and closed her eyes. Inside her chest she could literally feel her heart breaking for her kindhearted brother. At the same time, she didn't want Josh's neighbors to feel they'd done something to upset her and her mother. She opened her eyes and managed a teary smile. "Thank you for sharing that story with us."

"I like the happy ending." Daisy seemed a little nervous in light of the sadness in the room. "Right, CJ? It's a happy ending."

"Very happy."

A happy ending? Lindsay stifled a series of sobs that threatened to drop her to the floor. Her brother had saved the lives of two teenage girls, yes, but he had suffered a life-changing injury that eventually killed him.

"See the little girl?" Carl Joseph carefully took hold of one of the other framed photos on Josh's mantel. "Our good neighbor never told us that story."

Daisy wrinkled her nose. "Not a happy ending, that's what Josh said."

"So...do you know that story? About the little girl?" Carl Joseph raised curious eyes to Lindsay's mother, and then to Lindsay.

"Josh was right." Lindsay took the photo gently from Carl Joseph. "That story doesn't have a very happy ending."

"I bought her a present." Daisy looked slightly uncertain about her gift. She took the beach bag off her shoulder, rummaged through it, and pulled out a new Minnie Mouse headband. She looked to Carl Joseph for help. "You tell it, CJ."

He looked at the mouse ears and then at Lindsay and her mother and once more he pushed his glasses up on the bridge of his nose. "Me and Daisy went to Disneyland."

"Our favorite place." Daisy smiled.

"And we wore our ears. I had Mickey Mouse and Daisy had Minnie."

Daisy set her beach bag down and held the ears up in front of her face. "With these ears, me and CJ had the happiest day of all."

"A real-life happy ending."

"So, I was at the store and I saw this new pair of Minnie ears." Daisy's shyness wore off as she got caught up in her story. "And I thought if I buy these ears for the little girl in Josh's picture then maybe a happy ending would happen for her, too."

Lindsay kept the tissue pressed to her face. This couple had clearly loved Josh. Everything about him mattered deeply to them. "So...you bought the Minnie ears for the little girl in the picture?" Lindsay lightly touched Daisy's arm. "You know who the little girl is, right?"

"No." Carl Joseph's answer was quick. "Because Josh

said that story could wait because it doesn't have a happy ending."

But Daisy looked at the picture a little longer and her eyes filled with a gradual understanding. "Well...she looks a lot like our good neighbor."

"Yes." Lindsay sniffed, struggling to speak. "That little girl is Josh's daughter. Her name is Savannah."

"Savannah?" Carl Joseph seemed stunned by the revelation. "He never said she was Savannah."

"That's a pretty name for a pretty girl." Daisy's eyes glistened with tears as she turned her face to Lindsay. "Why didn't she live here with Josh?"

"Yeah, why only a picture?" Carl Joseph put his arm around Daisy. "Because that's why no happy ending if she didn't live here."

Lindsay saw her mother look away from the photo and turn toward the patio door. Her shoulders shook from the quiet sobs washing over her. Lindsay dabbed beneath her eyes again and she cleared her throat. "That's the sad part. Savannah lives somewhere else."

"Oh." Daisy let the Minnie ears fall to her side. But after a moment, she held them out to Lindsay. "Well...when you see her I still think she'd like these. Because if she has the Minnie ears she'll have a happy ending, like me and CJ."

Lindsay took the headband and held it to her chest. "Thank you, Daisy. I think she'll like these very much."

"It's not Disneyland." Carl Joseph shrugged. "But it's close."

"Also..." Daisy looked at her friend. "We'll pray for Savannah. That she'll come out of the picture and into your arms."

Lindsay stared in awe at the young woman. Out of the picture and into their arms? What a beautiful way to pray for Savannah. She thanked Carl Joseph and Daisy once more and before they left she told them they could stop by any time in the next two weeks while she and her mother were cleaning out Josh's apartment.

"And let us know if you need anything." Lindsay's mother was still crying, but she was more composed than before. "Thank you ... for being Josh's friends."

Carl Joseph's eyes filled with fresh tears. He crossed his arms firmly in front of his chest and stared at his feet for a few seconds. "Josh—Josh was a hero and a very good neighbor."

Daisy nodded. "We miss him a lot. We tell God all the time, right, CJ?"

"Right." He gave both Lindsay and her mother a quick hug, and Daisy did the same. The two of them left arm in arm, their heads hung, tears on their cheeks.

Lindsay watched them go and she fell into her mother's arms. They stayed that way a long time, holding on to each other so they wouldn't drown in the sea of sorrow churning around them. And they thanked God for the gift of Carl Joseph and Daisy—a couple of handicapped adults who knew more about Josh than his own family did.

All because they'd taken the time to listen.

FIFTEEN

Annie was still reeling from the visit, but she needed answers. She pulled back from her daughter and searched her eyes. "The story about the girls? Is it true?"

"It is." Lindsay walked to Josh's computer desk and picked up a stack of papers. "I found these just before you got here. A newspaper article about the accident, and a couple of letters from the girls' parents." Lindsay's voice was still thick with sorrow. "The story calls him a hero."

"And we never knew?" Annie wrestled with a mix of emotions. She was proud of Josh but her pride was tempered by pangs of anger and hurt. She motioned toward the door. "He told strangers what happened, and he didn't tell us?"

Lindsay's answer was quiet. "They asked." She handed the documents over. "Every Saturday, apparently."

Annie hated the way she felt, like she'd missed some great and marvelous opportunity to connect with her son over something good in his life. And in his last years there had been little good. She looked at the headline spread across a page that included Josh's picture and a photo of the two girls. *Tow Truck Driver Hailed as Local Hero.*

"He knew you didn't like his job." Lindsay didn't sound accusing, just honest. "He probably didn't think it would matter how he was hit that day or why. He was doing his job and it cost him his health. That made the job seem like a mistake, however the accident happened."

Annie sank into the nearest chair, the clipping and the letters still in her hands, and she stared at her son's face in print. *Dear God…I need one more chance, just one more chance. Please….* If only she had the last three years to do over again. She would have asked more questions about the accident or come by his apartment and noticed the photograph on his mantel. *Tell me about the girls,* she would have asked him. And—as he'd done for his neighbors—he would tell her how he'd pulled the girls out of harm's way and taken the hit instead.

But none of those closest to him heard about his act of courage.

Annie felt like bits of herself were breaking off and scattering around the room and she couldn't do anything to bring them back together. She'd missed the chance to celebrate Josh within the family and among their friends, to share his act of courage and give him the credit he deserved. *God…why am I finding out now, when there's nothing I can do about it?*

Ten more minutes, that's all she wanted. Ten minutes to hug him and look into his eyes and tell him that she knew the truth about the accident, about what he'd done. Ten minutes to tell him she was proud of him and not disappointed, no matter how she'd acted in the past. Just ten minutes.

Lindsay seemed to understand that her mother needed

time to compose herself. She touched her mom's shoulder. "I'm going to finish going through his file cabinet."

Annie nodded, but she didn't look up. And as Lindsay set about the job of sorting through Josh's things, a thought occurred to her. What else didn't she know about her son? He'd been a hero, and she hadn't known that. So what else? Suddenly, she knew how she was going to spend these next two weeks. Not in a fog of sorrow, boxing up what remained of Josh's life. But in a quest to learn all she'd missed along the way.

My Lord...how could I have missed the fact that Josh saved the lives of those girls? What sort of mother am I? She squeezed her eyes shut and willed herself to pull the pieces together, to collect herself so she could set about her quest. *Help me find out everything about him, Father. He was my only son....I love him so much, but—but if I didn't really know him, please let me know about him now.* She covered her face with a fresh tissue and let the tears come. *And could You do one more thing? Could You tell him I'm proud of him, God, please.*

"Mom, look at this." Lindsay walked over and handed her a full-page note in Josh's handwriting. "It's dated ten years ago, the summer after Josh graduated from high school."

And with that, her tears slowed and she embraced the task at hand. She took the page and saw it was a photocopy of a letter Josh had written to Becky Wheaton. Annie looked at Lindsay. "Did you read it?"

"I did." She sat back against the edge of the computer desk. "It's heartbreaking."

Annie stood and walked with the letter to Josh's patio

door. Leaning against the cool metal frame, she started at
the beginning.

> *Dear Becky,*
>
> *It's been two weeks since you broke up with me, and I still don't blame you. I need to get my act together, you're right about that. Last night you called and told me you loved me and that you're praying for me to figure things out. Well, I stayed up all night thinking about what you said, and I've decided to make you a promise.*
>
> *I, Josh Warren, promise you, my first and forever love, that I will stop smoking cigarettes. I watched my uncle die of lung cancer, and I won't be like that—dead before I'm forty, wasting my life on some terrible addiction. I also promise to stop drinking and get serious about my life. Whatever else happens, I want my college degree. I want to be successful so that one day I can marry you and support you and have a family with you.*
>
> *Believe me, Becky, you deserve someone successful, and that someone is going to be me. I promise you here and now.*
>
> *This summer will be hard, because I know you need some space. Maybe I do, too. Space so I can have the time I need to figure out these changes. But the changes will come, you'll see. And one day you and I will have the life we've both dreamed about.*
>
> *I'll never love anyone like I love you, Becky. Pray for me, that I can be the man you need me to be.*
>
> *Love forever,*
> *Josh*

Annie read the letter over again, racked by the sincerity of Josh's great intentions, the tragedy of all he'd failed
to accomplish. He had wanted to stop smoking, but that
didn't happen until four years later. The drinking with

his buddies continued through that summer and the next. He tried college, but only because he wanted to impress Becky and Annie and Nate. His grades were weak his first year and dismal his second, and by then Becky was seeing someone else. Josh moved to Denver and took a job at the garage, and the years began to pile up.

"I need to meet with her, show her this letter." Annie said the words more to herself than to Lindsay.

"You should." Her daughter was sitting at the desk again, going through Josh's files. She looked up and blew at a loose strand of hair. "I wonder what would've happened if Becky had been more patient."

"Or if Josh had taken life more seriously." Annie folded the letter and put it in a stack with the newspaper clipping and the letters from the girls' parents. Nate would want to see everything she found today.

As the day wore on, Annie kept her resolve, that these two weeks would be about learning whatever she could about her son, everything she hadn't known, good or bad. She especially wanted to find whatever she could about the woman Josh had been with in Vegas. Maria Cameron. And any documents or proof that would explain why Josh felt so strongly that the child was his daughter.

She and Lindsay found photos of Becky and Josh, and stacks of deposition documents related to the court case. The testimony ripped at Annie's soul for the way the insurance company's lawyers tormented Josh on the witness stand. After ninety minutes of reading through the transcripts, Annie was ready to call Thomas Flynn and ask him to file a second lawsuit—this one against the attorneys for harassment of her son.

She moved on to a broken-down box on the top shelf of Josh's bedroom closet. There were old yearbooks and awards from his participation in football and baseball, and at the top she found a thank-you card from Keith, Josh's best guy friend from high school.

Annie read the note written inside:

Hey, man… thanks for getting me those miles. You gave me something I would've missed otherwise—a chance to tell my dad I loved him before he died. You're the best, Josh… no one like you anywhere.
Keith

Again, Annie felt she was learning about a young man she'd never known. She remembered Keith's father dying a couple years back, and she knew Keith and his dad weren't close. The man rode Keith relentlessly about his sports, yelling at him in front of the other parents if he struck out. That sort of thing. When Keith was a teenager, he spent a lot of time at the Warren house, confiding in them that he was sure his father didn't love him.

Though she and Nate made a few attempts to help Keith and his father reconcile, the efforts never seemed to amount to anything.

What she didn't know, until now, was that Josh helped his friend with airline miles. Josh didn't fly, so how in the world did he come up with enough miles to get Keith back home from Ohio before his father died? However it had happened, somehow Josh had found a way to help his friend, and because of his efforts, Keith had gotten a priceless chance to reconcile with his father.

You were a hero two times over, my precious son. And

I never got the chance to know that about you. Never got to tell you how proud that makes me. She held the card to her heart and for a priceless moment she had the distinct feeling she was holding Josh instead, holding him close against her the way she had when he was a little boy, when his future was still one long trail of endless possibilities.

The search continued until Annie was too emotionally exhausted to look through another envelope or file or dusty cardboard box. They would pick up the job again later, and maybe then they would find some sign that Josh was right about the girl being his daughter. But Annie doubted anything would come of the matter. If she was his child, Josh would have found out definitively by now.

In light of all Josh had hoped for his future, the child probably gave him what Becky Wheaton gave him: a reason to believe that someday the pain and torment from his accident would end. He would find a new career and financial freedom and the life he'd always wanted. That's all the little girl in the photograph really was. A reason for Josh to believe that tomorrow would be better than today.

SIXTEEN

Savannah wasn't sure what happened, or how come her life seemed so different now, but she believed the change had something to do with her daddy. Her mama didn't grab her arm like before, and twice she even let Savannah sleep in the big bed with her instead of under the desk.

"The good times are just beginning, Savannah," her mama told her this morning on their way to a place called the clinic. "A few more weeks and we'll have a big house and a maid and the best food and clothes and cars."

Savannah listened with wide eyes, and sometimes she wondered if her mama was crazy or just kidding about all that. But one thing she wasn't kidding about was the clinic. They walked from the subway to the small building, where her mama filled out a piece of paper. The place smelled like the bathrooms in Central Park, and Savannah's tummy felt topsy-turvy. Why were they here, anyway? Was this where her daddy was going to find her?

She had her little plastic cross from Grandpa Ted in her pocket and she felt it through her jeans, just to be sure it was there. Her mama finished writing on the piece of paper, and together they sat in a little room full of people who looked sad or hurt or sick. An old man sitting next to them had a cut across his arm and blood was coming through his Band-Aid. Savannah tried not to look. She leaned up to her mama's ear. "Why are we here again?"

"For the test." Her mama seemed a little nervous. Not as happy as she was when they had their hot dogs in the park or when they went to the zoo yesterday.

"What sort of test?" Savannah crossed her ankles and swung her feet. She was thirsty, but she didn't want to drink too much water. Her mama said she didn't have time for the bathroom until after the test.

"A blood test." Her mama picked up a magazine from a table next to her and she started flipping the pages.

A blood test? Savannah's stomach felt sick, because what sort of test was that? She glanced next to her at the man's reddish Band-Aid. Was he here for a blood test, too? Because she didn't want to look like that when she left. She remembered the cross in her pocket and Jesus, who was always with her. *Jesus, it's me, Savannah. I'm sort of scared about the blood test, so can You stay with me, please?*

She was waiting for an answer in her heart when a big lady in a tight white dress stepped into the little room. "Savannah Cameron?"

"Here." Her mother stood and smoothed the wrinkles in her short skirt. She reached for Savannah's hand and pulled her to her feet. "This is Savannah."

The woman looked at her notes. "Follow me."

Savannah tried not to think about the man and his bloody arm. She stayed close to her mama and the big lady took them to a room the size of a closet. "Sit here," she said. The woman and Mama talked about how "'rangements" had been made and some other words Savannah didn't understand. Then the woman rolled up the sleeve of Savannah's sweatshirt and rubbed a wet little ball of white fur over her arm. "This won't hurt much." She opened a small white bag and took out a sharp needle and a plastic tube the size of a pencil. "Hold still."

"Very still." Her mama raised one eyebrow the way she did when Savannah had better listen, or else.

The big lady stuck the needle into Savannah's arm and held it there. "You don't have to watch, sweetie."

But Savannah did watch, because little by little her blood came from her arm into the tube. The lady was right, the needle didn't hurt too bad once it was in her. When the tube was filled, the woman pulled out the needle and put a Band-Aid on her arm—a smaller one than on the man in the room full of people. "There you go."

"The blood test is finished?" Savannah felt her stomach settle down a little.

"All done." The lady ripped a few smiley stickers from a roll on the wall. "These are for you."

"You did good, sweetheart." Her mama smiled at her.

Savannah wasn't sure what to do with the stickers. "Thank you, ma'am." She peeled off one and then the other and stuck them to the backs of her hands. She could see them there and remember that she'd done a good job on her blood test. The big lady was telling her mama that something would be sent to her in a few days.

When they were back outside in the sunshine, her mama gave her a happy squeeze. "Savannah, I have a feeling about that blood test. I think this is the beginning of a very happy time for us."

Savannah felt a little shy of her mama, this new way her mama acted around her. She nodded her head and smiled. Then she looked back down at her happy face stickers.

"Here, baby"—her mama reached for her—"take my hand."

Savannah did as she was told, and together they started walking. "Are we going to the park?"

"Yes. It'll be a beautiful day in the park, don't you think?"

"Are we gonna beg money?"

"We are." Her mama seemed less happy for a few seconds. But then she smiled big again. "Not for long, though. Your daddy is going to take care of us real good. Then we'll never beg for money again."

Savannah's heart felt suddenly light and free, like she was one of the birds over Central Park, the ones that landed on the top of the fountain and flew away whenever they wanted to. Her daddy was going to take care of them! Ever since the changes in her mama she had hoped in secret that it had to do with her daddy. She breathed in a very big breath and held her head high. The good things were finally going to happen! She was going to meet her daddy and he was going to take care of them. After so much waiting and talking to Jesus and hoping, all her dreams were finally going to come true.

Her mama stayed happy that day, even while they begged money. She waited until they were on the subway on the way home, then she decided this was the right time to ask a few questions. "The good things that are going to happen are because of my daddy, right?"

A little laugh came from her mama. "Yes, sweetie. All because of your daddy."

Savannah felt a little shiver of excitement. "So when will I meet him? Today or tomorrow? Or later this week?"

Her mama's smile fell back to a straight line. "Well… you're not exactly going to meet him." She had a worried look in her eyes, but then she smiled again. "He's going to send us a gift instead. A very, very nice gift."

Savannah didn't want a gift. She already had the plastic cross from Grandpa Ted and the framed picture of her daddy, which was all she needed. What she wanted was her daddy, not a present from him. She felt tears in her eyes and she wiped at them real fast so her mama wouldn't think she was ungrateful. "Will—will I meet him later, then?"

"Much later." Her mama patted her on the head. "Don't worry, Savannah. Your daddy's gift will be enough for now."

She didn't ask any more questions on the ride home. For now? She settled back against the hard, cracked seat and stared out the window at the walls rushing past. All day she'd been happy because sometime very soon she might meet her daddy. She was still going to meet him, but "much later" was a long time away. A whole week or a month, maybe. She was puzzled about her daddy because his eyes and his smile were very kind, and he wanted to send her a gift—which was also very kind. But didn't he know that all she wanted was him? A daddy to hold her and swing her around and take care of her so her mama could have the break she always talked about. Her very own Prince Charming daddy.

What could be a better gift than that?

SEVENTEEN

After one week of sorting through the pieces of Josh's life, Annie had learned much about her son, and she had a strong feeling her quest wasn't yet complete. She talked to Thomas Flynn and learned that Josh had contacted him about his friend Keith's need for airfare.

"I had a million extra miles," Thomas told her. "It was no problem donating some to Josh's friend so he could get home to see his sick father."

But the trip never would have happened if Josh hadn't made the phone call, if he hadn't cared enough to put his own pride on the line for the sake of his friend's great need.

On Annie's second day of searching through Josh's apartment, Ethel, the old woman who lived in the apartment above his, made her way downstairs and sat with Annie and Lindsay for an hour.

"I have no family," the woman explained. "Josh was like the grandson I never had. It's hard for me to get out, so one week a few years ago he asked if he could pick up a few groceries for me." She had tears in her eyes as she talked. "After that it became a routine. Every Saturday he picked up just what I needed to get through the next seven days, and sometimes he brought me an extra little surprise—a box of fresh cookies from the bakery or a small bouquet of flowers for my kitchen table."

Annie hung on every word, sometimes jealous that Josh had lavished his attention on this stranger when he might have brought the flowers to her instead. But she quickly corrected her attitude and became overwhelmed with pride over her son's decision to help a neighbor. "And you would pay him when he dropped off the food, is that how it worked?"

"Never." She touched her fingertips beneath her eyes, wiping at her tears. "Josh never let me pay for anything."

The woman's story filled Annie's heart with wonder. Her son was on an extremely tight budget, so tight that regularly he had to call her and Nate for an advance toward his settlement. Yet with what little he had, he made a point of buying the old woman's groceries every week.

Annie thought about the people who ran in their circles, the socialites and political types. Not long ago, the superintendent of Nate's school district donated five thousand dollars of his own money to the local PTA. In doing so, he threw a party for the entire PTA, complete with a free barbecue dinner for the community and a speech midway through the night. The man himself contacted the media, and Lindsay had been assigned to the story, "Local Educator Gives Gift to PTA."

No one seemed to think anything of the man's efforts to be noticed, but at the time Annie mentioned to Nate that the man's gift seemed awfully self-serving. "The Bible says when a person gives something, the right hand shouldn't know what the left hand's doing."

Nate laughed. "Every hand in the PTA knew about this one."

But not so with Josh's gift to his elderly neighbor. It was as though Josh inherently knew that the only way to feel good about a gift was to give it in such a way that no one else knew. It was a lesson Josh had no doubt heard again and again in Sunday school through the years, but until now Annie would have sworn her son had forgotten every valuable bit of Scripture from his childhood days.

Now she knew differently.

Everything she found she shared with Nate. Last night, when they were talking about the miles for Keith's flight back home, Nate's eyes welled with tears and, for a long while, he didn't say anything. When he could talk, he took hold of her hand. "Like I told you, not everyone is an all-star in sports or in life. But that doesn't mean Josh was a failure." His chin quivered and he scrunched his face, fighting the breakdown. "I always believed in Josh, that he was a good boy, a good son." He shook his head, getting a grasp on his emotions. "I appreciate these details, but they don't surprise me, Annie. Not like they surprise you."

She wanted to argue with him, but she couldn't. He was right, and rather than deny the light her discoveries were shedding on the memory of their son, she embraced it. Even the more painful pieces of information, like the letter she'd found from Maria Cameron stating that Josh couldn't have visitation or any other rights to Savannah until he figured out a way to send her four thousand dollars a month.

Your hundred dollars will never cut it, the woman wrote. *I'll keep Savannah from you until you figure out your finances. Savannah needs money, not some sentimental father figure. You won't hear another word from us until you get the money. Otherwise I'll tell her you're a loser like every other guy.*

The letter was bathed in venom. Annie felt sick to her stomach just touching the paper, as if the woman's filth might still be on the edges of the page. After reading it, she set it aside for the attorney. Her belief that the woman was nothing more than a gold digger looking for any man to bail her out doubled after finding the letter. The girl wasn't Josh's child. At the same time, she grieved the fact that her son had ever been tricked into sleeping with a woman like Maria Cameron. Josh knew better. The lessons about purity had come right along with the lessons about helping others.

For two hours after reading Maria's letter, she allowed herself to wonder where she and Nate had gone wrong that their son would go to Las Vegas, of all places, and spend the night with such a woman. But then gradually her heart softened, and she caught herself creating scenarios that might've explained Josh's poor decision that weekend.

He'd lost Becky Wheaton by then. She was tired of waiting for Josh to quit smoking and drinking, for him to get serious about life, and so she'd taken up with a young man in law school. Josh couldn't compete with that, and after moving to Denver and taking the job at the garage, he must have been very lonely. The weekend in Vegas had probably been an impulsive decision, some way to forget about the emptiness in his heart created by Becky's absence.

Who knew what Maria had told Josh? She might've had some sad story about being lonely, like him. If she needed a friend or an ear or a place to stay, Josh would have helped her. She thought about the couple with Down syndrome, and Ethel from the apartment upstairs. Yes, certainly Josh would've helped her. He wasn't wise enough in the ways of the world to recognize a trap like the one the woman had clearly set.

The entire situation was too sad to dwell on, so Annie had moved on to other boxes of belongings, other memories that made up her son's past.

Now it was Tuesday, and she was at the apartment by herself. Nate and Lindsay were coming by later that day with more empty bags for Josh's bedding. They were moving most of his furniture into an empty room at the back of their house in Black Forest. The room would be a guest suite now, a place where Josh's memory could live on.

Annie slid two more boxes into the entryway of Josh's apartment and then stood to catch her breath. As she did, she looked at her son's computer and she realized this was one area they hadn't looked at yet. She sat in his chair and reached down to hit the power button. A minute later, the screen came to life and Annie wondered where to begin. She opened Microsoft Word and checked his list of documents.

One of them read simply, "Savannah."

Annie's heart missed a beat, and she felt the blood leave her face. Was he that certain about the little girl that he'd created a document about her? How sad that he believed someone like the Cameron woman enough to care this much. She double clicked the document and it appeared on the screen. The font was small, and the text was single-spaced.

Dear Savannah, the last entry read. *It's been three days since I've written to you, so I thought I better catch up....*

Annie's stomach dropped to her feet. Her son had kept an ongoing journal for the girl? As if she really were his daughter, and someday she'd actually read everything he'd written to her? Annie checked the bottom descriptor, the line that contained the information about the document. What she read took her breath away. Fifty-three pages? Her son must have been keeping the journal ever since he found out about the girl.

Everything in this document was what he might've said if he'd lived long enough to be a father. The photo on the mantel, the document tucked away in his Microsoft Word program, all of it allowed him to think and act and feel the way he might have if he'd been blessed with children. And since he never had that chance, Annie was sure every word would speak straight to her soul, to the place that would always belong to Josh.

She checked the paper supply in Josh's printer, and after a few clicks the machine came to life and the pages of his journal began falling gently onto the paper tray. But even as the document was printing, Annie finished reading the last entry:

Dear Savannah,

It's been three days since I've written to you, so I thought I better catch up. I know I've told you this a lot lately, but I'm really feeling closer to God these days. He's getting me through this trial, this stage in my life, and somewhere I know He's getting you through something, too.

I found a Bible verse I want to share with you, sweetheart. It's from Psalm 119:50, and it says, "My comfort in my suffering is this: Your promise preserves my life." You know about my accident, and how I've been in a lot of pain. But lately I've been reading from the Bible more and I find that this promise is true. Beyond true, even. God's Word is reviving me, Savannah, and one day soon when I get my settlement, I'll come find you. Together we can learn about Jesus and the promises in His Word.

Annie felt tears on her cheeks, and she reached for a tissue. Lately, she kept the box within reach. The journal to a child who probably wasn't his daughter was one thing. But when had her son gotten closer to God? And how come she and Nate hadn't heard about this? She scanned the next few pages and saw that many times over the weeks that led up to his death, Josh talked about Jesus.

She found an entry from two months earlier, and her eyes fell on a paragraph halfway down the page.

I was watching country videos one night and Wynonna Judd came on, singing a song about heaven. "I Can Only Imagine," it was called. Savannah, I can only tell you that in those next few minutes I realized I'd been running from God for too long. It was like I finally got it about having a relationship with Him, and how He wanted me to rely completely on His strength. I've been going to church every week since then, and I can feel God changing me. I love Him more than life, Savannah. One day you will, too.

Annie sat back and a scene came to life in her mind. It was the week before Josh died, and Lindsay had stopped by to talk. But Annie was busy on a phone call, and then in a rush to get ready for another dinner, another event to help Nate get reelected to the school board. Lindsay had said something about Josh finding a song about heaven, and how he was going to church again and he was changed. The memory of Annie's response hit her like a sucker punch. She'd dismissed everything Lindsay was trying to tell her, refusing to hear the news as anything other than one more empty promise by Josh.

But here was proof that Lindsay had been right, that Josh really had found a closer relationship with God in the weeks before his death. That explained something Carl Joseph had said on his second visit this past week. He said Josh had gone to church with him and Daisy and his family. Again Annie had dismissed the idea, thinking Carl Joseph was confusing intent with action. She looked at the journal entry again. Apparently not.

Her heart warmed with the reality of what Josh had found in his renewed faith, but at the same time the guilt of her disbelief all but smothered her. What would it have taken for her to listen a little more carefully, to call Josh and congratulate him or ask for details about the change in his heart? Since Josh's death, Annie had been burdened by all her son had missed out on. But now the loss was hers alone.

She thought again about having ten more minutes with him. On top of everything else, she could talk to him about his faith and what led to his changed attitude. What a joy to have shared such a moment with him, in light of all the pain he'd been through. But Annie had missed her chance, and the reality was sadder than anything so far. *Josh, my son...I'm sorry.* She hung her head. *Dear God, I missed so much. What sort of mother misses moments like that?*

The only answer she had was the one that Josh had written in the last journal entry: *My comfort in my suffering is this: Your promise preserves my life.* God's Word. Yes, that's where she would find healing and comfort in the weeks and months and years ahead, in the lifetime ahead when missing Josh would be a part of every day. She would spend more time in God's Word, picking up the journey Josh had begun in the weeks before his death and finding comfort in the truth of Scripture.

Her sorrow subsided enough so she could breathe again. Josh's journal was finished printing, so she scanned the rest of the list of documents. Every one of them needed to be looked at in case somewhere in the middle of one of them there might be another detail about her son's life. For now, she wanted to check the Internet.

She opened the Safari browser at the bottom of his screen and looked at the list of bookmarks across the top of the page. Facebook was first, and Annie clicked it open. Instantly she was on Josh's personal Web site, a page with more information than she could take in at a single glance. Almost at the same time a box appeared in the lower right part of the screen. In it was a series of messages from someone named Miss Independent. The last one read, *J, I'm serious. What's wrong with you? I haven't heard from you in a week! It's like you cut me out of your life or something. Please! Write to me now!*

Annie had the strangest feeling as she scrolled down through the messages. This was a friend she knew nothing of, someone who clearly was in daily contact with her son. Was she another Maria Cameron, or even maybe someone worse? Annie felt dizzy, but as she read through the messages she discovered a beautiful and innocent friendship.

The woman's name was Cara Truman, and she was a single mother who lived in Arizona.

According to the messages, Cara had given her life to the Lord because of what she'd seen God doing in Josh's life. Here and there Annie saw a hint of romance in the messages, but nothing overt, no plans in the making. Again she felt the weight of losing Josh. This was one more detail she hadn't known about his life, one more aspect of her son she hadn't been aware of. He wasn't only a great neighbor, a giving young man, a hero, and a rededicated follower of Christ. He was a true friend as well.

In all the messages Annie saw, there was no phone number listed. Annie positioned her fingers over the keyboard. *Hello*, she typed. *This is Josh's mother, Annie. Please call me as soon as possible.* Then she typed her cell phone number and hit the send button.

An hour later she was sorting through more of Josh's computer files when her phone rang. The number on the caller ID was one she didn't recognize. "Hello, this is Annie."

"Hi. This is Cara Truman. You left me a message." There was fear in her voice, and a breathy hesitation.

"Cara, I'm afraid I have bad news about Josh." Annie expected the conversation to be quick and to the point, the way it had been when she called other old friends of Josh's or acquaintances listed in his cell phone. But Cara Truman was different. She took the news hard, as though losing Josh was one of the greatest tragedies in her life.

"He—he was the best friend I ever had," she said in a voice broken with grief. "No one ever cared about me like he did."

The young woman spilled her heart about finding Josh

during an online poker game, and then connecting with him when the game was over. "He wasn't like other guys. He wasn't looking for anything from me."

"That sounds like Josh." She closed her eyes, picturing her son and all she'd learned about him. "I'm—I'm very proud of him."

By the end of the conversation, Annie had promised to stay in touch with Cara. They both agreed that was what Josh would have wanted. Before she hung up, Cara had one question. "What about his daughter?"

Annie felt her heart lurch forward. "His daughter?" What had Josh told Cara about the girl?

"Savannah. He talked about her constantly." Cara's voice filled with fresh tears. "That's all he wanted, to get his settlement and find his little girl so he could buy a house and make a home for her—however much time he could get with her." She sniffed. "Is someone going to contact her?"

For the first time since Annie had become aware of the little girl, she felt ashamed of her attitude. However wrong it had been for Josh to go to Vegas and connect with Maria Cameron, his actions did not negate the fact that somewhere a little girl existed who possibly might be Josh's daughter. Her head spun with the admission of this new possibility. "We, uh, we aren't sure the girl is his." But even as she said the words they felt lame and rife with excuse.

"Oh." Cara's tone became kindly adamant. "Well...Josh was sure. I can promise you that. It seems someone should look into it, because Josh lived for that girl. Some days all that got him through was the hope that he could be her daddy."

The heartbreak surrounding her son's death seemed to know no limits. Annie sighed in a way that gave a window to the pain inside her, pain that had reached flood level. "We'll keep that in mind," she finally said. "Thank you, Cara, for being his friend."

"It's the other way around." A few stifled sobs sounded over the phone line. "Thank you for having such an amazing son."

The call ended and Annie stood and walked to the fireplace mantel. How often must her son have stood in this very spot, looking at the picture of the two teenage girls and knowing without a doubt that no matter how much pain he was in, he'd saved two lives. And how much time did he also spend looking at the family photo and yearning for the time when his parents would be proud of him? And then turning his eyes to the picture of the child. Savannah. She didn't want to see it before, but there was something in her face that reminded her of Josh. Or maybe Annie was just too overwhelmed with guilt to deny for one more day the possibility that the girl was Josh's. She picked up the picture and studied it.

Savannah Cameron.

If she was Josh's daughter, then she would be Annie's granddaughter. It was more than she could take in, and with heavy hands and a heavier heart she returned the photo to the mantel. Cara was right about one thing. They needed to finish going through Josh's things in case somewhere there was information that might lead to the whereabouts of the girl's mother.

Annie returned to her son's bedroom. So much loss made her unsure if she could survive another day of this quest, this discovery process. She comforted herself by remembering the one shining bit of information that today's search had brought to light, the fact that Josh had reconnected with the faith he'd had as a child. The joy of that was enough to help Annie draw one more breath, take one more look into a box of her son's belongings. He had missed out on his settlement and the success he hoped to have. He'd missed out on a deeper friendship with his friend Cara and on being the father he wanted to be.

But he hadn't missed out on heaven.

EIGHTEEN

Thomas hung up the phone and sent a message to his secretary to hold his calls. He needed a few minutes to process what had just happened. The notice came to him through e-mail, but just to be sure he'd called the clinic himself. He probably shouldn't have been surprised by the news, but the finality of it knocked the wind from him. The test had come back positive.

Josh was Savannah's father. There was no debating the fact now.

He covered his face with his hands and pictured Josh, the earnest way he'd looked sitting in the chair opposite his in this very office, talking about Savannah as if he'd already seen the test results. She was his daughter, he never had any doubts. It was why he'd talked about her from the witness stand, why he had gone to his grave desiring mainly one thing—the chance to be Savannah's father.

Thomas drew a long breath and leaned back in his chair. If only this news had come when Josh was still alive, when he still filled the spot across from him. His pain would've taken a backseat to the thrill of knowing Thomas had found the girl, and that she was officially his.

Instead, so much about the news was unfair. Josh had been denied the chance to know her, and now Maria Cameron was going to walk away with the settlement money. The money Josh had given his life for. He stood, but he could barely straighten his shoulders under the burden of the news. He needed to tell Annie and Nate now, before another hour passed.

He called Annie's cell phone and wasn't surprised to learn that she and Lindsay were at Josh's apartment. It was Tuesday, the third week after Josh's death, and Annie had spent nearly every waking minute looking through her son's things. Annie sounded like a different person in light of all she was learning about Josh. Like the revelation was from God alone, and day by day it was changing her, making her softhearted and kinder. Less ambitious about things that didn't really matter now that Josh was gone.

"I found out more today," she told him. "I met a friend of his I found on his computer and we talked for an hour. She says Josh taught her about Jesus. Isn't that something?"

Thomas leaned his elbows on the desk. "That is."

"And she told me that she was a single mom and Josh had given her the courage to be a better mother, to put her kids first, and—"

"I'm sorry." Her words reminded Thomas that he wanted to make it to his son's piano recital that night. Josh had made the same impression upon him. "I don't mean to cut you off, Annie. But we need to talk. Is it okay if I head over?"

Annie paused, and her tone filled with a fresh sense of alarm. "Is this good news, Thomas?"

"Let's talk about it in person."

"Okay. I'll look for you."

Thomas gathered his briefcase and his car keys and told his secretary he was leaving for the day. He would have liked Nate to be there, too, but Annie could pass on the information. The important thing was that they get the news as soon as possible.

Even if their lives would never be the same afterward.

❧

Something in his voice told Annie there'd been a dramatic and maybe terrible development in Josh's lawsuit against the insurance company. The moment they were off the phone, she called Nate and asked him to leave work, to get to Josh's apartment as soon as possible. Whatever the news, she didn't want to process it without him.

Lindsay came to her side midway through her quick conversation with Nate, and when Annie hung up, her daughter's questions came immediately. "What's wrong?"

"That was Thomas Flynn. He's on his way over." Her heart felt numb. "Some sort of news."

"Something bad?"

"He didn't say." But her tone told Lindsay what Thomas hadn't come right out and said. The news couldn't be good.

"Maybe they've reached a settlement, or an offer, at least." Lindsay took the chair closest to her mother and tucked her legs beneath her. "It's supposed to come sometime soon, right?"

"Thomas would've said so, he would've said a decision was reached. Even if he didn't want to talk about it on the phone."

"And he didn't say that?"

"No." They talked another few minutes about the possibilities. "A week ago he said a speed bump had come up regarding Josh's estate, a question of some kind."

Neither of them could make sense of that, so they waited, talking instead about Cara Truman and Keith and Ethel, and what a good guy Josh had been. Nate arrived at the apartment first. He came in, his eyes wide, face paler than usual.

Again the small talk continued, nervous and empty, anything to fill the time. In a few minutes there was a knock at the door. Lindsay opened it, and Thomas's face assured Annie that whatever was coming wasn't good. They repositioned themselves so Annie and Nate were on Josh's sofa, and Lindsay was in the matching armchair. Thomas pulled up the computer chair and for a long moment he only looked at them. In his hands was a folder, but he didn't open it.

Thomas turned to Nate. "Annie tells me you've learned a lot about Josh these last ten days."

"Yes." Nate's voice was patient, even though everyone in the room wanted to ask the obvious. What had happened that the attorney would drop what he was doing and head straight for Josh's apartment? Nate clasped his fingers and leaned over his knees. "God has been...very good to us, letting us see a picture of our son that we might've missed otherwise."

Thomas nodded slowly and let his eyes fall to his hands for a few seconds. When he looked up, his eyes glistened with a deeper sorrow Annie hadn't seen in the man until now. "I'm afraid I have more information about Josh."

The three of them were silent, unblinking, waiting. The

only sound was the whir of Josh's refrigerator and the subtle tick of the second hand on the clock that hung in the
kitchen. That, and Annie's pounding heart. Surely everyone in the room could hear that.

Thomas released a long sigh. "In the last deposition, the
one Josh gave the day before he died, he told the court that
he had a daughter. That would make her his only heir."

Annie felt the room begin to spin. She slid closer to Nate
and leaned on his arm, so she wouldn't slide off the sofa
and pass out on Josh's beige-carpeted floor. Still, none of
them said anything.

"Because of Josh's testimony, I was obligated to do my
best to find the girl's mother, Maria Cameron of New York
City." He pursed his lips. "I found her the Friday after
Josh's death, and left her a message later that day. By law I
was required to tell her that the girl could be the heir to a
settlement." His disdain sounded in his tone. "Needless to
say, she contacted me first thing the following week."

"Why...didn't you tell us all this?" Nate didn't sound
angry, just baffled.

"I wanted to believe the search would lead to nothing."
Thomas breathed in through his nose. "I didn't want to
worry you over nothing."

"But..." Nate didn't need to ask, really. Everyone in the
room could see where the conversation was headed.

"I ordered that the girl be subjected to a paternity test.
We had Josh's results already. Standard in a case like this
where he suspected he was the father of a child and where
paternity hadn't been established."

His words ran together, and Annie felt her world slipping off its axis.

"The woman was very compliant, of course, and very sure that Josh was her daughter's father." He lifted the file in his hand and let it fall again. "The results came in right before I called you." He made eye contact with each of them one at a time. "Without question, the girl is Josh's daughter."

Annie grabbed on to Nate with one arm and the edge of the sofa with the other. No—no, it wasn't possible. All this time Josh had been right? He'd had a daughter and he'd been denied the chance of seeing her or holding her or knowing her? She sucked in her next few breaths and then stood and paced to the patio door and back. "You're sure?"

"The test is conclusive." Thomas handed the folder to her. "The details are all there."

She dropped the folder on the sofa and crossed her arms. The results must have had a million implications, but the first one, the one that stabbed straight through her heart, was this one: Josh had a daughter, but he'd missed out on being a father.

Thomas was going on, saying something about the settlement, and the girl being Josh's only heir, and how the entire amount minus any debt Josh had incurred would now go to Josh's daughter, and—

"Wait." The room stopped spinning. Annie drilled her eyes into those of the attorney. "Are you saying that we won't have control over Josh's settlement?"

"That's right."

"The entire amount will go to this—this child?" Nate's voice was incredulous.

"Yes. But her mother will be in control of it until she turns eighteen."

"But my parents are the executors of my brother's estate. Can't they determine whether the girl should really be an heir in this situation?" Lindsay was on her feet, her voice slightly raised. "I've written stories about things like this." She turned to Annie and then to Nate. "We can fight it."

"You can certainly try." Thomas sat a little straighter. He nodded, still in the game, not quite ready to throw in the cards. "Your case would be better if Josh hadn't said on the witness stand that he had a daughter, if he hadn't acknowledged her."

Annie remembered something. She hurried to Josh's bedroom and returned with the letter from Maria Cameron, the one where she threatened never to let Josh see the girl unless he paid her thousands of dollars per month. "Listen to this." She read a few choice paragraphs from the meanest sections of the letter. "The woman blackmailed Josh. She refused to even let him meet the girl. There's no way his accident money can go to her and a daughter he never met."

"Actually," Thomas said, sounding more tired than hopeful, "the law is pretty clear in this situation. In the case of estate law, any money belonging to the deceased automatically goes to the heir of the estate unless the deceased stated in writing before a witness that he or she did not want any or all of the estate to be given to that heir."

"In other words, if Josh had put in writing that he didn't want his money going to this girl, or rather her mother, then there wouldn't be an issue." Nate was still sitting on the sofa, but he'd slid to the edge, his back straight, clearly doing his best to understand the situation they were suddenly in.

"Exactly." Thomas looked like he wasn't sure how to say this next part. "The thing is, I had this talk with Josh a number of times. I advised him not to mention the girl on the witness stand, since there had never been a paternity test and since he had no idea where she was or any other details about her."

Annie knew where Thomas was headed with this. She closed her eyes and she could hear him still, hear the pleading in her son's voice as he tried to convince her and Nate that the child was his daughter.

"Josh wouldn't hear of it. He told me that Savannah was his daughter and he would never deny the fact, not in court or anywhere else."

Her eyes opened and she looked at the photo over the fireplace. For the first time in all these years she saw the resemblance as clearly as if she were looking into the face of her son at that age. They had the same eyes. Annie must've seen it all along, seen it and denied it all at the same time so that her brain wouldn't allow her heart to acknowledge the obvious. That this little girl was Josh's daughter, their granddaughter.

"I'll look into case law on the matter first thing tomorrow." Thomas pursed his lips.

"I can check on the story I wrote, the one about a case like this," Lindsay said. "The woman already tricked Josh once." She looked at Annie and Nate. "I don't think any of us can stand back and let her trick Josh again. Not when that settlement meant so much to him."

The conversation continued another five minutes, then Thomas left with promises to call sometime around lunch tomorrow. If they were going to contest the idea that the child was Josh's rightful heir, they needed to form a battle plan as soon as possible.

After Thomas was gone, Nate pulled Annie into his arms. "I have a few more hours left at the office." He nuzzled his face against hers. "Don't worry about this. We'll get everyone at church praying and God will help us. The right thing will happen, I have no doubt whatsoever."

Annie nodded, too weary to speak. The news had knocked the wind from her, and after the initial burst of indignation, she was unable to feel anything but one very clear emotion: doubt.

Lindsay needed to go, too, and she asked Annie to join her. "Come to my house, Mom. We'll pick up a few salads on the way and you can spend a little time with Ben and Bella." Lindsay leaned in and kissed her forehead. "They miss you."

"I'm not hungry." Annie looked past her daughter to the boxes that still hadn't been sorted through. "I'll come over later. In an hour or so."

Reluctantly, Lindsay left, but only after Annie promised she wouldn't stay more than an hour longer. Annie understood her daughter's concern, but being here among Josh's things, his words and music, his greatest treasures, had become almost enjoyable, a routine that made Josh a part of her life again.

When she was alone, Annie returned once more to the picture on the mantel. Savannah was Josh's daughter, and neither she nor Nate had ever wanted to admit that fact. But what if they had? What if they'd taken the time to hire an investigator and search out Maria Cameron? They might have forced a paternity test based on Maria's own admission that the girl belonged to Josh. And then with the results in hand, Maria would've had no choice but to allow Josh a role in the girl's life.

Which meant Josh might have had his daughter after all. If only she and Nate had once, just once, believed him.

Her tears came in convulsive spasms, taking over her heart and soul, her lungs, and her ability to think clearly. What had they done? So what if the woman had slept around? Did it really matter that she'd been married at the time of her Vegas tryst with Josh? Even if she'd been with a hundred men that month, there was a chance Josh was the father. A single chance, and that chance was worth exploring, wasn't it? Didn't Josh deserve at least that? He didn't have any resources to wage that sort of search, that type of custody battle. The only way would have been if he'd received help.

Help that Annie and Nate had unequivocally denied him.

Dear God, what have we done? She took hold of the photo and slowly, painfully, she dropped to her knees. The little girl in the picture had never known her daddy, and now it was too late.

Josh had never gotten to cradle his newborn daughter, never spoken to her in the quiet coos and gentle whispers that existed between a father and his child. He had been robbed of the chance to hold her hand while she toddled across the room, and he'd missed the drive to school on her first day of kindergarten.

She had never known her father's hugs, his strong arms. Never had she run to him down the hall of her home when strange noises made her frightened in the middle of the night. She'd never walked hand in hand with him to the park or giggled out loud while he pushed her high on a swing until her feet brushed against the sky.

Josh had known she was his little girl, and there'd been nothing he could do about it. So he'd kept the journal and fought the lawsuit, knowing that the moment he had the settlement he would do what he'd longed to do since he first heard about the girl. He would fight Maria Cameron for custody. Annie remembered one time when the subject came up, the earnest look in Josh's eyes, the passion with which he talked about the child.

"Even if I get only one week a year, I want her to know me. I want her to know she has a dad who loves her."

Annie swallowed another sob. What had she done when Josh said that? Change the subject? Ask Josh if he wanted a second helping of spaghetti? Nothing about the child seemed even a little real. People didn't go off to Vegas, have a one-night stand with a married woman, and wind up the father of her child. Annie couldn't bring herself to acknowledge the possibility.

And now it was too late.

She held the photo close to her heart. "I'm sorry, Josh. I didn't know."

The conversation from earlier played in her thoughts again—the news from Thomas and her reaction, the way she was instantly sure she wanted to fight the girl's mother. Nate's comments, too, about how nothing had meant more to Josh than receiving this settlement.

That's where she stopped. She struggled to her feet, her eyes never leaving those of the girl's. No wonder she'd been feeling overwhelmed with doubt, both then and now. She'd denied the truth for seven years, denied that even a possibility existed that this child was Josh's daughter. She caught herself, forced herself to rethink the way she viewed the little girl in the photograph. She wasn't *that girl*, or *that child*. She was Savannah, Josh's daughter. *From now on I'll think of her by her name,* Annie told herself. *I owe Josh at least that much.*

If Annie was sure the settlement would go to Savannah, then there would be no war to wage, no battle to fight. Josh loved her, even if he never met her, and he would have wanted her taken care of. But that wouldn't happen. Thomas said so himself. The money would go to Maria Cameron as Savannah's guardian. By the time Savannah turned eighteen, the money would be gone, the insurance money wasted in the hands of a woman who had done everything in her power to ruin Josh's life.

That was something worth fighting against.

But even so, Annie asked God for wisdom and understanding greater than herself. *Please, Lord, lead the way in this legal nightmare. I've spent the last seven years denying even the slightest chance that Savannah was Josh's daughter, and I was wrong. I don't want to be wrong again. Please, God, lead us.*

"Josh, I promise I'll never forget that you're Savannah's father. Not ever again." She whispered the words through a fog of agony and she silently prayed at the same time that somehow God would let Josh hear them.

Especially after so many years of denying Savannah's relationship to Josh.

She and Nate and Lindsay could form a team and fight for Josh's settlement, and even now she was convinced that was the right thing to do, the only way to keep his money from falling into the hands of a woman who did nothing but hurt him. But they couldn't tell themselves that nothing mattered more to Josh than the settlement. That was hardly true.

Josh cared about the settlement, certainly, and the decision that the drunk driver's insurance company should pay for the losses he'd incurred. He cared about getting the money and buying a house and building a future for himself. But his top concern wasn't the settlement. That spot belonged to one person and one alone. Cara Truman had confirmed the fact again in their conversation earlier today. The answer was obvious to everyone who knew and loved Josh. What mattered most wasn't the lawsuit but his daughter, Savannah Cameron.

And now, one way or another, Savannah would have to matter to the rest of them, too.

NINETEEN

Cody Gunner couldn't shake the feeling that he needed to contact Josh Warren's parents. It was Wednesday, more than three weeks after Josh's death, and every day since then the thought had all but consumed him. He hadn't slept well once since hearing the news, because he knew a truth that maybe Josh's parents should know, too. On the other hand, the situation really wasn't his business. He waffled between whether to say something or not, and the inner conflict left him a little more worn out each day.

Now he sat on the front porch of the ranch home he shared with his wife, Elle, and once more he voiced his feelings. "I keep telling myself it's none of my business." He reached for Elle's hand and stared out across their property. "I mean, what if his family doesn't even know about the little girl?"

"What did Josh say, exactly?"

"It was a talk we had on the way home from church, the last time he went with us. You were in back with Carl Joseph and Daisy, and Josh looked like he had the weight of the world on his shoulders."

"That's right. I thought something was wrong with him."

"I saw it, too, so I asked him. I told him he looked like he had a lot on his mind." Cody remembered the conversation perfectly. He could hear Josh's voice, see the lines on his forehead all over again.

"My lawyer keeps asking me about Savannah," he had said.

"Your little girl?" Cody knew her name because Josh had talked about her before.

"Yeah. He thinks the subject might come up in court soon. If the other lawyers ask about her, he wants me to say that as far as I know I don't have any children." Josh's eyes narrowed with his concern over the issue. "You know, because there's never been a paternity test or anything."

Cody remembered how his heart went out to Josh. He and Elle had been married for just over two years and she was expecting their first baby—a boy, if the ultrasound was right. Already the protective feeling he had for their first-born surpassed any emotion he'd ever known. He could only imagine what it would feel like to be Josh, to be sure that the child was his and then advised by his own attorney to deny his relationship to her in a court of law. Cody had pushed the issue a little further, curious about the intentions of Josh's lawyer. "Why wouldn't he want you to tell it like you believe it to be, that as far as you know you're Savannah's father?"

"Because of the settlement." Josh had squinted against the glare of the sun in his eyes. "If I tell the court I have a daughter, and if something happens to me, then Savannah will get all the money."

"All of it?" The thought had concerned Cody, especially

since there was no real proof of Savannah being Josh's daughter.

"My debts would be repaid first, so my parents and my sister would be taken care of for everything they ever loaned me. And they'd do a paternity test before Savannah would get a dime, that sort of thing." He shrugged one shoulder. "But yeah, after all that she would get the rest."

"Is that what you want?"

"If I die before I get the settlement? Yeah, it's what I want." He had never sounded so sure about anything since Cody had met him. "That little girl hasn't had her daddy all these years. If something happens to me, I at least want her taken care of financially. So she can grow up knowing I cared that much about her. You know?"

Cody understood better now that he was about to be a father. Coming back from the memory, he looked deep into Elle's eyes. "At the time, I let the conversation end without giving it another thought. I mean, Josh was in a lot of pain, but I didn't think he was about to die."

"Of course not." Elle's expression told him she understood his dilemma. She put her hand on her stomach. "The baby's kicking a lot tonight."

"Is he?" It was the third week in October and temperatures were cooling down at night. He put his arm around Elle's shoulders.

"I think he's gonna ride horses like his daddy."

"Bulls, you mean?"

"Horses." Elle raised her eyebrows at him. "We have a deal."

"I know." Cody smiled. He moved closer and kissed her

slowly, enough that it left them both breathless. "No bulls for this baby. I promise."

They kissed again, and Elle drew back first. "What are you going to do?"

"About the conversation with Josh?"

Elle nodded. "His parents need to know their son's wishes."

"You're right. I'll call them tomorrow." He thought about Carl Joseph. "My brother's having a hard time with this."

"Daisy, too."

"Yesterday he called and asked me about heaven." Cody drifted as the conversation came to life again.

"Heaven's where Ali is, right, Brother?" There'd been uncertainty in Carl Joseph's voice.

"Right. Ali's been there almost five years."

"That's a long time."

"It is." Cody rarely hurt over the loss of Ali anymore, but in that moment the pain was as fresh as the day his first wife had succumbed to cystic fibrosis. He swallowed his sorrow. "A very long time."

"You think maybe my good neighbor is getting to know Ali in heaven?"

Cody had smiled at the picture. "That would be nice, wouldn't it?"

"Yeah, because Josh was a really good neighbor, Brother. And if Ali needed a good neighbor in heaven, I wish God would put their houses right next to each other."

"Me, too."

"But I really wish Josh still lived across the parking lot

in Apartment J-8, because we can't exactly stop by on Saturdays and visit him in heaven."

"Not yet."

"One day?" Carl Joseph let a little hope creep back into his voice.

"Yes. One day when we're all in heaven together I'm sure Josh will be your neighbor again."

"I hope so, Brother." Carl Joseph sighed. "He was a very good neighbor, and he gave us eggs for late breakfast and he didn't even put them all in one basket. He used a plastic container instead."

Cody's heart had been touched by his brother's description. "Josh was a good guy."

"Yeah, so the people in heaven are lucky to have him."

Cody pulled Elle close against his side. "That brother of mine has a good heart. He was the one at Ali's funeral who told me he hoped God would give Ali a horse in heaven. Because she was a good horse rider. Now he's hoping that Josh can be a good neighbor in heaven the way he was here."

"I love that guy." Elle pressed her cheek against his. "Daisy has called me three times in the past week, crying. She tells me she's worried Carl Joseph will die, because maybe dying is contagious." Elle sighed. "Other than when our father died, Josh is one of the only people Daisy has ever lost. It's been hard on her."

Cody could only imagine how hard the past few weeks had been on Josh's family. And if his family did, indeed, include Savannah, then somewhere a little girl had lost her daddy. Whether she knew it or not. There was nothing he could do about the pain Josh's loss was causing the people around him, but he could do something about the conversation he'd had with Josh on the way home from church. He'd make the call first thing in the morning tomorrow.

Maybe after that he'd be able to get a good night's sleep.

❧

Annie and Nate were at home that night going over the paperwork from the lawyer's office. Thomas had gone over the documents contesting Savannah's position as Josh's heir, and now it was up to them to sign the papers. When they signed and returned the papers to Thomas tomorrow morning, the battle would officially begin.

A hearing would take place, and evidence would be presented. Annie found another letter from Maria, this one stating in more specific terms that it would cost Josh dearly if he wanted even an afternoon with his daughter. That correspondence would be presented, as would a number of witnesses who could state Josh's determination to find Savannah and accept her as a daughter, all to no avail because of Maria's decision to keep that from ever happening.

Unless and until Josh could come up with the money.

Beyond that, they would hire a private investigator who would show the judge the sort of person Maria was, how she'd tricked Josh into sleeping with her even though she was married. When it was all said and done, the investigator would know exactly how many men Maria had been with, lending credence to the fact that Savannah's father could have been any of the men her mother had bedded, the point being that Maria Cameron hadn't been interested in establishing Josh's paternity until there was money at stake. And since at the same time she refused Josh access to his daughter, Thomas thought they had a chance of winning the case.

If the situation had been different, if Maria had been in contact with Josh and if she'd been a more fit mother, Annie and Nate wouldn't mind letting the money go to Savannah. But the woman's greed and character had already been established. Now Annie and Nate sat across from each other at their kitchen table and talked about the battle ahead.

"What did Thomas say about setting up a college fund?" Annie's head was swimming with the legalities of taking on the system. In the meantime, the attorneys for the insurance company were nearer every day to a settlement. Thomas would have to make his case about Savannah not being a legitimate heir quickly. Otherwise, the money would go to Maria Cameron without a fight. Once she took hold of it, the chances of winning it back from her were almost non-existent.

Nate locked his fingers behind his head and leaned back in his chair. "It's possible. We can tell the judge we'd like to put an amount, a hundred thousand dollars, say, in a trust fund for Savannah's college years. Two hundred thousand, even. Her mother couldn't touch it because the money wouldn't be for Savannah's care and support. It would be only for her college expenses."

"Then that's what we'll do. That way everyone wins." She thought about that. "Besides, the judge will be more likely to see things our way if he knows we're willing to help Savannah. It's her mother we're trying to avoid."

They'd been home for several hours, but not until Nate stood for a glass of water did he notice the blinking light on their home phone answering machine. He pressed a series of buttons and a tiny voice filled the room. "This is Mary-beth Elmer, manager of your son's apartment buiding. We've spoken before. I need to tell you that a Cody Gunner is looking to talk to you. He left his phone number." The woman went over the number twice slowly. "Maybe you can give him a call and see what he wants. His brother is one of our tenants."

Nate played the message again and wrote down the phone number of Cody Gunner. Annie had never heard of the guy, but if he was the brother of one of the tenants, maybe he knew something about Josh—another detail that would add to the new way they'd come to see and know their only son.

"It's too late to call him tonight." Nate set the piece of paper with Cody's number on the counter next to the phone. "Remind me to call him in the morning."

"Okay." Nate sat back at the table and pulled the paper-work close. He flipped through the top five pages and took a little longer with the sixth and final page. "I think we should sign it. We're doing the right thing, Annie."

"There's no way Josh would've wanted that woman tak-ing his settlement."

"Absolutely not."

In the distant rooms of her heart, Annie remembered her prayer, her promise that she would let God show her if at any point in the battle for Josh's settlement they were doing something that went against the Lord's plan in all this. But today there had been no voice advising them not to move ahead with their motion. Maria Cameron had used Josh one too many times already, without her walking off with his money.

After all, the accident cost him his life, his chance for a future with Becky Wheaton, his dreams of making a new career for himself, and saddest of all, his opportunity to be a father to Savannah. It belonged to Josh's family to decide where Josh would have wanted the settlement money to go—not to a stranger like Maria Cameron.

For a slight moment, Annie wondered what it would be like to meet Savannah, to look into her eyes and see a part of her son looking back at her. If they lost the battle, Annie had every intention of asking for visitation rights. If the courts deemed Savannah to be Josh's rightful heir, then the privilege would have to come with a responsibility on the part of Maria Cameron—to connect her daughter with Josh's family.

At least Annie hoped that would happen if they lost.

But what if they won? Would that mean they'd never have the opportunity to meet the child, to hug her even one time the way Josh had never been able to? Annie didn't like the way that felt, as if winning the legal battle was more important than meeting Savannah. But maybe somehow God would allow both—their rightful victory in court, and a meeting with Josh's little girl.

She wasn't sure about much of anything except that they needed to sign the papers. Nate went first, and then it was her turn. But as she signed her name on the line clearly marked by their attorney, it took everything Annie had to remind herself that this battle was against Maria Cameron.

And not against Josh's precious Savannah.

TWENTY

The twitches and rapid heartbeats were happening more often, constant fleshly reminders that she had to play it straight. Very straight. At least until the settlement came. Maria looked at the glowing red numbers on the table next to her bed. Seven-fifteen. She sat on the edge of her bed and stretched her arms over her head. Life had become crazy and she had no idea how to handle the pressure. At least not sober.

Maria had an attorney now, someone Freddy had recommended. The attorney was his idea after a call from Thomas Flynn last Thursday telling her that Josh's family was fighting for the money. Of all the nerve. Savannah was Josh's only kid, his only heir, as Josh's lawyer liked to say. The case should be open-and-shut, and three months from now she and Savannah should be sitting in the lap of luxury. That's what her attorney said. He'd found out the numbers Thomas wouldn't tell her during that first phone call: a cool two million dollars. That's what she and her baby girl stood to win if things went right. Two million. Josh had finally reached the big time. He'd gotten himself hit by a rich drunk driver, and now the payout was weeks away.

Maria picked up the business card on the table next to the alarm clock. "Harry Dreskin, Attorney-at-Law," the card read. Harry was a good guy. He worked out of a tiny office on the Upper West Side. Maria had met with him twice already and as far as she could tell Harry was beside himself to be working on a respectable case like hers. Helping his client rope in a settlement for a kid without a father? What could be more honest and good than that?

Harry didn't want money up front, which made him the perfect lawyer. But he'd hinted around that a little bedroom action could cut his fees quite a bit once the settlement came. Maria was mildly interested, but she turned him down because mothers—real mothers like the ones she saw playing with their kids in the park—didn't sleep with men as a way of bringing down the cost of legal fees, or rent, or blow, or anything else.

Maria thought about the day ahead. She and Savannah couldn't sit around Freddy's place. Not today. They had to clean it and get lost. Freddy had a business deal with a group of characters who scared even Maria. After that, more scary was the trip she had to take to Denver tomorrow. First time she'd flown anywhere since the junket to Vegas eight years ago.

The trip was part of this new fight for the money, naturally. Her attorney said it would take some time since they couldn't afford the airfare and would have to borrow a car and drive to Colorado, so Josh's attorney bought tickets for her and Savannah. He was even going to put them up in a fancy hotel—a Holiday Inn with a free breakfast. The trip wasn't the scary part. The reason she was going, that's what made her afraid. Some judge in Denver said she had to come and testify about Savannah being Josh's daughter, and how come she never let Josh visit her.

She'd come up with one lie after another since she got news of the trip. The attorney would ask her why she hadn't let Savannah see Josh, and she would smile sweetly and say, "I gave Josh the chance to see his daughter, but he wasn't interested." Maria's heart picked up speed. No, maybe that lie wouldn't work. Josh's family probably knew how hard he'd tried to see Savannah.

She bit her lip. There was the other lie. "I gave Josh the chance to spend time with his daughter, but he could never afford to make the trip." Again, she would give the attorney her sweetest smile. "I kept hoping he'd find a way to visit us, to connect with Savannah, but it never happened."

Somehow between today and Wednesday—two days from now—she would have to come up with something solid, a believable story that would prove she hadn't intentionally kept Savannah from her father. Otherwise, there could be some question as to whether Savannah should be his rightful heir.

She reached out her toe and nudged Savannah's foot. "Wake up, sleepy. It's a new day." Maria's heart was still racing, her right eye still twitching just beneath her lower lashes. Every part of her body screamed for a drink or a hit—anything to dull the anxiety closing in around her. But even so, she silently congratulated herself at the way she talked to Savannah just now. She almost sounded like a real mother.

Savannah sat up and moved her blankets to the corner of the room, far enough beneath the desk that they were out of sight. " 'Morning, Mama." She yawned and blinked a few times. "Is there breakfast today?"

The question frustrated Maria. "When have we missed breakfast? Not for two weeks now, right?" Maria started to roll her eyes but she caught herself. Harry told her that the attorneys for Josh's family would probably put everyone breathing on the witness stand. That meant some stranger could come sniffing around asking Savannah what sort of mother she had, and whether Savannah was happy living with Maria.

If she was going to be in charge of the girl's two million dollars, then Maria didn't want a single doubt about whether her daughter would tell the lawyers she was happy. Happy and well fed. Maria led the way out of the bedroom. They needed to clean the place today. Freddy's orders. Keep Savannah happy, keep enough food in the kitchen, pay the rent, clean the place. So much to worry about. Maria walked to the cupboard and pulled out a box of Cap'n Crunch. The pressure would be a lot easier to handle if she could drink just a little. A swig of whiskey now and then.

They were finished with breakfast and halfway through the cleaning job when the phone rang. Normally, Maria avoided Freddy's phone, but since the whole settlement thing had come up, she didn't miss a call. She picked it up on the second ring and reminded herself to use her best motherly voice. "Hello?"

"Maria, it's Harry."

"Hey." She relaxed. "I got Flynn's package in the mail. I'm all set for tomorrow's trip to Denver."

"Right, well, that's why I'm calling. I filed a motion with the court and the judge thinks he can resolve the case without your testimony."

Maria's eye stopped twitching. "What does that mean?"

"It means you don't have to fly to Denver." He allowed only a quick break in between sentences. "That's not saying you won't have to fly out some other time to testify, but for now you can stay home. We'll be talking to the judge and I'll call you later this week."

The thrill of victory rushed through Maria's veins like a drug. "Well, that's the best news of the day."

"I'm sure it is. I'll be in touch." When he hung up, she eyed the whiskey bottle tucked back in the corner of the kitchen counter. "Savannah?"

"Yes, Mama?" Her voice came from the bathroom upstairs. "Do you need something?"

"Are you almost finished up there?"

"No." Her voice sounded closer and there was the sound of her feet on the stairs. When she was in sight, she gave Maria a nervous look. "I still have to wash the windows and the sink."

"Okay." Maria gave a lighthearted laugh. "Just checking. I want to make sure we have plenty of time in the park later. Plus Freddy has that meeting here."

"I'll hurry." Savannah's eyes were wide with concern as she hurried back up the stairs.

Maria waited until she heard the girl working in the bathroom again, then she grabbed the whiskey bottle and jerked the top from the glass neck. Being sober was one thing, but no one would know if she took a small drink. How else could she celebrate the attorney's great news? Whatever had happened between the two lawyers, Harry Dreskin had clearly won this first battle. She didn't need to fly to Denver, which meant she didn't need to lie about letting Josh see Savannah.

This legal thing was a breeze, and one day soon she'd get a check in the mail for two million dollars. She held the bottle of golden liquid to her nose and breathed deep. The whiskey smelled wonderful. She could feel herself relaxing just from the intoxicating scent of it. She glanced up at the stairs one more time and reminded herself to hurry. She couldn't have Savannah find out she'd been drinking again. Even Harry Dreskin told her to stay clean if she wanted the money.

This was different, though. She had a reason to celebrate, and besides, no one would ever know. She put the bottle to her lips and took a small sip. The liquid felt smooth and seductive on her tongue, and it burned deliciously as it slid down her throat. She took another sip and another. Already the alcohol was spreading through her, warming her and slowing her heart rate. She needed this—she deserved it. But if she was going to soothe her cravings she needed more than a few quick gulps. Who knew when she'd have the chance to drink again?

Once more she looked for Savannah, listened for her footsteps. When she was sure the girl wasn't going to catch her, she turned the bottle bottom side up and guzzled several long swigs. Enough so that she'd really feel it. Then she quick twisted the top back on and slid the bottle back to its place on the counter. The dizzying euphoria flooded through her, over her. This was the life, filling herself with warm, welcoming whiskey and having all day ahead to enjoy the feeling.

She finished tidying the kitchen, cleaning the counters and sweeping the floors. She wasn't quite steady on her feet, but that part would wear off before they left the apartment. Maria remembered the routine, even if it had been a while.

Savannah came down after a while and for a long moment she studied Maria. Finally, a nervous laugh came from Maria's lips, a laugh that was probably too loud. "What ya lookin' at?"

"Mama? Are you—are you okay?"

"Jus' tired, baby girl." She laughed again, quieter this time. "All this work has me tuckered out."

Savannah looked doubtful. She looked around the kitchen until her eyes seemed to fall on the place where the whiskey bottle sat. "Did you drink, Mama? Is that what you did?"

"Of course not." Maria turned her attention back to the broom in her hand. How could a seven-year-old be so smart, anyway?

"Did you drink Freddy's whiskey?"

"Listen!" Maria spun around and glared at her daughter. "Are you callin' me a liar?"

"No, Mama." Savannah took a step back.

Maria hated this, when Savannah acted afraid of her. She closed the distance between them and grabbed Savannah's arm. "Don't call me a liar, you un'erstand?"

"Sorry. Sorry, Mama." Savannah started to cry. "You told me you weren't gonna drink."

"And I didn't drink. You never saw me drink, okay?"

"Okay." Savannah jerked her arm free and rubbed the place where a line of red marks stood out. "I'm sorry."

"You better be." Maria gave her daughter a shove for good measure. Brat. Trying to ruin a perfectly good day. She was about to say so when she remembered she was supposed to be treating Savannah differently. Better than before. She swept the other half of the kitchen floor, and she was almost done when she realized how dizzy she was. The whiskey was making the room tilt, and Maria was angry at herself for drinking so much. She could have done with half of what she'd gulped down. The floor felt wobbly beneath her, and suddenly she leaned wrong on the broom and wound up flat on the floor. Quickly, she lifted herself to her hands and knees and cursed softly.

"Mama." Savannah rushed to her side. "Are you hurt?"

"No." She used her daughter's shoulder to stand up and then she smiled her nicest smile. "Mama's sorry about earlier. I'm jus' tired, like I said." She messed her fingers through Savannah's reddish-blond hair. "Let's get ready for the day, okay?"

Savannah still looked nervous, but she nodded. They got dressed and took the subway to Central Park, same as always. Halfway to their spot, Maria grabbed a fistful of dirt and rubbed it on her face and Savannah's.

"I hate this, Mama. No more dirt, please!"

"Shhh." Maria put her hand against her daughter's mouth. The effects of the whiskey were already wearing off, her body already craving one more swig, one more rush. "We won't beg much longer, baby girl. We have to have the dirt or people won't give us anything."

She had made a sign last week that read "Please help me feed my daughter." She carried it in a grocery bag and when they found their spot on a bench across from the zoo entrance, Maria pulled it out. It seemed to work. People tossed fives and tens their way without thinking twice. Yesterday they'd brought home more than a hundred dollars, most of which she gave to Freddy for rent. She was paying her way now. It was more respectable that way, more like a mother should be. But today the money would be hers, and she could take Savannah out for pizza later or maybe to a movie. That would keep the kid happy, and keeping Savannah happy was very important now.

That's what mothers were supposed to do, keep their kids happy. But Maria had to be honest with herself, trying to be a good mother had to account for at least some of her twitches and racing heart. They begged for five hours without a break. After that, they went out for pizza, and when Savannah took a trip to the bathroom, Maria ordered herself a pitcher of beer.

When Savannah returned she noticed right away. "You said you weren't gonna drink alcohol."

"This is a party." Maria kept her tone happy, but under the table she dug her fingers into Savannah's arm, to warn her against saying anything else. "We made a hundred and twenty-two dollars today, baby girl. I'll drink what I want."

One pitcher became two and then three and the room was spinning hard. A waitress told her it was time to leave, but Maria didn't want to go. She was having a party with her daughter, and what was wrong with that? But then the waitress had two people with her, two big ol' guys, and they told her she needed to pay for her tab and be on her way.

"Listen!" She stood and pushed the nearest guy in the shoulder. "No one tells me what to do!" She was yelling, but she didn't care. "I'm a millionaire. I do what I want!"

Savannah shrank down in her seat and covered her face.

"Ma'am, if you don't pay your tab and leave, we'll have to call the police."

"Mama!" Savannah shrieked at her. "Please just pay him."

"Shut up." Maria was sick of the girl, sick of playing the role of perfect mother. She slapped Savannah hard across the face. "I hate being your mama, can't you see that?"

The man from the restaurant grabbed her arm. "That's enough," he hissed at her. Then he turned to the other guy. "Call nine-one-one."

Nine-one-one? The police couldn't come or everything would be ruined. They wouldn't give two million dollars to a drunk who slapped her daughter. And if the guy called the police then everyone would know that's what she'd done. "No, you don't!" Maria screamed right in the man's face. Then she reeled back and took a swing at him, but she missed. Somehow the action sent her spiraling to the floor, and on the way down she hit her head on something sharp and hard. The table, maybe.

When she next opened her eyes, a roomful of policemen stood around her. They pulled her to her feet and put handcuffs on her. Maria cussed and kicked at them, but they took her anyway, threw her into a police car, and drove off with her. Not until they pulled into the precinct parking lot did she remember Savannah.

"My little girl!" she screamed. She leaned as far forward as she could. "Where's my little girl?"

"We took care of her." The policeman behind the wheel glared at her. "Sit back and shut your mouth."

Maria realized how badly she'd blown it. She would have to work harder than ever to make the lawyers and the judge believe she was a good mother now. Her head hurt as she pressed herself into the back of the cruiser. On the good side, she was getting a break from Savannah, from

KAREN KINGSBURY

the girl's constant questions and scrutiny. The kid was more a spy than a daughter. But she'd have to find a way to make the girl happy, to keep herself sober and in line, or Maria knew she'd lose everything.

After they booked and printed her, they pushed her into a stinky cell and slammed the door shut. Maria felt afraid and alone, drunk, and depressed over the mistakes she'd made that night. She curled up on a wooden bench along one wall of the cell and hoped she hadn't blown it. Because for the first time in her life, she had reasons to believe things would be good again, reasons to believe she would have the house and the car and the future she'd always wanted. With or without Savannah. If she could get herself out of this mess, she had reasons to believe in tomorrow.

Two million wonderful reasons.

❧

Savannah lay in the dark in the strange bed and held tight to the only thing that mattered. The photograph of her daddy. After the trouble at the restaurant, a nice policeman had taken her to Freddy's house. Savannah wasn't sure how they knew where to go, but they looked through her mama's wallet and maybe something in there told them the directions.

At Freddy's, the lights were out and the nice policeman took her hand and walked her inside so she could get her things. He turned on the bedroom light when they reached the room Savannah shared with her mama. Savannah got down on the floor and crawled under the desk. One at a time she pulled out her pillow and her blanket and her pile of clothes.

"Is this your bed?" The policeman pointed to where Mama slept.

"No." She felt shy about not having a bed, because maybe other kids her age didn't sleep on the floor. She pointed to the spot beneath the desk. "I sleep down there."

The nice man's face said that he wasn't happy with that news. Savannah was scooping her things into one pile, but the officer said she didn't need her blanket or pillow. "Your foster parents will have all that, sweetie."

Foster parents. Wasn't that what Mama had always said might happen? If Savannah complained too much, then the police would take her to foster parents? She was suddenly very afraid about that news. "Who are the foster parents?" Her voice sounded quiet and little and scared.

"They're very nice people." He patted her on the arm. "Don't worry, Savannah. It'll be okay."

"I want Mama." She wasn't sure why she said that, because her mama didn't want her. She even said so out loud in the restaurant. But Mama was all she had until the day her daddy came to get her.

The policeman looked closer at her arm. "What's this?" He ran his finger over the marks on Savannah, the ones her mama had put there.

She tried to be brave, but she moved a little because the spots hurt. "Nothing."

"Your mother did this, didn't she?"

"She didn't mean to."

The officer shook his head and said, "I'll bet." Then he

took Savannah's things from her so she didn't have anything to carry except her small bag with the plastic cross and the picture of her daddy.

They drove for a long time and crossed two bridges before they pulled up in front of a nice house, nicer than anything Savannah had ever been inside. She heard the officer tell someone on the radio that the foster family lived in Queens, so that's where they must be. Together they went inside. An old man and lady lived there. They showed her to a room upstairs with a bed that was just the right size for Savannah, gave her a new toothbrush and some toothpaste, and said it was time to brush. Then they gave her a new nightgown and told her it was bedtime.

"Do you believe in Jesus?" the old woman asked her. She had nice eyes.

"Yes." Savannah remembered Grandpa Ted. "Are we going to talk to Him?"

"We are." The old couple sat together on the edge of her bed and talked to Jesus for a long time. "We know You have plans for Savannah. We pray that You protect her and help her find those plans. Please be with her mother and let her know that with You she can find true and lasting change."

After that they said good night and sweet dreams and they left her alone. But they kept one small light on. "Just in case you're afraid," the old woman told her.

As soon as she was alone, she snuck out of bed and pulled the picture of her daddy out of her bag. She had Jesus in her heart, but when she was really afraid she would sleep better if she had Daddy in her hands. She looked at his smile and his friendly eyes. *Daddy, where are you? Why aren't you coming for me?* She felt little stinging feelings in her eyes and she blinked back some wetness. *Dear Jesus, it's me, Savannah. Can You tell my daddy that I'm waiting for him?* She sniffed real quiet, so the nice people wouldn't come back in the room. *Tell him I'm at the foster house and Mama doesn't want me anymore. So now would be a good time to come find me.*

She talked a bit more to Jesus, and then she yawned two times and looked at the picture again. Her daddy was so handsome, so strong. He never would have let anyone put marks on Savannah's arms. She yawned once more, and her eyes started to close. The picture was rough around the edges, but Savannah didn't care. She hugged it close to her heart and pushed her face deeper into the pillow. Her mama's voice came in all around her, all the mean things she'd said at the restaurant.

Shut up! I hate being your mama!

The words lined up again and again in her mind, until finally she thought about Jesus again. Because Grandpa Ted said Jesus loved her, and that meant it was up to Jesus to bring her daddy to her. As she fell asleep, she begged Jesus to love her enough to make that happen. Because she needed to be with her daddy right away, before the foster people gave her back to Mama and something really bad happened. Her daddy better hurry and get here, because she needed her Prince Charming to rescue her.

Even if she had to find him herself.

TWENTY-ONE

Annie was aware that she'd lost the first round. Maria's attorney was some creep from Manhattan, and he'd insisted that Maria was a single mother whose routine couldn't be disrupted simply because some jilted family members didn't want their son's settlement money going to his own daughter. At least that's the way Thomas had depicted the scenario to them. Apparently, the judge was convinced, because he ruled that more evidence would need to be presented, enough to make a decent argument that Savannah wasn't Josh's daughter in any way other than by blood.

If they could make that argument strong enough, then the judge would consider ordering Maria out to Denver for a hearing.

Annie was reading through the documents on Josh's computer, and her determination had never been stronger. How dare the woman get an attorney and battle for Josh's money? Could she honestly sleep at night knowing she was fighting for money that should never be hers? She rubbed her eyes and looked around the apartment. They'd moved Josh's furniture out this past weekend. Nate rented a U-Haul and took his bedroom set to what would now be the guest room in their house in Black Forest. The rest—the sofa and chair, his pots and pans and dishes and linens—all had been donated to Goodwill.

When the place was empty except for Josh's computer and desk and several boxes of things they'd already gone through, she and Lindsay and Nate spent a day cleaning. It was important that they leave the place the way it had been given to Josh. He would have wanted them to do that much for the manager.

Now, with only a few days left in October, Annie was glad they were nearly finished. She still had to decide which boxes of his personal belongings they should keep, and which—like the box of hiking magazines—should be dropped off at the recycling center. When she needed a break from the paperwork, she spent time on Josh's computer, opening one document at a time and either printing or deleting it.

She opened Josh's iTunes library, selected his Favorites playlist, and hit the play button. The heartrending, haunting sounds of Josh's favorite song filled the space around her. The plink of the piano chimed in, and then the words that Josh loved.

"I can only imagine, what it will be like...when I walk by Your side...."

Sorrow, like an old friend, put its arms around her, and for the hundredth time since her son's death, she felt tears in her eyes. *You don't have to imagine anymore, Josh...never again.* She pictured her baby, her son, walking alongside Jesus, looking long into His face. Was he hurt that his own parents hadn't really known him? Was he angry, disappointed in her the way she had once, a life-time ago, been disappointed in him?

She knew him so much better now. Her discoveries made her want to have Lindsay write a story about his life for the *Gazette*. That way the busybodies with the public library and the teachers union and the PTA could know that Josh Warren had been a success in all the ways that mattered. No matter how his life looked to people who didn't know him.

Shallow people, like Annie had been.

She breathed in deep and let the words of the song fill her soul. A ray of light warmed the cold, dark sadness inside her. Josh wasn't angry with her or disappointed, he had no regrets. His only concern now was whether to dance for Jesus or fall to his knees in awe of a God so merciful, so loving. Josh was okay, and one day she'd have the chance to hold him in her arms and tell him what she hoped he already knew.

That she couldn't possibly be prouder of him.

The music kept playing, but she returned her attention to the files on Josh's computer. The next one was marked Hours. She opened it and saw a spreadsheet with Josh's assigned hours for the month. Next to each calendar date, Josh had added a check mark—designating, it seemed, that he had completed the shift in question.

Thomas had told her to print anything dealing with his work as a tow truck driver, so she hit the print button and waited. As she did, someone knocked at the door. Carl Joseph and Daisy had been by several times now, once with a plate of cookies and most recently with a seedling pine tree. "Because when you see it you'll remember Josh," Daisy had told her.

"And Josh was too good to forget." Carl Joseph's earnestness was refreshing.

She figured they were probably back again, maybe to check if she'd enjoyed the cookies or to bring her a pitcher of iced tea. Daisy had asked last time if she liked iced tea on hot days. Annie smiled to herself as she turned the knob and opened the door. But standing there instead was a striking dark-haired young man with high cheekbones and eyes deep enough to fall into. "Mrs. Warren?"

"Yes." She stepped aside. "How can I help you?"

"I'm Cody Gunner, Carl Joseph's brother."

"Ah. Your brother speaks very highly of you." Annie made the connection immediately. "Come in." She motioned to a couple of bar stools that remained along Josh's short kitchen counter. "I'm afraid there aren't many places to sit."

"That's fine. I won't be long." He gave her a polite smile and moved to the closest seat. He waited until she was seated opposite him before he began. "My wife and I were talking recently about a conversation I had with Josh a couple of weeks before he died." The grief in Cody's eyes told Annie that he, too, had cared about her son. "I left a message for you. I'm not sure if you got it."

Annie didn't remember the message from the apartment manager until just then. She frowned. "We got the message. I meant to call you the next morning, but..." She looked around.

"I know, you've been distracted." He gave her a sad smile. "I was at my brother's and I saw your car. I decided to take a chance."

"I'm glad you did." Annie was no longer surprised by anything she might learn about Josh. Whatever piece of

Josh's life story Cody was bringing with him now, Annie didn't fear it. She craved it the way women in wartime craved the next letters from their sons on the battlefield. "Can I get you some water?"

"No, thanks." Cody put his hands on his knees and looked at the mantel over Josh's fireplace. The photos were still there, where they would stay until they closed his door behind them for the last time. Cody turned his eyes to her. "What do you know about the little girl in the photo?"

"Much." Annie sighed. She turned her attention to the picture of her granddaughter. "Our attorney had a paternity test done, and it was conclusive. She's Josh's daughter, Savannah."

They were quiet for a few moments. "That's what Josh believed—that she was his." Cody seemed uncomfortable with whatever he was about to say. "This is none of my business, Mrs. Warren, but Josh's settlement...Has there been a determination about where the money will go?"

Annie was surprised by Cody's question. He was right, the topic was none of his business, but if this had something to do with a conversation he'd had with Josh, then...Her insides tightened sharply. "Actually, we're working with Josh's attorney on that. The money will automatically go to Savannah by way of her mother unless our lawyer can convince the judge otherwise." She felt the strange need to defend herself. "Obviously, we're contesting the fact that Savannah is a rightful heir to the settlement. We're trying to set up a college fund for her, anything to keep the money out of the hands of her mother. We don't think she'll use it for Savannah at all."

"Yes, well, that's what Josh and I talked about that day. We were on our way home from church."

Again Annie felt the loss of all she'd missed out on. She never believed Josh had found his way back to God, and so her son had spent his last two months attending services with people who were virtually strangers. She hid her heartache and forced herself to listen.

"We were talking about Savannah, how Josh's attorney didn't want him to mention her if the subject came up during one of his depositions. That was before anyone knew for sure whether she was his daughter."

Annie wondered if they might have avoided all this if Josh had only taken his lawyer's advice.

"Josh said he knew why his attorney wanted him to deny having any children. It was because of the settlement, so the money would go to his family if something happened to him before the case was settled."

Annie felt for her son, troubled by the conflict between his certainty that Savannah was his daughter and the urging of his lawyer to publicly say otherwise for the sake of a pile of money. She could almost sense where Cody's story was headed. "Did he—did he tell you his wishes?"

Cody hesitated. "Yes, ma'am. That's why I'm here."

"Hold on." Air, that's what she needed. She stood and slid the patio door open and breathed in until her lungs were full. Then she returned to the seat opposite Cody. She had prayed for God's wisdom, His leading. Now she needed to listen very carefully, no matter how she thought things should go. She searched Cody's eyes. "Tell me. Please."

"He wanted you and your family to be repaid.

Everything you ever loaned him." Cody narrowed his eyes, empathy flooding his voice. "But after that, he wanted the money to go to Savannah."

"All of it?" Annie felt suddenly light-headed, as if the moment were something from a dream or a nightmare. She had ideas for how to use the settlement, once Josh's debts were repaid. She pictured setting up a college fund for Ben and Bella, and of course for Savannah, and then maybe they would use the money to help Nate get reelected one more time. There would be money for their church and several of their charities, and something for Carl Joseph and Daisy, so they might never have to pay for bus fare again. She and Nate would pay off their house, because Josh had worried about their retirement when he'd had to borrow so much from them, often bringing up the financial concerns that plagued some retired people. That sort of thing. She asked the question again in a tortured whisper. "The entire settlement?"

Cody nodded. "I'm sorry. I figured this would be hard for you. I was surprised, too."

Annie wondered if Josh was upset with them, if that was why he could fathom giving his entire settlement to a child he'd never met—whether she was his own daughter or not. "Did he say...I mean, was he angry with us? Was that why?"

"It wasn't like he actually thought it would happen. He was in a lot of pain, but he didn't think he had weeks to live." Cody's tone told her that he'd thought all of this through a number of times already. "Like I said, he wanted his debts repaid. But I think he just loved that little girl with all his heart."

Annie could almost hear the Lord telling her to pay attention. "Did he say anything else?"

"He told me Savannah hadn't had her daddy all these years. If something happened to him, at least he wanted her taken care of financially." Cody sat up a little straighter. "He said he wanted her to grow up knowing how much he cared for her—whether he was alive or not."

Just like that, Annie felt everything change, felt the fight drain from her body like water from a sink. She'd asked God to show her the right thing, and now through Cody's words He had. She kept her thoughts to herself as she and Cody talked a few more minutes about Josh's renewed faith, how he loved singing along during the worship part of the service, and how he hung on every word the pastor said. "My wife and I had the feeling Josh was just starting to live." Cody gave a sad shake of his head. "I'm sorry, Mrs. Warren, for your loss."

She saw him to the door and thanked him for his honesty. After he was gone she stood unmoving in the silence of the empty living room. The settlement belonged to Josh. Until now they could tell themselves that Josh would have wanted Savannah's college education taken care of, but not her current needs, not if they had to go through Maria first. Until now they could have made themselves believe that he wouldn't have wanted a dime going to Maria Cameron, not after what she'd put him through.

But now...

The conversation with Cody was all the proof Annie needed. When Nate heard what their son had said about Savannah and the money, Annie was sure her husband would see things the same way. God might as well have come through the door and told her the news Himself. The message was that clear.

She started the song over again and closed her eyes, picturing Josh walking the streets of heaven free from pain and worry over when the lawsuit would be settled and how he was going to connect with his daughter. He'd left them to sort through what remained of his life, and they would remember him differently because of that. But he'd also left behind a daughter, and his wishes that she receive his settlement money. Even if her mother spent every dollar before Savannah's eighteenth birthday.

Annie wandered to the photograph on the mantel one more time. She picked up the wooden frame and stared into the eyes of her granddaughter. If Josh wanted her to have all the money, then so be it. She would call Nate, and then call Thomas Flynn, and the fight against Maria Cameron would be officially dropped. But she would demand one thing before walking away from the matter forever. Something that was almost worth two million dollars all by itself.

A visit with Josh's little girl.

TWENTY-TWO

The call to Josh's lawyer was merely a routine favor Lindsay was doing for her mother. Her parents had been through so much in the past month that, even with her workload at the newspaper, she tried to do everything she could to help.

Lindsay dialed Thomas Flynn's number and waited while the line began to ring. Already this morning they'd all met at Josh's apartment to load the rest of his things in the back of her father's pickup truck. The last things her mother packed were the three photographs that had sat over Josh's fireplace. She wrapped them in a pillowcase and set them on the front seat of the truck.

Before they left for the last time, she and her parents stood in the doorway and her father had prayed. "Lord, You showed us so much about our son this past month." His voice was strained as he continued. "Thank You for giving us this time and place so we could learn what we didn't know about our son."

Lindsay and her mother both had tears on their cheeks as Nate continued, thanking God for the neighbors who had known Josh and for the ways in which they'd come forward to fill in the memory of all Josh had meant to this world. "A person doesn't have to have a college degree or an investment portfolio or a big house to be successful, Lord. You showed us that this past month, and in the process You gave us a season of grieving and discovering that none of us will ever forget."

When they finally closed the door and locked it, they took Josh's keys to the apartment manager and returned to their separate cars. Lindsay's parents looked emotionally exhausted. They took Josh's final belongings back to their house, and Lindsay returned to her home to make a few phone calls. This was one of them, to see if there'd been any response from Maria Cameron since she'd gotten the news that Josh's settlement money was hers.

A secretary patched Lindsay through to Mr. Flynn, and Lindsay kept her question short and to the point. But even before she could finish, Josh's lawyer cut her off. "I was just going to call your parents." His words came fast and colored with concern. "I got news from Maria Cameron's attorney. She's been arrested and put in jail for two weeks. Apparently, she got drunk and put on some public display." His tone fell. "She tried to hit a waiter, and she slapped Savannah with a whole restaurant full of people watching."

Lindsay was on her feet, pacing from the kitchen to her dining room and back again. "So where's Savannah if her mom's in jail?"

"In foster care. Her lawyer says the district attorney is sorting through a stack of warrants trying to figure out what to charge her with." Mr. Flynn barely broke for a quick breath. "This could change things. Here's what I'm thinking."

For the next fifteen minutes, Lindsay listened, and when the call ended, she picked up the phone and dialed her parents. Her mom answered almost immediately. "Lindsay? Did he have any news?"

Lindsay steadied herself against the doorway in her dining room. "In fact, he did. How soon can you meet me?"

"I was headed to the cemetery." Her mom still sounded tired, drained. "I bought flowers for Josh's grave."

None of them had spent time at the graveside. They'd been too busy sorting through Josh's life to spend much time dwelling on his death. "Meet you there in an hour."

Her mind raced with the details Thomas Flynn had shared with her. With Savannah in foster care, Lindsay was still trying to absorb the fact that her mother's prayers might be answered sooner than any of them thought.

If Mr. Flynn was right, a visit with Josh's daughter might be only an airline ticket away.

Annie reached Josh's grave first. She didn't bring a chair or a blanket, because this wasn't a long visit, more just a chance to pay her respects. Josh's stone should be marked by flowers at least, so that people who passed by would know he was missed and that he mattered. If there was one thing Annie knew now, it was that single truth.

Josh's life did matter.

She studied the temporary marker. Nate had ordered a permanent stone and an inground container to hold flowers, but they wouldn't be ready to install until Thanksgiving time. For now there was only the simple piece of cement with Josh's name engraved across the top: *Joshua David Warren.*

"I miss you, son...so much." She closed her eyes and lifted her face to the breeze drifting down from the mountains. Sometimes on days like this the light wind felt like Josh's presence beside her, like she could reach out and touch him, his memory was so close. If she could—if she could have just one more time with him she wasn't sure she would even know what to say. Carl Joseph had said it all, really. Josh was a hero, but as wonderful as that was, Annie had missed the fact. Tragically and completely, she'd missed it.

"Mom."

For a fraction of a second, the voice belonged to Josh. Not Josh the way he'd sounded the last time she talked to him, but Josh the way he'd sounded when he was ten or eleven and he had a frog or a flower to show her. But before the thought had time to root itself, Lindsay's voice was soft beside her. "Sorry...I didn't want to frighten you."

Annie opened her eyes. "Sometimes I can feel him." She smiled—that painful sort of drenched-in-sadness smile. The one that would be her trademark whenever she thought about Josh for the rest of her days. "As close as wind against my skin."

"Hmmm." Lindsay folded her hands and stared down at Josh's marker. "I feel it, too. But it's not the same."

"No." She breathed in slowly through her nose, savoring the smell of evergreen on the breeze. "Thomas had news for us?"

"You're sure you don't want to sit down? We could talk about it in the car."

Annie cocked her head and took another look at her son's name on the temporary stone. "I'm okay. I need this time, the serenity of it."

Lindsay looked like she wasn't sure where to begin. "He got news about Maria Cameron. Mom...she's in jail. Public intoxication, and she has a list of warrants for her arrest. I guess she hit Savannah."

The details kept coming, but Annie couldn't get past that one. She felt something fierce and protective come to life within her, and in the middle of Lindsay's story she held up her hand. "She hit Savannah?"

"With everyone watching." Lindsay bit her lip. "Mr. Flynn says Savannah has bruises on her arms. She's in a foster home for now."

Annie wasn't sure whether to scream or break down in light of this latest sad development. All this time she'd had nothing but disdain for Maria Cameron, but only because of the way she'd treated Josh. Until now she hadn't thought for a minute about how she'd treated Josh's daughter.

The truth nearly dropped her to her knees. What sort of life had Savannah lived? As Lindsay shared the rest of what the lawyer had told her, a frightening picture came into focus. Savannah and her mother lived with a known drug dealer, and Savannah slept on the floor beneath a desk—which was an improvement from the three times when police had picked the pair up in Central Park where they sometimes slept beneath a bridge near the pond.

Annie wasn't sure how much more of the story she could take. If Josh had known these details, he would have found a way to reach Savannah if he had to walk across the country. Again she was hit by the truth that if she and Nate had paid more credence to Josh's insistence that Savannah was his daughter, then together they might have found out about her situation sooner, gotten the paternity test, and figured out some way to rescue her.

Annie's determination to find and help her granddaughter grew like a wildfire within her. Maria Cameron would never hurt Savannah again, not if Annie had anything to do about it. "If her mother isn't fit, then Savannah should come live with us. What did Thomas say about that?"

"Well, that's the worst part." Lindsay folded her arms. Her voice blended with the wind, every word washing over Annie whether she wanted to hear it or not. "Mr. Flynn says that Maria hasn't been arrested in more than a year, and her landlord says that she's usually a model mother."

"Which is clearly a lie."

"But the system is bound to pay attention to that. If her attorney can get the warrants dismissed, then she'll probably get Savannah back. That's what he said." She took her mother's hand. "But he also said that if you act fast, you can meet Savannah while she's still in foster care."

"What?" Annie couldn't explain the sense of joy that burst through her pain in that single moment. She was going to get to meet her granddaughter. Her dream of looking into the eyes that were so like Josh's was going to come true. God had heard her prayers, and now in a matter of days she would meet the girl Josh had loved for the past seven years.

She called Nate while she and Lindsay walked back to their cars. Once she had his okay, she called Thomas and then the airline. Lindsay and Nate wanted to go, too, so she booked three flights to LaGuardia. Thomas recommended that all of them go, because there was no telling what Maria would do once she had custody of Savannah again, once she had the money. The woman was under no obligation to stay in contact with the Warren family, despite the fact that they had willingly dropped the fight for Josh's settlement.

Thomas felt strongly that once Maria had the money, she and the girl would disappear, move to another state or another country, and that would be that. Which meant this might be their only chance to meet the girl Josh had longed to hold, the one he had planned to love and care for as soon as he had the chance to meet her. Annie tried to imagine what might have happened if Josh and Becky had gotten back together, if he'd finished college and if they'd married. Her grandchild would've had a different mother and a different life, and Josh would never have been working for the garage that night. Never would have had a reason to find himself suddenly in the path of a drunk driver.

Annie drove home from the cemetery lost in a maze of questions. What would the girl be like? If she'd been abused or neglected, would she be quiet and withdrawn? Would meeting Annie scare her or confuse her? Did she love her mother despite the life she'd lived? Was she being treated kindly in the foster home where she'd been placed? But the question most pressing on Annie's heart was the obvious one, the one she had thought about ever since the results of the paternity test came in.

Did Savannah know about Josh?

TWENTY-THREE

Some nice people were coming to see her today, that's all Savannah knew. Her foster parents bought her new clothes—a sundress, they called it, and a sweater. The sweater was white, and the dress...the dress was white with little purple and green flowers across it, and best of all, the sundress was brand-new!

"Who are these people?" she asked her foster mother.

"They're very nice from what I understand, and they love Jesus."

That part made Savannah less scared about the meeting. But still it didn't answer her question. "How do they know me?"

"They'll explain it to you, sweetheart." That's all her foster mother would say. The people would explain it when they showed up after lunchtime.

It was after lunch right now, so Savannah sat on her knees on the sofa next to the front window and studied every car that passed by. There would be three of them. That's what her foster parents said.

Savannah had wondered something ever since she knew the nice people were coming. What if one of them was her daddy? He was out there somewhere, and her mama said she was going to meet him later. Much later, but still...this was much later than then. Maybe her daddy had a family and he was bringing them along. That's what other people did, because when she and her mama were in Central Park and other people walked along with their kids sometimes there was a whole group all together.

She had always wondered what it would be like to be part of a whole group.

"You okay in there?" Her foster mother poked her head into the room. "You need anything, Savannah?"

Just my daddy, she wanted to say. But she gave the old woman a nice smile. "No, thank you." Then she thought about kneeling on the sofa and maybe that wasn't allowed, so she covered her mouth real quick and felt her eyes get big. "Want me to get off the sofa?"

The woman laughed real soft. "No, sweetie. You go right ahead and kneel on the sofa. The thing's old as time anyway."

Savannah smiled. "Thank you." She felt better now. Her foster mother was nice. At first Savannah thought about running away and finding her daddy, because that was all she really needed. Then she wouldn't be a trouble to her mama, and she wouldn't take up the time of the foster parents. But her foster mother was very nice, and she probably would've been sad if Savannah ran away. So she stayed and asked Jesus every day to bring her daddy very soon.

Her foster mother walked back into the kitchen and Savannah looked out the window again. Just then, a blue car stopped in front of the house, and after a few loud heartbeats, a man got out from the driver's side. Savannah made her eyes squinty and looked at him real hard. He sort of looked like her daddy, but not really because he had gray hair. Mostly gray.

Next came a woman from the other front seat, and a younger woman from the backseat. Savannah sucked in a little gasp, because the first woman, the one from the front seat, was very pretty. Like the queen in *Sleeping Beauty*, but with hair down to her shoulders. The three of them talked for a minute by themselves and then they started up the walk.

Savannah quick ducked down beneath the windowsill. Why were people who didn't know her coming for a visit? Were they friends of her mama's? Or maybe friends of Freddy's? Savanna poked her head up just enough to see them. No. They weren't friends of either her mama or Freddy because they dressed in nice clothes and their eyes looked different. More like the people who gave them money when they begged in the park.

"They're here!" She shouted the news because she wanted her foster mother to answer the door. That was the right way of things for regular people, and Savannah wanted these nice people to think she was regular. When her mama drank too much whiskey or stayed up too late, she was the one who answered Freddy's door. But that wasn't regular at all.

Her foster mother came into the room wiping her hands on a towel. She moved to the door and all of a sudden Savannah had a warm feeling inside her. So many times when she and her mama begged money, she wondered what it would be like to spend time with the people who *gave* the fives and tens, instead of always being on the taking side.

And now, even though she still didn't understand, she was about to find out.

❦

Annie had never been so quiet in all her life.

The whole way here—on the trip to the Denver airport, during the flight through O'Hare to LaGuardia, while they waited at the rental car counter, and during the drive here to Queens—she had no interest in making small talk. All she could think was that this should have been Josh's trip. Now that they'd found Savannah, now that they knew for sure she was Josh's daughter, the chance to meet her and get to know her even for a short time belonged to Josh.

So she spent the time wondering what he would have been thinking, and anticipating the moment when she would first see Savannah the way Josh would have looked forward to it. This was the single goal through all of his pain and suffering, the one moment that mattered more to him than any other.

Annie linked hands with Nate, and a few steps behind them came Lindsay. That moment was finally here, and Annie wondered if she'd remember to breathe. It was the first Wednesday in November, but the afternoon was still warm, the leaves every shade of orange and yellow and red. Twenty years from now Annie knew without a doubt she would remember everything about this minute. The way Nate's hand felt in hers, the clutter on the front porch of the foster family, the colors in the leaves, and the feel of fall in the air. Her heart beat so hard she wondered if it would burst through her chest. Nate went to knock on the front door, but before he could reach it, an older woman opened it and smiled at them. "You must be the Warrens."

"Yes." Nate fell back beside Annie. "Thank you for making this possible."

"Anytime I can be part of something good for these kids, it makes my day." She held out her hand. "I'm Marti." The three of them introduced themselves, and Marti explained that Savannah didn't know who they were or how they were connected. "I figured I'd let you take care of that part."

The questions came again in a wild rush. What if she didn't understand? What if she had no idea who Josh was or that he was her father? How could they erase seven years of having no relationship in a single afternoon? Nate must have seen her anxiety, because he squeezed her hand and gave her a look that said not to worry. Everything would be okay.

Marti welcomed them in and moved aside. There, standing at the far end of the room, was Savannah, the girl from the picture. She was older now, her eyes more guarded than they'd been when she was four. But they were Josh's eyes. Annie was sure that Nate and Lindsay could see that as easily as she could. Marti stepped into another room, saying something about leaving them alone so they could get to know each other.

Annie couldn't focus on anything but the little girl, Josh's daughter. "Hi, honey." Annie took a few steps closer to the girl and then stooped down so she was at eye level with her. "I'm Annie."

"Hi." Savannah gave a little wave of her hand, but she kept her chin tucked down, too shy to make a move in their direction. "I'm Savannah."

How often had Josh longed to hear those simple words? Annie pressed her finger to her upper lip, refusing the tears lining up along the back side of her soul. "Nice to meet you, Savannah."

Nate and Lindsay took turns introducing themselves, and then Annie motioned for the three of them to take seats around the room. Savannah stayed standing in the far corner. Nate coughed a few times, and Annie could tell he was fighting tears. "Would you like to sit for a minute?"

"No, thank you." Savannah did a half twirl one way and then the other, and though she still had shy eyes for them, a smile tugged at her lips. "I got a new sundress and a new sweater."

Annie wanted to take her to FAO Schwarz and let her buy whatever she wanted. She dismissed the thought. If this was their only chance to meet Savannah, her attention couldn't be on all the girl didn't have. Nate nodded at her, silently asking her to take the lead in the conversation that needed to happen before they could spend the afternoon with her.

Annie slid forward a few inches and looked at her granddaughter, at the eyes that were so familiar. "Honey, you don't know who we are, right?"

Savannah shrugged one dainty shoulder. "You're nice people, that's what my foster mother said. And you love Jesus."

"Right." Annie appreciated the woman's comments. They needed all the help they could get to make this little girl understand who they were and why they were here. She exhaled, silently begging God for the right words. "What do you know about your daddy, Savannah?"

As soon as the question was out of her mouth, Annie

saw the child respond. Her eyes began to dance and she clasped her hands the way young children do on Christmas morning when they wake to find the rocking horse or doll or train set they'd always wanted. That's how Savannah looked, and she moved her gaze from Annie to Nate to Lindsay, and back to Annie again. "Can you wait a minute?"

"Sure, honey." Annie glanced at the others while Savannah ran off down the hall toward the back of the house.

"At least she knows who he is." Nate dabbed his knuckle beneath one eye and then the other. "Did you see her light up? I think she knows, don't you?"

"Definitely," Lindsay whispered. "I can't believe how much she looks like Josh."

"She looks like you, too." Annie had realized it as the girl reacted to the mention of her father. Her excitement changed something in her face, and suddenly Annie felt like she was looking at a mix of Josh and Lindsay at that age.

They heard Savannah's feet coming down the hall, running as fast as she could by the sounds of it. *Breathe,* Annie ordered herself. *Breathe so you don't pass out on the living room floor. Please, God, help me breathe.*

Savannah rounded the corner and stopped short. In her hands was a framed photo—a five-by-seven. She held it out in front of her and with a look that was pure adoration, she studied the picture. Then she turned it so they could see the photo.

Annie gasped softly and put her fingers over her lips. The picture was Josh a few years ago, before the accident. Savannah's eyes shone as she looked from the picture back to Annie. "This is my daddy." She smiled with a pride that knew no limits. "He's a Prince Charming."

Across the room, Lindsay looked away, probably so Savannah wouldn't see her tears. Annie felt Nate put his arm across her shoulders. She hadn't counted on this; none of them had. The idea that Savannah might not only know who her dad was, but that she'd have a picture of him, that she'd so completely adore him.

Annie could barely force any words from her mouth, let alone her heart. The image of Josh's daughter holding his picture and calling him a Prince Charming would stay with her forever. She locked eyes with her granddaughter. "How do you know about him, Savannah? Who told you?"

A ribbon of fear wove its way through Savannah's smile. "My mama." She squirmed as if maybe that part wasn't quite true. "I think she knew him a long time ago, because she had this picture. She put it in the trash one day when she was cleaning out our room, way back when I was a little girl. She said once it was my daddy." Savannah swallowed hard and her eyes found Josh's in the picture again. "She told me he was a real Prince Charming. Since she didn't want the picture, I took it." She held it close to her chest. "Mama doesn't know, but...I've kept it ever since then."

A few seconds passed while Annie processed what her granddaughter was saying. Basically, Maria had tried to end Josh's presence in Savannah's life, but she'd found the picture and asked about it. All Annie could figure about the Prince Charming bit was the obvious—Maria had meant the comment sarcastically. But Savannah had been too young to understand sarcasm, so she'd taken her mother's comment to heart. She'd also taken the photo and kept it in hiding every day since then.

Annie wanted to take the little girl in her arms and tell her the truth about Josh—that he really was a Prince Charming. That he had lived for the chance to meet her, but that he'd lost that chance forever. And the worst part of all—that her daddy from the photograph was dead.

Nate leaned closer to Savannah. "Your mother doesn't know you have the photograph?"

A worried look darkened Savannah's countenance. "You're not going to tell her, are you?"

"No, dear." Nate's answer was quick. "Definitely not."

"Mama told me I would meet my daddy later. Much later." She looked out the window to the street beyond. "I thought maybe you were going to bring him to me."

"Well, that's why we asked you about him." Annie slid over and patted the spot on the sofa between her and Nate. "Want to sit here with us?"

Savannah hesitated, but then she tucked the framed picture beneath her arm and slowly crossed the room. She sat on the slightest edge, half standing, and she studied the picture. "He looks like a Prince Charming, don't you think?"

Annie could hardly believe they were sitting here with Josh's daughter. "I can tell you this, honey. Your daddy was definitely a Prince Charming. We just learned that about him."

Savannah's eyes lit up again and she turned fully toward Annie. "You know him? My daddy?"

Annie wondered how many times a person's heart could break. How could they be the first real connection to her daddy the child had ever known, and in the same breath tell her that he was no longer alive? *Tell me what to say, God.... Help us get through this time with Savannah.*

I am with you, daughter.... I will give you the words.

The peace of God's promises gave Annie the strength she needed.

Even if it was only enough to survive a few minutes at a time.

TWENTY-FOUR

The time had come to tell Savannah the truth about who they were. Annie wanted to take hold of her grand-daughter's hand, but it was too soon, so she stayed in her spot. On the other side of their granddaughter, Nate did the same. Lindsay was still crying softly across the room, taking in the scene.

Savannah was waiting for an answer.

"Yes, honey, we know him." She could feel herself being led along by the Holy Spirit, feel God leading her in what to say and when to say it. "Your daddy is our son—mine and Nate's."

"And he's my brother." Lindsay touched her fingers to the place above her heart. "We all love him very, very much."

Savannah was on her feet. Her smile took up her whole face and she ran to Lindsay, putting her small hands on Lindsay's knees. "You're his sister?"

"Yes. He's always been my best friend."

"Really?" She raised her eyebrows high up into her fore-head. "Mine, too!" She darted back to Nate. "And you're his daddy?"

"Yes, honey." Nate touched the girl's shoulder. "You know what that makes me?"

She looked like she might have an idea, but she wasn't sure enough to voice it. Instead, she shook her head.

"It makes me your grandpa, Savannah."

"Like Grandpa Ted!" Savannah gasped and put both her hands over her mouth. When she dropped them she rushed into Nate's arms and flung her hands around his neck. "Grandpa Ted's in heaven, but you're right here. I didn't even know I had another grandpa, so now you can be my grandpa Nate, okay?"

Nate's chin was quivering. He had one hand on Savannah's back, and with the other he squeezed the bridge of his nose. He nodded, and Annie knew it was because he couldn't say anything. After another big hug, Savannah turned to her. "Then...are you my grandma?"

Annie wanted to freeze the moment. She held out her arms toward Josh's daughter. "Yes, honey. I'm your grandma."

Savannah didn't rush into a big hug the way she had with Nate. Instead, she seemed mesmerized by Annie, by the idea of having a grandmother. "I never had a grandma before."

"You do now." Annie couldn't fight the tears another minute. They came despite her smile. "I'll always be your grandma, because your daddy is my son."

Savannah nodded slowly. "You're"—she reached up and gingerly touched her little girl fingers to Annie's dark hair—"you're very beautiful, Grandma Annie."

A small sob escaped from Annie and she tenderly took the girl into her arms. "You're beautiful, too, Savannah. I see your daddy in your eyes." They hugged for a long time, and Annie wanted the moment to end right there, without the admission of anything so sad as Josh's death. The ending was all wrong. She sniffed and ran her hand along Savannah's small back. "Would it be okay if we took you to the park?"

"Central Park?" Savannah looked suddenly afraid. "You mean, to beg for money?"

Annie was horrified. "No, honey. The park at the end of the street. So we can play on the swings and talk about your daddy."

Again the girl's smile was as wide and innocent as a sunrise. "I'd like that very much."

They told Marti they were leaving, and the four of them climbed into the blue rental car. A few minutes later they pulled into the lot of Maple Leaf Park, and once they were outside they headed for the swings. Annie whispered quietly to Nate and Lindsay. Sometime in the next hour she wanted a few minutes alone with Savannah, so she could tell her the truth about Josh in a way that wouldn't seem overwhelming. It was what they'd agreed to before the trip, and Nate and Lindsay both whispered their agreement.

Annie wanted to delay the news as long as possible. Savannah held her hand as they walked to the playground and when they were ten yards from the swings, she broke free and ran to the closest one. "Can I ride one, please?"

"Of course." Despite so much that was sad about the visit, Annie couldn't help but be filled with happiness at the sight of Josh's daughter begging for a ride on a swing. Like their time together was as normal as that of any other grandparents spending an afternoon with their granddaughter. "Go ahead." Annie laughed. "Climb on and I'll push you."

Savannah grabbed hold of the metal chains and sat

down awkwardly, as though she wasn't sure the swing would hold her up. "Not too high, okay? I've never been on swings before."

The news shifted Annie's emotions one more time, and hit her hard. Her granddaughter had never been on swings? "I thought you said you and your mother spent a lot of time in Central Park."

"We beg money there." Savannah looked embarrassed at the fact. "Mama always said that people wouldn't give money if we looked like we were at the park for fun. So no swings for us."

Annie was glad she wasn't meeting Maria Cameron on this trip. She wasn't sure she would be responsible for her actions if she had a chance to address the woman in person. She let go of her anger and frustration, so that Savannah wouldn't think for a second it was directed at her. "Here." Annie put her hands around Savannah's smaller ones. "Hold tight to the chains and I'll push you really slowly. Just tell me if you feel like you're going too high."

She moved around behind her granddaughter and gave her the most delicate pushes. "Don't let go."

"I won't." Savannah was clearly petrified, but as the ride continued she relaxed and began to giggle. "I like this, Grandma Annie. It's like I'm flying."

"Tell me if you want to go higher."

"Okay." Savannah's giggle became a full-fledged laugh. "Higher, please."

Annie did as she was asked. This was how all of life might have been for Savannah, only Josh should have been the one pushing her, and Annie should have been on the park bench next to Nate and Lindsay. She was a delightful child, and if Josh had known her these past seven years, no doubt the five of them would have shared countless happy times like this one.

They moved from the swings to the monkey bars, and then to the double slides. Annie even climbed up and rode down next to her granddaughter until she felt brave enough to tackle the slide on her own. After her fifth time down, Savannah set her feet in the sand and caught her breath, her narrow sides heaving with the exertion, her cheeks red and full of life.

She angled her pretty face at Annie. "Did my daddy like going to the park when he was a little boy?"

"Yes." Annie sat on the end of the second slide. She pictured the free spirit Josh had been at Savannah's age. "He would run from the swings to the slide and back again until he could barely take another step."

Savannah giggled. "I can't wait to meet him." She put her hand on Annie's knee. "Do you think he could push me on the swings when he comes here?"

For a crazy instant Annie thought about keeping the charade going. What was the difference whether Savannah knew about Josh's death? Could any harm come from her holding on to the image in the photograph, believing her Prince Charming daddy was going to come for her one of these days? The answer was as obvious as daylight. Annie reached for Savannah's hand. *God, please....I can't do this without You.*

"And hey"—Savannah grinned at her—"if you know my daddy, could you tell him to hurry? I don't want to meet him much later, but right now. Today, if that's okay with him."

"Savannah"—Annie felt God giving her the ability to

speak the words that had to be said—"honey, your daddy isn't coming for you."

The news seemed to hit her slowly, like a gradual rain, the kind where it took several drops of wetness before the reality of the storm sank in. Her thin shoulders slumped forward a little and her eyes held a mix of shock and betrayal. "Why not?" Her mouth hung open, and the beginning of tears sprang to her eyes. "I've been waiting for him a very long time."

"I know." Annie wondered how much her heart could take. "You see, honey, a month ago your daddy went to sleep and he never woke up. He went to heaven instead."

"To heaven?" Savannah stood and stared at Annie. "My daddy is in heaven? Like Grandpa Ted?"

"Yes, baby." Annie reached for Savannah's hand.

But the child took a step back and shook her head. "No." She scrunched up her face and began to cry. "No, he can't be in heaven. That's too far away." She shook her head harder, faster. "He's my Prince Charming, and he was going to come for me and...and..." She turned around and ran across the sand to the swings. She flung herself onto the farthest one, grabbed the chains hard, and hung her head halfway to her lap.

Annie caught a look of pity from Nate and Lindsay. The two of them stood and started walking along a path in the other direction. They could hear the details later. These next few minutes were for Annie and Savannah alone. Annie stood, and as she trudged through the sand toward her granddaughter she wore her son's loss like a heavy coat.

He should have been here right now, to take Savannah in his arms and soothe away her hurt and sadness. Annie stopped a few feet from the girl, and again she knew she'd remember the sight of Savannah—sitting on the swing weeping, her heart breaking—for as long as she lived. Although she was only seven years old, the child under-stood the significance of Josh being in heaven.

Annie took the swing beside her and waited several min-utes until Savannah's angry sobs eventually subsided. Finally, she sniffed and turned her red eyes to Annie. "Grandpa Ted told me sometimes things don't go the way we want this side of heaven."

"That's true." Annie wasn't sure who Grandpa Ted was, but she had a feeling he had been Maria's father. "This side of heaven can be pretty sad sometimes."

"So here's what I want to know." She sniffed again. "How do I get to *that* side of heaven? So I can be with my daddy?"

Annie couldn't talk through her tears. *That side of heaven.* If she could take Savannah there now she would. "Ah, Savannah, baby. If only there were a way to make that happen."

"Grandpa Ted said there was." She had fresh tears on her cheeks, but her anger was gone now. In its place was a sad desperation, a last-ditch hope that she might somehow find a way around the terrible news. She wiped her nose. "He told me if I loved Jesus, then one day I'd go to heaven, too. So then I'd be on that side with my daddy."

"Your grandpa Ted was right." Annie brushed her wrists across her cheeks. "One day you'll be on that side of heaven with your daddy and your grandpa Ted and—and all of us who love Jesus. Just not until you're much, much older."

"But"—her voice broke and she looked smaller than she

had an hour ago—"my daddy wasn't old. So how come he's on that side of heaven and I'm here on this side?"

Annie swallowed a sob before it could consume her. "I don't know. I've wondered that same thing."

When Savannah saw that Annie didn't have any more of an answer than that, she squeezed her eyes shut and lowered her head again. "I was going to live with him, and he was going to give me hugs, and…and…" Her tears came harder, and it was difficult to understand her. "He was going to take me to his house and bring me to school and push me on the swings and race me down the slide. And everything was going to be happily ever after." She lifted the saddest eyes and looked deep into Annie's face. "What about that?"

"I'm sorry, Savannah." Annie reached out her hand once more, and this time Savannah stood, and after a few seconds of inner struggle she came to Annie and flung her arms tight around her neck.

"I wanted to meet him so bad, Grandma Annie." Savannah nuzzled her face in close against Annie's neck. "Now I have to wait for heaven."

"Yes." Annie let her tears come. "We both have to."

They hugged for a long time, until finally Savannah pulled back. She searched Annie's face. "That's why you came, isn't it? To tell me my daddy was in heaven?"

"Yes, honey." Annie didn't want to mention the rest. "And because we wanted to meet you and tell you about your daddy. He loved you very much." Annie had made a copy of Josh's journal. It was in an envelope in the car. "Before we go I have something for you. Lots and lots of letters your daddy wrote to you from the time you were a baby until the day before he died."

"Why—why didn't he come see me before he went to heaven? Before it was too late?"

The afternoon sun was slipping behind the trees that lined the playground, and the temperature was falling. Annie wasn't sure how much to say. "He wanted to, baby. Every day he wanted to."

The pieces seemed to come together slowly but surely in Savannah's mind. She thought for a long time, and then she bit her lip. "It was 'cause of my mama, right? She didn't let him come, because she threw his picture in the garbage."

"That's right, Savannah." She didn't want to turn the girl against her mother, especially when the woman was most likely all she would ever have in the years ahead. But the truth needed to be spoken. "Your mother didn't want Josh to be a part of your life."

"Josh?"

"That was your daddy's name. Joshua David Warren."

Savannah repeated his name slowly. "I like Prince Charming Daddy better."

Annie smiled. Her tears were drying in the late afternoon breeze. "I like that, too."

"My mama shouldn't have kept him away from me."

"No." Annie ran her hand along the back of Savannah's head. "But she can't keep him away in heaven. So you'll always have that to look forward to."

They talked a few more minutes about heaven and how Josh had loved Jesus very much. Then they met up with Nate and Lindsay, and Savannah hugged each of them. "Grandma Annie told me about my daddy. I'm sorry he went to heaven so soon."

"Us, too." Nate held her hand as they walked to the car. "We miss him every day."

When they got back to the foster home, Savannah found Josh's picture on the sofa where she'd left it. "Is it okay if I still keep this picture? So I can think about my daddy and what it's like on that side of heaven?"

"Yes, sweetie." Lindsay hadn't said much, but now she knelt near Savannah and touched the girl's strawberry-blond hair. "My brother wanted to be your daddy so much. I want you to know that."

"He is my daddy. It doesn't matter if it takes a long time to meet him." Savannah was accepting the situation a little better now. "Plus, I have my picture, so he'll always be close by, even if he's in heaven."

"Right." Lindsay kissed Savannah's cheek. "We have to go now. But I want you to remember us, okay?"

Savannah moved on to Nate and hugged him, too. But as she pulled away she looked confused by the good-byes. She turned to Annie. "Are you leaving, too?"

"I have to, honey. We live in Colorado, on the other side of the country."

Her eyes lit up, but not like they'd done earlier in the afternoon. "How 'bout I go with you? My mama doesn't want me." She glanced at Nate. "She told me in the restaurant. She doesn't want to be a mama anymore."

The admission ripped at Annie and made her want to pack up the girl's things and take her home. Let the courts figure out a way to make the arrangement legal. If Maria didn't want her daughter, then Annie and Nate would be happy to step in. But Maria definitely wanted her daughter. As soon as she was sober, she would certainly come back to her senses. There could be no settlement money if she gave up Savannah. Thomas figured Maria and her attorney would pull out all the stops so that Maria could regain custody and get her hands on the money.

Annie gave her granddaughter one more long hug. What she was about to say next was only what she had to say, so that Savannah wouldn't fear the life that lay ahead of her. "Listen to me, honey." She searched Savannah's eyes, the eyes that were so like Josh's. "Your mother didn't mean what she said. She's sick right now, but when she gets better she'll make things right with you."

"Know something?" Savannah's voice was too soft to hear across the room.

"What?" Annie touched her finger to the tip of her granddaughter's nose.

"My mama doesn't love Jesus. She told me she doesn't believe like Grandpa Ted."

Another blow, not that Annie was surprised. "Well, honey, maybe one day you'll help her believe." They needed to go. One afternoon was all Child Protective Services would allow given that Savannah was in emergency foster care. And now their plane was set to leave in just three hours. Annie cradled her hand around the back of Savannah's head. "I'm going to ask Jesus every day that we have the chance to see you again. Okay?"

Savannah nodded. She looked shy again, her expression a mix of hurt and disappointment and a sorrow that seemed all too familiar. "I'll ask Him, too." She took a step back and gave each of them a little wave—Annie last. Then she hugged the picture of Josh to her chest. "Thank you for telling me about my daddy."

Annie had brought the envelope from the car and now she handed it to Savannah. "Can you read, sweetie?"

"Not yet." Again there was shame in her voice. "Mama said I could learn later. Right now we have to beg for money."

Anger threatened to taint the moment. Annie gritted her teeth and made a mental note to talk to Thomas about Savannah's living conditions. If the courts returned the child to her mother then the entire system was flawed. She put the thought out of her head for now. "Inside that envelope are the letters I told you about." Her face softened and she squeezed Savannah's hand once more. "The letters from your daddy. Keep them with your picture of him, so that one day you can read for yourself how much he loved you."

"How much he still loves me." Savannah held the photo tighter to herself. "People can love all the way from heaven."

"Of course." Annie kissed the top of Savannah's head. "Inside the envelope is our phone number. In case you ever need anything."

Savannah nodded, but the confusion in her eyes told them she didn't really understand. She couldn't possibly have understood how far away Colorado was, or why her daddy's family was leaving so soon after finding her. When Annie couldn't take another moment of the good-bye, she turned, left the house, and walked to the car. Nate and Lindsay followed, and the last image they saw as they pulled away for the airport was Savannah's sweet pixie face in the front window of the foster parents' house. Marti was beside her and Savannah wasn't somber or pouting or indifferent.

She had one hand raised to the glass and she was sobbing.

TWENTY-FIVE

Back in the Springs the days passed slowly, each one drenched in the sadness of Josh's absence. Every few afternoons, Annie called Thomas for an update, and one week after their return home from the quick visit to see Savannah, Thomas passed on word that a local judge had ruled Maria fit to regain custody of the child. No surprise, Annie knew. But when she read in Scripture that week about God's faithfulness, she remembered the song at her son's funeral service and the little girl on the other side of the country praying for a happy ending, and she had to wonder.

God had a plan, no doubt, but in this case she was better off not trying to make sense of it.

Annie debated the situation with Thomas, because she needed to talk to someone about the insanity of it. "The woman told Savannah she didn't want to be a mother anymore."

"I know."

"She hit her on the face in front of a crowd of people."

"The judge was aware of that."

"So how, Thomas . . . how can they overlook her warrants

and the fact that she begs for money and return Savannah to that environment?"

Thomas could only release a sigh that sounded drenched in futility. "I wish I could explain it, Annie. I'm sorry."

The outcome for Savannah was exactly as they feared it might be, and as the day of the settlement neared, Annie was sure that Maria would do just what they expected— flee the city and any ties to the court or to the Warren family, most likely in case she might have to share the money if she kept in touch.

Now, with each day that passed, she not only missed Josh, but his little Savannah, too. She would always be glad for the few hours they'd had with the child, but it made the grief she and Nate and Lindsay shared even stronger than before. Annie kept her word and prayed every day that Jesus would allow them the chance to meet again, to know each other. But Jesus hadn't let Savannah see her daddy, and now it didn't look like the rest of them would ever get to see Savannah again, either.

The settlement came in late November. After three years of updates, depositions, hearings, and meetings, Thomas called with the news they'd been waiting for. The decision had been made. The judge had analyzed the accident, the damage caused by the insurance company's client, and the fact that Josh's need for pain medication had ultimately led to his death. Instead of the two million dollars Thomas asked for, the judge ruled that the insurance company pay out $2.3 million.

The case was a landslide victory for Josh's estate, and one of Lindsay's colleagues at the *Gazette* covered the story.

A few days after the article appeared, Annie spent an

afternoon in what had become a new kind of routine. She brought two Starbucks soy lattes to Carl Joseph's apartment and talked for an hour with him and Daisy.

"We saw the story about Josh." Carl Joseph pointed to the bulletin board on his kitchen wall. "Daisy cut it out for me."

"Yeah, but"—Daisy wrinkled her nose—"it wasn't long enough. It didn't say that Josh was a hero, and Cody says that's bad journalism."

"Because bad journalism isn't good." Carl Joseph shook his head. "You should've written the story, Annie."

She wished she could have. But what she knew now about Josh would have never fit in a single newspaper feature. She could have written a book about her son's life, and once in a while she almost convinced herself she should do just that, even if their family and Josh's friends were the only ones who ever read it. She could always use the book as a reason to find Savannah again, years from now.

After her visit with Carl Joseph and Daisy, Annie went to the local Whole Foods and picked up the same items she'd been buying every week since the end of October: a half gallon of milk, a loaf of bread, two small containers of strawberry yogurt, a bag of frozen salmon fillets, a bag of rice, and an assortment of fruit and vegetables. The food fit neatly into two grocery bags, and Annie carried them easily up the steps to Ethel's apartment.

"Hello, dear." The woman smiled as she opened the door. She took the groceries, clucking her tongue about how Annie didn't need to do this and how she'd be happy to pay for the food if only Annie would let her. "Have I ever told you," Ethel said as Annie set the groceries down on the small kitchen table, "every time I open the door and see you standing on the porch with my groceries, for just a short minute I can see Josh again. The two of you have the same eyes."

Ethel said the same thing each time Annie came, and always Annie left with a promise to be back the next week. Not on Saturday, but on Monday—the day she'd set aside to keep in touch with the people she'd met because of Josh. Today she had more than her usual stops to make. She drove across town to a small café at the foot of Black Forest. The meeting was set to take place at one of the tables near the window. It was the first week in December, and snow was forecast for that night.

Annie parked and thought about all she wanted to say, all she never would have had the chance to say if the person she was meeting hadn't pursued this private, early dinner, hadn't been willing to drive in from Denver. Annie spotted the young woman as soon as she entered the restaurant.

Becky Wheaton raised her hand so Annie would see her. As she reached the booth, Becky stood and gave her a quick hug. "Thanks for coming. I—I felt bad asking."

Annie took her seat opposite Becky and once she was situated she reached across the table and briefly took hold of Becky's hands. "That's why I wanted to come here today. I think we have a few things to talk about."

"I thought you'd think it was awkward, sitting down with me after all these years."

A sad smile tugged at Annie's lips. "That's one of the things Josh taught me. The only awkward thing between people who care about each other is missing out on the chance to sit down and talk things out."

"Yeah." Becky was wearing her blond hair shorter these days. She was already sipping a cup of coffee. "I see what you mean."

They ordered dinner, and then Becky got to the point. "Ever since Josh's death, I've been buried under, I don't know, a sense of guilt. Like maybe if I'd stayed with Josh none of this ever would've happened."

They were the same thoughts Annie had experienced at first, but not in a long time. "You did what you had to do, Becky. No one faults you for that. Josh certainly didn't blame you." Annie had come today with one goal in mind—to give Becky the freedom to move on with her life. But first they had to talk through the things Becky was feeling.

"I asked him to stop smoking and stay in college." She set her coffee cup down and leaned on her forearms. "But every night I fall asleep thinking I never should've expected that of him." Her eyes glistened. "I loved him so much. I still haven't ever felt that way about anyone else."

Annie had wondered whether she should share with Becky just how much Josh had still cared for her. As long as Becky was being painfully honest, Annie figured she might as well tell the whole story, too. She settled back into the booth. "Josh didn't blame you, Becky. He respected all you wanted from him. He stopped smoking a few years after he moved to Denver. I wasn't sure you knew that."

Her eyes showed her surprise. "I had no idea."

"He heard your engagement fell through, and he was hoping to get his settlement and open a business. He needed back surgery and he was trying to lose the last forty pounds he'd gained. But once he had all that figured out, he was planning to call you." She studied the young woman across from her. If things had been different, she might have been her daughter-in-law.

"I—I didn't know any of that."

"Josh loved you. He had a lot to work through, and he wanted to find his daughter. But he always saw you as part of his future plans. At least he prayed you might be."

Becky dropped her gaze to her hands. "That only makes it worse."

Annie understood what she meant. All along the process of discovering who Josh had really been, she'd experienced that same feeling: that the depth of Josh's loss grew the more good she found out about him. But that's not the way God wanted either of them to feel about Josh, and now it was Annie's responsibility to help relieve Becky of the burden she was carrying.

"You need to understand something." Again Annie put her hand over that of the young woman across from her. "You'll keep Josh in your heart, the same way I'll keep him. But you need to let your guilt and regrets go." Annie hoped she sounded sincere. "Josh made his own decisions, and it took him a little longer to understand the sort of life you wanted."

"I didn't want any sort of life, though." She looked up and there were tears on her cheeks. "I wanted Josh. That's all."

"I want him, too. Just for ten more minutes so I can tell him how proud I am of all he was, all I didn't know about him." Annie gave a slow shake of her head. "But that isn't going to happen for either of us." She thought about Savannah. "Not this side of heaven, anyway."

"I feel like I missed out on a kind of love I'll never know again."

"But you will." Annie wanted the young woman to believe that. Otherwise she would be paralyzed by her past. "You'll love again, but first you need to let go of Josh and everything you're feeling about him."

"How?" Her question seemed trapped in a heart that had never rebounded from a love she'd found when she was only fifteen years old. "How do I move on?"

"You tell yourself that you can only keep those times you and Josh *did* have. Beyond that, you can't grasp at days that never existed. For all you know, you and Josh might've been too different to make another go at things."

Becky seemed to ponder that for a few seconds. "Maybe. Still, I don't know if I can go a day without wondering."

"Wondering is part of life. As long as it doesn't keep you from living."

Their dinners came and they talked about Becky's job as a therapist, and a young man at the practice who'd asked her out to dinner twice in the past month. Josh didn't come up again until the end of the conversation, after the meal was over. "I still see him, this dark-haired gorgeous guy sitting in the stands at the first football game our sophomore year." Becky's eyes grew distant, the memory clearly alive again. "Everyone was talking about him, but after the game he came and found me. He said it'd been a long time." She laughed.

"Let me guess—the two of you had never met until then." Annie would always remember her son's sense of humor.

"Not once." She lifted her hands and let them fall back to her lap. "He was making the whole thing up, pretending that we'd met at a game the previous year, when he attended the school across town. By the time I figured out he was only teasing me, it was too late. I'd already fallen for him."

"And he for you." Annie remembered. "He came home after one of the football games that fall and told me he'd met the girl he was going to marry. She had blond hair the color of sunshine and her name was Becky."

A wistfulness clouded Becky's eyes. "I guess we'll never know."

"Which is why you can't spend today wondering about yesterday, my dear. Josh is gone." The words would always hurt to voice them. "He's gone and you have to let him go. It's what he would've wanted for you."

She still didn't look sure.

"You believe in God, right?"

"Of course. I talk to Jesus all the time." Becky's cheeks grew slightly red in anticipation of what was coming. "I ask Him to tell Josh how sorry I am, and that I never stopped loving him."

"Okay, then...I want to give you something." She pulled a small greeting card from her purse and handed it over. "Read it."

Becky opened the envelope and read the inside of the card. Besides restating everything Annie had already said, the card contained the Bible verse that had meant so much to Josh in his final days. Psalm 119:50.

"'*My comfort in my suffering is this: Your promise preserves my life,*'" Becky read the verse out loud. "Really? That verse meant a lot to Josh?"

"Right up until his death." Annie crossed her arms, warding off the sadness that threatened to consume her. "I think Josh would want you to take that verse to heart. Stay grounded in God's Word, Becky. Let the Lord's truth revive you so that you can date that young man from your work, and so you can let Josh take his rightful place in your life. As a part of your past, a very fond part."

For the first time since Annie had spotted Becky sitting at the booth, the young woman's eyes looked less troubled, as if a cloud had lifted from her heart. The process of letting Josh go wouldn't happen in an instant or overnight. But this was a beginning, and Annie felt sure she'd done the right thing by meeting with her. They said their good-byes and agreed to stay in touch. Annie had a feeling that someday in the not too distant future, she and Nate would be invited to Becky Wheaton's wedding.

Night had fallen as she drove home to Nate. They had plans to watch *Monday Night Football* that evening and go over the last phase of Nate's reelection plans. The election had taken a backseat in their lives since Josh's death, and neither of them felt driven to return to the frenzy for votes that had defined their lives prior to losing their son. They were involved in their church's Bible study again and were planning to take meals to the homebound starting in January.

The settlement funds had been transferred to Savannah in care of her mother, and at any time she expected to hear from Thomas that Maria had changed her phone number or moved without any forwarding address. Thomas explained how at the last minute he'd worked out the settlement so that Maria couldn't have access to all of it right away. But the details no longer mattered. The money was gone, and very soon Savannah would be gone, too.

In the meantime, she comforted herself with something Cody Gunner had told her that afternoon in Josh's apartment. In light of Josh's faith, Cody and his wife had figured Josh was just starting to live. Annie understood now how true that was.

He really had just started to live. Just not the way she and Nate and Lindsay and the others had expected.

The beautiful thing was this: She hadn't only discovered what her son meant to other people, the sort of true success he'd been while he was alive, but she'd discovered something about herself, as well. In taking over the love and friendships Josh had begun, Annie had become a better person in the process. More of the person God had intended her to be.

If only she could have forced Maria Cameron into a shared custody arrangement with Savannah. Then she could be absolutely sure that not only would she spend the rest of her days proud that Josh was her son, but that he would spend eternity proud that she was his mother. She pulled into the driveway, parked her car in the garage, and found Nate waiting for her inside.

"How was dinner?" He pulled her into his embrace and rocked her slowly.

"Good. I told her she needs to move on. Let Josh go because that's what Josh would've wanted for her."

Nate nodded. "The game's already started."

"I figured." She set her purse down. "Any score?"

"Not yet." Nate moved to sit down, but then he stopped himself. "I almost forgot. There was a message for you on the machine when I got home. Thomas Flynn. He wants you to call him first thing in the morning."

Annie nodded absently as she took her place beside her husband. Thomas was good about giving her updates on the case, even now, after it was long since settled and the funds dispersed. She stretched out her legs and focused her attention on the football game. When it came to the lawsuit or the painful time after Josh's accident, Annie believed God wanted her to take the same advice she'd given Becky. Let it go and move on.

No matter what bit of information Thomas had for her this time.

TWENTY-SIX

Maria didn't want to admit to herself that she was worried. Harry Dreskin would take care of the mess she was in. Ever since she met him, Harry always took care of her messes, right? She gripped the bars of her jail cell and shouted at an officer as he walked by. "Where's my attorney? He should've been here an hour ago."

The officer scowled at her. "When he shows up, we'll tell you."

"That's not good enough." She cursed at the man and stormed to the opposite side of the boxy cell. She'd been sitting here for nearly three days, and she hadn't talked to Harry Dreskin since she was arrested. How was she supposed to get out of here if he didn't make more of an effort?

Two men were fighting in a cell across the hall, yelling at each other, getting on Maria's nerves. "Shut up!" she screamed. "Officer, get back here and tell them to shut up!"

They turned on her instead, shouting vile things at her. Maria didn't care. She tuned them out and sat on the wooden bunk bed in the corner of the cell. Ever since her arrest she'd done everything in her power to get her attorney back to the jail, back into a conversation about what might happen next.

What worried Maria was Harry's attitude. Normally, her lawyer was as cocky and full of himself as any man she'd ever met. Harry prided himself on finding ways around the system. Creative representation, he called it. Caught writing a bad check? Harry could make it look like a mistake. Public intoxication? A case of depression gone bad. The slap across Savannah's face? An exaggeration on the part of the restaurant employees. Harry hated judges, all judges. If he thought he had even the slimmest chance of winning a case, he made promises and predictions and he bragged about his abilities until the victory was his.

But this time Harry had promised her nothing.

An hour after her arrest, he'd met her at the jail. They sat in a windowless conference room for thirty minutes. Harry had spent half the time poring over the booking sheet, stopping only to ask a snappy question or two. "You kiddin' me, Maria? You stole two grand from a pawnshop in Harlem?"

"I needed start-up money." Maria was indignant. "I told the guy I'd pay him back in a week. So what?"

"You tried to buy a bag of coke from a cop?"

"He wasn't exactly wearing a uniform, okay?"

He read a little more and his eyes opened wider. "With your kid standing there watching?"

Savannah was a sore subject right now. "Keep her out of it." Maria had wanted to kick the guy in the leg. "Come on, Harry. Give me a pep talk. That's what I need, because you're the best, right? Isn't that why I hired you?"

Harry didn't respond. He read the details on the booking

sheet again, pointing at a line here and there and shaking his head. "This is bad stuff. Real bad."

"Quit it, Harry. You're scaring me." She gave him a light shove in his shoulder. "This is just like the other times. No big deal, right?"

"First"—Harry's tone changed—"don't shove me." He straightened his coat sleeve. "Second, hittin' up a pawn-shop and dealing to a cop's a very big deal. Especially with your rap sheet. You could lose your kid for good this time, Maria. I mean it." He raised a wary eyebrow at her. "What kinda down payment you got?"

Maria had been stumped by the question. "I just paid you thirty grand. What do you mean down payment?"

"That was my cut a' the settlement." He thumped his chest. "I earned that. This"—he flicked the booking sheet—"is a new case. I don't work for free, got it?"

"Okay." Maria thought about the money. "I can afford you. So get on it, already."

"I need up-front money. When I come back I want two g's to get started on this mess."

Their thirty minutes was up, and Harry told her he'd be back in the next day or two. Only she hadn't heard a word from him since then and it was going on the end of the third day. She dropped her head in her hands and tried once more to shut out the shouting from across the hall. What had she gotten herself into? This was supposed to be the beginning of the big time, the best days of her life.

She went over the series of events again and tried to figure out where things had gone wrong. The answer was easy.

Josh Warren.

The guy had been bad news from the beginning, talking

about his plans for success and then failing to see a single one of them come to pass. He'd gone and knocked her up, and once her old man ditched her she was nothing but a single lady with a kid on her hip. Savannah was a nice girl, but she'd cramped Maria's style long enough. What sort of big time was she going to find trying to make a living for the two of them?

She'd believed Josh Warren, thought he'd be good for eighteen years of monthly payments, but he'd let her down. And since she couldn't count on him for child support when Savannah was a baby, what was she thinking to count on him for the settlement money? Maria rubbed her thumbs into her temples. Her head pounded, her body screaming for a drink. Sure, the settlement seemed like the answer to all her cares. Like she'd hit the lottery without buying a single ticket. But when the money finally came there were more strings on it than a frayed sofa.

Thomas Flynn saw to that.

Right off the money went into an account with Savannah's name—not hers—on it. Maria told Harry to fix the problem, but he told her his hands were tied. The money belonged to Savannah, not Maria. Then she found out about some guy called an administrator who had the job of giving Maria a couple thousand dollars a month. Pennies, really.

"The stipend is intended so that Savannah is taken care of. The rest of the money can only be withdrawn by Savannah, and only on or after her eighteenth birthday," Harry told her.

"How 'bout if I'm the administrator?"

"Flynn said you can't be because you have a criminal

record. I checked it out, and he's right. Nothing I can do about it."

Thomas Flynn had a lot of nerve, rubbing that in her face. Everyone had a past. With two million dollars she had every intention of being a respectable mother. But on two grand a month? What did the system expect, that she'd get a job waiting tables to supplement the money?

Harry suggested she draw up an expense sheet, prove to the judge that she needed more money to keep Savannah comfortable. Five g's or maybe seven a month. But Maria never got around to writing up the details. She ran into one of Freddy's guys first. Big Pete was his name, and he gave her an idea for making money all on her own, without Savannah's help or the administrator's permission. A career only she could take credit for. "It's a business venture," he told her. "But you'll need start-up cash."

The venture turned out to be dealing drugs to high rollers, guys who took the subway each morning to Manhattan's financial district. "We got no one running drugs for that crowd." Big Pete winked at her. "With your looks, shouldn't take no time to get clientele."

It was Big Pete's idea that Maria hit the pawnshop. "I know the guy who runs it." Pete shrugged. "Go in on a Friday night. Make like you got a gun in your pocket and when he gives you the cash, tell him you're good for it. You'll pay him back in a few days."

Big Pete set up the buy. Maria would take the money and meet secretly with one of the biggest drug dealers in the city. She'd buy a half-gallon bag of coke and break it into smaller bags. "You'll triple your investment in a week," Big

Pete said. "Oh, and I'll get twenty percent of everything you make—since you're using my contacts."

Maria wasn't sure what went wrong. She got the money without a hitch, wore the ski mask, kept her identity a secret, the whole nine yards. The day of the big buy, she went to the right corner, looked for the guy with the right description, and used the right code words. Only instead of some big-time drug dealer the guy she tried to buy from was an undercover cop.

A frustrated sigh slid through her teeth. Figures. And now even Harry was worried. Maria stood and walked from one side of the cell to the other. Harry was wrong. She'd get through this and find the big time on the other side. Big Pete had given her an idea. If the high rollers from the financial district took the subway every morning, then she could do the same thing. She could take some of the monthly stipend money and fix herself up real nice. A better haircut, better clothes. And then some morning soon she would hit on the right guy and all her problems would be solved.

All except two.

When was she going to get out of jail, and what was she going to do with Savannah?

☙

Two weeks had passed since Thomas learned of Maria Cameron's arrest, and as he hung up the phone with the social worker, he could hardly believe how quickly the system was working. Especially less than a week before Christmas. The way things were happening, it was like God was moving heaven and earth to help Savannah find her way home for the holidays.

Thomas stared out the window at the rainy Denver sky and reminded himself of all that had transpired in the past fourteen days. After Maria's arrest, the investigating officer found evidence on more than just the crimes in question. Maria was now being charged with enough to send her to prison for at least twenty years. She'd confessed to using a gun in the robbery and, on top of that, the investigating officers were able to connect her with a bad-check writing ring. All that combined with her attempt to buy from an undercover officer, and no one thought Maria would see the light of day before Savannah turned eighteen.

Thomas even called Harry Dreskin, Maria's less than reputable attorney, and the man had been straight about his client. "She's got no money. I'm repping her as a favor." He sounded weary of the case. "I'm gonna try to cop a plea for five years, but I'll be happy with ten."

Harry said he'd shared the information with Child Protective Services for two reasons. "First, the kid deserves a family if she can get one. Second, Maria doesn't want to be a mother. Not in prison or out. She's tired of pretending."

Under other circumstances, Thomas would have been heartbroken for the little girl—living with a new set of short-term foster parents and without a mom or dad to love and care for her. But Savannah wasn't any other child. She was heir to a multimillion-dollar estate, and her very existence came with a stipend for care that would put to shame the typical monthly amount given to foster parents. It was a detail Thomas wanted CPS to keep secret from any potential long-term foster or adoptive parents.

But mostly Thomas wanted CPS to keep quiet about the money because he had a different plan for Savannah, a plan he hoped God was orchestrating. Before he could say anything to Annie or Nate Warren, he wanted to make sure Maria's case couldn't slip through the cracks, that Maria wouldn't wind up Savannah's guardian again in a few weeks or a month.

Now that problem had been solved for good.

The phone call he just ended was from the social worker, with the best news Thomas Flynn had heard in a very long time. "Savannah Cameron is officially a ward of the court," the woman said. "I thought you'd like to know."

"So"—he pushed back from his desk, adrenaline flooding his veins—"her mother's rights have been severed?"

"Forever."

Thomas closed his eyes. *Thank You, God.... You're doing this; I can sense Your presence opening the right doors.* He drew a steadying breath. "So you're saying Savannah Cameron is legally available for adoption?"

"Yes." The woman's voice held an undeniable smile. "Let me guess. You have someone in mind?"

Thomas grinned at the memory of the recent conversation. He picked up the phone and dialed Annie Warren— first her home number, and then her cell. Both times he left her the same message. "I have an update on the situation with Savannah. Call me as soon as you can."

It was lunchtime, and Thomas ordered chicken salad to be delivered to his office. Otherwise he might miss Annie's call, and this was one connection that couldn't wait. His eyes found the plaque on his desk and he was struck by the faithfulness of the promise. For indeed, all things had worked to the good for the people who loved God—Annie, Nate, Lindsay, and Savannah. Even for Josh, who was safe in heaven.

Thomas was halfway through a slice of sourdough bread when his secretary alerted him, "I have Annie Warren on the phone."

"Thank you." His throat was suddenly thick, and as he reached for the receiver, he thanked the Lord again for all that lay ahead, all the good that would happen now because of these recent developments. Most of all, he thanked God for hearing the prayers of sweet Savannah, a fatherless little girl Thomas would meet one day soon.

And for loving her enough to give her a second chance.

TWENTY-SEVEN

Annie and Nate were by themselves this time. They'd arrived in New York late yesterday, and after lying awake most of the night, they were sitting in the waiting room at the Manhattan office of Child Protective Services trying to believe this wasn't all some wonderful dream. Especially three days before Christmas.

"I can't believe she's going to be ours." Nate could hardly sit still. "I prayed for this, but still...Josh would be so happy, Annie."

"I keep picturing him, all those years wishing Savannah could be a part of his life and ours, a part of her cousins' lives." She couldn't stop smiling. "Everything he wanted is going to happen."

She didn't state the sad obvious—that Josh was the only one who would miss out. All that mattered now was Savannah. Annie leaned against her husband and remembered Thomas's phone call. His question was a simple one. "Would you and Nate be interested in adopting Savannah?"

Annie would always remember what she did next. Nate was sitting across from her at their dining room table, and

Annie let out a happy cry as she placed the call on speaker-phone. "Say it again. Please, Thomas."

And Josh's wonderful attorney had laughed. "I said, would you and Nate be interested in adopting Savannah?"

The question was a rhetorical one, of course. Annie had talked about pursuing a custody battle for Savannah from the moment Josh's wishes became clear, after the conversation with Cody Gunner. But always the answer was the same—if the local Child Protective Services didn't deem Maria an unfit mother, then no one could force her to let Annie have custody even one day a year.

Ironically, when it came to establishing paternity, the courts didn't care if Josh had been denied access to his daughter. Savannah was his heir and with the exception of only the rarest cases, nothing would change the court's mind. But when Annie talked about seeking visitation rights or custody, those same facts worked against them. Thomas had explained that since the girl had no prior relationship with Annie and Nate, no one could force her to have one now.

Up until the call from Thomas, it looked like their family wouldn't see Savannah again, at least not until she was an adult. Even then there would be the matter of finding her. Annie folded her hands in her lap and tried to keep from giggling out loud. Those days were behind them now. Thomas had worked quickly, filing the right paperwork and requesting a rushed adoption.

Even Thomas was surprised when the judge oversee-ing the adoption agreed, under the circumstances, to sign paperwork on Monday afternoon. There would be a home study conducted and other paperwork to complete in the months ahead, but the documents she and Nate would sign later today would give them temporary custody until then.

Annie remembered Josh's funeral service and the words of the song played at the beginning and the end. *Great is Thy faithfulness…Oh, God my Father…there is no shadow of turning with Thee….*

The words were true, after all. His mercies really were new every morning. Today was tangible proof. And no matter what happened from here, Annie would never doubt them again. God's good plans for Josh, His faithfulness to her youngest child, had taken him straight to heaven, to a better life than this one. And now Annie and Nate would care for his daughter all the days of their lives.

Annie tapped one toe on the dingy carpet that covered the waiting room floor. She wished the social worker would hurry. It was hard to think of Savannah in a room behind the closed door. After all she'd been through in the past few months, she needed the love of her grandparents more than ever. She thought about the other details Thomas had shared with them. He expected that sometime before the end of the year, Annie and Nate would be named coadminstrators of Savannah's settlement. In light of all they now knew, they told Thomas they would only take the monthly stipend if Savannah needed it for clothing or a car when she was a teenager. Otherwise, the money would wait for her—the way Josh intended.

Annie stared at the brand-new pair of Minnie Mouse ears sticking out of her purse. She hadn't brought them the first time they'd come here to see Savannah because she couldn't have faced Daisy with the sad ending. Daisy, who had prayed every day that Savannah would come out of the picture and into Annie's arms.

But now...

Annie heard the sound of a door handle, and she and Nate looked up at the same time. The social worker opened the door and smiled at them. "Mrs. and Mr. Warren?"

"Yes?" Nate was on his feet.

Annie stood at his side. "Is Savannah ready?"

"She is." The woman motioned to someone in the other room, and after a few seconds Savannah appeared in the doorway holding a small worn plastic Little Mermaid suitcase. The zipper was broken on one side.

She set the bag down and put her fingers to her mouth, her chin tucked against her chest. In her eyes was the same shy uncertainty she'd had the last time they met—nearly two months ago. This time Savannah wore jeans that were an inch too short and her rumpled white sweater hung on her skinny frame. Someone had placed a blue bow in her hair, and the effect made her look closer to six years old than almost eight. "Savannah"—the social worker put her hand on the child's shoulder—"you remember your grandparents?"

"Hi, honey." Annie gave her a little wave. "It's Grandma Annie and Grandpa Nate. Remember us?" Only then did Annie realize that the look in Savannah's eyes wasn't shyness or uncertainty. It was a hurt, borne from feelings of abandonment and betrayal. With her eyes, Savannah seemed to ask, "How can I trust you again? You left and look what happened."

Nate must have recognized the look, too, because he got down on one knee and held out his arms. "We're very sorry, Savannah. About what's happened to you."

She searched his face, and then she lifted her eyes—the eyes so familiar to Annie. Gradually, like the break of day, a sparkle came to life in her eyes, and when she couldn't hold back another moment, she ran to them, ran for all she was worth, and flung herself into their arms. They circled her, holding her close and giving her the security she'd never had for a single day in all her life.

Sobs came over their granddaughter, the same heart-rending sobs that had marked her when they'd said good-bye back in early November. Annie pressed her face in close to Savannah's. "Oh, honey. We're never going to leave you again." Annie felt tears in her eyes, but she couldn't cry—not with the joy consuming her. Still, for all the good ahead of them, Savannah needed to cry, needed to grieve all she'd lost before she could embrace all she was about to have.

Annie and Nate stayed that way, knees on the floor, their arms around Savannah, and they let her cry. The whole time, Annie couldn't stop thinking about Josh and how she had held out unrealistic expectations for her only son. Every mistake she ever made with Josh she promised herself and God she would never make with Savannah. Whatever the girl wanted to do when she grew up, Annie and Nate would love her and encourage her. They would tell her they were proud of her as often as they had the chance. The way Annie had failed to do with Josh.

The social worker left the room. The legalities had been cleared and they could take Savannah whenever the three of them felt ready to leave. After a few minutes, Savannah dragged her fist across her face. "Can I have a tissue, please?"

Nate hurried to the receptionist's desk and snagged several from a flowered box. "Here, sweetie."

"Thank you." She dried her face, blew her nose, and then stood and dropped the crumpled tissue in the trash can. When she came back to them, she put one hand on Annie's shoulder, the other on Nate's. "I'm glad you came back. Know why?"

Annie ran her thumb ever so gently beneath Savannah's eye, catching one last wayward tear. "Why, honey?"

"Because remember how my daddy is on *that* side of heaven?"

"Yes." Nate was completely enamored of their granddaughter. He soothed his hand over the back of her head.

"Well"—she looked at Nate and then at Annie—"since I can't go there yet, I need you both to tell me stories of my daddy. So I can know everything about him." She sniffed. "Okay?"

The tears Annie didn't plan to cry came unbidden. What would her answer have been several months ago? If Josh's daughter had asked for stories about him, Annie would have treated the question the same way she treated the inquiries from people like Babette. She would have had to work to find something good, and stretch the truth to keep from dwelling on all the bad.

But now—now she could spend the rest of her life telling Savannah about how her daddy had rescued two girls from certain death, and how he'd told the hurting people in his life about Jesus, and how he could find friendship with a person even if they were handicapped or too old to drive to the market. How he would go the distance so a buddy might have a final conversation with a father he'd never connected with. How he'd helped a friend find Jesus. All that and so much more.

Annie brushed the tears from her cheeks with her fingertips and smiled at Savannah. "Actually, honey"—she coughed to clear her voice—"I've learned a lot about your daddy since he died." She fought her emotions so she could finish her thought. "He was a hero, did you know that?"

"Really?" Her eyes danced. "So he was a Prince Charming *and* a hero?" She grinned. "I bet that's a really good story, Grandma Annie. The kind with a happy ending."

"Yes." Annie breathed in sharp through her nose to keep her control. And in that split second she knew, with everything in her, that one day she would write Josh's story, even if no one but her family ever read it. She sniffed again. "Yes, a very happy ending." Savannah tilted her head and patted Annie's hair with the softest little-girl touch. "I'm glad you can tell me about him. Because those stories about my daddy are all I'll have. Those and my picture of him and the letters." She smiled. "I still have the letters. They're in my Mermaid suitcase."

Annie pulled the Minnie Mouse ears from her purse. "Here." She handed them to Savannah. "These are from some friends of your daddy's. You'll meet them soon." Annie felt her throat tighten again. "They're a special gift."

"They're pretty." She turned them one way and then the other.

"Want to wear them?"

"Okay." She handed them back to Annie. "I never had a pair of Minnie ears before."

Annie steadied her hands and slid the headband into place. "There. You look beautiful, Savannah."

"Thanks." She felt lightly against the ears. "I think I'll like Daddy's friends."

Annie smiled. "You will." She gently patted her arm. "Ready to go home, Savannah?"

"Really?"

Nate rose to his feet, grabbed her pink suitcase, and reached out his hand. "Really."

"Forever? Until heaven, I mean?" She tucked her fingers into his. She still looked wary.

"Yes, honey." Annie took hold of her other hand. "You're our little girl now."

Savannah smiled and nodded. "I'm ready." The three of them headed for the door, and even before they reached the sidewalk, Savannah was talking about Josh again. "Maybe you could tell me the hero story on the subway. We are taking the subway, right?"

Annie cherished the full feeling in her heart. What more could God have given them in light of all they'd lost? The chance to know that Josh was with his Savior, and the opportunity to raise his daughter with the love and acceptance she deserved. And most of all the great privilege of teaching Savannah everything she could ever want to know about her daddy, her Prince Charming.

This side of heaven.

༄

Already Savannah loved her grandma Annie and grandpa Nate more than anyone except Jesus and her daddy. They had wonderful stories about him, and on Christmas morning Aunt Lindsay and her husband and her two kids came over and everyone sat around the tree and Grandma Annie read to them out loud.

The letters her daddy had written to her, every single one of them.

She knew so much more about her daddy, because Grandpa Nate found lots and lots of pictures and so now she didn't just have her favorite one with the wooden frame, she had a whole stack of books with pictures. Her daddy was handsome and happy and he loved Jesus. He also loved her, because he said so in the letters a hundred million times.

Savannah still couldn't wait to meet him, one day on that side of heaven. She had seen a few videos of him, and she was pretty sure she'd know him right away because she would recognize his laugh. And of course he would look like a Prince Charming, which he was.

But in the meantime she felt like Snow White, living out a fairy tale. Because all those years when she prayed to find her daddy, she was never really sure if she ever would, and so she didn't know how her own story was going to end. But now she knew, because she had so much love, more than she could believe. She had new friends, Carl Joseph and Daisy and Mr. and Mrs. Gunner, and a pair of Minnie Mouse ears prettier than any she could have dreamed about.

But most of all she had Grandma Annie and Grandpa Nate and Aunt Lindsay and Uncle Larry and Ben and Bella, who were like built-in best friends. All that, and one day heaven, and a Prince Charming daddy who was a real-live hero.

And what could be a happier ending than that?

Dear Friends,

I'm not sure about you, but having just finished *This Side of Heaven*, I have tears streaming down my face. I long for the chance to hold Savannah in my arms and love away all her sorrow and loneliness, and I would pay dearly for a front-row seat to see that far-off reunion between her and her daddy, her Prince Charming who loved her so much.

My characters always feel real to me. That's why my husband can catch me at a moment like this and temporarily feel a great sense of alarm. Why in the world would his normally happy wife be sitting at her computer crying her eyes out? It's why he teases me that one day I'll make a very interesting old lady—when I can no longer tell the difference between my kids and my characters, and I pester him with questions about how come Carl Joseph hasn't been by to borrow eggs in a while.

Yes, the characters feel real to me.

But in this book, the characters, the story line, the haunting sorrow, and the bittersweet triumphs were very close to home. You see, *This Side of Heaven* was inspired by the story of my brother, Dave. Like Josh, Dave chose to forgo college to become a tow truck driver. And like my main character, Dave pulled two teenage girls out of harm's way and took the blow from a drunk driver one cold, wet New Year's Eve seven years ago. The story line about Maria Cameron is entirely fictional.

After that, the lines blur between Dave's real story and the one that came pouring from my heart and into the pages of this book. In the real story there was no major settlement, no multimillion-dollar windfall. The lawsuit and depositions in Dave's case all amounted to nothing more than so much extra heartache. And rather than my mom, it was I who wondered about Dave's life—whether he had sold himself short and settled for mediocrity when he could have really been something.

Dave had struggled in his faith for many years, despite prayers and efforts on the part of me and my family and so many extended family members. We all have people in our lives like that, don't we? People who seem determined to take the hard road in life. But for Dave, the change happened as it happened with Josh—through a Wynonna Judd country music video late one night in the solitude of his lonely apartment.

She was singing "I Can Only Imagine," and at the end of the video, she raised her hands to our mighty God—God who in that moment became deeply real to Dave. He searched for the song and found the MP3 by a group many of you are familiar with, MercyMe. Afterward, he played that song all day and into the next, and that's when he called me.

By then, when it came to Dave, I'd grown a little jaded. He had rejected every offer to attend church or join our weekly Bible study, so when I saw his name on the caller ID that Wednesday afternoon I figured he'd be calling for one reason—to borrow more money. I almost walked away, almost missed out on one of the greatest moments in my life. But by God's grace and mercy, I was compelled to pick up the phone.

"Hello?"

"Hey, Karen." I could hear the song playing in the background. "You won't believe it." He talked loud so he could be heard over the music. "I found this song, and it's like I finally get it about God."

I had to sit down just so I could process what was happening. My brother was not speaking to me in his usual stifled grunts and distant tones, but he was pouring out his heart about a change that was dramatic and undeniable. He told me about the video and about finding the song, and finally he laughed with unbridled joy. "Can I go to church with you this weekend? I mean, really. I can hardly wait."

Dave had been hooked on OxyContin for three years by the time he found that deeper faith. He would be at one of our family get-togethers, and I'd head into the kitchen to refill the water pitchers, and he'd be standing in the kitchen, unshed tears in his eyes, gritting his teeth and clutching the countertop. Sweat would have broken out across his forehead and he'd give me an apologetic look. "I'm sorry...the pain is so bad, Karen. I can barely stand it."

But once he developed a craving for God and His Word, once he found the joy of singing worship songs to the Creator of the universe, Dave no longer talked about his pain. Oh, it was still there, I'm certain of that. But it no longer defined him the way his faith and hope for the future defined him.

Every weekend for six weeks in a row, Dave attended church with us at our favorite Saturday night service and again with my parents at their service Sunday morning.

I remember the service that sixth week like it was yesterday. We were running late—three of the boys still in their soccer uniforms and one holding a napkin to a suddenly bloody nose. Amid the chaos and the rush of getting the younger four boys signed into Sunday school, we hurried into the darkened sanctuary after the first song was already in progress. People were on their feet, but my brother was six foot six, and I could easily see him near the front, in the third or fourth row.

He was doing what any of us do when we're at church waiting for someone to join us. Every few seconds he was glancing over his shoulder, searching the back of the church, looking for me. Donald and I and our two older kids took a row in the back, and I excused myself. I had to at least tell Dave we were there, and since everyone was standing, I didn't think anyone would notice.

No one except Dave.

He saw me coming, and as I came nearer he stepped out into the aisle and pulled me into his arms. "I love you," he whispered near my ear. "Thank you for never giving up on me."

Our hug lasted a few more seconds, and then we shared a smile and I returned to my family at the back of the church.

It was the last time I ever saw my brother.

I was at a book signing the next Saturday, a beautiful sunny morning in October, and Dave had planned to attend my nephew's football game. Only he never showed up. I was ten minutes into meeting with a hundred or so readers when I suddenly noticed that my husband was there. He had a strange look on his face, and my first thought was something must've happened to one of the kids. They were busy with soccer and theater and any number of things could have gone wrong.

I asked my next reader friend if she could wait a few seconds, and then I stepped close to Donald. "Is everything okay?"

"No, honey. It isn't." He took my hand and led me a few feet away, never breaking eye contact. "Your brother's dead. He died in his sleep last night."

What happened next was a beautiful picture of the family of God. That bookstore became a church, the readers gradually sharing the awareness of what had just happened. In no time they circled me and prayed for me, giving me the grace to spend a few minutes in the store's break room to call my parents. In the end, I decided to stay and finish the signing because, after all, that's what I write about—the heartache of real life, the hope of the Cross. The promise that in the end all things really do work to the good for those who love the Lord.

My reader friends that day were kind and compassionate, hugging me and telling me how sorry they were. One lady had tears in her eyes after I told her that my brother had a daughter, but that he never had the chance to know her. "I lost a grandbaby last week," she told me. "Maybe tonight your brother is holding her in heaven."

But even with that, and with the firm knowledge that Dave was with the Lord and no longer in pain, I had regrets. In the weeks after his death, I learned much about the goodness of my brother, his care for others and his compassion for the weak. I wondered why we didn't take the whole family up front and sit with Dave that last time in church. And how come I'd grown distant and jaded by my attempts to invite him to Bible study, when God never grows distant and jaded with me? The one consolation that remained, the one that remains with me now, comes in the form of my brother's final words.

"Thanks for never giving up on me."

And so, my friends, that brings me to the reason I wrote this book. I wanted to share the story of a character like Dave who maybe wasn't an all-star or a first-place winner or a financial success. Someone who didn't earn a degree or gain a title or write a bestselling novel. Someone who wasn't popular and successful the way the world defines those things. Because all of us have people in our lives like Dave, people like Josh. My challenge to you—the one that comes at great personal cost—is to look for the good in these less-noticed people.

Our pastor, Matt, said something last week that stays with me still. "Jesus was about the least, the last, and the lost."

Yes, and we ought to be about those people, too. I would encourage all of us to renew our love for the least and last and lost in our lives, and most of all—no matter how jaded we might have grown—to never, ever give up.

For only if we keep on loving, keep on believing in these precious people, will we allow God room to work a miracle the way He did with Josh.

The way He did with Dave.

∞

Always, as I finish a book, I spend many hours praying for you, my reader friends. Sometimes God needs to take us back in time to the place where one of our relationships became strained, to the place of new love and second chances, before we let go of our own ways and grab on to Him for life. At some point, all of us will hear the voice of God calling us back or drawing us closer in some way: through a conversation with a friend or a sermon on the radio or the loss of a loved one.

Maybe even through Life-Changing Fiction™.

If during the course of reading this book you, like Annie Warren, found yourself crying out for God to give you strength, for Him to find you again, for the chance to become the person deep inside your heart that once upon a yesterday you used to be…then I pray that you will connect with a Bible-believing church in your area. There, you should be able to find a Bible, if you don't already have one. That life-saving relationship with Christ is always rooted in His truth, the Scriptures.

If you are unable to purchase a Bible or if you can't find one at your local church, and if this is the first time you are walking into that relationship with Jesus, then write to me at my Web site, www.KarenKingsbury.com. Write the words "New Life" in the subject line, send me your address, and I will send you a Bible. Because between the covers of that precious book are all the secrets to a new life.

For the rest of you, I'd love to hear your thoughts on *This Side of Heaven.* My guess is that there are a great many of you out there who can relate to having a person in your life like Josh Warren. Tell me how Josh's story and Annie's new understanding about her son spoke to you, and how it maybe even changed you.

Contact me at my Web site, and while you're there, take a moment to look at the ways you can get involved with the community of other Karen Kingsbury readers. You can leave a prayer request or pray for someone else, tell me about an active military hero or a fallen one, and send me a picture so that all the world can pray for your soldier. You can also join my club and chat with other readers about your favorite characters and books.

If this is your first time with me, thank you for taking the time to read. My Web site lists my other titles in order, as well as by topic, in case you're looking for a specific type of Life-Changing Fiction™.

Again, thank you for your prayers for me and my family. We are doing well and trying to keep up with our kids, all of whom are growing up way too fast. In addition, we are making that special determination to be proud of them— regardless of their trophies or lack thereof.

We feel your prayers on a daily basis, and please know that we pray often for you, too.

Until next time,

In His light and love,

Karen Kingsbury

www.KarenKingsbury.com

DISCUSSION QUESTIONS

Please share these questions with your book clubs, church groups, friends, and family. Discussion makes the experience of reading so much richer!

1. Talk about Annie's relationship with her son prior to his death. What was her opinion of him, and why?

2. Nate plays a lesser role in this story. What was his relationship with Josh, and how did it differ from Annie's relationship with him?

3. Talk about a time when you or someone you know has been tempted to value the people in your life based on performance or perfection. What was the outcome of that attitude?

4. How do you define success in the lives of the people you love? How important is it to tell the people you love that you're proud of them?

5. Have you ever experienced a loss that made you doubt God or feel angry toward God? Explain.

6. Annie was struck by the song at Josh's funeral, "Great Is Thy Faithfulness." Have you ever doubted God's faithfulness? Talk about that time.

7. Lamentations talks about God's mercies being new every morning. How was that true for Annie? How has it been true in your life?

8. Explain the emotions Annie went through as she made the series of discoveries about Josh after his death. When have you or someone you know been wrong about the way you viewed someone you love? How was the discovery made of that person's real character?

9. Maria Cameron made many poor choices in her life. What were some of those choices? Talk about how those choices can affect people in real life.

10. What common theme seemed to dominate Maria's life? How can greed get in the way of loving the people God has placed around us?

11. Thomas Flynn was a good and godly attorney. Why do you think so many attorneys have a bad reputation? Talk about a situation that may have tainted your view of lawyers.

12. Why is it important that we have people of integrity in the field of law? Tell about a situation where a lawyer of great virtue made a difference.

13. The sign on Thomas Flynn's desk reads, *"In all things God works for the good of those who love him, who have been called according to his purpose,"* a Scripture found in Romans 8:28. How have you seen that verse apply in your life and the lives of those you love?

14. Tell about a time when you doubted the promise in Romans 8:28. How did that situation resolve, and if it hasn't, how might you find a way to apply that Scripture to your life?

15. Josh prayed daily for the chance to meet his daughter, Savannah. At the same time, Savannah prayed that she would meet her daddy. Neither of those prayers seemed to be answered this side of heaven. Talk about a time when your prayers weren't answered the way you wanted. How can we see God in moments like that?

16. Becky Wheaton had regrets about her relationship with Josh. Explain Annie's advice to Becky. Tell about a time when you or someone you know had regrets about a relationship. What are some ways to handle that type of situation?

17. Annie was willing to fight to the end to protect Josh's settlement. Why was this? Do you think Annie was a greedy person? Why or why not?

18. Cody Gunner wasn't sure about going to Annie with the story of his last conversation with Josh. Tell about a

time when someone came to you with life-changing news. What did Cody's admission mean to Annie?

19. Annie's prayers that she would have time with Savannah were answered very dramatically. Talk about that. Whom are you praying for right now? What can you focus on so that you'll be encouraged to continue to pray? Tell about a time when a prayer in your life was answered after someone spent time praying for you.

20. Many different types of love are illustrated in this book. Talk about a few of them, and explain what types of love are illustrated in your life.

Karen Kingsbury's
Complete Book List

Redemption Series—Baxters 1
Redemption—Book 1
Remember—Book 2
Return—Book 3
Rejoice—Book 4
Reunion—Book 5

Firstborn Series—Baxters 2
Fame—Book 1
Forgiven—Book 2
Found—Book 3
Family—Book 4
Forever—Book 5

Sunrise Series—Baxters 3
Sunrise—Book 1
Summer—Book 2
Someday—Book 3
Sunset—Book 4

Above the Line Series—Baxters 4
Take One—Book 1
Take Two—Book 2
Take Three—Book 3
Take Four—Book 4

Bailey Flanigan Series—Baxters 5
Leaving—Book 1
Learning—Book 2
Longing—Book 3
Loving—Coming 2012

Lost Love Series
Even Now—Book 1
Ever After—Book 2

September 11th Series
One Tuesday Morning—Book 1
Beyond Tuesday Morning—Book 2
Remember Tuesday Morning—Book 3

Timeless Love Series
A Time to Dance—Book 1
A Time to Embrace—Book 2

Cody Gunner Series
A Thousand Tomorrows—Book 1
Just Beyond the Clouds—Book 2

Forever Faithful Series
Waiting for Morning—Book 1
Moment of Weakness—Book 2
Halfway to Forever—Book 3

Standalone Titles
Unlocked
Shades of Blue

Divine
Like Dandelion Dust
Oceans Apart
On Every Side
Where Yesterday Lives
When Joy Came to Stay
Between Sundays
This Side of Heaven (with friends
    from Cody Gunner series)

Red Glove Titles
Gideon's Gift
Maggie's Miracle
Sarah's Song
Hannah's Hope

Treasury of Miracles Books
A Treasury of Christmas Miracles
A Treasury of Miracles for Women
A Treasury of Miracles for Teens
A Treasury of Miracles for Friends
A Treasury of Adoption Miracles
Miracles Devotional

Children's Books
The Brave Young Knight
Let Me Hold You Longer
We Believe in Christmas
The Princess and the Three Knights
Let's Go on a Mommy Date
Let's Have a Daddy Day

Gift Books
Forever Young
Be Safe Little Boy
Stay Close Little Girl

www.KarenKingsbury.com
Life-Changing Fiction™